BLOOD VOWS

BLOOD VOWS

THE DIVINE VAMPIRE HEIRS, BOOK SIX

by

GINNA MORAN

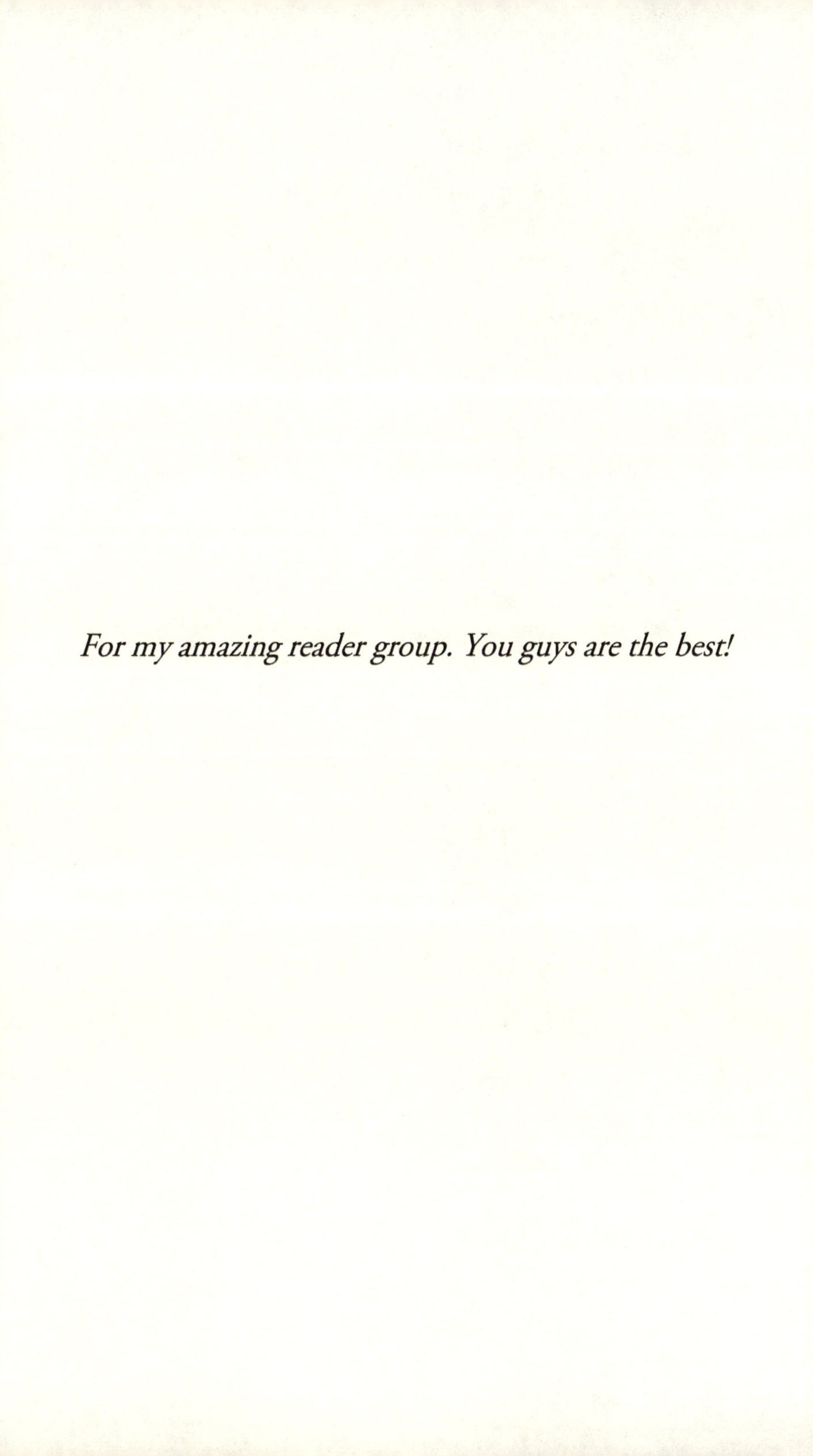

For my amazing reader group. You guys are the best!

HEART ATTACK

ICE SLIDES THROUGH MY VEINS, sending a shiver over my body. At least I think it does. I can't seem to move on command. The disconnection between my mind and body ignites the kind of fear I've only experienced in the face of death.

Light. Dark. Light. Dark. My vision refuses to focus, only allowing the blending and moving of shadows above me. Figures, I think. I can't be certain. None of them get close enough for me to get a clear glimpse of, but I can hear them. The whispering. The pleading of my name. Music hums over the sound of a heart beating. The rhythmic melody thrums over and over, slow and steady, dragging at my soul. But it's not mine.

"Her body is burning through the sedation faster than I can safely administer it." Austin's soft voice trickles to me. "She's waking up."

"How is she healing?" It's Orlando.

"Slower than I'd like. I'll check again in a few minutes when she's more aware..." Austin's words trail off. "The last time she awoke, she was in a lot of pain. I doubled the sedation to get her body to calm down. Any sort of exertion puts a strain on her. Stalls her healing almost."

"Can we give her more blood to drink?"

My muscles tense at Orlando's question, the pounding of my own heart now surpassing the beating of Austin's in volume. Numbness clings to my fingers, but I manage to move them, touching the softness of the blanket around me.

"Any more might cause her discomfort or make her vomit. I don't think we should try just yet." Cool fingers touch my cheek, and the light dancing in front of my eyes darkens with another figure. "Jewel, hey. I know you're hurting and confused, but please try to stay calm, okay? I'm right here."

A hand gently covers mine. "As am I," Orlando says.

Austin strokes my jawline over and over. "We're not going anywhere. I had to sedate you, so you'll feel out of it for a bit longer."

I open and close my mouth, my throat burning as I try to push the stuck words free.

Austin leans in closer until I catch a flicker of silver through the blurriness of my eyes. "Kingston and Diego will be back in a few minutes. We're all safe. Please, breathe slowly. Don't try to get up on your own. Your body is working hard to regenerate. You suffered some serious blood loss and damage to your chest. Broken ribs and sternum. Bruising to your heart."

Orlando squeezes my hand. "It sounds worse than it is. You've always been such a fighter. You should've seen the other guy. Your matches served you well. I'm proud to call them my brothers."

The two of them stare at me, each holding my hands as I remain lying down for another few minutes until my vision clears and my head stops spinning. The coolness dripping through me subsides, and the numbness in my fingers turns into tingles.

I let go of Austin and Orlando and grip the blankets again, trying to push up. My body wants nothing more than to stand and get a better look around. Fragments of my memory whirl through my mind. Something happened. An explosion? I can't be sure.

"Jewel, let me take a look at you again," Austin says, firmly touching my shoulders to keep me in place. "I don't want you sitting up until I'm sure you're okay to do so."

Orlando tightens his jaw. "We wouldn't want your heart to fall out now, would we?"

Austin growls and glares at him. "He's kidding, Jewel. Come here. I'll be fast."

"Not w-with—" I snap my mouth closed as Orlando disappears, leaving me alone with Austin. He could already tell what was on my mind before I said the words out loud.

Leaning forward, Austin blocks the overhead light from my vision again. "This will only take a second. I'm just going to take a quick peek."

I reach out and grab the hem of his shirt, clenching it between my fingers. Austin stops short of the blanket and peers into my eyes. He offers me a small smile despite the worry lining his forehead.

My breath comes out in a pant, my tongue dry. I desperately need something to drink. I lick my lips and swallow, tasting something sweet. Austin leans over and grabs something from above my head. He brings an ice cube to my lips and lets it melt a few drops of water onto my tongue.

Austin allows me to suck on the ice cube for a moment longer. "I'm sorry you're thirsty, but your stomach is too full right now. I don't want to chance you getting sick."

I close my eyes for a second and swallow again, the dryness slightly subsiding. "Thanks."

"Now for your checkup."

I stop him again, digging my fingers into his stomach to push him back, though he doesn't move. "I want...to see."

Austin raises his eyebrows at me. "Are you sure?"

I bob my head.

Disappearing for a second, Austin shuffles across the room and back to me. He appears in my view again and holds up a small mirror. I blink a few times at the silver in my eyes, the constant color making me nervous as all get-out. I can't even see a speck of blue in my irises. Despite feeling disgusting and achy, I don't look as bad as I feel. The sweetness on my lips wasn't from blood but lip balm, probably to help with the dryness of my mouth.

"Your dhampir mutation currently suppresses your human side. Your blood work is quite interesting. If I didn't know any better, I'd have assumed you fully transitioned into a vampire." Austin runs his finger over my bottom lip. "But you still don't have fangs...much to Kingston's disappointment."

"Can you blame me for wanting our girl to get her bite on with me?" Kingston materializes over me and beams me a smile. He flashes his fangs and snaps his teeth before leaning down to kiss me on the forehead. "I still might let you," he whispers into my ear.

"Kingston, we're in the middle of an exam," Austin says softly but doesn't push him away.

Diego appears next to Kingston and slings his arm over his shoulders. He offers me his gorgeous smile, and I try my best to stretch my mouth into a smirk. "We'll wait outside."

I reach out and grab Diego's shirt because he's the closest. "It's fine. You guys can stay. Kingston can't control his reaction, so this way I can know how bad it is."

Kingston purses his lips, clenching his jaw.

Austin remains expressionless. "You'll completely heal in no time. It's honestly not that bad. The worst is already healed."

I inhale a small breath. "Okay, go ahead and show me."

Austin hands the mirror to Kingston to hold, and Diego slides his fingers through mine. The tingling sensation melts into warmth as he cups my cold fingers in his hand. This might be one of the few times I'm actually colder than he is.

Gently easing up the blanket, Austin reveals my chest. Tears burn my eyes at the blood soaked gauze that hides whatever wound heals beneath it. I knew I was impaled but shit. My guys and I have completely different definitions of what is considered bad. I guess I should've expected as much since they treat bullet holes and knife wounds like scraped knees and mere inconveniences.

"See, it's not bad, babe. Your tits are so fucking amazing that I can't even see where the asshole tried to remove your heart." Kingston grips the mirror tighter, managing to keep his hands to himself.

"He's right about that, beautiful," Diego says, squeezing my hand. "It's so hard to keep my hands off you. Torturous. I've missed you."

I laugh softly and groan. "You guys."

Kingston breaks and reaches out, but he only touches my cheek. "You have no idea how good it is to hear you laugh, especially after all the banshee screaming. Worst. Ever. I swear, you will never scream like that again. It'll only be the good kind...the second you're healed enough."

Austin carefully pulls away the bandage from my chest,

and I wince and squeeze my eyes shut. "Does this hurt?" he asks.

"No, it's just gross as all get-out." I slowly open my eyes to peek at myself in the mirror again, but Kingston hides it away from me.

"If you think that's gross, you haven't seen anything," Kingston says.

Diego nudges Kingston up toward the top of my head. "It really isn't bad."

The three of them continue to smile at me as Austin carefully redresses the wound and deems me okay enough to sit up. I clutch my stomach at the movement and frown, feeling the liquid sloshing around inside me.

A small tap on the door draws my attention away from my full belly, and I spot Orlando leaning on the doorframe, keeping his gaze trained on the rug. It's now that I realize we're in his room, but things have been moved around. The bed sits in the middle and away from the wall to make room for Austin's medical equipment.

"May I come back in?" he asks.

Everything catches up to me so quickly that it feels like my heart actually ricochets around my ribcage, making me bring my hand up to touch my chest. The sensation freaks me the hell out, and I tip my chin down to see if it's about to crash through to spill on my lap at any second.

"Jewel?" My name sounds softly on Orlando's lips.

I turn my attention from my chest to him. "What?"

"May I?"

My eyes widen. "Oh, you're asking me. Eff. I'm sorry. I—"

I shift in my spot, my stomach sloshing again, and I gaze down at my body. Something is most definitely wrong with my insides. I can't stop myself from freaking out a bit as everything jiggles around.

"What's wrong with her, Austin?" Diego asks, keeping his voice low but not quiet enough for me not to hear.

"What he said. Am I really okay? I feel weird." I hold the blanket out just a little bit, making sure to block any chance of giving Orlando a view of my breasts and use my free hand to gently shake my stomach. "Do you hear that?"

Kingston chuckles and has the nerve to reach out and poke my belly. "Blood bloat. You know I had to drink twice as much gen. pop. to keep up with your need. And not just any gen. pop. blood. From Midnight Valley. Subpar."

"Kingston is right," Austin says. "You don't have to worry. You're healing just fine."

"Benefits of regeneration." Diego touches my other side through the sheet. "And you'll feel better in a few hours. Blood bloat is the worst."

"Many new vampires experience it. It's your body's way of teaching you better control. Your matches have been rather cautious in your blood consumption, so you've been fortunate until now," Orlando says from the doorway.

Ugh. I do not want to talk about the way my body works

with all of them. Kingston can't keep his amusement under control and chuckles to himself, which makes Diego laugh. Austin looks ready to smack the both of them. And Orlando? I don't even know what he's thinking about. But his attention focuses on me even though he continues to stare at the floor.

I heave a few deep breaths and jerk my attention to Orlando. "Enough about my body. What exactly happened besides being friggin' impaled? Why am I in your room?"

Orlando takes my questions as permission to enter. "It seems that word finally got out to Mitchell about our official alliance with the Vaduva Region. But worry not. Everything has been handled for now. The board rushed to approve my authority, and the system is pushing through new resident approvals as we speak. I think they're scared he'll go after other regions next."

Damn. I gape at the four of them, not sure how I should process this. I knew that things were going to get rough after we formed the alliance with Viorica, but it's been months. Mitchell has basically been in hiding, and the board cautiously continues to move forward—slow as hell, but still actively. It's why it's taken longer to turn official. "Oh."

Austin climbs onto the bed behind me and rubs his hand up and down the length of my back. "Calm breaths. I know all of this is overwhelming, but you don't have to panic. Promise."

"Yeah, babe. We got you." Kingston touches my chin to get me to look at him. "You haven't even missed much while

Austin kept you knocked out. Only our coven union, your birthday, the celebration of Winter Nights, and—"

My mouth drops open. "Shit. What year is it?"

Diego punches Kingston hard, sending him flying off his feet and into Orlando. Orlando catches him midair and spins him by the back of his jacket, throwing him through the double doors of the study. Kingston lands on top of...a bed? From my spot on Orlando's bed, I notice his study has been arranged into another bedroom with three extra beds.

"Kingston is joking with you, Jewel. It's only been a few days. We're all currently staying in Orlando's wing due to the damage in ours."

I glare at Kingston. "Dude."

"Payback for the prank you and Diego played on me in Haven Springs, babe."

"I guess I deserved it," I say, motioning for him to come back to me. "Makes up for this...sleeping arrangement. Has it been weird?"

"A real fucking bonding experience," Kingston mutters, dodging around his brothers. "I'm just so happy that you're awake."

"Me friggin' too, dude. And I'm glad I didn't actually miss your coven union." I rub my hands into my eyes. "A few days? So does that mean it's this weekend?"

"Mmmhmm," Diego hums.

"But that's not the only thing, babe." Kingston carefully sits next to me. "There has been a slight change in plans."

"What kind of change?" I prop up higher, accidentally shoving my elbow into Austin in the process. Austin helps me get comfortable and kisses my bare shoulder.

Kingston glances at Orlando, which makes me glance at him. He remains a few feet away from the bed where my guys crowd me. His blue eyes flash silver, and he licks his lips. Rocking back on his heels, Orlando shifts under my gaze. I can't help but think something horrible must be coming if he's nervous.

I tip my head to rest it on Austin. "Someone spit it out already."

This time, the four of them look at each other.

"You're freaking me the hell out." I grab Diego's hand. "Diego? Tell me. Please."

He clears his throat.

Orlando steps closer and touches Diego's shoulder, stopping him from telling me what's up. Sitting on the bed next to us, Orlando rests his hand on my knee through the blankets. Austin adjusts me in his arms again, hugging me without squeezing too tightly. Kingston and Diego each hold my hand.

"Because of the attack, Viorica put a rush on our Blood Vow application. The majority of the board agreed that it was in our region's best interest to ensure your place as an Ortega immediately. They would like us to proceed with our Blood Vow following the union of our coven."

I blink in surprise a few times. I thought I had months. I

thought that maybe Brayla would return and we wouldn't have to ever go through with it. But now? Ah hell. "What about the party? Isn't there supposed to be a celebration? I—I'm not good at that kind of thing."

"It has been taken care of. The Vaduvas—"

I grimace. "The Widows are planning it?"

Orlando leans closer and brushes fallen strands of my dark hair from my face. "It's going to be lovely. I promise that it'll be everything you've imagined."

I press back harder into Austin. "Doubt it. I haven't imagined anything."

Kingston snickers, shaking the bed. I jerk my attention to look at him, and he offers me a pouty lip. "I told them you wouldn't go for this."

"It doesn't matter if Jewel will go for it or not. It's not an option," Orlando says. "Our vows are happening."

I flare my nostrils.

Kingston pulls my hand to his mouth. "Now you've done it."

My heart aches, beating so quickly that my eyes water from the pain. I bend forward, but it does nothing to help. And now my stomach twists and turns. My breathing comes in quick pants, and Austin motions for everyone to step back.

"Jewel, look at me," Austin says.

I can't find the strength to lift my chin to turn to him.

"I need more sedative." Austin gently lays me back. He shines a light in my eyes. "This was too much. Her heart's still healing."

Kingston growls. Something shatters.

Four forms hover over me, blocking the light above. Dizziness washes over me as ice travels through my veins. Then all I see is flashing silver eyes.

"Kingston, stop!" Diego yells. "Don't pull him off. He has her heart!"

I scream in pain, staring up at the flashing silver eyes of the snarling vampire. He snaps his teeth at me, trying to bite my face. Squeezing my eyes shut, I tense through a wave of agony that steals my breath. Fire burns through me. My heart thumps so hard that my whole body jerks with the movements.

"Diego, hold Jewel still," Austin says, coming into view. "Kingston, don't let him go. Don't let him jerk his arm."

Kingston roars, extending his fangs longer than I've ever seen them. He locks his fingers to the strange vampire's arm, stopping him from yanking it back from my chest. Diego presses his big hands down on my shoulders, pinning me. I kick my legs, trying to thrash, my body wanting to do everything it can to escape the pain.

"Orlando, Jewel needs blood." Austin kneels next to me, a sparkling silver blade in his hand. He looks to both his brothers. "On the count of three."

Sweet liquid fills my mouth, and I automatically latch onto Orlando's arm. He blocks my view of everything, keeping his blue eyes trained to mine. A loud ass scream rips through the air, making me wince. I release Orlando to gasp and cry, the pain in my chest intensifying.

"Stop! I'll let her go!" The loud, masculine voice pulls at my consciousness.

Orlando holds his arm to my mouth again. "Drink, Jewel. It is important. Bite me if it hurts too much."

"Hold him tighter, Kingston," Austin demands.

"Please!" the strange vampire begs.

Austin ignores him and starts counting. "One. Two. Three—"

I bite down hard on Orlando's arm at the high-pitched wail that startles me. Blood splashes across my face, and Orlando uses his sleeve to swipe it off. Diego's big hands ease off my shoulders, and all three of my guys disappear.

"Jewel, look at me," Orlando says, drawing my eyes back to his. "I need you to fight, okay? I did not go through all of this just to lose you. Do you understand?"

I don't respond. I can't.

Instead, I lose myself in the sounds of the horrifying screams.

NO BIG DEAL

"IF YOU WANT IT, YOU'RE going to have to come to me, beautiful." Diego stands next to the new table my guys temporarily set up in Orlando's room for me.

I guess I should've expected to have them go into complete protective mode, limiting where I stay in this huge, confusing as all get-out deathtrap of a mansion, but seriously. Orlando's room doesn't even have a window. I know the reasoning, and it's not like my personal room in my wing had one, but I feel like my guys have unintentionally imprisoned me.

Sprawling back on the pillows, I heave a sigh. "How can you resist feeding me in bed? I won't even ask to hold the utensil."

Diego releases a small growl before chuckling. "You're

torturing me. I want nothing more than to slide into that bed next to you, but I was given one job. Don't make me fail."

I raise an eyebrow. "Your job is to feed me. In this bed. Naked."

Diego's smile turns serious as he drinks me in. Shifting onto my side, I pat the spot next to me, inviting him over. He closes the distance and stands over me, brushing his fingers along my cheek to comb the hair spilling into my eyes out of my face.

"I've missed your playfulness," he murmurs. "And I want nothing more than to give you what you want."

I hold out my hand. "Then come here."

Perching on the edge of the bed, he bends down and kisses me softly, just grazing his lips to mine. A moment later, he disappears.

"Sorry, beautiful. You have to come to me." Diego waves his hands, encouraging me to roll out of bed.

I groan. "I don't see what the difference is between me eating here or there. Kingston and Austin didn't make me."

"Which is why I'm here. They couldn't resist giving into you."

"And you can? The guy who promised to give me everything I want?" I bite my lip as I say it. "Who had accepted and come to peace with the fact that he could never deny me."

Diego steps a few feet closer and stops himself. "I can't deny you. But..."

"But nothing. Just come here and feed me in bed."

A loud laugh resonates from the study, and I catch sight of Kingston and Austin standing nearby. I didn't hear them come, and I wonder how long they've been standing there. Diego sighs and links his hands behind his head, plopping down in one of the chairs at the table.

"Stubborn as fuck, right?" Kingston asks. "I think we have to accept that this is our life now. Jewel living in bed with us. Forever."

I open my arms to invite Kingston closer. "Well, you did say that's what you wanted from our eternity."

Austin cuts Kingston off. "I would love that, but the Vaduvas have been here for an hour. They're expecting you to make an appearance at some point. Plus, you haven't even tried walking yet. As much as I love carrying you everywhere, I need to make sure you still can."

I purse my lips and curl my knees to my chest. "If I prove I can, then there's no backing out of my Blood Vow."

"There *is* no backing out, babe," Kingston says softly.

"We're going to get through this," Austin adds.

"Maybe if you..." I let my words trail off. There's no point in arguing.

"Beautiful, I know this is all sudden, but I promise you everything will be perfect with us and even Orlando. We realize you have your doubts and hesitation in regards to him, but he's determined to prove himself worthy of this vow."

"And if he doesn't, we'll hold him down while you devour him," Kingston adds.

No matter how much they reassure me, I can't help feeling off. Nervous. Not only am I vowing myself to Orlando, but I'll also officially have to pass as a vampire, something I'm not so sure I'm capable of. It takes a lot to get me to move and act like one, and even then, there is the whole lack of fangs thing. Also, Orlando will have to bite me.

I shiver at the thought and tug down the front of my shirt. "Tell the Widows I'm still not feeling well. I mean, look at this nasty scab."

Kingston releases a cross between a hum and purr from deep in his throat. "Maybe pull the shirt up instead so that I can get a better look. Right now, I see nothing nasty about your sexy, kissable tits, babe."

Austin closes the space to me. "Does it still hurt?"

I shake my head, realizing my words flicked on Austin's health keeper switch. He looks ready to start an exam, and right now, I don't want him to see me as a patient. "It's fine."

He touches my forehead. "You don't feel hot. I can get you some—"

Grabbing his hand, I pull Austin hard enough to make him climb into bed. I cup his face and kiss him, sucking his lip between my teeth. He only lasts a few seconds before Diego drags him out and nudges him back. My guys know how easy it is to get carried away with me, especially when I want them to. The two of them growl at each other, looking ready to start a fight.

Swinging my legs over the edge of the bed, I drag the

blankets with me and stand between them. "Please, don't."

"It's a miracle," Kingston says. "It only took three attempts and four hours to get our girl out of bed. Something I never wanted to do or participate in, if I might add."

Austin laughs. "We were about to call in Orlando if Diego didn't succeed."

I roll my eyes and take a few steps to flop onto the mattress. "I'd like to see that."

Diego intercepts me and blocks my way. I jab my finger into his taut chest, trying to get him to fall back, but he holds strong, even when I slide my arms around his neck and push my body to his.

"I promise I'll give into your every want and desire, beautiful...tomorrow." He gently grabs my shoulders and spins me around. "But right now, I'd like for you to give into mine."

I peer over my shoulder at him. "When you put it like that."

"It's all of our desires, Jewel," Austin says, holding a fork with a piece of pancake on it. He cups his hand beneath it to catch the dripping syrup. After he feeds it to me, I bring his hand to my mouth and glide my tongue across his palm, making all three of my guys suck in a breath.

"Mmm, delicious."

Diego beats us to the table and places a piece of pancake on his palm, pouring extra syrup over it. I grin and go along with his game. Slowly drawing my tongue over his hand, I lick up the syrup and suck his finger into my mouth.

Kingston materializes at the table with his vampire speed and rips his shirt off to throw it at me. I crack up as he swipes the dishes to the edge of the table and lies down, hanging his legs off. He slaps down a pancake on his chest and drizzles syrup down the hard line of his stomach to his navel. Grinning, he wiggles his fingers to get me to come closer.

"Had I known this is how you wanted breakfast served, we could've had you out of bed so much sooner," Kingston says. His muscles tense as I give him a once-over.

"Don't make any sudden movements, bro," Diego says, placing his big hands on my shoulders.

Austin steps between us, blocking my view. "She looks fully set on devouring you and not your offering. Look at how crazy her eyes are."

"Shit," Kingston murmurs, sitting up. "This is why I'll never be her damn nutrients match."

I stand on my tiptoes and peek at him from over Austin's shoulder, eyeing the syrup pooling along his waist. "I think you two are in more danger since you're blocking me from devouring my breakfast."

Austin and Diego both laugh and move out of the way. I rush Kingston, startling him, but he doesn't move out of the way. He lets me push him back, remaining completely expressionless as I lean over him and trail my gaze across his body.

He swears something back-world under his breath at my sudden closeness. I keep my face straight by biting my lip and use the chair to climb onto the table next to him. Placing my hands on his chest, I pin him in place and gaze into his eyes. His whole body tenses, tightening up under my fingers. He braces himself to be devoured by me without even a fight.

"You have to relax, bro," Diego says. "Tensing makes it tougher for Jewel."

I nearly lose my composure, a laugh building in my chest to shake the rest of me. Kingston mistakes it as me trying to control myself, and he releases a small breath, finally relaxing. I slide on top of him, straddling his waist, still pressing my hands firmly into his sticky chest, drenched with sweet syrup.

Easing myself lower, I playfully pick up the pancake with my teeth and drop it onto his face. He releases another breath, tensing for only a second until he feels my tongue glide slowly from his chest and down the hard planes of his stomach. I lick the syrup from his waist and release a moan before pulling myself up.

I smile at Kingston. "That's for the joke you played on me."

He playfully growls and tries to hook his hands around my waist, but Diego snatches me away and sets me down on the chair. Austin chuckles, grinning at me, and feeds me another bite of pancake.

"Joke's still on you, babe. I knew you wouldn't devour me," Kingston says, wiping his stomach off. "And that was fucking hot. I'll risk your zombie bite to experience that over and over."

"The wonders of our girl's mouth," Diego says. "I'm pretty sure we're never using plates again, beautiful."

Austin feeds me another bite. "So sexy."

I shake my head and laugh. "I'll most definitely bite next time."

"I plan on it," both Diego and Austin say at the same time. They look to each other and laugh.

Kingston groans. "Damn it. You guys are going to ruin it with your freaky ass shit."

"Definitely," I say, smiling. "Good thing you're not my nutrients or body match, dude."

Releasing a playful growl, Kingston throws a napkin at me and disappears into the bathroom to get cleaned up. He returns and heads into the wardrobe to pick out a new shirt and brings an off the shoulder, boat-neck dress that'll still expose a lot of skin, just not the healing wound left behind by Mitchell's minion.

I hold my arms up, and Diego eases the shirt off me. Kingston hovers his fingers an inch from my boobs, looking like he'll die if I don't let him touch them. I straighten my shoulders and graze my nipples against his palms, and he takes a moment to lean in to kiss me, playfully fondling me at the same time. I return the favor, cupping him through his pants, making him disappear only to flop on the bed.

"All right. Jewel is not feeling well," Kingston says. "Bring her back here."

"We could probably stall for another hour," Austin says, smirking at me. "If our girl needs us to satiate her a bit more."

"I suppose it's a good thing I've come when I did." Orlando's voice sounds from the study. "Is everything all right with Jewel?"

Kingston steps in the doorway to block his view while Diego helps me finish getting dressed. I inhale a few breaths through my nose as my nerves get the best of me. I nod to Kingston, and he moves to let Orlando into the room.

Orlando's eyebrows pinch together, noticing my inability to smile, even to fake one. "What's wrong?"

"Nothing. Just taking my time with breakfast," I murmur, twisting my shaking hands together.

Orlando glances at Austin, who shrugs. Diego reaches out and touches my knee, and I grab his hand to pull it to my chest to hug against me. Kingston puffs out his bottom lip. Everyone knows I'm full of shit, and that something bothers me, but I don't want to get into it.

"Brothers, will you please check on the Vaduvas? I need a moment alone to speak to Jewel." Orlando tilts his head, peering at me.

None of my guys move right away, expecting for me to argue.

For once, I don't.

I don't know if it's because I nearly died or what, but I'm tired of constantly keeping my walls up. Or fighting with him. How can I ever be okay if I don't allow myself to be? We've decided on this life together after all.

I nod my head and put on a smile for them. "It's fine.

You can tell Viorica I'll be there shortly."

Kingston raises his eyebrows but doesn't comment. Diego offers me an easy-going smile while Austin leans in and reminds me that they won't be far if I need them.

The three of them hug and kiss me before leaving me with Orlando. I sit quietly at the table and shove a few more bites of the pancakes in my mouth. Orlando takes a seat at the table next to me and sinks his fangs into his arm, drawing my attention to the rivulets of blood seeping from his bite mark.

"Would you like to—"

Before he can finish his sentence, my body reacts without consulting my mind, and I hook my fingers to his arm and bring it to my lips. I don't latch on or suck, though. A dozen memories flicker through my head, all moments from our times in the shadows where I drank from him like it was no big deal.

But now? It feels huge.

Orlando picks up my empty glass, ready to drizzle his blood into it because I hover my mouth an inch from his skin, just inhaling deep breaths of the tantalizing scent. My hesitation arises from the part of me that doesn't want to let myself give in, but that part of me can't win for much longer. There is no turning back with a Blood Vow.

"Jewel," he whispers, my name hanging in the air as he watches me. "It's okay either way, but if you have any doubts at all, let me give you the glass. I don't want you to feel like you have to do it this way with me because of the vows."

It's like he's read my mind. Or he knows me. Of course he does.

I lick my lips. "I want this to be okay. I *need* for this to be okay. You've done so much for us that—"

"Please, Jewel. If you feel like you should because of what I've done for you, then I want to put it in the glass. I want you to want this." He reaches out and gently touches my knee. "Because you owe me nothing. I'm grateful that you even allow me this chance after everything."

I don't respond. Instead, I swallow and close my eyes. Everything about Orlando feels so utterly familiar in this moment that any doubt I carry vanishes the second a drop of his blood coats my bottom lip.

I give into my body's need to drink and caress my mouth to his skin. Tingles dance across my tongue and down my throat with my first swallow. I can't stop the soft moan from escaping my lips.

"Jewel."

My name sounds like a plea on his lips, and I flutter my eyes open, nerves coursing through me at the thought of meeting his gaze. Orlando's eyes flash silver, his fangs peeking out from beneath his lips, a look of longing darkening his sharp features.

It's enough to ease myself away.

"Thank you. I feel a lot better," I say, leaning back in my chair, pretending that this is no different than the hundreds of times before.

I turn my attention to the food on the table and stab the last bit of pancake with my fork and shove it in my mouth so that I don't have to say anything more.

Orlando presses his lips into a thin line, but I know it's only to combat his oncoming smile. "I'm always happy to give you what you want and need."

"Just don't get too ahead of yourself, okay?" I don't know why I say it. He hasn't done anything to show that he plans to.

"I'll let you lead this in any direction you want. This feels new to me too," he says, resting his arm on the table to staunch the bleeding from his bite.

"This?" I motion between us. "This isn't something yet. This was me getting what I need in a way I like. Now please don't make this weird or anything. I'm already freaked out enough as it is." And I'm pretty sure it's taking everything in Orlando not to frown. I didn't mean to make it sound like this step meant nothing, but hell. I'm—I'm so friggin' confused.

I push back the chair and stand up, trying to escape his sudden intensity. My heart thrums in quick beats, and I can't stop myself from easing the collar of my shirt back to take a peek. I hate that it already looks better than it did a few minutes ago because of the strength of Orlando's blood.

"Freaked out?" Orlando blocks my way, attempting to get me to stop before I stride out of the room to find my guys.

Again, I try to push past him. "It's nothing. I'll get over

it."

Instead of grabbing onto me, he holds his hands up. "Please, Jewel. Just wait a moment. I didn't come here with the intent to give you my blood. I wanted to talk."

"Then maybe you shouldn't have offered me a drink." I shift on my feet and hug myself. "The side effects aren't strong like with my nutrients match, but I still feel something. I need space."

"That's not due to my blood," Orlando says.

"The hell it's not."

I try again to shove past him, but the world around me blurs. I land on the bed, my body bouncing a foot in the air with Orlando's sudden action. I grab a pillow and hug it against my chest, scrambling back a bit.

"You did not just throw me," I say, scrunching my nose.

"I'm nearly certain I did."

He clenches his jaw for a moment, narrowing his eyes at me, but then he breaks and releases a chuckle. I gape at him in shock. It's been so long since he's laughed with just me and not because he was amused by something my guys did. The gesture takes me by surprise, and I can't stop staring at how handsome he is with his whole face lit up.

The melodious sound of his voice digs into my heart, and I close my eyes, just absorbing the softness that reminds me of how he used to always speak to me.

I thought for sure he was going to growl or some shit because I let him in only to knock him right back out in a way I know he desires to be. But my nerves got the best of me. I thought I wanted to try with Orlando, to remind myself that we have history, but I'm terrified.

"And I apologize," he adds, filling the silence I let arise. "You've been nothing but one fight after another with me, Jewel. I do get it—I deserve it—but I just want you to humor me and give me a couple more minutes of your time. You haven't said much since I told you about the sudden approval of our Blood Vow. I know you well enough to know that you were hoping for Brayla to return, but I want you to know that a vow with me doesn't have to be much different."

I groan and sink deeper on the bed. Covering my face with the pillow, I release a small screech to sooth the nerves tensing my muscles. "Orlando...I love my matches. I—"

"You've made it quite clear, and I've accepted that. I depend on it to make our coven strong." His light footsteps tap closer, but I still don't look at him. "It's like how they depend on my love for you. I also depend on their love for you as well."

"You do?" I ask, my voice muffling into the pillow.

"Is that so surprising? Their love for you makes them strong, determined. It's what has cemented our bond as brothers. We don't want you to be miserable with this vow. You shouldn't dread it."

I heave a breath. "I don't dread it—much. It's not that."

The bed jostles as Orlando sits on the edge. "I think it is. At least partly. And because of that, we've asked Merrick and

Samantha to arrange the ceremony to make it as pleasant as possible. It's supposed to be an exciting moment for you, Jewel. You're trading your life as a donor for eternity."

"I'm not, though," I say into the pillow.

"To the world you are."

I ease the pillow away from my face and meet Orlando's gaze. "I don't understand why it has to be a big deal. Why can't we just tell them we want a private ceremony with just our coven? You were able to do that with Brayla."

"I'm on the board now, Jewel. You're not only fulfilling a place in my coven, you're also accepting a prestigious part of my life, one with power. You could ultimately be next in line to take control of the Ortega power."

"You're shitting me," I say. "That's the worst idea ever."

He chuckles. "Well, it might be if I planned on something happening to me."

I throw the pillow at him, and he catches it. "Hey! You're not supposed to agree."

"Oh, precious Jewel. I'm only teasing. You'd be a magnificent leader over our coven. Your vision of our future together reminds me of what I wanted all along. I thought I'd be content to have you alone, to..." His words trail off, his voice growing soft. "No matter. You've given me a better purpose, one I can only fulfill with your matches. I thought I wanted to use them against Mitchell on your behalf, but it's so much more than that."

"So you really aren't just inviting them into your coven to

keep me around?" I ask.

"I know you struggle to trust me, but my offer has always been genuine to them." Orlando scoots closer so that he can place his hand over mine. "I don't know if it's because they're who your heart wants or if it's because they truly are matches worthy of you, but I want nothing more than to assure our coven's happiness. I feel fortunate that you allow me such the honor."

"Orlando." I place my free hand on top of his and sandwich his between mine. "This is—"

"Still a lot to process. I know. But you'll see that it'll be okay."

"Our Blood Vow...I'm scared." My admission hangs in the air, and I throw myself back on the bed and stare at the ceiling. "I know I agreed to it, but you have to bite me."

"Oh."

"In *front* of people. With venom."

He releases a breathless laugh and groans, covering his face with his hands for a second. "Austin and I discussed this, and we agree that the risk is minimal. If you can handle all their venom at once, mine shouldn't be much different. Better if anything."

I crinkle my nose. "Of course you discussed this with Austin."

"Your wellbeing is important to us, Jewel."

"Then what about the other stuff? I mean, we've never gone *there*." I don't have to say the words again for him to know what I mean.

Leaning closer, Orlando uses his free hand to draw his fingers across my jaw. "That can change quite easily."

Holy shit balls. My dumb body. What a traitor. Excitement blossoms through me, and I squirm under the weight of Orlando's stare. Heat prickles across my neck, and I feel like my face will explode into flames at any second.

Scrambling up, I hop off the bed to put some space between us. "Uh, shit. Um. I need to go."

Orlando doesn't block my way this time. He lets me jog into the study, though he calls for Diego.

I rush from the room, my heart threatening to spill out onto the floor, it's hard rapping testing the new skin healing over my chest.

I'm so focused on keeping my feet going that I don't see one of the hallway doors open. Orlando yells my name, and I spin and meet his wide eyes too far away.

Strong arms wrap around me and tug me into the room. I kick and buck, doing everything I can to escape, but the world suddenly drops out from under me. A hand covers my mouth to stifle my screech, and my legs buckle under me when I land on something soft. A mattress.

"Be quiet, Jewel. We only have a few minutes before they find the trap door. Come on. This way."

I jerk my arm back to punch Hayden, but he holds a small light between us, and I stop short, staring at his glossy eyes.

"Please, Jewel," he begs, offering his hand.

My good senses stop working, and I find myself running with Hayden, his hand tight around mine.

And then we're outside.

SURPRISE VISIT

HAYDEN HOLDS HIS INDEX FINGER to his lips and motions for me to follow him around the front of the mansion and to the sleek, silver car parked out front. He waves for me to open the door, and I unlock it using my handprint like all of the other locks on the premises.

I get behind the wheel, and Hayden signals for me to start the engine. I swivel in my seat and meet his gaze dead-on. "You're out of your damn mind if you think I'm driving anywhere with you."

He sighs. "Not anywhere. Just into town. It'll give us enough time to talk. Orlando hasn't even let me in the same section of the house as you since the attack."

"Not like you could've talked to me." I tug my shirt

down just enough to show off the top of my scab. "I nearly lost my heart."

"So it is true. You do regenerate like a vampire," he says, leaning back in the seat.

I stare at the lights flickering on through the crystal windows. "Not as quickly, but yeah. Shouldn't you know this? You said Blood Rebels have located other dhampirs before."

"I haven't personally. But the rumors. Fuck. Jewel, you have to help me get to The Orchards. Ramona—"

I put my hand on the door. "I told you no. Ramona doesn't want my help."

"What about your cousins? You're just abandoning your family now? Have they really gotten so far into your head that you don't care about—"

I slap Hayden across the face, sending his head jerking to the side. "How dare you!"

"Shhh!" he hisses. "They'll hear."

"I don't care! You can't come here and ask me for help and then insult me. You know how friggin' important my family is to me, but this—" I wave my hand around the car, motioning to the world outside us. "This is important too. We're trying to establish a region. My guys are joining the Ortega Coven. I'm going through with a Blood Vow to Orlando. You already told me my cousins were safe. Obviously, wherever my dad took them is dangerous for vampires. If it wasn't, my guys would have agreed to help."

Hayden releases a strangled laugh and hits his palms on

the dashboard. "You're crazy, Jewel. I thought that your dad's idea was dangerous, but you have no idea what you're getting yourself into. If anyone finds out about you, they'll kill you. Your life would be a waste. All for what? This idea of a future with vampires? Do you even know what is happening in Haven Springs?"

My throat dries at his words. No matter how hard I try, I can't even form a response.

And then the front door bangs open.

Hayden rushes to exit the vehicle, yanking his gun free to aim at Austin. Thrusting the door open, I hop out and catch Austin by the back of his shirt while he lifts Hayden off his feet. He snarls, releasing a scary ass growl, and I slide my arm around his chest.

"Let him go, Austin," I say, trying to pull him into me. "Please, just let him go."

Austin drops Hayden to his knees and spins around to lift me into his arms. Kingston, Diego, and Orlando materialize from inside the house, and I hold up my palm, stopping the three of them in place. Hayden stumbles to his feet and rushes down the path and past the fountain, disappearing from view.

"I'm going to murder him," Kingston says, growling deep in his throat.

"Dude, calm down. We were just talking."

Kingston points his finger in Hayden's direction. "He kidnapped you."

I twist my lips to the side. "He didn't. Not really."

"What?" Kingston, Austin, and Diego say in unison.

"I'm sorry I scared you." I turn my gaze to Orlando. "I needed some fresh air, and Hayden just kind of led the way."

"Why did you need fresh air? Are you still not feeling okay?" Austin asks. We all know that I was fine when my guys left me, but he's trying to get answers as to why I'd do something crazy after spending a couple of minutes alone with Orlando.

Orlando and I glance at each other.

"It's a personal matter between Jewel and me," Orlando says, speaking up first.

I frown. "No, it's fine. I'm just freaking out about being bitten by him. He offered to...never mind. It's nothing. I'm being ridiculous."

Turning my back on the four of them, I hug myself and stare into the darkness, training my eyes on the glittering stars until they blur with my watery eyes. I blink a few times, feeling the weight of everyone looking at me, though no one moves or speaks.

"I'll get over it," I add to fill the silence. "I've been bitten by other vampires before."

A gentle hand touches my shoulder. "Orlando's obviously different than other vampires." Diego slides his arms around me from behind when I don't turn to face him. His taut chest presses into my back, and he bows low enough to rest his chin on my shoulder. "And I don't think you're acting ridiculous."

"None of us do, babe," Kingston says. He steps up next

to me and takes my hand. "We know how much you hate feeling vulnerable."

"It's not that." My voice barely sounds above a whisper. "I don't know what it is."

"If it's about us and our feelings, you don't have to worry, Jewel." Austin comes up to my other side and links his fingers through mine. "The last thing we want is for you to be afraid or nervous. I can't speak for my brothers, but you ever being in the position of getting bitten for anything other than pleasure and enjoyment kills me. I hate that you went through that. If you think it'll help to let Orlando bite you beforehand, you should do it."

"What if I like it?" I ask, rubbing my lips together.

Kingston groans. "As much as it pains me to say this, I hope you *do* like it."

"You do?" I finally break my gaze on the night to look at him.

He nods, smirking at me. "Fuck yeah. I'm not even jealous of the idea. All I want is for you to be happy and content. Feel loved. I don't want you to worry about us. You're our girl. This is our coven. Our future. It's going to be amazing."

Orlando joins our circle and steps in front of me. Kingston and Austin slide their arms around me and Diego to free my hands for Orlando to take. He brings them up to his chest and holds my fingers over his pounding heart.

"Kingston is right. We want the same thing in regards to you. I might not regret putting you through what I did because of where it led, but I do regret that you will never hold me as dear to you as your matches. I'm okay with that, though. Just being around you is enough for me. I want you to know that. All of you."

I open my mouth to tell him that I know he's trying, that I want to give him a chance, even after everything, but a loud pop sounds through the air. Hayden's familiar yell echoes out, and I push into Orlando to break our circle faster than my guys can react.

I don't get far as Orlando spins me back around and into Diego's arms. Kingston and Austin take their places beside me while Orlando blocks my view. I bump into a whole lot of hot muscle as I try to get a better look. A light flashes through the air, lighting up one of the tall palm trees at the end of the pathway before the gate that leads out of the property.

Another gunshot pops.

"Take Jewel inside," Orlando commands, unsheathing a knife from beneath his jacket.

Fear clenches my chest. "Are we under attack?"

Orlando peers at me from over his shoulder. "I only hear one vampire, and he seems to be rather taken by Mr. Andrei."

I pull away from Diego and grip Orlando's shoulders. "You have to do something."

"Yeah, like reward the outcast with residency if he manages to get ahold of Hayden," Kingston mutters.

I swat him. "Dude."

"What? He kidnapped you," Kingston says, releasing a

growl.

Austin tries to put his arm around me. "It would teach him a lesson."

I catch sight of a figure running in our direction at a human's pace. Hayden slams the gate closed, and the metal rattles. He risks his safety by turning his back on us, leaving himself open. Holding his gun steady, he aims it at the gate as another figure materializes. I expect the vampire to ignore it, but he stops short and just clamps his fingers to the wrought iron.

"I think I agree with my brothers," Diego says from behind me, keeping his voice even.

I step on his foot. "Seriously?"

Orlando straightens his shoulders. "You have my permission to enter the premises."

My mouth falls agape as I realize that Orlando totally just told the stalking vampire he could enter our property. I smack him in the shoulder and glare.

"You guys," I say. "This is wrong."

"But it's entertaining as fuck. Look at Hayden go." Kingston bumps his shoulder into mine.

"I know that Hayden is an asshole, and he pisses me off as much as he pisses you off, but this is not cool."

Diego covers my ears for me, anticipating another round of gunfire as the vampire closes the distance to Hayden. I push harder into Orlando's back, trying to get him to budge from his spot. The vampire flies at Hayden, surprising him by sneaking up and materializing in front of him the second he tries to look over his shoulder.

Hayden shoots the vampire at close range, sending blood spraying through the air. And eff. I can smell it.

"Take Jewel ins—"

I shove so hard into Orlando's back that he nearly eats shit on the walkway. Something intense snaps inside me, hearing Hayden yell out again. Kingston snatches me by the back of my shirt while Austin grabs Orlando's hand and sends him up into the air to land in a crouch.

Silence draws through the night, Hayden and the vampire no longer making any noise. Diego lifts me up onto his shoulder, dangling me upside down, and I smack his ass.

"Mr. Ortegas," the vampire says, speaking to all of them. "I heard the Blood Vow ceremony wasn't until the weekend. Does this mean we'll be getting early entrance? If so, I'd like to put my claim on this donor I've caught."

"Fuck, he saw her," Kingston says.

Diego flips me off his shoulder to stand me in front of him. "He'll spread the word to the new arrivals."

The vampire disappears from on top of Hayden and closes the space to us inhumanly fast. He offers Orlando a deep bow and nods to my guys. Then he catches my gaze from over Orlando's shoulder.

"Allow me formally to congratulate Mrs. Ortega," the vampire says, flashing his fangs. "I would love to offer her a taste of the donor."

"Yeah, no thanks," I say, speaking up.

The strange vampire growls. I'm nearly certain I just offended him. His gesture makes everyone react. If I closed my eyes, I might think I was standing amid a pack of ferocious beasts.

The strange vampire jerks his hand out and grabs onto Orlando's shoulder.

Huge friggin' mistake.

One second I'm in the middle of a delicious, even if a tad noisy, vampire sandwich, and in the next, I'm lying on top of Orlando's back, digging my fingers into the vampire's throat from over Orlando's shoulder. The jerk flashes his fangs, attempting to bite Orlando. Strong hands grab me by the waist, yanking me up. I drag Orlando with me, and the vampire disappears.

Another round of gunfire pops through the air, and Hayden screams.

"Orlando, do something!" I yell.

He's not quick to react. None of my guys are. They remain surrounding me yet keep a few feet of space between us.

"Jewel, please take a breath," Austin says. "You look ready to attack."

"Then stop him," I say, waving my hand at the vampire.

Austin, Diego, and Orlando disappear. Diego and Austin rip the vampire off of Hayden, and Orlando helps Hayden to his feet. He stumbles in my direction, a scowl distorting his already hard features.

"You're hurt," I say, motioning to the blood soaking

through the sleeve of his shirt.

"Nothing I can't handle," he mutters, pushing past Kingston.

I grab Kingston's hand to stop him from reacting.

"Kingston, incoming," Orlando shouts.

Kingston spins me so fast that it takes me a second to realize another vampire enters the property—actually, two vampires. Orlando holds another by the throat.

A deep, guttural noise trickles through the air, and Kingston tenses. Ah, hell. The noise comes from me.

"Control yourself, babe," Kingston murmurs. "I got this."

But so do I.

The second Kingston grabs the intruding vampire by the shoulders, I charge at the two of them. How dare they come onto our property and threaten us. How dare they try to test me after everything?

Blood sprays across me, and I heave a few breaths and lick my lips.

I didn't even get within a foot of the vampire in Kingston's arms. A hard chest presses against me, and Austin whispers for me to calm down in my ear. I stare in shock and surprise, watching Kingston drop the body to the ground while he still holds onto the severed head.

"Holy shit balls," I say, eyeing Kingston.

He grimaces. "Sorry, babe. I know how much you wanted to rip his heart out...but no. Not when I got it."

"Uh-oh," Diego says, his voice light, pulling my attention

away from Kingston and the head dripping dark blood to the ground. "You better brace yourself, Kingston. I think you're making Jewel hungry."

"Someone take care of our girl," he says, dropping the vampire's head.

I flare my nostrils at him and narrow my eyes. He holds up his bloody hands to me, and I close the space. Kingston remains utterly still as I tighten my fingers around his wrist and bring his hand to my mouth.

Kingston jerks me to him and hugs me against him, stiffening as I bury my face into the crook of his neck. "If you can't resist, just bite, but keep your eyes closed. Merrick is coming in—"

A soft hum trickles through the air. "So this is what was taking so long. You should have told us. You know we like having fun too."

"It was an unexpected encounter," Orlando says. His footsteps softly tap nearby and he touches his hand to my back. "Thank you, brother. I can take Jewel from here."

I squeeze Kingston tighter for a second and then relent and let him go though I want nothing more than for him to carry me back inside.

Orlando doesn't let my feet even touch the ground. He gathers me in his arms and strokes his fingers up and down my back in such a way that leaves my body at war with itself. Because I hate that I love how good it feels.

Orlando clears his throat. "You'll have to excuse us for a

bit longer. My brothers must reset our security. It seems this coven wanted to test us before our coven union."

"On Mitchell's behalf?" Merrick says.

"Don't know," Kingston says. "Didn't ask."

"This one went after one of the staff members Jewel wants to keep around," Diego says, motioning to a bloody heap.

Merrick sucks air through her teeth. "Hopefully not that handsome man you just sent in to entertain us."

"What?" I ask.

Orlando squeezes his arms around me.

Merrick tips her head back and laughs. "I'm only teasing, Mrs. Soon-to-be-Ortega. I can see why he's your favorite. Once you transition, he'll satisfy your hunger any way you'd like, considering a love vow is exclusive between vampires and not the donors who serve them."

Damn it do I have a lot of friggin' questions.

I don't get the chance to ask them, though. Instead, Orlando says, "Jewel hasn't chosen her personal donor yet. If Mr. Andrei agrees to accept your company, I grant you permission to taste him. But you mustn't put his life in jeopardy."

"Oh, I'm always nice," Merrick says. "And take your time. Mother is rather patient."

Kingston laughs, the noise echoing through the air. "If you say so. Enjoy the commodities while you wait."

"I plan to." Merrick's footsteps disappear along with her soft humming.

Orlando finally sets me on my feet. "Austin, please take Jewel back to our suite. Assure she's unharmed."

I don't even get a chance to look around before Austin sweeps me off my feet and the world blurs.

HEART-TO-HEART

A KNOCK SOUNDS ON THE BATHROOM door. "Looks like the Vaduvas are staying the day," Kingston says. "So no rush."

"We didn't plan on it." I tilt my head and meet Austin for a kiss. "Why don't you come in and join us?"

He groans. "You love testing me, don't you?"

"It's not a test."

"I really fucking want to, but I have to go suffer through showing the Vaduvas to their rooms." It sounds like Kingston thuds his head on the door. "Invite me again next time?"

I slide my body slightly sideways to glance at Austin with my silent question.

He shrugs and kisses me. "The thought makes you happy.

How could I deny you?"

I giggle and blush, turning my attention to the closed door. "You bet, Kingston. I will figure out the seating or buy a bigger tub."

Kingston's laugh fades away and silence falls on the other side of the door. I turn and kiss Austin again, smiling against his mouth. A bath with him was exactly what I needed to shake the weirdness of the night so far.

"How's this?" Austin asks, gently lathering soap across my skin. He insisted we just rinse off in the shower because he wanted to take his time making sure to take care of the rest of me the way he wants. His fingers slide under my wet hair, shifting it from my back to rest on my shoulder.

"Mmm," I hum, scooting forward to allow him to massage the length of my back.

Hot water runs down my skin as Austin rinses me off before moving closer to brush his lips against the crook of my neck. The scent of fresh flowers permeates the air, and I lean into his muscular chest and peer around the dimly lit bathroom. Bouquets litter every free spot of counter space along with glass sconces with lit candles, setting the room aglow.

"This is perfect." I squirm a bit, slipping my hip against Austin's thigh to stretch just enough to glance at him. "Thank you."

"No, thank you for letting me join," he whispers. "I've missed you, Jewel. I love taking care of you, but not in the way I had to the last couple of days. It was...I guess it was worse for you than it was for me."

I link my fingers with his under the water and guide them slowly up my stomach to map across my skin. "Let's not think about it anymore. I just want to forget everything and enjoy this."

His breath quickens as I bring his hands up to the curves of my breast. "It's already forgotten," he murmurs, gliding his fingers higher to caress my sensitive skin, my nipples hardening with my desire as Austin exposes my breasts to the cool air.

I moan and sink back, relishing the feeling of his hands rubbing across my body, memorizing every inch of me without getting carried away. Austin breathes against my damp hair, leaning to suck my earlobe into his mouth. The sensation makes me squirm between his legs until I feel the pressure of his growing arousal against my lower back.

"Jewel," he whispers. "Let me help you out of the tub."

"Just a bit longer." Reaching down, I stroke my fingers along Austin's legs, turning his touch from gentle to desperate. "It feels so good."

Austin relaxes behind me, his heart thrumming against my back. His exploration of my body continues, his fingers teasing me in circles between my legs in the best way possible. I arch my back, resting my head on his shoulder. Tingles wash through me, and I shift slightly to reach Austin, making him moan into my hair, the sound sending my heart racing.

"You'll tell me if you experience any pain, right?" he asks breathlessly, building more pressure between my legs.

I nod my head, rubbing against him. "The only thing my body aches for is you."

Austin shifts me in his arms and kisses me deeply, sliding his tongue into my mouth. Hooking his arm under my ass, he picks me up with one arm, steadying the both of us with his free hand on the wall. I cling onto his side, hooking my arms around his neck. I trail kisses down his throat, tasting the sweet tanginess of his skin.

Water drips across the floor, and Austin snatches a towel from the rack and manages to drape it around the both of us. He carries me across the bathroom to the door and stops short. Through the soft music, voices sound out from Orlando's room.

"Here's fine," I whisper, bringing my mouth to his. "I can't wait a moment longer."

Austin sprawls out a towel with one hand and gently sets me down on my back, not letting any space get between us. My whole body hums in anticipation, feeling Austin align his body to mine. He kisses the moan from my lips, slowly rocking his body to test me, teasing me enough to hook my legs around him.

His green eyes capture mine, watching my face as he eases inside me. His eyes close at his torturously slow pace, just letting me experience every inch of him until I pull him close to where our pelvises meet.

Leaning down, he brushes his lips to mine and works his way across my jaw, moving his body in a rhythm that's quick to draw short gasps from me. His torso slips up and down against my thighs, still damp with water, and I stretch up to nip the skin of his shoulder.

I clutch onto him, goosebumps prickling over my skin at the cool air around us. His panting matches mine as I press my back into the ground to create more resistance. Austin leans close, caging my head with his elbows, pressing our wet bodies together. Meeting me for a kiss every few seconds, he satiates my craving for his mouth on mine, his tongue caressing mine, turning our love into passion and need.

His motions ignite warmth inside me, building a pleasure so intense that I arch my back. Sliding his hand between us, he works his fingers over my buzzing body, sending me on the verge of exploding. I squeeze my eyes shut, my muscles clenching and releasing from the heart-pounding sensations exploding through me, and I can't stop from moaning so embarrassingly loud as I come to the point of release.

Austin brings his lips back to mine to feel the vibration of my voice on his mouth. He smiles through kisses, molding his mouth so fervently to mine that I suck his lip to graze my teeth over until he bites it for me to tease me with his blood.

He hums my name, his voice deepening with the desire I elicit from him. I love my name on his lips and pull back to meet his vibrant green gaze. His lips puff with his breathing, his eyes narrowing, making him sexy as hell, and I cup his face, unable to resist trying to steal his breath again until he breaks away and closes his eyes, his face scrunching with pleasure.

He rolls his body through a few more powerful thrusts, releasing a sexy noise into my ear, until he sinks his weight onto me just enough that our hearts thrum against each other. We lie together for a few minutes with only the sounds of our breathing, just being together, soaking in the love we share, the passion and relief we give that makes me know that we're always going to be amazing.

He rests on his elbow and caresses his fingers across the skin on my chest, now nearly healed apart from a pink shininess that should disappear in a few hours. Rubbing his lips together, Austin searches my face. A dozen thoughts dance across his soft features, and his eyes flash silver.

"What?" I ask, smiling at him. "You look like you have something you want to say."

"Just how much I love you."

"I love you too," I say. "More than I ever imagined. I wish it were you standing before me with the board this weekend. It kills me, you know."

He doesn't let his smile falter, though his jaw twitches. "We'll still get our vows."

"I know. It's just…" I let my words trail off for a minute. "I wish Brayla were here. It would be so much easier if she were."

With my admission, a dozen thoughts cross my mind. Everything has been so overwhelming since I woke up from sedation that I haven't even thought much about Brayla or my family for that matter. About the Blood Rebels. Ramona. If Hayden hadn't appeared tonight, I might not have. It bothers me too much, and right now, I need a clear head to get through what the board has to throw at me.

Austin shifts off of me, resting on his hip. "I do too, but it's just not going to happen. Not any time soon at least."

I groan and rest my head back on the towel. "Hayden is pissed at me. He thinks I don't care about my family."

Austin touches my cheek. "So he was trying to get you to convince us?"

"He worries about Ramona...because of everything with me." I pucker my lips, wondering what my family is thinking right now. What and how Ramona is dealing. I wish my mom were still here. She would help her the way she needs. My dad? I'm afraid even to imagine. "I feel like an awful person, Austin. My sister—ugh, I can't believe she's pregnant. I was hoping I dreamt that."

One frown from Austin proves that I didn't, and Hayden did knock her up. And since Ramona's a carrier of the dhampir mutation, it could mean their child has a chance of being like me. Ah hell.

"We'll worry about it when that time comes. The average human gestation period runs about two-hundred and eighty days. Orlando told me that Hayden said they're guessing she got pregnant in Haven Springs since they didn't have intercourse here, so she has at least four months left."

I frown at him as he goes into health keeper mode. That's

way more information about my sister and Hayden than I wanted. And Kingston was totally wrong.

"That gives us a bit of time to figure things out if the fetus is in fact female." Austin slides his arm under me to pull me more against him. "I can go over everything with you if you want."

My cheeks burn, and I lean back to draw my gaze over the length of our entwined bodies. "Maybe not while we're in this position."

Austin blushes next and chuckles. "I'm sorry."

I bite my lip and smile at him. "But thanks for offering. I'd rather teach the new human residents of our community. Provide preventative measures if they want it."

He groans under his breath. "That goes against Donor Life Corp's territory law."

I grimace.

"I know it bothers you, but with our up-and-coming region, it's important to show a growth in population," Austin says.

I roll closer and cuddle against him, so I can brush my lips to his throat. "That doesn't make me feel better, so hug me more."

He tightens his arms around me. "I promise you things will be nothing like Dark Terrace Ranch. We know better now. We don't have to appease anyone here."

"Good. I can't wait to see that. All the other stuff? I just want to get through it."

"We'll get through it together."

Austin sits upright and helps me from the floor. We spend a few extra minutes warming up in the shower, and he carries me out wrapped in a fluffy towel and sets me on my feet in the wardrobe. Kingston, Diego, and Orlando murmur to each other from the study, and I peek my head through the doorway to catch sight of them sitting on the three beds, facing each other. None of them look up at me, giving me and Austin pretend privacy, and Austin slides his hands around my waist and pulls me to him to kiss me again.

"No need to dress up now," he says, picking out a pair of jeans and a cotton shirt for himself. "We'll share a meal with the Vaduvas later, but it's not a formal occasion. Viorica won't care if you show up in your pajamas if you want to. This is our house and region. We're never to be uncomfortable in our own home."

I do my best not to react to the idea of waltzing in front of the gorgeous Vaduva Coven in my PJs, because that feels like a nightmare thought, and instead peer around for something that doesn't make me seem like I'm trying too hard. I stroll along my section of the wardrobe, which takes up more than all of theirs combined, and run my fingers across the dresses before I skip them completely.

I purse my lips and look to Austin again. He looks incredibly kissable in his casual clothes. I peek out at Kingston and Diego, and they're also in jeans. Even Orlando is.

Easing the top drawer open, I pick out a pair of cotton

and lace undergarments and stare at the few shirts hanging that I haven't worn yet. I spot a familiar blue T-shirt and laugh as I pull it off the hanger.

"Close your eyes," I say, hiding it from Austin.

Austin does as I ask and shuts his eyes while I pull on the *Book Nerd* shirt I picked out from the ancient clothing store in town. I shimmy into a pair of jeans and laugh as I spot the glasses Diego tucked among my shelf of accessories.

I pose with my finger in my mouth, laughing to myself. "Okay, I'm ready."

Austin gawks at me for a second, sweeping his gaze from the glasses to the rest of me. Tipping his head back, he releases a laugh and shakes his head. His smile widens when he actually reads the T-shirt.

He closes the space and plays with the hem. "You're making it incredibly hard to find it in me to step even an inch away from you."

I place my hands on his shoulders and hop into his arms to meet him for a kiss, bumping the glasses against his eyebrows in the process.

"I was going to save this for a trip into town," I murmur into his mouth. "But I doubt you guys will want to go there with me now. When are the new residents officially moving in? What happens with the old stores?"

Austin kisses me again. "Hold that thought and wait here."

One second I'm in his arms, and in the next, I'm on my

feet and staring at the empty space in front of me. I frown and stroll to the doorway to peek out. I find Austin leaning in close to Orlando, and Kingston and Diego both wave at me. I run my hand through my damp hair and lean in the doorway, posing for them.

Diego howls a laugh while Kingston raises an eyebrow. Orlando turns his attention to me and smirks. I flush and swivel back into the wardrobe. Leaning my back on the mirror, I take a deep breath. I don't know why I'm suddenly feeling shy. Awkward as hell too.

"Babe, come back out here and let us take another look at your sexy nerdy self," Kingston calls.

I swipe off the glasses and cross my arms over my chest. "You just wait until you see what I have in store for you."

Kingston stands up. "I can't. This is way hot. I want you to put me in detention or something."

I scrunch my nose. "You know, detention wasn't a real thing. At least not at my school. I only saw it once in a movie."

"Oh, it most definitely was. But it wasn't as fun as this." He twirls his finger at me. "So punish me."

Austin chuckles, cutting Kingston off before he can reach me, and gathers me to him in a hug that steals the breath from me. "That can be arranged. Jewel, tell him he can't go...on our field trip."

I tilt my head and gaze up at him. "Field trip? Those aren't real either."

Diego laughs again and materializes next to Austin to offer him his hand. "We're making them real for you now. Your health keeper seems to think you might need some fresh air without all the fighting off of new arrivals."

Orlando joins us in his room. "The Vaduvas should be fine alone here for few hours, and Austin suggested we take you into town one last time before the renovations. That is, if you want to."

"We'd all go together," Austin adds.

I twist my lips and turn my gaze to Kingston, who dares me with his midnight eyes to say something. "Except Kingston. He's in trouble—" I can't hold a straight face and laugh, motioning for him to come closer. "I can't do it, dude. You're too cute to punish."

"Damn straight," he teases.

I rock on my heels and look at the four of them. "So, a sort of night on the town, huh? Are you sure about this? You guys complained about all the close bonding during my healing."

"It was more of a complaint that you didn't get to enjoy it with us," Diego says.

I stick my tongue out at him. "Mmmhmm."

Kingston pokes my nose. "I'm fucking not sure about this, and not because of our coven bonding time. You're all sorts of trouble and not always the good kind."

"But we think we can handle you," Austin says. "I can't imagine someone will offer you a taste of a human again."

"At least not tonight," Kingston murmurs.

"It doesn't happen that often. Vampires don't like to share," Diego says.

Orlando squeezes his shoulder. "Most vampires."

Damn it if their attempt to ease my worry about having to fake a life as a vampire doesn't freak me out more. I know they think I can handle it, but I'm not so sure. "That's good, I guess. Because we're going to have to figure this shit out."

Kingston pokes me in the shoulder with his finger. "We will, babe. And if not, I have so many plans on how to entertain you in this room."

I beam my biggest smile. "I'm holding you all to that. And as for the rest of the night, I'll behave. Promise."

Kingston attempts to steal me from Austin. "Doubt it but okay." He turns to Orlando. "You're probably going to regret agreeing to this."

Orlando offers me a smile. "I regret a lot of things, but this, brother, will never be one of them."

"You hope," I tease, letting Diego help me onto Austin's back.

Orlando touches my cheek. "With everything in me."

FIELD TRIP

I STAND IN THE MIDDLE of the street and glance around the old storefronts. "Do you think our rooms can fit it all? I'd hate to see everything just trashed."

Orlando steps closer. "We wouldn't throw away perfectly fine goods, Jewel. We can take whatever you want and then distribute the rest. I want the human residents of Ombre Noire to feel lucky to have been chosen to live here."

I frown. "Chosen? They didn't get to apply?"

No one responds to me right away.

"Shit. They're going to be scared that this place remains in the shade nearly all day. Will they be told in advance?" I ask, prodding for answers.

Austin slides his arm around me. "Let's save all these

questions for later. Right now, we're here to enjoy this. It'll be the last time this place will be just our coven."

I open my mouth to argue but stop short and bob my head. Austin's right. Big changes are coming, changes out of my control, and I should take a moment to appreciate that we're here, being together, just enjoying each other's company. Even Orlando doesn't get on my nerves that much. I can't actually think of a time he got on my nerves lately. Just under my skin in a good way that scares me.

Orlando catches me staring at him and offers me a smile. My rebel mouth responds without my permission and smiles right back at him, sending my heart racing.

"So, where to first, beautiful?" Diego asks, pulling my thoughts to him. "The bookstore? Movie place? Music shop?"

"There's an old art gallery too," Orlando says.

"You like art?" I ask.

His continuous smile at me softens his hard features. "Would that be surprising?"

I straighten my back and try my best to capture a piece of Kingston's cockiness. "Not if the pieces were painted with the blood of your enemies."

Orlando breaks into a wider smile, and Diego smacks him on the back and laughs so loudly that I'm certain all the vampires in the area can hear him. Austin brings my hand to his mouth to kiss, and Kingston offers his hand out to me to high-five.

"Our girl is never going to let you live your assholeness

down," Diego says.

"'Cause he deserves it," Kingston says.

Orlando shakes his head and groans. "I hope not forever."

I shrug. "That's still up in the air, but I hope so too. I don't like feeling so confused."

Closing the space, he extends his hand for me to take. I stare at his proffered hand for a moment and decide to slide my fingers between his to hold his hand. I'm nearly certain that the only way I'm ever going to get over my nerves about the Blood Vow is to give Orlando the chance to make it right with me. To stop fighting with myself. I didn't always feel so conflicted about him. I know I had—have—some sort of feelings for him. If I'm committing to forever with his coven, with my guys, then I want to allow him into this version of me.

I tug Austin along with us, swinging our arms to distract me from my nerves. No one treats me holding Orlando's hand as weird, so it helps a bit. Even Kingston winks at me in an attempt to show me he's good. We're good.

Diego leads the way, and Kingston follows behind, the four of them strolling with me along the cracked sidewalk in what I'm sure is battle-ready formation. But none of them makes me feel on guard. My fear instincts remain in check.

"Oh, oh. Let's stop here," I say, pointing to the music store where Diego gave up one of Kingston's secrets about him being able to play any instrument. I glance at Kingston over my shoulder. "This place is for Kingston."

Kingston furrows his brows. "For me? Why me?"

Diego closes the space to Kingston and wraps his arm around his neck, rubbing his knuckles into his head. "I already told Jewel you play, bro."

"But I don't play...anymore." Kingston's eyes flash silver, and he flicks his gaze from me and to the dozens of instruments still hung on display from a time long ago. "The hobby was not beneficial."

I tap my finger to the glass. "Fine, whatever." I look to Diego. "Can you grab me that guitar? Maybe I'll teach myself how to play."

"That's a bass, and if you want to learn how to play guitar, you want that one over there, babe," Kingston murmurs, sliding up next to me to stare into the window. "The acoustic one."

"Maybe I want something I can blast everyone's eardrums off with," I say, smiling.

He chuckles. "Diego, let me help you."

Diego grins at me and holds his fist out to bump against mine. We both thought that Kingston would deny ever playing, and the fact that he's even humoring me makes this night out already feel like a success.

"While you guys pick out the best—and I mean *the best* for me—Austin, Orlando, and I will head to the bookstore," I say, hugging my arms around Kingston and Diego. I don't actually want to learn to play, but I can already see how excited Kingston is at the thought. I want nothing more than to give him something back that Mitchell stole away from him.

I tug Austin and Orlando away, peering over my shoulder once to watch Diego and Kingston break through the metal gate blocking the entrance. Austin smiles at me and squeezes my hand, swinging our arms for a moment.

"You might've created a monster, Jewel," Austin says. "If Kingston is one thing, it's determined. You're going to have to break it easy to him that you don't want to learn."

I smirk. "It's not that I don't want to. I just might prefer to listen to him. Sing along."

"He does love hearing you sing," Austin says, squeezing my hand.

"Is that so?" I tilt my head to peer at Austin. I knew that about Kingston but hearing Austin confirm it makes me grin like crazy. Kingston has been rebuilding his playlist, and I have seen one on his tablet titled *Songs Jewel Sings*. There's one for dancing and...banging. My cheeks warm just thinking about it.

"That used to drive your father crazy," Orlando says, pulling me from thoughts of Kingston. He brings my hand up to draw me a bit closer to him. "He was afraid you were unintentionally calling vampires to you."

Austin scrunches his nose. "That's an interesting thought. Luring instead of hunting."

I groan. "Austin, really?"

Orlando leans forward to meet Austin's gaze. "That's exactly what Noah feared."

I tug both their hands and pick up the pace. "Can we not talk about my dad? I bet he was the one who put Mrs. Peppers up to constantly yelling at Ramona and me for singing too loudly. But living in The Boxes was boring. Especially during Winter Nights. It was movies and music and talking. That was it. Without that stuff, it would have sucked even more." I suppress the anger over my dad rising through me. I still struggle with my real memories about him. How different he is than what I thought I knew.

"And I'm so glad to have finally helped change that for you, Jewel." Orlando motions for me and Austin to stop a few feet from the bookstore.

He peers around, searching the area, and Austin slides a dagger out from beneath his jacket. I tense at the sight of it, caught off guard. My fear instincts aren't even going off or anything. Closing my eyes, I listen for anything strange. All I can hear is Kingston and Diego whispering from inside the music store while messing around with instruments.

"What do you guys hea—"

Something crashes nearby, and Austin releases me to rush toward the broken door of a store. A hiss sounds through the air along with another crash, and I break out into a jog. Orlando has no choice but to run at a human's pace with me or risk losing his arm because he refuses to let my fingers go. Austin holds up his hand.

"It's nothing, Jewel. An animal," Austin says.

I ignore his gesture to stop next to him. "That's not just

any animal. It's my cat. I can't believe he came back here. Diego looked everywhere for him."

"*Your* cat?" Orlando tilts his head to the side and gives me a questioning look.

I hum my agreement and slowly tug the broken door of the movie store open. I spot the orange and white cat disappear from on top of the counter and through the door to the backroom. I click my tongue. "Aw, come on, baby. Don't be scared. Remember, I was going to take you home and feed you before that asshole Hayden showed up and scared you away."

"Damn, babe," Kingston says from behind me. "Why don't you ever talk to me like that?"

"So hot, right?" Diego says, chuckling. "I'm still so damn jealous of that cat."

Kingston releases a small growl. "Which means no, babe. We're not taking it home."

I place my hands on my hips and glare at him before turning to Diego.

Diego smiles and nods at me without me even having to say anything. "I did tell our girl I'd catch the cat."

"If it's that important," Orlando says.

I beam him a smile and throw my arms around him. He accepts my gesture without even tensing in surprise, reminding me of the last time I hugged him in Dark Terrace Ranch before he told me that he took my dad and changed everything.

I tilt my chin up and meet Orlando's blue gaze. "It's not,

but I really want you to say yes anyway."

He rubs his lips together, glancing at my mouth before returning to stare directly into my eyes. "Perhaps this is the perfect vow present for you."

"It better come with a human to look after it," Kingston says, grimacing.

I laugh, pulling myself from Orlando to stick my tongue out at Kingston. "I look after you fine, don't I?"

Kingston releases a growl and darts at me to throw me over his shoulder to spin me around. I screech and clutch onto him until he finally sets me back on my feet. Sliding my hands around his neck, I narrow my eyes at him and silently dare him to tell me no.

He huffs a dramatic breath, deciding against taking my dare. Pulling me closer, he pushes his hips and chest into mine to assure no space gets between us. "Fine, babe. I'll catch you the cat, but I expect twice as many cuddles as the mini-beast gets."

I bob my head, grinning. "Deal."

"That is, if you catch it first," Diego says, knocking his knuckles into Kingston's arm to get him to release me.

Austin playfully punches Diego. "Oh, it's on."

The three of them look at Orlando and he shrugs. "I'll stay with Jewel. I don't think we're quite at the place of bribing with affection."

Kingston flashes his fangs at me. "If she really wanted something..."

Diego whacks Kingston, and the two of them laugh. Austin shoves the both of them and takes off to find the cat. Diego and Kingston race each other inside the store, and something crashes. I bare my bottom teeth and suck in air through my mouth. Turning it into a competition might not have been such a good idea.

"If you guys traumatize my cat and make it hate you, you're going to have to sleep on the floor while it gets your spot on the bed," I call, making Orlando chuckle.

"Watch your mouth, babe," Kingston retorts. "This cat is gonna love me so much that you'll be the one sleeping on the floor."

"Or in my bed," Diego says.

Something crashes again, and I shake my head. Orlando squeezes my hand, drawing my attention to him. He offers me a smile, and I find myself grinning right back. If I didn't know any better, I'd think he was suddenly nervous.

"How about I show you the art gallery while we wait for my brothers?" he asks.

"I guess that would be okay. Might be better than watching a cat defeat my matches." I laugh when three playful growls echo through the air. A door slams, and I think the three of them might have exited through the backdoor of the building.

Orlando motions for me to walk with him, and we stroll down the block and cut down an alley between the buildings. I haven't been anywhere in Ombre Noire off the main street, and I can't help the jitters coursing through me. Exploring a new-to-me place with Orlando leaves me a bit anxious.

He notices, his smile faltering. "You're safe with me, Jewel. I won't let anything happen to you."

I lick my lips. "I know."

"You also have it in you to defeat any enemy who tries to test you," he says.

I release a breathless laugh. "If only I could control my inner savage. I hate feeling so out of control. I worry about you guys."

Orlando stops and turns to face me, his blue eyes lighting up at my words. I realize that I included him in my worry, but I can't deny that a part of me does. I just wish I could tell if I worry because I'm afraid of what will happen to us without him or if Jewel Jordan from Dark Terrace Ranch sneaks from her hiding place in the back of my mind to remind me of my history with Orlando.

"It might not feel like you have any control, but you do. You're stronger than you think, Jewel." Orlando reaches up and brushes my hair from my shoulder so that it spills down my back. His gaze trails from mine and slowly down my jaw to my neck. My breathing quickens under his intense scrutiny, and I find myself leaning closer, drawn to him.

"I want to kiss you," he says, his voice low and smooth. The words surprise the hell out of me. I know he wants more with me. I know that he desires to mend our relationship and to shower me with the same affection I receive from my guys—it's written on his face all the time—but this is the first move he's made, telling me exactly what he wants.

And shit balls.

Heat floods my face at the thought, at the memory of our one kiss before in front of the board. How it dragged so much from me that I felt out of control but in a good way. "I—"

"It's okay, Jewel. I'm not going to pressure you." Thank friggin' God. Orlando breaks his gaze to peer around the alleyway. "Come on. The gallery is just around the corner."

Instead of taking my hand, Orlando touches the small of my back, guiding me with him. The thought of kissing him lingers on my mind, drawing silence between us. I swore to myself I'd never do it again. That his kiss might destroy me. But now? Fuck me. Am I willing to risk it? I'm going to have to. I can't imagine a Blood Vow to lack that sort of connection. I just wish it could be on my terms, when I'm a hundred percent in.

But maybe that's my problem. My confusion and the hurt I still cling to might not allow me to ever be a hundred percent in. Orlando is infuriatingly unapologetic about what he put me through to get me from the Divine name. He went so far as to relent to bring my matches too. A part of me can't help thinking about what would've happened had they not agreed. Had they never given up their loyalty to Mitchell...

I shove the thought away and lock it up tight in the back of my mind. There is no point of thinking about the what-ifs. Because my guys aren't loyal to Mitchell. They'll never be again. We have chosen a life together. Sure, they might have originally agreed to accept Orlando's offer to join his coven as a way to ensure power and protection, maintain status, but I know their reasoning has shifted. I know it's more than about me. It's about them too. I can already see the bond they formed to include Orlando, and it was to be expected. It's how it's supposed to be.

A coven united by more than selfish interest stands strong.

That's why Mitchell failed. He insisted that all loyalty remain with him. Now with Orlando, our loyalty will remain with each other. With all of us.

"Jewel?" Orlando asks, pulling me from my thoughts.

I turn my attention to him. "Huh?"

"I asked you if you were ready to go in."

Shit. Talk about being lost in my head. I hadn't realized we were already here.

"Oh, yeah. Sorry. I have a lot on my mind," I say, stepping back so that Orlando can open the door.

He pulls the handle, and it opens with ease. It's one of the first places I've been here that didn't require us to break in. It might never have been locked. "You can talk to me, Jewel. About anything."

"Is it safe to go in first?" I ask instead of responding to his comment.

He nods. "No one is here."

"What about human remains from when the human

population was decimated?" I shiver at the memory of finding the remnants of a body at the movie store with Diego.

"Not unless someone died here in the last week." He inhales a long breath. "But fortunately, I don't smell anything."

I scrunch my face, making him chuckle. Reaching out, he pokes the tip of my nose so that I smooth out my features. We stand in silence, staring at each other for a long moment. He looks like he has just as many thoughts on his mind as I do, but we both refrain from speaking our minds.

I break away first and turn to peer around the room. A thick layer of dust coats the light wooden floors, but dozens of footprints scatter about with tracks leading along the walls and around the displays encased in glass.

"Show me your favorite pieces," I say, rocking on my heels. "Or actually, let me try to guess."

Orlando waves his hand, and I stroll in front of him, following the first line of shoe prints that leads to a painting unlike anything I've ever seen. It lacks any real detail but bursts with colors.

"This is kind of pretty," I say, trying not to give away the fact that it's not as interesting to me as some of the other stuff around us.

He chuckles. "I'm not much of a fan of abstract art either."

I laugh and continue on, following the footprints until I come up to a painting where several tracks lead to it. I stop in front of it and cross my arms, just gazing at it for a long moment. Reaching up, I trace my fingers along the couple without touching the piece. A woman and man cling onto each other amid a crowd that attempts to pull them apart. Dark, stormy clouds fill the sky, and streaks of paint blur across the painting almost as if it's melting.

The longer I gaze at it, the sadder I feel. I wonder why the artist chose to create something so dark and foreboding.

"It's rather striking, isn't it? One of the few pieces I've ever seen depicting The Divide in such a way."

"Because the artist was human," I say, my voice cracking. It's obvious without having to even know who painted it. I force myself to turn away from the painting and hug my arms around me.

Orlando gently touches my shoulder. "How about I show you something more light-hearted?"

I spin around to face him, my stupid eyes threatening to spill tears. I can't believe I'm actually upset over a painting. "I'm sorry. This is so stupid."

"Your empathy is far from stupid." Orlando surprises me with a hug that I can't help but sink into. He strokes his hand along my back, smoothing my hair without smothering me. I press my cheek to his chest, listening to the quickening beats of his heart.

Tilting my face up, I meet his intense gaze. "I know we can't change the past, but I want to make sure that shit like that doesn't happen again in the future."

He rubs his lips together. "I promise you we will do

whatever it takes."

His eyes break from mine to trail down to my lips. My heart picks up speed, crashing around my chest. His promise ignites something wild and uncontrollable inside me that I can't stop myself from imagining the feeling of his mouth against mine, the touch of his fingers around my waist, how sweet I know his lips are.

"Jewel," he whispers breathlessly, my name a plea on his lips, begging me to give in to my sudden desire.

I swallow and stretch up to close the space, grazing my lips to his. His hands tighten around me, moving from my back and to my hips, pulling me closer into him. Heat travels from my heart to spill through the rest of me, and I push him toward the wall, kissing him deeper, trailing my hands up his chest to wrap around his neck.

Our hearts beat against each other through our shirts, and I glide my tongue between his lips, tasting his spicy sweetness, feeling how soft his tongue is as it caresses against mine. His fangs extend slightly with his desire, and I ease away to meet his silver flashing gaze.

He doesn't let the inch of space last between us for long. He brings his fervent mouth to my jaw and kisses down my neck, lighting a fiery trail that makes me moan softly under his kisses. Sliding his arms lower, he picks me up to straddle against him, and I arch into him, feeling his body, his hard desire, press into me.

"Jewel," he whispers again, grazing his teeth along my

throat. "I've been waiting so long for this. It's better than I imagined."

I pant with desire, nearly asking him to bite me. Doing so here, experiencing a new level of intimacy with Orlando while I feel so connected with him, sounds and feels a helluva lot better than exposing my neck in front of the board.

Tipping my head to the side, I let my hair fall away from my neck. Orlando sucks in a soft breath, tightening his hands around me. "Are you sure?" he asks, questioning my silent gesture of permission.

I don't get the chance to nod. A soft meow sounds through the air, and the orange and white cat pads from the back of the art gallery in our direction. Something crashes outside, and I hear Kingston and Diego murmur something to each other.

"Where did it go?' Austin asks.

I wiggle in Orlando's arms until he sets me on my feet. Crouching down, I hold out my hands for the cat, and it closes the space to me. I rub my fingers into its head, and it pushes its head harder into my hand with a purr. I gaze up and smile at Orlando as the cat lets me pick it up to hold in my arms.

"Hey, baby," I say to the cat. "Do you want to go home with me?"

"Fuck yeah, I do." Kingston's voice sounds through the air, and he appears in view. He stops short as Austin and Diego come up behind them, and the three of them stare at me and Orlando.

I adjust the cat in my arms. "I won...and I kissed Orlando. I almost let him bite me." My mouth. I know my guys agreed that they couldn't ask me questions about stuff I do in private with them, but it's like I need to really know they're okay. And apparently my rebel mouth thinks surprise info bombs are the way to check for sure.

The three of them remain utterly expressionless.

I wish they didn't. I wish I could read them.

"What you and Orlando do is none of our business, Jewel," Austin finally says. "You don't have to tell us or explain anything. You know that, right? We've agreed to try to keep a bit of privacy for your sake."

I bob my head. "I'm sorry. I know. I just—I always want to be honest. And I want you to be too."

"Well, I'm not going to lie. I'm slightly jealous. Mostly that you caught the damn cat," Kingston says, smirking at me. He closes the space and lets the cat sniff his fingers before scratching it under the chin. It purrs like crazy at Kingston, making him chuckle.

I release a small breath and stretch to kiss him. "Don't worry. Extra cuddles for everyone. But at home. I'm ready to go." Turning to Orlando, I add, "Will you bring that painting? And the first one we looked at too."

"The first one?"

"Yup."

"May I ask why?"

"It reminds me of you. Confusing, unreadable, and it kind of pisses me off that I can't figure it out."

He chuckles. "Whatever you want, Jewel."

My smile falters. "I don't know what I want. All I know is that I'm ready to let my guard down just a little. Don't take advantage of me."

His face falls serious, and he turns his gaze to Kingston, Diego, and Austin. "You have my word. If I fail you, your matches can rip me apart."

I gape. "Really?"

He shrugs. "At least they can try."

WEIRD-ASS TRADITIONS

"WHAT ABOUT THE DESTROYER?" DIEGO asks, reaching down to let the cat nuzzle its head into his hand.

"The cat is female," Samantha says, speaking up.

"How do you...never mind," Kingston mutters.

Layla tips her head back and laughs, her dark blond hair cascading in shiny waves down her back. "If we have to explain that to you, I'm rather relieved you're not the one on the other side of Jewel's Blood Vow."

Kingston growls and throws a butter knife in her direction. She catches it midair and stabs it into the table. I startle at the sudden action, and the cat jumps into my lap and releases a hiss that might be even scarier than a Vaduvas'.

"Layla," Kingston says.

She glares at him. "What?"

He flashes his fangs. "That's what we should call the cat. Possibly Merrick."

I roll my eyes at the same time as Layla, and she looks smug as all get-out that I wipe my hand across my face and turn away from Kingston's death glower. Both Diego and Merrick laugh, and I just gape at everyone.

Austin enters the dining room, followed by Viorica and Orlando, turning everyone's attentions from each other. Samantha and Evora slip in and head to the opposite end of the grand table. Lastly, Heidi enters carrying a tablet in her hand.

Orlando leans down and presses a kiss to my cheek and takes a seat beside me. Austin sets a tray in front of me and arranges a few plates onto the table. He stops me from dragging one with what looks like a plain piece of chicken closer and scoops it back up to set on the floor in the corner of the room.

"That's for Baby," he says, grinning at me.

"Baby?" I ask.

Kingston releases a small growl. "No fucking way. I'm not going to get turned the hell on every time Jewel calls the cat."

"You better get used to it, Kingston. You won't be able to act on your desires in a few days," Merrick says. "But you know, my offer of a good time always stands."

I slam my hands on the table and push to my feet, but I don't even get a second to react. My back hits the cool wall in the hallway, and Orlando leans down and cages me in with his body. I heave a few deep breaths, trying to pull my shit together.

"I never thought I'd have to protect a Vaduva," he murmurs.

I shiver. "I'm sorry. I didn't mean to let her get to me."

"You must better control yourself, Jewel. I don't want to have to force you into wearing the contacts any time we're around others. Our secret cannot get out. The consequences—"

"I said I'm sorry. Jeez, give me a friggin' break. I'm doing my best."

He lowers his hands to cup my cheeks, meeting my gaze. "I know. But if this was any other time—"

"It won't happen again." I close my eyes and place my hands on his chest, pushing him back to give me space. "Now, if you'll excuse me. I don't want my dinner getting cold."

Orlando steps out of my way and follows me into the dining room. Everyone gawks at me as I slump into my chair and lean my elbows on the table. I don't meet anyone's gazes, feeling awkward as eff under their scrutiny. It doesn't help that it feels like Orlando pulled me away for a timeout. Yeah, it kind of was, but still.

"She really can't take a joke, can she," Merrick whispers under her breath to Layla.

I shove a forkful of food into my mouth to stop myself from reacting. They don't know I can hear them. I'm already over this dinner, wanting nothing more than to get through it so I can be myself with my guys.

"Maybe because your jokes are rude and unfunny," Samantha whispers from her end of the table.

I set my fork down and sit up straighter. Orlando touches my shoulder in an attempt to get me to look at him. Austin squeezes my knee under the table. Diego and Kingston both gently kick my feet from their spots across from me. I'm too embarrassed to look at any of them.

I turn my attention to Viorica and force myself to smile. "I can't wait until my transformation so that your daughters will refrain from talking about me." Petty and passive aggressive to point it out like this? Maybe. But I don't give a damn now.

"There are dozens of other things more important to look forward to, Jewel," Viorica says, smirking. "And my girls will have better manners by then, seeing as you'll gain the power of the Ortega name. I look forward to seeing who you become."

"As do I," Orlando says.

"I doubt it will change me that much," I say, keeping my mouth tight. Viorica doesn't know that it will do nothing to me, but I feel like I have to point out the fact that a Blood Vow doesn't automatically mean I'll just change.

Kingston snickers.

"We shall see. Regardless, congratulations. I know it must be difficult to give up a part of yourself, including your fondness over your matches in the public eye." Viorica glances at

Kingston, Diego, and Austin. "It's a shame the board still won't agree to a status or loyalty vow."

I frown. I had no idea that Orlando even tried to persuade them again.

Kingston puffs out his bottom lip. "We weren't surprised. The board members have always loved their games."

"And what they do not know won't hurt them," Orlando says, bumping his shoulder into mine. "Jewel is free to do what she wants in the privacy of our estate."

"You mean she's free to choose whom she wants to do," Merrick says, flashing a smile at me.

Orlando prepares to rush me from the room again, but I take a deep breath and return her smile with my own.

"So please stop trying to seduce my lovers," I say, glancing around the table. "It won't work. They're mine. Forever. As long as you respect me and them, our alliance will be envied by all."

The Vaduvas all stare at me without reacting, and it takes everything in me not to sink lower into my chair. I guess my best Vaduva impression needs work. I thought being under the weight of my guys' gazes without reacting was hard. Being under the Vaduvas' scrutiny is damn painful.

Viorica reacts first, releasing a small hum under her breath before she smiles. "It's still quite the shame you didn't match into our household, though we do love Evora." Viorica makes a point to smile at Samantha's Blood Match. "Perhaps while you prepare for your ceremony you'd allow her to watch and help."

I shrug. "I don't see why not."

"But no guys allowed," Merrick says, parting her plum lips into an evocative smile.

"Yeah-fucking-right," Kingston says. "She's our girl. We're going to make sure it's what she wants and not what you imagine as you live vicariously through her."

Layla tosses her napkin at him. "I'd never dream of a life such as that."

A knock on the doorframe draws our attention to five human men standing in the hallway. Viorica rises to her feet and waves for them to enter. Merrick flashes her fangs and nudges Layla with her shoulder. Kingston and Diego raise their eyebrows. Austin holds a forkful of meat to my mouth, encouraging me to take a bite, probably in an attempt to assure I don't react.

Orlando stands and touches my shoulder. "Viorica, you didn't have to do this."

Viorica pulls one of the guys forward. He smiles and puffs his chest out, slightly opening the fabric on his short silk robe in the process. And then all five of them remove their robes and drop them to the ground, revealing their speedos.

"What the fu—" I slap a hand over my mouth to shut myself up.

"I know you can't enjoy these donors now, but I wanted to give you and your matches some of the best donors Midnight Valley has to offer to celebrate your upcoming union and Blood Vow," Viorica says.

"Oh." I bare my teeth in what I hope is an acceptable smile.

"Aren't they all so handsome?" Merrick asks. "Delicious too. Might I suggest choosing Joaquin as your personal donor?"

"Uh, sure," I murmur. "Suggest away."

"I know Jewel's transformation will be an adjustment for everyone, considering how much you enjoy her, but I hope this helps." It's the first time Heidi, Viorica's first in line, speaks up. "It did so with me."

"How thoughtful," Orlando muses, glancing at me. "Isn't it thoughtful, Jewel?"

How he keeps a straight face? I have no friggin' idea. Kingston loses his shit, though, releasing a loud laugh before coughing into his hand. It makes Diego snicker and kick me under the table. Even Austin chuckles, breaking his even expression.

"So thoughtful," I say, shaking my shoulders with the laugh that builds inside me.

Orlando waves at the table. "Come now, gentleman. Please join us."

The second the muscular human that Merrick called Joaquin lies down in front of me, I lose all composure, staring at his hardening erection.

"Holy shit balls," I say, jerking back in my seat. Either Austin or Orlando's foot sticks under the leg of my chair, preventing me from sliding away. I tip back on two legs in the process of trying to escape, screeching as I wave my arms in search of something to hold on to before I fall.

"Got ya, beautiful," Diego says, catching the back of my chair and balancing it.

I heave a breath. "Fuck. I'm not ready for this shit."

"Of course you're not, babe," Kingston says, standing next to Diego to peer down at me.

Diego pushes my chair back up, and I hop to my feet, nearly eating shit on the ground as I rush to escape the table again and the sudden array of boners. And I can't blame the guys—I mean, the Vaduvas are gorgeous and charming. They make all of their personal donors feel like they are living their best life, but damn.

"I—I need to be excused," I say, clutching my hands together. "I'm really sorry."

"You'd think she's never seen the magnificence of a male body before," Merrick whispers to Layla under her breath.

"If she's been with her matches, that's obviously not the problem. I mean..." Layla's voice trails off at the fact that Kingston and Diego listen.

"Jewel isn't used to a live feeding yet. Nor a group one," Austin says, standing up to come to me.

"Yeah, that's it. I'm not feeling like eating my chicken with a centerpiece of raging boners right now," I say, clearing my throat.

Kingston laughs harder.

"And we rather you not introduce our girl to your traditions just yet," Diego adds.

Samantha makes a weird coo sound. "That's really sweet to try to preserve Jewel's innocence."

Merrick lifts Joaquin's arm to her mouth and bites down, making him groan and tip his head back. "Or incredibly hindering."

Orlando stands and takes my hand, kissing the back of it. "I have a few more things to discuss with Viorica if you don't mind."

I nod. "I don't."

He looks at his brothers. "No need for all of you to escort Jewel."

Diego scoops up my plate from the table. "I got it. Call us if you need anything."

Kingston swears under his breath.

Austin kisses my cheek. "Have fun, Jewel."

Diego hooks his arm around me and carries me from the room just as several sensual moans echo through the air. I shudder, wishing I could've lived my life without hearing the amount of pleasure the Vaduvas' bites bring to their donors.

"Damn," I murmur into Diego's ear. "Do I sound like that?"

He chuckles. "Depends. Sometimes you're far louder."

"Ugh. I'm going to practice controlling my rebel mouth."

He adjusts me in his arms and kisses me sweetly. "I volunteer to assist."

"It might be a losing battle," I tease.

"That's what I hope for."

I nuzzle my nose to his neck and kiss along his throat and up his jaw. He quickens his pace, rushing through the maze of hallways and low rise stairs until we reach our temporary room with Orlando.

Diego tenses, his muscles bunching as he flexes his arms. He releases a low growl in his throat, and the familiar click of his fangs extending sound in my ear.

"Jewel, please control your match." Hayden's voice draws my attention from Diego's body reacting to a threat and to him sitting on the loveseat now pushed against the wall of the study to make room for the three beds.

"Maybe if you didn't command shit like that or talk to me like he's not right here, I wouldn't have to ask him nicely not to throw you into a wall." I push against Diego until he sets me on my feet. "What are you even doing here?"

Hayden looks like he wants to retort to my comment, but with one look behind me at Diego, he refrains. Diego stands so close that I can feel the muscles of his chest ripple against my back. Hayden was lucky it was Diego and not Kingston who returned to the room with me.

"I wanted to talk," he says. "I didn't get to say everything I needed to say."

"I told you—"

Hayden throws his hands up. "Damn it, Jewel. It's not always about you and your family."

Hayden grunts and crashes into the wall. It happens so fast that I don't get a chance to react. Diego lifts him off his feet and shoves him into the wall again. Rushing forward, I close the space and lace my arms around Diego's chest, getting him to relax.

He drops Hayden and picks me up again to carry me out of the room.

I pat Diego's chest. "Wait."

"Jewel, please don't ask me to humor him," Diego says, meeting my gaze with what looks like lightning in his stormy gray eyes as they flash silver.

I blink a few times and frown. "Um, okay. How about you humor me then?"

Sighing, Diego turns me in his arms but doesn't let me down. If I didn't know any better, I'd think he's been taking lessons from Kingston lately. Diego's usually the least likely to be overprotective. He's also more likely to let me do things the others might find too dangerous.

"Make it quick, Hayden," Diego says. "Raise your voice at Jewel again, and you'll—"

I press my finger to Diego's lips. "Threats are unnecessary. If he talks like that to me again, he'll realize that I can take down more than vampires."

Diego's serious face breaks into a smile, and he kisses me. "My badass."

I turn my attention to Hayden, his face now a series of sharp curves and lines. He looks more annoyed than I feel, and it takes everything in me not to mess with him some more. Because shit. Intense doesn't look good on him, not like it does with my guys.

"You have three minutes," I say. "My dinner has already been ruined by one surprise dick interruption."

Hayden tightens his jaw. "I need your help. The attacks at Haven Springs have gotten worse. We've lost twenty people since I told Orlando. The board isn't doing shit to keep their word. You know as well as I do that participants join the Blood Match Program to grant exemption and safe living to their heirs. It's falling apart. Something has to be done."

"We're working on it, Hayden," Diego says, speaking up for me.

"Bullshit! Those vampire guards do nothing." Hayden balls his hands into fists.

"I'll let Orlando know so he can bring it to the board's attention."

"We're running out of time," Hayden says. "By the time they do something, everyone will be dead or taken. Don't you think Brayla will care if something happens to her mom and brother?"

I inhale a small breath. "Shit. I thought Mr. Diggs would go for her."

"He's in as deep as Noah. We make sacrifices for our cause all the time." Hayden rubs his hands up his face and into his hair. "They were one of them. No one could have predicted that Mitchell would start a war, going against the board and using the exiled against us."

I turn to Diego. "We have to bring them here."

"I'll talk to Orlando. We don't have enough night to make the trip tonight, but we can do it tomorrow. You'll be busy with the vow prep, so you'll have to stay," Diego says, keeping his face expressionless.

I frown. "Really?"

He nods. "Sorry, beautiful."

"And what about everyone else?" Hayden asks.

I shift on my feet. "There has to be something else we can do."

Diego frowns and glances at Hayden before meeting my gaze. He looks like he's ready to deny me, the action hurting him before he even admits that he doesn't want to handle Haven Springs. "It's not so easy, Jewel." Uh-oh. He's using my name. This can't be good. "We have to go through the proper channels. Right now, our coven union takes precedence with the board. They won't move forward with anything until it's all set."

I tighten my jaw, trying to keep my face even. I know it bothers my guys that I even carry a semblance of pity for the exempt, but they're not all bad. They're just not.

"I know of something you can do," Hayden says, speaking up.

We both turn to look at him without a word, waiting for him to spill his plan.

"Allow me to bring some people here. Those who face the

most risk," he says.

"I don't know," Diego says. "I have to discuss it with my brothers."

"Bring them," I say to Hayden, unable to remain calm and expressionless. I know the people most at risk are women. I can't just deny them if Mitchell keeps sending in outcasts to prey on the community. It isn't right. "You'll have all day to travel here."

"Jewel," Diego says.

"Diego, if we can help them, we should," I argue.

"My brothers might not go for it."

I wrap my arms around his neck. "How about you leave that part to me?"

DISTRACTIONS

"YOU SHOULD TAKE ADVANTAGE OF this moment alone with me. I've missed you," I say, strolling from the wardrobe in only a skimpy, sheer, soft lace nightie.

Tugging my hair from my messy bun, I let it spill across my shoulders and down my chest to purposely block Diego's favorite view of me. It took some convincing, but I managed to get him to postpone calling Orlando to tell him what I've done. The last thing I want is everyone to come rushing in here, especially now with how Diego drinks me in.

"With all this space, I'm not so sure you feel the same," I add, smirking.

His entire face lights up, and he graces me with the smile I love. I don't even see him hop from his spot at the table before his arms encircle my waist and pull me to him. Leaning down, he caresses his lips to mine so softly that I crave a thousand more.

"Let me convince you otherwise," Diego says.

I release a breathless laugh and pull away. "I'm waiting."

Smiling again, Diego trails his gaze from my mouth to my neck, taking me in inch by inch without touching me. I squirm under his hot intensity and sweep my hair to my back to show off my cleavage. I start to pull the strap down on my shoulder, but Diego gently grabs my hand and stops me.

"Not yet," he whispers. "Let me appreciate your sexiness for a bit longer."

I exhale softly, goosebumps prickling over my skin at just his words. He sucks in his bottom lip between his teeth and tilts his head before he lifts his hand to trail his finger along my jaw and down the sensitive skin of my throat. My heart picks up pace, and I lick my lips and attempt to reach for him.

He captures my hand in his other one and kisses it, slowly working his lips up the inside of my wrist and to my elbow, creating tingles that ignite desire through me. I full-on pant in anticipation by the time he reaches my shoulder and uses his teeth to draw my strap down to kiss my heated skin under it. My legs tremble, my knees turning weak under his touch.

"Diego," I murmur.

He kneels in front of me. "Just a little longer."

"I don't know how much longer I can resist."

Smiling, he undresses me at a painfully slow pace, kissing

his way down my boobs to glide his tongue over the sensitive skin of my nipples. His fingers ease down my nightie, the soft sensation of the fabric gliding down my skin making me moan. I run my fingers through his hair, playing with the short strands as he works his mouth across my stomach, stopping at the band of my lace thong. His fingers move to hold onto my ass, and he kisses each of my hips, testing me for my reaction, seeing if I'll let him continue.

I respond by combing my fingers through his hair again and parting my legs just enough to let him undress me completely. His eyes flash silver with his hungry desire, and I grip onto his shirt and hold onto him as he grazes his tongue between my legs, just tasting me until I'm trembling with so much anticipation that Diego sweeps me off my feet to set me on the bed.

I tug his shirt off him and graze my hands along the taut planes of his muscles, tensing and relaxing under my fingers. I unhook his belt and tug his pants down to lace my fingers over his hardness.

"Not yet, beautiful," he whispers, kneeling between my legs. "You should come first."

I release a cross between a laugh and a moan at his double entendre. Diego smiles at me and pulls me a bit closer by my hips. He kisses inside my thigh, positioning my legs to rest on his broad shoulders. I press deeper into the soft bedding and clutch the fabric, twisting it in my fingers, my back automatically arching as pleasure erupts through me at the pressure of his mouth, his tongue flicking against my buzzing skin. I moan so friggin' loud and squeeze Diego's head between my thighs, making him moan, the vibration across my skin sending my hands reaching for something to grab onto.

"Diego," I say, his name a loud plea on my lips. "I'm—mmm—fuck—" The words don't manage to escape, my body on the verge of exploding in the best way possible.

Diego keeps going, sliding his fingers through mine. He uses his free hand to hold my wiggling body in place as my muscles tighten and relax while my moan turns into a shout of pleasure that I'm sure even the Vaduvas can hear. My heart thrashes against my ribs, threatening to break free. Diego slows down, softly kissing my humming sensitive skin a moment longer.

Pulling himself to his feet, he rests his hands on my bent knees, just drinking in my reaction like it's the best thing he's ever seen. He licks his lips, his gray eyes narrowing with the same desire hardening his every muscle.

"Jewel, that was...indescribable," he says, standing at the edge of the bed, stroking his hand across the length of his massive friggin' boner. "I want you so badly."

I smirk and push myself upright, tilting my head up to gaze into his eyes. "Not yet."

Hooking my fingers to Diego's hips, I tug him closer. His breathing quickens with his anticipation, and I lace my fingers around his shaft and bring his tip to my lips. He tastes even sweeter than his blood, the good surprise teasing my tongue until I draw him into my mouth and suck just hard enough to make him moan.

Diego combs his fingers through my hair, gently guiding me in the motion he prefers. I peek up at him, and he greets me with a longing smile, his fingers growing more desperate as they move down to my shoulders.

"Jewel," he whispers with a moan. "I want you. I *need* you."

I ease away, and Diego rubs his thumb across my lips as I stretch them into a smile. "Is that so?"

"Desperately."

I hold my hands out to him. "Show me."

Diego kneels on the bed and picks me up from the edge to set me down so I can lay my head on the pillows. He sinks onto me, the weight of his body feeling so good against mine. I kiss his shoulder and graze my teeth along his skin until I reach his mouth. He kisses me so passionately that I have to pull away to gasp for breath. He doesn't let my mouth stay away for long and grazes his tongue to the seam of my lips until I part them and let his tongue caress mine.

My body warms his, and he shifts to graze his body against mine until I gasp again, wanting so badly for him to hurry. The anticipation makes it hard to stay still.

His erection teases me more, sliding over my tingling skin, and I adjust my body to open my legs to feel his hips against my thighs. Diego smiles and lifts my legs up as he continues to kneel, finally giving me what I want and need and love so intensely. He starts slow, sinking into me with a moan that matches mine in volume. Lust flashes silver in his eyes, but he doesn't break them away, devouring me with his gaze.

"I love you, Diego," I say breathlessly, my body rolling with his thrusts that grow more powerful and passionate by the second.

"I love you, beautiful." His voice comes out deep and raspy, so friggin' sexy. "You are the most spectacular, incredible, delicious woman in the world. I could survive on your smile, you know."

"And I can survive on yours."

Diego rocks against me, our bodies in perfect rhythm. My moans come in quick, short hums of pleasure as I pant, my body aching in the best way possible. Diego leans forward, placing his hands on both sides of my head and pushes so deeply and fervently into me that if the pillows weren't under me, my head would bang into the wall.

Tingles wash through me again, growing between my legs and building a pressure so intense and I dig my nails into Diego's shoulders hard enough to break his skin. He wraps my legs around him to bend down to kiss me as I reach the point of release, my body clenching and relaxing, electricity zinging through me, making me jerk up to press my face to his chest, warmed by my skin.

"Bite me, beautiful," he whispers, feeling my tongue glide over the small beads of blood seeping from my scratching.

The second I sink my teeth into him, he cums, moaning

through his heavy breathing before he slows to lie on top of me.

"Damn," he whispers. "That was so hot."

I hum in my throat, sucking on his shoulder for a moment longer, just satiating every single one of my desires. His hands slide around me to hug me close, and he kisses my bare shoulder, grazing his fangs along my skin, his own deep-seated need to bite me clear in the desperation of his kiss.

I arch my neck in silent permission, and Diego sinks his fangs quickly into my shoulder before working his mouth over my skin. We stay together, enjoying the intimacy and love we share, the ability that we can survive on each other being the most incredible thing in the universe. Something I feel so grateful that I never have to give up. I can't imagine drinking blood from someone other than my guys.

I finally manage to pull my mouth away from Diego, and he tugs me in for another kiss that I can lose myself in.

"Bath or shower?" he asks, nuzzling his nose to my throat. "Or stay here and cuddle until someone interrupts?"

"How long do you think that'll be?" I slide my hands up and down Diego's sides, just hugging him against me.

He reaches over to look at the tablet on the nightstand. "Probably soon."

"Then I'll stay here. I'm sure your brothers are hungry unless..." I frown, not even wanting to think about what the hell is happening in the dining room with the Vaduvas.

Diego smirks. "They're going to want their mouths all

over you."

"The way I like it."

Sliding from the bed, he gathers enough clothes to cover us without getting fully dressed. I hold open my arms and invite him back to the bed to pull the blanket around us. Diego was right about his brothers' arrival being soon. Soft voices sound through the door before a knock thuds against the wood.

"It's awfully quiet in there," Kingston says.

"Which means you guys can come in," I call, smiling at Diego. "I've been waiting for you...mostly. I bet you're starved."

The door swings open, and an orange blob bolts inside the room as fast as a friggin' vampire. The cat jumps up onto the chair before crossing the table to inspect the leftover food from my half-eaten dinner.

"Come here, Baby," I call, puckering my lips to make kissing noises.

Kingston materializes in front of me and meets his mouth to mine.

I giggle and pat his chest.

"Were you not talking to me?" he asks.

I curl my finger at him to come closer. He climbs onto the bed, sinking me back into the pillows until I slide my hands under his shirt and tug it off him. He pulls back and chuckles at my surprise undressing of him and then kisses me again.

"I don't mind who responds," I murmur into his mouth. "And I'm pretty sure our cat's name is officially Baby."

He groans. "Fucking fine. I'll live with it. My babe and damn Baby. You kill me."

"That's too bad. You need to be alive to enjoy..." I drop the blanket a bit to show off the lacy bodice of my nightie. "This."

"How could you resist leaving it on her?" Kingston asks Diego.

Austin smiles at me, giving me a long look, making me flush. "He couldn't. Take another look at our girl."

Kingston gives me a once-over. "I fucking love you for putting it back on so we could enjoy it too. You're sexy as hell in only a T-shirt, but this? Let me ravish you. Right now. I can't wait. I don't even care if Diego's all over you."

OhmyfrigginGod. "Dude."

He chuckles. "I love you that much."

Orlando clears his throat from the doorway, drawing my attention to him. "May I leave some of my blood with you, Jewel?"

I sit up straighter, his question flitting through my mind. I don't have to be a mind reader to know that this is his way of asking me whether I want him to stay or go. Thoughts of our kiss earlier tonight send goosebumps over my skin, and I twist the blankets in my hand.

"Did you get enough to eat?" I ask, licking my lips, trying to stay calm against the unexpected excitement coursing through me. It helps that Kingston slides on the bed next to me, and Austin perches on the edge, running his hand up my leg.

"I'll manage. I don't want to ruin whatever idea you had by asking Austin to draw your blood." He leans his arm on the doorframe, turning his attention to his brothers for a moment.

None of them react, waiting for my response.

Diego squeezes my hand. "Whatever you want, beautiful."

"We don't mind," Austin says.

I bob my head, licking my lips. "You don't have to go. I have something I need to tell you all first."

Austin, Kingston, and Orlando glance from me to Diego, looking to him to see if he knows what I'm about to say.

Diego twists his lips and takes my hand. "Maybe they should eat first."

I bring his hand to my mouth and kiss it. "And mess up a moment between us? No friggin' way. Plus, if they're hungry, they'll be distracted easier."

"One of you two need to spill it. You're freaking me out, and I want to destroy the universe when I'm freaked out," Kingston says.

Austin touches my cheek. "You can tell us anything, you know."

I turn my gaze to Orlando. "Try not to overreact. Everything is going to be fine. I know it."

Kingston growls. "What happened? We just came from

the Vaduvas, so I know you didn't accidentally kill one of them in a sexy rage of jealousy."

"Maybe I should," I whisper to Diego, making him chuckle. "It'll distract him."

"Brother, tell us what's going on since Jewel's too scared to," Orlando says, his soft features suddenly hardening.

I hold my hand up to Diego. "I got this, Diego. I don't want them to get mad at you even though you'd only be the messenger." I glance at the rest of them. "I mean it. I didn't give him a say."

Kingston releases a soft growl. "Shit."

I sit up, leaning forward to rest my elbows on my knees. "It's really not a huge deal...but I invited some guests to stay in Ombre Noire. At least temporarily."

"Guests?" Orlando asks, tilting his head curiously at me, never leaving his spot from the door.

I swallow my nerves. "Hayden's bringing people here from Haven Springs."

"Jewel," Kingston, Austin, and Orlando say in unison.

"It's just until the board gets things situated. Did you guys know that Mrs. Diggs and Dougie are there? We can't just leave them." My voice rises at the thought. "There are other kids, too."

Austin hugs me. "Jewel, children are the safest out of anyone. Vampires, no matter who they are, respect the young. That's a death sentence even to try such a thing."

He sounds so certain that I believe him despite knowing

that he can't be a hundred percent positive. No one can.

I tighten my mouth. "Still. There are women too. I already told Hayden yes. It's only temporary."

"The board won't like this," Kingston says.

I nudge him with my knuckles. "Then don't tell them."

Kingston sighs and rubs his hands over his face and into his dark hair. "That could jeopardize our standing."

I close my eyes, curling in on myself. "Please."

Silence falls between the five of us, and I don't look up to give them pretend privacy as they quietly converse with their eyes. After another minute, Diego touches my chin to get me to look up.

"If this is that important to you, Jewel, then I'd be willing to risk it," Orlando says.

"As are we," Austin says.

"Really?" I ask, a smile lighting my face.

Kingston groans. "Yes, really. But I swear, babe. You need to work on discussing this kind of shit with us."

I nod. "I know. I'm sorry. Let me make it up to you all?"

Kingston flashes his fangs. "What did you have in mind?"

"Just wait and see."

NEW BONDING EXPERIENCE

ORLANDO HOVERS IN THE DOOR, drinking me in as I sit between Kingston, Austin, and Diego. A dozen silent thoughts flicker through his eyes as they search over me.

"Orlando, I wasn't kidding or just being nice. I want you to stay," I say. "I'm still feeling kind of hungry. If it's okay with my matches, I'd like you to join us."

"Like we said, we're good, babe. But please, just let me see the rest of you already." Kingston tugs at the blanket to gaze at my body and hums his enjoyment under his breath. "Damn, it is your lucky day, brother," he says to Orlando. "Do you know how long it took Jewel to get into some sexy lingerie for me?"

"Probably not as long as he's been waiting," I say, crossing my legs at my ankles. I can't stop myself from joking around. It helps with the nerves building inside me. It's not often that we partake in this kind of bonding, and it's the first time I've even considered inviting Orlando. The last few days have worn on me, and not in a bad way—just in a familiar way.

Kingston kisses me. "Thank-fucking-God for that."

Baby darts away and through the door next to Orlando's legs, and he looks into his study to watch the cat pounce and lie down on one of the beds. He turns back to me like he needs one more confirmation that I'm really okay with him staying, so I wiggle my fingers at him.

"I hope it's okay that I don't want to drink from a glass," I say, my voice coming out low and unintentionally sultry. "I need to be comfortable."

"Whatever it takes," Orlando says.

Austin rubs his fingers over my leg, squeezing it. "You know that's the way we like it, Jewel."

I lick my lips and motion to Orlando. "Don't forget to shut the door."

Orlando raises his eyebrows in surprise, and I wave my hand at him to get him to hurry up. A part of me is nervous as all get-out the second the door locks, but a more dominant part of me, the part tethered to my very nature, ignites with excitement.

He was probably expecting to treat this moment like another dinner, though in bed, and I want to use it as a way to gather my nerve to be bitten with the love and support of Diego, Austin, and Kingston so that I can better prepare myself for the Blood Vow.

"Damn, babe. You look starved," Kingston says, brushing my hair off my shoulder. He leans in and kisses my cheek. "Insatiable."

Orlando smiles and closes the space, standing before me with his intense gaze roving over my face and to the skin Kingston exposed on my neck.

"Allow me to help. I want nothing more than to see you get everything you need." Orlando bites his arm, sending rivulets of blood toward his elbow from the bite.

I shift and sit on Kingston's lap to dangle my legs over the edge. Orlando steps even closer to me, pressing his legs against my knees. He stands straight and extends his arm to me, his sharp features smoothing out the longer he watches me watch the blood. I don't react right away, just working myself up to taste him. The eagerness building between us is so strong that my body trembles enough to make Kingston hug me tighter.

"You guys, breathe," I say. The sudden silence of everyone seemingly anticipating this moment does nothing for my rapid heart. Their gazes penetrate me, and I squirm a bit, wondering if I should get off Kingston before I drive him too crazy.

Diego chuckles, his soft voice loosening my tight muscles. "Sorry, beautiful."

"This is new for all of us," Kingston adds, kissing my shoulder, obviously not wanting to let me off him. I can't tell if it's because he's trying his best to control his possessiveness or he just wants to support me through this, but either way, it helps. It can't be easy to watch me drink from Orlando in the privacy of our room in a situation that isn't life or death.

I suck my bottom lip between my teeth. "If it's awkward—"

Austin squeezes my leg. "It's not. Just new."

"With the Blood Vow coming up, I—" I pause without finishing my thought. "I'm sorry. I'm nervous." I want my mouth to stop talking. I don't want any of them to think this is a big deal for me, but my damn mouth won't quit. "I don't want this to be a big deal." Great, way to make it into something.

Orlando touches my cheek, getting me to stop talking. He holds his arm closer, keeping it still to not spill the pooling blood. "If this is too much—"

I inhale a long breath and bring Orlando's arm to my mouth. I glide my tongue along the sweet stream of blood to lick it off before I mold my lips over his bite. My guys release their breaths at once, and Diego leans in to kiss my bare shoulder, showing me that he's here for me.

Kingston hooks his hands to my hips, moving my ass in slow circles over his lap until I feel his body stiffen with desire. His teasing does the trick to throw out the rest of my nerves. Such a Kingston action, showing that he really doesn't care because he knows I love him and crave him lets me lower my guard and enjoy myself. I push all my chaotic thoughts away and sink into the present to just be with my guys, with my soon-to-be official coven the way I want—the way they want me to be.

I suck harder on Orlando's arm, pulling a soft moan from him. He reaches out to me, wanting to connect with me on a new level not based on my need to drink his blood to survive.

Because this, our upcoming union to his coven, is more than just keeping power and gaining protection. At least, I want it to be more. I want so badly to capture my feelings for the part of Orlando I knew before my dad messed things up. Before Orlando grew desperate. But I also want to familiarize myself with the man standing right in front of me, changed by my relationship with my guys. Changed by their relationship with him as brothers.

I lace my fingers through Orlando's and hold his hand to my heart so that he can feel the soft thuds against his palm. Diego and Austin each rub a hand over my leg, remaining as quiet as Kingston.

Something ignites inside me, a desire unlike anything I've experienced before, and I push into Kingston. He scoots back on the bed, letting me direct him with what I want. Orlando reads my silent invitation and climbs up to sit between my legs, letting me relax more in Kingston's arms.

I release my mouth from Orlando, rubbing my lips together, still tasting his blood. "I hope this is okay."

Austin takes my free hand and kisses a trail along my wrist to my elbow. "It's better than okay, Jewel."

"I just wish I could lose the pants," Kingston says, kissing the side of my neck.

I don't respond to him, but my heart pounds harder at his desire. I mean, could I really survive such an adventure? With Orlando here?

My body tingles, totally willing to risk it, and I squeeze my legs together as I shift to smile.

Warm lips graze my shoulder, and Diego releases a small breath as he kisses up to my ear. "You know I'd never deny you from what you want."

I wriggle under his comment as heat blooms in my middle. "I don't want to deny any of you either."

Kingston hums in his throat, drawing his fingers between my legs for a moment. "Is that so?"

"Uh-huh." My words come out low and whispery, my lust pushing away every doubt I could possibly have. I want to go wherever this leads.

"I want to bite you," he says.

I tilt my head slightly for Kingston, exposing my throat to him. He gently bites down without hesitation, and I tip my head and moan as Kingston's tongue sends a burst of desire over me. I squeeze Orlando's hand, drawing it over my breasts, staring at him as Kingston drinks from me.

Orlando leans closer, licking his lips, staring at my mouth. Silver lights his blue eyes, his desire awakening the longer I capture him in my gaze. I release a breath and wet my lips, tipping my chin up until he meets me for a kiss. A dozen thoughts crash over me, my mind whirling as every part of my body feels like it's set ablaze in a desire so intense I'm not sure it'll ever extinguish. Not that I want it to.

Kingston's hands move up my stomach, sneaking under my nightie to roam over my skin. "Babe, you can tell us to stop at any time."

"Keep going," I whisper against Orlando's mouth to Kingston.

"Anything you want, beautiful." Taking over for Kingston, Diego runs his hand between my legs and trails his finger over the curve of my thigh to shift my clothes to tease me the way I like. I gasp and kiss Orlando harder, moving on Kingston's lap. Austin kisses the sensitive skin at the crook of my elbow and licks all the way to my wrist. His fangs graze my skin, preparing to bite me.

Orlando runs his tongue over my bottom lip, gently parting my mouth open to explore my tongue with his. Kingston eases his mouth away from my neck and staunches his bite with his fingers. Orlando breaks away from me to kiss my jaw. He works his mouth down my throat and over my chest, following the line of my bodice. I arch back into Kingston, and he snakes his arm in front of my mouth. I inhale a shuddering breath at the scent of his blood awakening my senses.

I moan in my throat, dozens of sensations tingling over my skin, my attention pulled in four directions but never fully apart as I lose myself to the ecstasy coursing through me, the love and lust I get from feeding my guys and accepting their affection and attention, drowning me but helping me breathe.

I break away from Kingston's arm and reach for Austin, pulling him closer by his shirt until I can slide between his legs to rest my back to his chest next. With one hand, he tugs his shirt off, letting me feel how my body warms his. He maneuvers to lay me down and smiles at me, brushing the hair from my face. Kingston shifts between my legs, massaging his fingers over my thighs, but he doesn't undress me. None of them do.

I rake my fingers over Kingston's chest, drinking in the hard muscles of his body and the bulge prominently wanting my attention.

"Jewel," Orlando says so softly, begging me with just the sound of my name to ask my permission to do something I've never allowed him to do before. Patting the spot next to me that Kingston left behind, I nod my head and meet Orlando's startling blue eyes as they flash silver.

I extend my arm to him and watch Orlando trail feather soft kisses along my wrist. I shift in anticipation, feeling everyone's gazes on me.

"You can tell me to stop at any time," Orlando murmurs, extending his fangs.

"Relax, Jewel," Austin says, feeling my body tense with nerves.

I inhale a slow breath and nod to Orlando again to tell

him I'm ready. His fangs pierce my skin, and I tip my head back and close my eyes for a second. Austin smiles at me from above when I peer up at him. He bites his arm and offers his blood for me to drink. Diego shifts and lies next to me, watching me while trailing his fingers over the lace of my nightie to caress my breasts through the fabric.

Kingston's hips press into mine, drawing my attention to him. I stretch my free hand out and stroke the length of his boner through his pants until he pulls down the zipper for me and exposes exactly what I do to him so I can explore him with my fingers. He moans, totally all in for whichever direction this leads.

I pull my mouth from Austin's arm. "Is this okay?" I ask breathlessly, my body completely ready to give in to Kingston as he kneels in front of me. "I mean, it's not, right? We haven't talked about this."

"Kingston, slow down," Austin says softly. "Jewel sounds nervous."

My heart crashes around my ribcage, and I swallow, my breath panting. "I am, but not in a bad way. I just—what are we doing? How far are we going?"

"Jewel, I'm perfectly content just enjoying whatever affection you offer me. If you want me to leave, I'll go," Orlando says.

Diego reaches over and caresses my cheek. "You've taken great care of me already, beautiful. I'm happy just to kiss you and touch you however you want."

I smile at him. "I'd like that." Turning to Austin, I meet his vibrant green eyes. "What about you?"

"Whatever you want, Jewel," he says, reaching out to graze his thumb over my lips.

I smile at him and hum under my breath. "Take off your pants."

Kingston rests his hands on my knees. "Command me next. I want to bang the hell out of you."

Blush creeps up my neck and burns my cheeks, and I prop up on my elbows and meet him with a serious look. Kingston's fangs peek out from his lips, and he meets my expression with a smolder that could probably burn my nightie right off of me if he stares for much longer.

"Kingston, this is up to Jewel and what she's comfortable with," Diego says softly.

Kingston breaks my stare to look at his brother. They share a silent thought, and I sit up higher and turn to Diego. "I want you naked, Diego."

Kingston purrs. "You're teasing me, babe."

I ignore him and glance at Orlando. "I want you to stay, but your clothes must come off too."

Orlando studies my eyes for a second, his eyebrows raised on his forehead. "I believe we're about to be the closest coven I've ever known."

I giggle. Full-on giggle. I can't friggin' help it. "And the strongest. The way I want."

Kingston squeezes my knees again, drawing my attention

back to him. I trail my gaze over his tight muscles, his chest rising in quick pants, his eyes flashing silver, just waiting for me to tell him what I want him to do.

"Okay, Kingston. Your turn. Slowly."

He chuckles and drops his pants, kicking out of them to join me on the bed. Desire pushes away my nerves, and I reach my arms up and let Diego pull my nightie over my head, exposing my boobs to the four of them.

I brush my hair away and lean back, feeling so sexy and wanted and loved. My skin buzzes, and I rub my legs together until Kingston moves first and bends in to kiss me. I ease up my hips for him, letting him undress me completely.

"So beautiful. Perfect," Orlando whispers, trailing his gaze over me.

"Better than you imagined, right?" Austin asks him.

"The best tits I've ever seen," Kingston says, smiling at me.

Diego reaches out and caresses my curves. "And I'm ready to give them all my attention."

My breath catches at Diego's words, and I reach out and grab him so that he brings his lips to mine. He breaks away, and Austin kisses me next, whispering for me to speak up at any time. I reach out and rub my hand down the hard muscles of his stomach and motion for him to lie down. I shift over to kiss him sweetly and trail my mouth over his neck and to his chest, working my way down the line of his stomach while teasing my fingers over his erection.

Kingston's hands slide around my hips, and he presses his body to mine, testing to see how I react to a position we've never tried. He prefers to face me unless we're drinking each other's blood, but he's clearly down for anything right now.

"Babe, are you sure?" Kingston asks. "I want you, but I can wait until we're alone."

"I love you guys. If you're good, I'm good. Happy," I say.

Kingston leans into me and kisses my shoulder. "I plan to make you happier."

I rest on my hands and knees, allowing Kingston to align his body to mine completely. He pushes inside me until his hips hit my ass, and I gasp at the amazing pressure. Digging his fingers into my sides, he rolls his body against mine. Austin plays with my hair, running his fingers over my scalp, and he arches up a bit to kiss me, smiling into my mouth because I can't stop moaning for more than a few seconds.

Sucking Austin's bottom lip into my mouth, I tug it gently between my teeth before I break away to kiss his jaw. He shifts onto a pillow to make it more comfortable for me as I trail my tongue over his stomach. The position blocks my body from rocking too much with Kingston's movements, making the amazing friggin' sensations more intense.

Austin guides my hand over him the way he likes until I do it on my own. I stroke my hand up and down with just enough pressure to pick up Austin's heartbeat and breath. Diego sneaks his hands beneath me and twirls his fingers over my breasts before lying down and shimmying his body to fit his head in the small space between my boobs and the bed to take over with his tongue. Orlando massages his fingers into my back until I feel the softness of his lips tasting my skin, just exploring wherever he can with his mouth, familiarizing himself in a way he's never had the chance to do before.

Austin's hand covers mine, slowing me down. I tilt my chin to look up at him, and he smiles at me and caresses my cheek with his fingers, hunger and need darkening his green eyes.

"Can I?" I ask him, gliding my tongue over my lip without saying the rest of my question.

His cheeks flush with the color I love to kiss at my suggestion. "I'd love that."

Bending down, I glide my tongue over Austin, tracing the ridge around his tip and down the length, tasting the sweetness of his skin. I kiss my way back to the top, licking my lips and moaning in the process through every wave of hot, sizzling sensations that blaze across my body—from Kingston's rhythmic motions and Diego's flicking tongue to Orlando grazing his teeth along my back.

Wetting my lips, I purse them to create pressure as I slowly part my mouth open to suck Austin into my mouth. He releases the sexiest noise, running his fingers through my hair, pulling it back so he can watch me work my tongue and mouth up and down him over and over in a way that turns his fingers desperate to touch me as time passes.

"Jewel," Austin whispers, his breath panting, his muscles

tightening. "If you want to stop..." His words trail off, letting me know he's about to finish.

I don't stop, my mouth practically drooling as I remember Austin's taste the first time we were intimate with each other. Austin digs his fingers deeper into my shoulders as I suck a little bit harder, stroking him with my thumb. He releases a moan, tipping his head back. The sweet, almost chocolatey taste of his release fills my mouth, and I slow down and ease my mouth away to swallow.

"Damn," Diego whispers. "Did our girl just...?"

"Original nutrients match. I bet she'd love you too," Kingston says, picking up speed.

I blush so hard and shake my head. "Dude."

He chuckles. "Don't be embarrassed. So hot, babe. But now it's your turn. There is no fucking way I'm finishing before you, so try not to bite Austin in the process," Kingston says. I don't even have to see his face to know he's smiling with the words.

Austin hums and massages his fingers into my shoulder blades. "I'm not afraid."

"Good. Then brace her for me."

I laugh before I moan and bow to rest my head on Austin's thigh for a moment. Kingston thrusts into me harder and deeper. His powerful movements cause my rebel mouth to scream out in pleasure. Diego slides his finger between my legs to help, drawing circles over what Kingston likes to joke and call my love button with enough pressure to drag another loud ass moan from my mouth.

"Damn," Orlando says lowly, his voice deep and husky, so full of desire I've never heard on him before.

Diego hums his agreement. "So sexy."

Austin kisses another breath from my mouth. Shifting slightly, he rests his hands on my shoulders, holding me in place to assure I get to experience every inch of Kingston without accidentally hitting my head or body against the wall. I pant, my skin buzzing, my body aching and yearning, begging to explode.

I release a cross between a whimper and plea, bowing to press my lips into Austin's thigh as pressure builds and builds inside me. My muscles tense and release, and I nearly knock Austin back as I scream a moan once more and fall into him. My arms completely give out on me, my body just wanting to sink into the bed. Austin cradles my head, holding my hands until the crazy good spasms settle, and I can finally breathe again.

"My favorite part," Diego says, lying next to me to gaze into my eyes. He beams his brilliant smile and runs his finger over my cheek to pull the dark hair from my face.

Kingston grunts in his throat like he's trying to suppress his moan and thrusts into me a few more times until he slows down and lies on top of me, pressing his chest into my hot back. He moves my hair and kisses the crook of my shoulder, catching his breath as I catch mine. No one says anything for a bit, Austin still cradling my head and Diego and Orlando holding my hands while Kingston hugs me.

"Thank you for trusting me, Jewel," Orlando says, squeezing my fingers. "I never knew how much I wanted your trust until I lost it in the first place. I swear to always do right by you. I will never make you feel vulnerable again."

I shift my head and look at him. "It's not so easy to forget, but I'm ready to move past it."

Austin continues to comb my hair. "And we'll get there, Jewel. Together."

"Yeah, we love you, babe," Kingston whispers, nuzzling his nose to my throat. "We will do whatever it takes. Plus, this was...fucking awesome."

I wiggle beneath him until he pulls himself off me so I can roll over to face him. "The things you guys do for me," I tease, drawing my finger across his stomach."

"Pretty sure you're doing plenty for us, beautiful." Diego motions for me to slide up to the head of the bed to settle in next to him.

"Want me to start the shower, babe? Maybe a bath?" Kingston asks.

I shake my head and extend my arms out to invite Orlando to settle in at my other side. I lie on my stomach and stretch my arms over Diego and Orlando's chests to let Kingston and Austin hold my hands. In this moment, I feel so incredible. So loved. So safe. I'll do anything to save these feelings and to experience them always.

"I just want to cuddle for a bit," I say, sinking into the

pillows.

Diego reaches down and grabs the blankets to pull them up. "I love the sound of that."

I close my eyes and listen to the beating hearts of my guys, of those who love and will do anything to protect me. "Me too. This is exactly how I expect our future together to be like."

Orlando touches my cheek to get me to look at him. And then he kisses me. "We'll do whatever it takes to make it happen."

NERVES

GROWLS SOUND OUT THROUGH THE air, prickling goosebumps over my skin. Icy wind whips my hair from my neck, and I shiver, pulling my jacket tighter around me. Four figures stroll ahead of me, and I try my best to keep up, but the distance grows farther between us until I lose sight of them.

"Guys?" I ask, my voice echoing through the air. "Wait. I can't keep up with you."

Silence greets me, my nerves bunching in my stomach. Quickening my pace, I jog forward, searching the desolate street for signs of life. Dozens of silver eyes glow in the shadows, but the vampires don't move or come closer.

"You can't keep this up forever, Jewel. You're not like

them." Dad's familiar voice draws my attention behind me, and I spin on my feet to face him.

"We're more alike than you think," I say, placing my hands on my hips.

Footsteps draw my attention from Dad, and I peer at a light growing from the shadows. Ramona appears from an alley, holding a tiny infant in her arms. She adjusts the baby on her shoulder and frowns at me.

"Jewel, it's time to feed the baby," she says. "It's been too long. She's starving."

I blink a few times. "She?"

"Please, you have to do this." Ramona steps closer, stepping up next to my dad.

Dad glowers at me. "She won't. Those vampires got into her head. They won't help you unless you give her to them."

Tears burst from Ramona's eyes. "I can't."

"Of course you can't," Dad says. "I won't let you. My granddaughter will fill the place Jewel turned her back on. She will fight. She will destroy our enemies. We will raise her to never turn her back on humanity and be such a disgrace."

Anger rolls through me. "She will grow up and die young, Ramona-babona. Dad will assure it."

Dad reaches out and grabs the infant from Ramona. He holds her out in front of him and gazes at her. A small cry sounds through the air, and I suck in a breath through my teeth as the shadows draw closer, the growls growing in volume.

"She will serve our kind well. It is her duty," Dad says. "I will not fail a second time."

"The only reason you failed is because you put the fight before us. Mom—"

Dad scowls. "Don't speak of your mother. She'd be so disappointed to find out that her beloved daughter now poses as a vampire. Treats humans like they're beneath her. For the first time, I'm glad Helena isn't here to see what a disgrace you've become."

"Shut up!" I yell. "You have no friggin' idea!"

Dad hands the infant to Ramona and yanks his gun from his belt and aims it at me. I freeze in place, my heart crashing against my ribcage. "I should end you for the greater good."

A figure blurs around us, drawing my dad's attention away from me. He pulls the trigger and shoots, causing Kingston to drop to his knees.

"Holy shit. Dude!" I call.

I don't get a chance to move before Dad fires at him again over and over. Kingston doesn't get up. He doesn't even move. Tears fill my eyes, and I try to close the space, but Dad swivels and points his gun at me again.

"Stay back," he commands. Glancing at Ramona, he says, "Take my grandbaby over there, Mona. Give her what she needs."

I stare in horror as Ramona closes the space to Kingston. She sets the infant on the dirty concrete and tugs a knife from beneath her jacket. She grabs Kingston by his black hair, pull-

ing his head up to expose his neck. She slices through and spills his blood right over her baby.

A small coo and laugh trickles through the air, sending a shiver through me.

Dad waves his gun. "See? This is how it's supposed to be. They're not the predators. You are. Your niece is. They should bow down to you."

I shake my head, swiping my hands across my cheeks to wipe away my tears. "No. I love them, and they love me. We don't have to be enemies. We can live together."

"That's what they want you to think," he snaps.

"It's not."

"And what happens when they decimate the rest of humanity? What happens when humans go extinct? That'll leave you. They'll cage you. They won't have a choice if they want to survive."

"You're delusional."

Another figure blurs around me, and I dig my nails into the palms of my hands. "Run," I say, unable to get a clear glimpse of who tries to get close. "He'll kill you too."

Dad shoots his gun again, but he misses, shattering the old glass window of a storefront. The growls draw silent with my ringing ears, and I clutch my head as dizziness washes over me. Dad shoots again, but the figure is too fast. A small cry breaks through my dizzying thoughts, and I nearly lose my shit as Mitchell materializes next to Ramona and the baby.

"How thoughtful," Mitchell says, flashing his fangs.

"You've taken care of my disgraced heir for me."

Ramona darts toward Mitchell, and I screech out, rushing forward. Dad fires his weapon, and I stop in my tracks, surprise washing over me. He doesn't try to shoot Mitchell. He actually aimed and shot the wall behind me.

"Accept this as a gift. In return, you'll provide my granddaughter what she needs," Dad says to Mitchell.

Mitchell links his fingers together. "If you take care of the rest of my disgraced heirs."

Dad waves his hand. "Already done."

I cover my chest with my hand, my heart faltering as dark shadows throw two bodies into the street. Gasping, I take in Austin and Diego's appearances, their lifeless bodies not reacting as Mitchell kicks them both onto their backs to look at their faces.

"And my enemy?" Mitchell asks. "Where is Mr. Ortega?"

"Here." Orlando materializes out of nowhere and rushes Mitchell. The two of them only blur for a second before Mitchell pins Orlando down, shoving his hand into his chest. Orlando's eyes flash silver, and he turns his head to glance at me. "I'm sorry, precious Jewel. This is the end."

My screams rip through the air as Mitchell removes Orlando's heart and gets to his feet. He closes the distance to me and holds out the bloody organ, still pulsing in his palm. Hunger burns through me, and I can't stop myself as I snatch it from him and bring it to my lips, my inner monster breaking free to devour Orlando's heart completely.

"Jewel, no. What have you done?" Brayla's voice sounds through the air. "How could you? They loved you. You were supposed to protect our coven."

My bloody hands tremble. "I—I'm sorry."

"Come now, Brayla. Leave Jewel. Your home is now with me." Viorica materializes and takes Brayla's hand. The two of them disappear, leaving me alone to face my dad and Mitchell.

"My heir," Mitchell says. "How foolish you were to think you could ever take what rightfully belongs to me."

Rage pushes my feet forward, and I launch myself at Mitchell. A loud pop sounds through the air, and pain explodes through my stomach, sending me to my knees. Warmth blooms in my middle, and I touch my hand to the blood pouring from me.

I gasp and look at my dad. "D-Dad. How c-could y-you?"

He lowers his gun. "How could you?" Turning away from me, he glances at Mitchell. "Our deal?"

"Done," Mitchell says. "Now bring her here."

I curl in on myself as my dad approaches. "No."

Dad links his fingers to my arm. "This is where you belong. Caged."

"No!"

Cool hands slide under me and turn me over. I open my eyes and gasp, the vivid dream whirling through my mind as I stare into Orlando's blue eyes. His brows furrow, and he touches my cheek and drinks me in.

Soft lips kiss my shoulder, and Diego slides his arms around my stomach. "A nightmare?" Diego asks, resting his head to my shoulder blade.

Austin props up on his elbows, peering at me from over Orlando's shoulder. "It sounded like a bad one."

Kingston stands next to the bed and bends over Diego to shift me slightly so that I look at him. I'm nearly certain he left the bed after I fell asleep. "Fuck, it was. Look at her."

I cover my eyes with my hands and take a deep breath, hiding from all of their intense gazes. Gentle hands slide through mine to pull my fingers away. I stare at Orlando, fear and despair crashing over me despite Diego trying to smother the bad emotions from me.

"It was about Ramona and her baby...my dad. Mitchell." I close my eyes again to compose myself. My mouth quivers as I try to suppress it the best I can. "It was the worst."

"And just a dream." Orlando touches my cheek.

"It felt real," I say.

Soft lips meet mine, and I release a quivering breath against Orlando's mouth. I let him and Diego hug me for a moment before I break away to motion for everyone to sit up. Kingston comes to my side and pulls me into him, snuggling his face into the crook of my neck. Austin strokes his fingers over my hand, pulling it to his mouth to kiss.

"You guys probably think I'm ridiculous. Scared of a damn nightmare," I say.

"Never, beautiful," Diego says.

"He's right, babe." Kingston drapes his arms over my shoulder, taking advantage of the fact that I'm half naked. He slides his hands under my boobs and jiggles them. Diego, Austin, and Orlando all gaze down to watch. I lean my head back for a moment, letting him have his fun, and laugh.

"Do you want to talk about it?" Austin asks, drawing his gaze back to mine.

"It's okay. I'd rather just forget about it."

Kingston grazes his fingers over my breasts. "Is this helping?"

I release another breathless laugh. "A little."

"What about—"

I snatch his hand before he can get carried away and hold it to my chest. "As much as I want to pick back up from where we left off last night, I'm starving. For solids." I don't mention that my body aches, and what I really want is to start the day with a soak in the tub.

Like he can read my mind, Kingston gets to his feet. "Austin, why don't you grab Jewel something while I start her a bath."

I smile. "Lots of bubbles."

"So no company?" he asks, smirking at me.

"I'd like to watch you take a shower," I tease.

He purrs and kisses me. "You bet."

"And if you'll excuse me, I need to check on the Vaduvas," Orlando says, climbing out of bed. "They might be allies, but some of the sisters lack impulse control."

"Why don't I go with you?" Diego asks, stretching his arms over his head.

He catches me watching him and smiles, arching his back to show off what waking up next to me does to him through his boxers. I crawl closer and kiss him sweetly, climbing on top of him for just a second to steal the blanket and wrap myself in it.

"Mmm," he whispers. "Careful, beautiful. I can't resist when you're playful."

I grin and wave him off the bed. I watch the four of them, appreciating the hard muscles of their bodies until they get completely dressed and ready...at least everyone besides Kingston.

"You're making it hard to leave," Orlando says, buttoning up his shirt.

I smirk. "Good. It should be."

"It always has been, but now?" He leans in and kisses me. "It's torture."

Diego kisses me next, and I hug him for a bit, making Orlando wait at the door to the study. I want so badly to have a moment alone with each of my guys to ask them what's on their minds. They're obviously good, acting as if this is just another great late afternoon as we prepare for the evening and oncoming night.

"Something sweet or savory?" Austin asks, taking me from Diego. I hug him and wave at Diego and Orlando as they leave the room. Baby bolts in and pads her way to us, rubbing the length of her body on Austin's leg.

"Savory," I say. "And don't forget something for her."

Austin bends down and scratches her ears. "I'd never."

I smile and kiss him, watching him cross the room with Baby following behind him. Kingston appears next to me and links his fingers through mine to pull me toward the bathroom. I let him pick me up and carry me over the threshold and to the tub, where he kisses me as he sets me into the steaming water.

I moan as the lavender-scented air wafts around me. Kingston turns on the shower head and soaks my hair, taking his time to lather shampoo over my dark tresses. I lean back and sink lower, tilting my head up to look at him.

He kisses my forehead and smiles. "Good?"

"Amazing. Just how I wanted to start my day." I lift my feet out of the tub and watch the water splash into the bubbles. Kingston moves to the other end to lift my foot up to rub his fingers into. "And I changed my mind about watching you shower. Join me."

He chuckles and slips into the tub, letting me lie between his legs. He continues to massage my feet and works his way up to put pressure on my calves. "I promise I won't get carried away," he murmurs. "I know last night was...quite a bit."

I stretch my foot out and touch his cheek. "I enjoyed it, but I definitely need you to continue to massage me."

His eyes flash silver. "With the way you're looking at me, I agree."

"Just pray that Austin hurries with my breakfast." I smirk and snap my teeth at him. "Otherwise, I'll try my best to be gentle."

"I'm tough, babe," he says, raising his eyebrow. "You want to bite me? I'm all in."

"Don't tease me," I say, licking my lips.

"I'm not. After last night, after everything, I'm so fucking ready," he says.

I lean forward and grab his hands in mine, pulling him closer so that my legs rest over his. "So you're good? I mean, *really* good? I don't just want to assume because you're willing to go along with things. I know you sometimes struggle with your jealousy."

"It's like you don't even know me." He smiles as he says the words. "I'd be the first one to tell you, Jewel. But since you need me to express it, yes. I'm fucking great. Inviting Orlando was not as awkward as I expected. I'd equate it to the first time you allowed Diego, Austin, and I to intimately bite you in Haven Springs."

I scoot even closer to feel his body press between my legs. Sliding my hands around his neck, I hold his gaze for a second and search his eyes. "I don't know exactly what I want from him, but thank you for being okay with me trying to figure it out, especially with the Blood Vow."

He kisses me, sneaking his hands under my ass to pull me onto him so that I straddle his waist. "What about you? Maybe I can help you."

"You want to help me?" I ask, scrunching my nose.

"I know I'm not Diego or Austin, and I might say things that piss you off, but yeah. I want to help you if you need it. You're my—and I swear you better not repeat this—my perfect personality match." He kisses the tip of my nose.

"And my perfect body match," I say.

"Damn straight."

A soft tap sounds on the door, and I call out to let Austin in. He swings the door open, pushing it with his shoulder while holding a tray. "I thought you might want to eat now without having to get out."

I grin and slide away from Kingston, waving my hands to Austin. "You're the best. Come feed me. Kingston still needs practice, and I don't want to bathe with my breakfast."

Kingston releases a playful growl, and I gently kick him, splashing water into his face. He chuckles and pushes himself toward me, sending a wave of water over the side of the tub. Austin laughs and throws a few towels down, setting up the tray while Kingston kisses me before returning to his spot and holding my feet in place to stop me from rubbing them over his now fully raging boner.

Austin brings a chair to the side of the tub and sits down, not even caring that I drip water on him as I reach up to squeeze his leg and smile. He offers me a forkful of pan-fried, seasoned potatoes, and I hum under my breath.

"Good?"

"So good," I murmur, covering my mouth with my hand.

Kingston flicks water at me. "Seriously, babe. Control yourself."

I stick my tongue out at him. "Are you jealous of these potatoes?"

"Fuck yeah. They're lucky to be in your mouth."

I crack up and splash water at him.

Austin chuckles and feeds me another bite. "I might actually be a little jealous too, Jewel. I mean, last night, you were...you are incredible."

"And you're friggin' delicious."

He leans down and brushes his lips over my shoulder. "I can say the same. Nothing in the world tastes as good as you."

"Fucking one percent," Kingston murmurs.

I reach underwater and graze my fingers over Kingston's leg until I find exactly what I'm looking for. "Doesn't matter, dude. I'll show you later. It is technically your night."

"Damn, babe. I'm ready now." He cups his hand over mine and helps me stroke him a few times.

"Dude," I say, kissing him. "I want to but—"

Kingston presses his finger to my lips, silencing my comment. "Austin, get undressed. I need you to take care of Jewel."

I tip my head back and laugh. "Ah hell. I created a horny, sexy, nearly irresistible monster."

Kingston grimaces. "Nearly?"

Austin laughs. "You make it too easy for our girl to tease you."

"Hopefully pity me, too," Kingston says.

I roll my eyes. "Pity you? Why?"

"Because we decided that we're not rotating nights again until after your Blood Vow," Austin says. "And then it's customary for Orlando to get the night alone with you."

My mouth falls open. "Oh. Well, I can still make time tonight."

"If the Vaduvas don't bore you to sleep early with all their planning. I volunteered to supervise, though I might have to trade with Austin since he's least likely to murder one of them," Kingston says. "Orlando and Diego will be preparing for the board tomorrow night."

I inhale a small breath. "Shit. Tomorrow? It feels like it's coming fast. I'm so nervous."

"Which is why you should try to talk to Orlando. We can only help so much when it comes to this," Kingston says.

Austin massages my shoulders. "But we are here to support you however you need."

I groan. "I just want to Blood Vow with all of you. No hiding. No secrets. No pretending to be something I'm not."

A hiss sounds out from the bedroom as Baby reacts to something, drawing our attention to the closed door. Austin jumps to his feet. He disappears from the room, and Kingston and I listen as Austin murmurs something that I'm pretty friggin' sure isn't to Orlando or Diego.

"Jewel!" Hayden's voice sounds over the soft music. "Jewel! Come talk to me."

"I said she's in the bath," Austin says, keeping his voice even.

Something crashes, and Kingston stands up, spilling water over the floor. He rushes out of the bathroom, leaving the door open. I gape at Austin holding Hayden up by the neck. Hayden's face turns red from the lack of oxygen. Rushing to them, Kingston yanks Austin back, and Hayden drops to his knees.

Hayden crawls forward while Austin and Kingston blur in a fight for a moment, and fear trickles through me. Austin knocks Kingston off his feet and charges toward Hayden. Yelling, Hayden reaches for his weapon, ready to fight Austin the best he can.

"Everyone stop!" I shout. "Hayden, close your damn eyes now."

I grab a towel and nearly eat shit trying to hurry out of the tub. Austin catches me, choosing to take care of me instead of restraining Hayden, and I let Austin gather me into his arms to breathe in my hair.

"I'm sorry, Jewel. I overreacted, but he was trying to come into our room," Austin says. "I will not allow anyone to disrespect you or try to barge in on you when you're indecent."

I snuggle against him. "It's okay. He deserved it."

Kingston comes up to us and pats Austin on the back. "Bro, sorry I did that. You still sometimes make me nervous as fuck, and I didn't want you to lose control in front of Jewel."

A weird ass coo comes out of my mouth, and I pull Kingston in and laugh as he sandwiches me in a wet, sexy ass hug between him and Austin.

"Jewel," Hayden says, drawing our attention to him. "I don't have fucking time to wait while you take a bath. My people are here, and the sun will set soon. I don't want to bring them into the shade until we have somewhere to go."

"Let me get Orlando," Austin says. "We'll figure it out."

Hayden rubs the back of his neck. "They're the innocents of Haven Springs. Some have never seen a vampire."

I hug my towel around me and look at Kingston. "Will you go inform Orlando? I'll take Austin with me to meet the newcomers."

Kingston flares his nostrils. "This isn't your job."

I touch Kingston's cheek. "But it is. This is my chance to show that we can accomplish amazing things together. They'll see you're not bad, and I'm not a traitor."

"Fine," he mumbles. He punches Austin's shoulder. "Take good care of our girl, bro."

"He will," I say, kissing Kingston once before he disappears.

Austin grabs me some clothes, and we meet Hayden in the study.

Hayden crosses his arms. "No fangs, Mr. Ortega. And don't scare anyone."

I roll my eyes. "He knows how to handle humans."

"I trust you, Jewel," Hayden says.

I link my fingers through Austin's. "I'll guarantee your people are safe."

Nodding, Hayden takes a step forward. "Good, then follow me."

NEW ARRIVALS

AUSTIN DRIVES ALONG THE ROAD that'll take us up the cliff that overlooks Ombre Noire. The light changes as we reach the top and drive away from the shade. The sun sets in the distant horizon, setting the sky aglow in fiery color.

"I can't handle direct sunlight for long, Jewel," Austin says. "Even completely covered." There's a reason vampires like the shade if they don't have shelter. They get hot, and after a short period of time, they can still burn under their clothes.

I swivel in the front seat and look at him. "You're not going to handle it at all. You're staying in the car where it's safest for you."

Austin slides his hand through mine. "I can't allow you to

face them without my protection. My brothers would murder all of them if you got hurt."

"I'll protect Jewel," Hayden says from the backseat.

Austin releases a strangled laugh, his eyes flashing silver. Twisting in his seat, Austin extends his fangs and scowls at Hayden. I grab his leg and dig my fingers into his thigh. He's usually more composed than this.

"Austin, hey. Look at me." Reaching out, I cup his face. "What's wrong? You usually don't let things get to you. If this is going to be a problem for you, maybe I need to call Diego." Because Kingston is out of the question. He gets scary as eff when annoyed.

Austin composes himself and retracts his fangs, covering my hand with his to press my fingers deeper into his cheek.

"I picked you to come with me because I thought you would be less threatening than your brothers," I add. "As friggin' hot as you are acting all protective, these people aren't fighters. Dougie is among them. Other kids."

Austin swallows, his Adam's apple bobbing in his throat. He stares at me silently and lets my words sink in. "I know, and I'm sorry. I just—I don't trust Hayden to protect you. I trust no one but my brothers."

"You trust me," I say.

"With my life."

"So then trust me with my own."

Austin pouts harder than I think Kingston ever has, and I can't resist leaning in and kissing it away. He wraps his arms around me and hugs me, not even caring that Hayden watches us. Pulling away, he slowly nods his head. I smile at him and kiss him once more.

Austin reaches into his jacket and pulls out a sheathed dagger. "My brothers will murder me if I let you out of my reach unarmed."

I stick the dagger in the front pocket of my sweatshirt. "I'm not going to need it."

He scrunches his face. "They might try to murder me for even letting you get out of arm's reach."

I shake my head, letting my hair sweep back and forth. "Murdering you is a deal breaker, so I highly doubt it."

That makes him chuckle. "I love you, Jewel."

Hayden clears his throat and leans between the seats. He points his finger and draws our attention out the tinted windshield to a caravan of old ass cars that remain idling on the stretch of broken road just outside the perimeter gate. The daytime guards remain at their post, training their weapons at the group.

One of the guards turns in our direction and jogs toward us to close the distance before Austin even parks. Austin pulls his hood lower and cracks the window so that the guard can hear him through the soundproof glass.

"Allow them entrance, Mr. Lee. They are invited guests of Ms. Ortega," Austin says. "I'd like you to stand by and escort her to meet with them."

"Yes, sir," Mr. Lee says.

He presses a button on his radio, and the other guard lowers his gun and opens the gate. He motions for the first car to enter and inspects each one as they pass through.

"How many people?" Austin asks Hayden.

Hayden keeps his eyes trained at the window, watching the tenth and last vehicle enter our property. "Around fifty."

Austin sighs. "I need an exact number and stats on them. Orlando will want to know."

Hayden pulls out a folded piece of paper from his pocket. "Twenty-one under eighteen, fifteen adults, and sixteen elderly."

"How many males?"

"Nineteen of the kids and twelve of the elderly. The fifteen adults are all women—the mothers."

"Health statuses?"

"No known illnesses or anything logged in. We didn't exactly have time to give everyone a physical before vacating."

Austin clenches the steering wheel, his knuckles lightening in color under the pressure. "I'll need to examine everyone."

"Not happening," Hayden says, raising his voice.

"Then you need to have them turn around."

My mouth falls open. "Austin."

He sucks in a breath and releases the wheel to take my hand. "We can't afford to let any sicknesses slip in. Look what happened with Dark Terrace Ranch with the flu outbreak. Something as little as a cold virus could put a complete stop to the authorization of incoming donors. We need a gen. pop. blood source, Jewel. We can't maintain power and support a community without one. Running a region is part of being on the board. Once Ombre Noire is up and going, we'll be starting more and assigning other covens leadership."

"Oh. No one told me." It's all I can think of to say. I had no idea that we'd grow. I mean, I was aware that there were more cities in the Divine Region run by other covens under the authority of Donor Life Corp that paid for power through gen. pop. donations, but I didn't really think much of it. All the board members have their main cities, leaving the rest to less powerful but still elite vampires.

Austin closes his eyes for a second. "I'm sorry. We were getting around to it, but then the attack happened, and the board threw your early Blood Vow at us. We didn't want to overwhelm you."

"Or you just didn't want her to know," Hayden mutters under his breath.

I twist and reach between the seats to smack him on the chest with the back of my hand. "Shut up and stay out of our business. Disrespect my match again, and you can take your people and fuck the hell off."

Hayden's eyes widen as he stares at me in shock. He can't even find the words to react.

"I'm putting my guys at risk to help you. You will be grateful and do as we ask. If Austin wants to make sure you don't doom our region with an illness, then you're going to let him. He is highly trained in human health and not only the most professional but the most empathetic person I know—human or vampire. I will assist him in the process and do everything I can within reason to assure your people are comfortable." I turn to Austin to make sure my offer to help was okay before looking back to Hayden. "Do you understand, Mr. Andrei?" I ask, purposely using his last name, knowing how it annoys him.

Hayden's chest heaves, his fingers curling into tight fists. I half expect him to thrust the door open and stomp away to abandon his plan, but he licks his lips and nods. "Yes, I understand."

"Now apologize to Austin."

"What?" he snaps.

"Or get out and leave."

Hayden flares his nostrils and draws his glower from me to look at Austin. "I'm sorry for disrespecting you."

Austin remains expressionless. "Thank you. Please go prepare your people. Jewel will join you in a minute."

Hayden abandons the car and slams the door. I watch him walk toward the security guard standing in front of the first vehicle. Austin touches my chin, turning my head to look at him, and he offers me the most amazing smile before kissing me.

"You know I'm going to have to replay this for my brothers, right?" he asks, releasing a chuckle.

My brows peak on my forehead as I lean in to look at the

tiny camera lens in the dash. "You guys really watch all the videos?" I had no idea that most cars came equipped with inside and outside cameras until Orlando and Brayla tried to use a video against me to breach my Blood Match contract.

"Not all. Just the entertaining ones."

I bring my hand up to my mouth. "Oh, shit. Diego and I..."

He frowns. "Diego would never allow you to be recorded like that without your permission. We uninstalled the cameras in our cars at the Divinity Estate, which was probably one of the first signs Mitchell took that we were pulling away and hiding things from him."

I shudder, thinking about even the smallest possibility of Mitchell watching me on any of the videos. I knew there were security cameras all over the Divinity Estate, but my guys were always good at avoiding them and deleting anything they wanted since they were in control.

"The staff—and sometimes Hayden—use the vehicles, so Orlando monitors them," he adds. "The only reason I knew there was one in here was because Orlando had Kingston check the footage from the other night."

"With me and Hayden?" I ask, grimacing. "Did you not believe me?"

"It wasn't that, Jewel. We definitely knew you wouldn't lie to us. Orlando was more concerned about Hayden. Just because the rebel helped us before doesn't mean he's our ally."

"Oh." I glance toward the window again.

"I'll talk to Orlando about this. He should've told you."

"Thanks," I say, opening my arms to hug him. "I mean it. You have no idea how much I appreciate you looking out for me."

Austin kisses me again. "If only you'd relent to my need to move things to the shade so I can do it now."

I pat his chest. "I'll be fast. Promise. Now, cover your face."

Austin does as I say, and I exit the car. Mr. Lee waits at the hood of the vehicle and strolls next to me as we walk the two dozen feet to meet with the people exiting the cars to gather around Hayden. I take a moment to look at each person, trying to recall whether or not I've seen them before from my time in Haven Springs. The place was big, but not as big as Dark Terrace Ranch. Even Ombre Noire is bigger.

I recognize two of the women from my last day in Haven Springs, but I can't remember if they were on my side or not.

Everyone looks nervous as all get-out, glancing around the vast, open field of nothingness, since the town can't be seen unless you walk to the edge of the cliff a mile away, and even then, it's so close that you can only see the outskirts.

A few of the smaller kids laugh and play around, starting a game of chase, and two of the women dart and lift them off their feet, covering their mouths like any sudden noise will destroy everyone. And I feel bad. These kids probably never experienced a life outside of Haven Springs. If they had, it might not have been for long.

"Noise is fine," I say, speaking up.

The crowd turns in my direction. A few of the women clutch onto their children and scowl at me like I just told their kids that it was fine to throw rocks at vampires. Hayden kicks up dirt as he stomps toward me. He drapes his arm over my shoulder, shocking me so much that I don't move, and I hear the familiar sound of Austin growling from the car. Hayden must not appreciate his limbs. My guys have never liked anyone touching me. The only people they've never reacted to were my cousins.

I wave my hand at Austin to tell him I'm fine, and he quiets down. His reaction must've been too low for anyone to hear because no one reacts. No one glances at the car. I bet they don't even know Austin is there.

"Listen up, everyone. Some of you might recognize Jewel from her stay in Haven Springs under the order of Mitchell Divine of Donor Life Corp," Hayden says, glancing to me. "As I've already told you, she is no longer in Divine possession. Anything that involved her in Haven Springs was not her fault. You will consider Jewel an ally and show her the same respect you do each other."

I force myself to smile, trying not to look as bad as I feel even remembering my time in Haven Springs.

"Jewel has also graciously invited us to stay in her coven's new and upcoming region until the threats have subsided in Haven Springs. You will not be responsible for donations as you are still exempt, but vampires do reside here. Jewel's protection will assure your safety, but please do remain alert and armed at all times. Do not attack vampires unprovoked. If you need anything, call upon me and I'll work it out with the Ortega Coven." Hayden glances at me. "Would you like to add anything else?"

I clear my throat. "Before you're granted temporary Ombre Noire residency status, everyone will receive a quick, non-invasive medical exam performed by our human health specialist under my supervision. As long as you have a clean bill of health, you will be permitted to stay."

"That seems reasonable," the nearest woman says.

"I must warn you. The doctor is a vampire," Hayden says.

"What?" another woman asks. "You don't have a human practitioner?"

I twist my lips to the side. "I'm sorry, no. There was no time to arrange one. I doubt you all would like to sleep out here for a few days while we request one from another region. We are not yet open."

"Ms. Penny, it'll be fine," a familiar female voice says. "Jewel will assure everything is good. This is my daughter's region, you know. I'll introduce you to her."

I jerk my attention to a van and catch sight of Mrs. Diggs sitting in the back with a few infants and toddlers fast asleep. It takes everything in me not to react to her words. I still don't think she knows that Mr. Diggs abandoned her or that he took Brayla with him. I'm not even sure if she knows her daughter was transformed into a vampire. Donor Life Corp messed with her head.

"Mrs. Diggs is right."

I gape at a familiar man standing at the back of the crowd. Mr. Barton was the last person I had expected to come, but I guess the old man would be considered elderly. He was also cut from the council the day I left. Either way, I can't stop the frown crossing my face. The guy was an asshole to me.

"Hayden, I'd like to return to Haven Springs," a soft voice says from the back. "You should have told me that a former Divine was the one assisting in our relocation."

OhmyGod. And I thought seeing Mr. Barton was surprising.

It's been months, and I only met the old woman one time, but I'd never forget Laurel's mother. While she was not as responsible as Laurel, who kidnapped me for Katherine Duchanne, the woman allowed her to do so.

"Ms. Mendoza, I'm sorry. That won't be possible." Hayden side-glances me. "But I assure you, whatever happened between you and the Divines will not affect your stay here. Jewel is an Ortega now."

"I was found guilty for treason. They murdered my daughter." Ms. Mendoza doesn't meet my gaze. "I'd be better off braving the night alone out here."

I clear my throat and lean closer to whisper to Hayden. "Technically, Ramona killed her daughter."

He narrows his eyes at me. "Because she was commanded to attack."

"No, she was commanded to protect me."

Hayden and I search each other's faces, drawing silence among the crowd. He breaks away first and clears his throat, turning back to Ms. Mendoza. "I assure you that all has been forgotten."

It takes everything in me to remain expressionless. "Yeah, what he said."

Ms. Mendoza purses her lips and hugs herself, and I swivel to glance at Austin, only seeing his silhouette through the dark tinted window. I better warn my guys beforehand, because a surprise like this might not end well.

"Does anyone else have any concerns?" Hayden asks.

The crowd remains silent.

He nods. "Okay, good. Everyone, grab your belongings. We'll be walking to town from here. The vehicles are too loud, and our arrival must be as discrete as possible."

"But the sun," Mr. Barton says, pointing at the sliver of golden light in the sky.

"Doesn't matter," I say. "Ombre Noire doesn't get much sun anyway."

He frowns. "I don't understand."

I smirk. I can't help that I find his worry a bit satisfying. He's not so tough now in the world outside of Haven Springs. "You'll see."

Dougie sits on my lap, and I bounce my knees, making the little guy giggle the sweetest laugh. As an heir to an Ortega

Blood Match, Mrs. Diggs gets to live on our estate while the rest of the exempt take shelter in an old warehouse off of the main street in town.

"Tin-tin!" Dougie stretches his arms out to Austin while he gathers the medical supplies he needs to perform the exams.

Austin grins and closes the space, leaning in to rub his nose to Dougie's, making him laugh again.

"Don't shake him too much, babe. He could explode," Kingston says, sitting on the opposite end of the couch in Austin's makeshift lab.

I get up, resting Dougie on my hip as I stroll over and plop down next to Kingston. "I don't think he will."

Kingston groans but doesn't move. "If he does—"

"You'll get to take another bath with me," I say, grinning.

He looks down at his lap. "What the fuck? Babe, take those words back right now. You will not use the grossness of a little human to seduce me."

"Here, let me take him," Austin says. "Kingston, you can carry the supplies."

"And I'll gladly take our girl." Diego materializes in the doorway and beats Kingston to snatch me off the couch. I hook my legs around him and laugh, kissing him hard enough to slide his big hands down my ass to pull me tighter into him.

"You all can't go," I mumble against Diego's mouth.

"Actually, Jewel. We can, and we will. I'd like to assess the humans myself." Orlando leans in the doorway, crossing his arms over his broad chest. He dares me to argue with him by lowering his eyebrows on his forehead.

I slump my shoulders and resist. "No fangs. No fast movements. You make a kid cry, and you'll be in deep trouble."

Kingston raises an eyebrow at me.

I point at him. "Not the good kind."

"I think we can all manage that," Orlando says before Kingston can joke around with me. "I'd hate to have to experience your wrath the night before our coven union. It should be one of celebration. We still must go over the arrangements."

I swallow, my sudden nerves getting the best of me. "That's probably a g-good idea. I'm still nervous as hell."

"Then let's hurry with this so we can meet with the Vaduvas early."

I nod and hold on tight as Austin leads the way out of the house to the idling car in the front. We drive into town instead of walk, and Austin surprises me by playing the earlier recording of me yelling at Hayden for everyone to see.

Diego howls a laugh so loudly that it startles Dougie, making him cry, and I nearly melt at the sight of Austin cuddling him and calming him down. While my cousins and Ramona have always been better with kids, I can't help the soft spot I have for Dougie because I watched him grow up. And seeing Austin like this? I love him even more.

"Uh-oh. Our girl has that look," Kingston mutters.

I turn in Diego's arms and smack Kingston's knee. "I do

not."

Austin looks at me. "You kind of do."

His words bring Orlando's attention to me, and he studies me for a minute. "What are you talking about? I'm not familiar with her current expression."

I groan and cover my face. "Kingston's just teasing me about kids. He thinks a part of me would love to expand the donor population, which is untrue. I only love how cute Austin is with Dougie. It's nothing more than that."

Orlando presses his lips together in a thin line. "I see."

I frown. "You look like you have more to say."

"I was just thinking about Jade. It wouldn't be that unreasonable if the desire to bear children did arise. It's also not impossible."

"Uh, yeah it is," Kingston says. "...right? If it was, Jewel would've been knocked the fuck up already."

"Kingston!" I say.

He shrugs. "What? You know how babies are made."

Blush warms my cheeks, and I cover my face with my hands. "Yeah, well, I don't want to talk about it."

"If you ever want to—"

I groan and cut off Orlando. "Seriously, no. I'm good. I get freaked out enough about making sure you guys are good."

"You say that like we wouldn't help out. Hello, babe. Your spawn could be like you and need vampire blood. Midnight feedings could be on us."

I burst out laughing. "Okay, that might change my mind.

I mean, in The Boxes most mothers were usually responsible in supplying the food, so this is kind of friggin' awesome."

Silence falls in the car, all of them missing that I'm totally kidding with them. The fact that my throat locks up, and a weird, unfamiliar feeling washes over me doesn't help. The thought of bearing a child is scary enough. Even thinking about Ramona gives me friggin' nightmares.

Austin reaches out to me and squeezes my knee. "I'm on board with whatever you want of our future together."

I bite my lip and laugh nervously. "Thanks, Austin. I'm good for now."

Orlando stops in the middle of the street outside a boarded up warehouse, and I fling the door open and slide off Diego's lap. He doesn't let me get far, hooking his fingers to my hips to study my face as I gasp in a few deep breaths of fresh air.

"Relax, beautiful," he says, kissing my shoulders. "You don't have to make any decisions yet or ever, and we didn't mean to freak you out. We just want you to know that despite Kingston's quips about our inability to procreate, it doesn't mean you still can't have what your heart might eventually desire."

"Or not," I say.

He chuckles. "That too."

Hayden appears from inside the warehouse. He draws my attention from my guys and the unexpected weird-ass conversation I had no idea would happen the night before my Blood

Vow and the union of our coven, but I guess I can't blame them.

"I need to warn you guys about someone," I say, getting the four of them to gather around me and to block Hayden out. "Laurel's mom is among the people here."

"What?" Kingston's voice rises. "You gotta be fucking kidding me!"

I reach out and grip his shoulders. "If you can't calm down, then you have to go home, dude. I don't like it as much as you do, but I can't blame the old woman for what she did. I also swore to myself that I'd show her some mercy because she pitied me and gave me the knife I used that helped me escape, even if her intention wasn't exactly for that reason."

Kingston spins on his feet and laces his fingers behind his head. "I don't like this."

"Kingston," I say softly.

He shakes his head. "I—I do have to go home. I don't trust myself right now."

I frown.

Diego laces his fingers through mine. "I think I'm going to stay out here too."

"What?"

Lifting me up, Diego relocates me a few feet away from his brothers and rests my back against the wall of the building. His gray eyes flash silver, and he tightens his mouth, obviously trying his best not to frown.

"I don't think I can face Ms. Mendoza, beautiful. I'm

partly responsible for Laurel's death. I didn't take the time to properly manipulate her mind."

I blink a few times. Diego's never mentioned his feelings about Laurel. My first visit to Haven Springs is such a blur now that it hasn't crossed my mind much. Laurel nearly got me killed. She purposely went against my guys after they did what they could to protect her from an awful fate. My sympathy wears thinner now for her than ever. Because I no longer believe that everyone does what they have to do to survive. I know that there is more to life than that.

I embrace Diego and nestle my head to the crook of his neck. "I can't tell you not to blame yourself, because I understand, but I want you to know that I don't blame you. You did your best in a horrible situation."

He tilts his head back to gaze into my eyes. "Thanks for saying that, Jewel."

"You don't have to thank me for speaking the truth. I love you, Diego."

Setting me on my feet, Diego strolls with me to his brothers. Kingston stands with his arms crossed, watching me, and I curl my finger to get him to come closer.

"You and Diego can wait out here. I don't really want to send you back to fend for yourselves against the Vaduvas," I say, arching up to kiss him.

"What? No pep talk?" he asks.

I smirk. "I think your feelings are warranted, so no. You're fine."

Hayden sighs, clearly annoyed by how long we take to get ourselves situated for the task at hand. Orlando retracts his fangs and fixes his jacket before offering his arm out for me to take. Austin slings his medical bag over his shoulder and nods at Kingston and Diego. Hayden leads the way inside, and the soft murmur of voices disappears as everyone notices our arrival.

"All right, everyone," Hayden says. "Lin—"

Commotion sounds from outside, and Diego rushes into the warehouse, his fangs extended and his eyes flashing silver. A few people shout, grabbing for their weapons. Hayden holds up his hands, trying to get people to calm down.

"We have a problem," Diego says to Orlando, ignoring the commotion. "It seems the Vaduvas thought we were busy entertaining Jewel, so they took the opportunity to come into town."

"Shit," I say. "Please don't tell me—"

Kingston growls outside and heaves a breath. "Widows incoming."

Viorica enters the building and peers around. She materializes in front of Orlando and flashes her fangs. "Mr. Ortega, it looks like we have quite a bit to discuss."

A shot pops through the air, startling me. I don't have time to react as I'm thrown against the wall, the breath escaping me. It takes everything in me not to scream.

OUT OF CONTROL SAVAGE

AUSTIN GRABS THE BACK OF Merrick's shirt and yanks her away from me. My feet touch the floor a second before my knees give out, and I fall forward. Orlando catches me, not letting me hit the ground and hugs me to him, placing his hand on the back of my head to press my face into his shirt.

And then I bite him.

His warm, sweet blood spills across my lips, and I lose all control of my body. I move the collar of his shirt away from his bloody skin and begin to suck on the crook of his neck. He sinks his fingers in deeper to my side, his hand sliding up my shirt to touch my skin in the process.

"Viorica, take your heirs and return to my estate immediately," Orlando says, his voice low and sexy as hell. His chest presses against mine with his deep breathing, doing his best not to react.

I moan softly, and he moves his hand from my hair to rub the length of my back to slide under my ass to hold me more firmly against him. And hell does it set me off even more. My body tingles with my oncoming desire. It takes Austin running his finger across my hair to spill it over my forehead to get me even to look up.

He sucks in his bottom lip, staring at me through the veil of my dark tresses. "Don't pull away," he whispers so softly. "They'll see you."

The fear brought on by his words calms my body the hell down just enough for me to get my shit together. I slide my arms around Orlando's neck and practically choke him as I try to conceal us even more.

"I'm so sorry," I whisper into his ear too quietly for anyone but him and Austin to hear. "She scared me. I couldn't stop."

Orlando shivers at the softness of my breath against his skin. "Just take a breath. You're shaking."

"Viorica, did you not hear my brother?" Kingston asks. The Widows are nearly impossible to hear over the crying of the exempt, the pounding in my head in rhythm with my out-of-control heart, or the ringing in my ears. "We will explain everything. At the estate. You're scaring Jewel's guests."

Orlando's stiff body relaxes, and I don't have to look to know that the Vaduvas disappeared. "Follow them, Diego and

Kingston. Austin and I will handle everything here and meet you there as soon as possible."

A soft hand touches my back. "My fucking sexy savage," Kingston says. "You were supposed to save those teeth for me."

"You better go," I murmur, trying not to panic over my actions. "You'll be next if you don't."

"Later."

Diego chuckles, the lightness of his voice settling my frayed nerves. "I'll believe it when I see it, bro."

The two of them disappear, and Orlando strolls with me to another part of the building away from the people. Hayden's voice hums through the air as he settles them down and tells them that it'll be okay, because I have it handled. Who knew he had so much faith in me. I don't even know what the hell will happen. Viorica wasn't supposed to know. I can only hope that she truly cares about our alliance.

Orlando sets me on my feet and inspects my face, running his fingers through my sticky hair to pull it out of the way. "Do you need more?" he asks, his mouth opening slightly with a breath.

I lick my lips, tasting the sweetness of his blood. "I think I'm okay."

Reaching up, I gently trace my fingers over the top button of his dress shirt. He stands utterly still as I unbutton it and ease the bloody fabric away to look at the still bleeding mark my teeth left behind.

He trails his hand to my waist, circling it around to the small of my back and pulls me into him. "I have to admit, that was quite the experience," he whispers, allowing me to feel the sudden extent of his desire at my closeness.

"Are you sure you're okay?" I ask, keeping my voice low.

"Better than okay." He smiles with the words and leans down, kissing me softly despite his blood being all over my face. "I rather enjoyed it."

"Fuck. Me," I whisper to myself, my body doing all sorts of crazy shit with my insides.

Orlando's eyes widen.

"Fuck," I say again. "Um, it's an expression, not an invitation." Though the building tingles between my legs would like to disagree.

He releases a small breath and steps back, straightening his shirt. "Austin?" he asks, turning my attention away from my racing heart. "Do you have something to clean Jewel up with?"

Austin strolls in from the warehouse to meet us in what used to be an old office. He closes the space to me, and Orlando takes another few steps away to give Austin room to look me over himself.

"You okay?" he asks.

I nod. "A little shaken."

"Just take a breath."

I breathe a couple times with Austin until he's certain I'm not going to flip my shit or try to attack someone again. Orlando helps me clean the blood from my face enough that we can manage if we're seen heading back to the estate.

By the time we're done, Austin's nearly finished with his exams, working faster than I've ever seen him. So much for human speed. I think for once the humans might be grateful. Hayden gives me a once-over as I approach, and I try my best not to look at anyone directly.

"Be honest, Orlando. Do I need to prepare my people for an evacuation?" Hayden asks quietly.

Orlando shakes his head. "I'll handle it, but do not allow anyone to leave this building until we say so. Do you understand?"

He nods. "Austin already told us. He said it would take a few hours to get the results of his tests back."

Orlando sighs through his nose. "Let's just hope you didn't lie about the health of your people. I'm counting on it as a factor to get Viorica to see reason. If you did lie, I don't know what I could possibly do for you. You'll leave us no choice but to inform the board that you trespassed without our permission."

"You'd seriously do that? These people—"

"Aren't my coven's responsibility. Now, I must warn you. If you attempt to use Jewel like this again, you will not live to see another day."

Orlando doesn't give me a chance to react. He gathers me into his arms and motions for Austin to join us. Austin ruffles Dougie's hair, leaving him with Mrs. Diggs to wait out their temporary quarantine before they can return to the estate, and together, we disappear into the night.

Viorica and her daughters wait for us in Orlando's study. Kingston sits on the edge of one of the beds, holding Baby on his lap, petting the cat like it's his sole purpose in life. Her purring is louder than anything in the room, sounding almost like one of Hayden's old cars, and I can't help smiling. The moment I do, Viorica glowers at me like it's against the law to have a soft spot for my vampire match who will deny the hell out of the fact that he's already attached to our cat.

"Thank you for meeting with us, Vi," Orlando says, calling Viorica by a nickname I've only heard my guys use a few times in an informal setting. "I'm sure you have a lot of questions and concerns about what you discovered tonight, and I wanted to assure you that the situation is handled."

"Those donors are unregistered, Mr. Ortega," she says curtly, straightening her shoulders and using Orlando's last name to show that she means business.

"Viorica, please," I say, unable to stop my rebel mouth from speaking out of line. "It wasn't his fault."

"Of course it wasn't. I don't have to ask to know that you were the one responsible for this," she snaps, her voice so sharp that if I didn't know any better, I'd think the pain in my chest was caused from it cutting me.

I clench my fingers into fists. "It wouldn't have had to come to this if Donor Life Corp would get their shit together and follow through with their promise to Haven Springs."

Orlando spins me behind him where Diego sandwiches me into Orlando's back. Kingston and Austin each take fighting stances on my sides, and the four of them release some scary, unsettling as all get-out growls at Viorica, who stops in her place, now standing in the middle of the room.

Merrick and Heidi materialize next to her, fully prepared to fight, but Viorica slowly raises her arms and nudges them back.

"Girls, sit back down, please," Viorica says. "Jewel will learn to harness her mortal emotions soon enough. The Ortegas will also remind her of the respect she must show me."

"As long as the respect for my beautiful Jewel is mutual. I will not allow you to treat her as if she's less than the powerful woman she is, even now before our Blood Vow." Orlando reaches behind him to grab my hand.

Viorica stands taller in an attempt to see me, but I keep my forehead pressed to Orlando's back. "Respect must be earned."

"And she earned it. Now, if you will excuse us, we need a few minutes as a coven. If you consider going against our alliance because of a few exempt humans, you will soon learn the mistake of your decisions. They will cause no trouble and have passed all qualification to stay here."

"Apart from board approval," Viorica says, meeting Orlando's threat without so much as shifting her feet.

Orlando squares his shoulders. "As soon as our union is

recognized by the board, I will register the donors through the proper channels and provide proof of good health. Most are under eighteen anyway, so they are free to stay under Donor Life Corp laws if properly provided for. I'll assure Mr. Andrei meets all requirements."

Viorica smirks, looking smug as hell. "I think you've forgotten the cost of so many young, Mr. Ortega."

"The cost will be covered."

"I hope so." Without another word, Viorica motions to Merrick and Heidi to follow her out. She stops in the doorway and glances in my direction. "And Jewel, be ready to meet at midnight. You must pick out your dress and approve all celebration details my daughters so kindly arranged on your behalf."

I nod and clear my throat, praying it remains even. "Yes, Ms. Vaduva. And thank you. I appreciate everything you've done."

The Vaduvas disappear, and I push through my guys' protective circle to walk across the study and to the double doors that lead into Orlando's room. They silently follow me and watch me kick off my shoes, yank off my sweatshirt, and flop on the bed.

"That was awful," I say, lying on my side. "I don't know how I'm going to survive this."

The bed shifts and Orlando sits next to me and pats my arm. Kingston climbs on the bed behind me and drapes his arm over my waist to cuddle against me in the way I love. Austin and Diego join us, and I stretch out to take each of their hands.

"You guys are going to just have to lock me up," I add when no one responds to my comment. "My dream was right."

"Your dream?" Diego asks, running his thumb in smooth circles over mine.

I release a breath. "Yeah, the crazy ass one I had about my family. My dad swore that you'd cage me."

"We'd never, babe," Kingston says, kissing my shoulder.

I turn and face him. "You say that now, but I *bit* Orlando. What if it was Merrick? I just—you guys might not have a choice."

"Jewel," Austin says, reaching out to get me to roll to my back so I can look up at him. "You're getting better."

"It sure doesn't feel like it," I say.

Diego shifts a bit closer. "You are, beautiful."

"But if I change. If I get worse, you have to promise me that you'll do it," I say.

"What? No," all of them say at once.

I sigh and flip over to lie on my stomach. "I could hurt you."

Kingston touches my back. "Babe."

"Just promise me," I whisper. "You said you'd do anything for me."

Diego sighs. "Except that."

"Never that," Austin adds.

"You have to trust that we can handle you," Orlando says.

"I do."

He pats my back. "Then trust yourself."

Unfortunately, that's going to be a huge friggin' problem.

BEST COVEN UNION CELEBRATION...EVER

I GAPE AT THE RACK of white gowns. What is it with vampires and their need to dress donors in fabrics that stain and show blood spill? The fact that they think it looks sexy as all get-out. I still blush every time I think about the one and only vampire party my guys threw on my behalf for Donor Life Corp and how Diego asked me to walk around with his blood all over me. Kingston might be a tad right about the two of us being freaky. Because now I can't stop my body from getting turned on thinking about doing it all over again.

Merrick sighs and leans her elbows on her knees. "Just decide already."

Samantha waves her hand at her sister. "Knock it off. This is the biggest moment of Jewel's life. Let her pick what's perfect for her."

"It's been an hour, and she's tried them on twice," Merrick says.

"What did you expect? Jewel's not known for her decisiveness. I mean, look at all of her guys." Layla whispers the words so low that I shouldn't be able to hear them. And I friggin' hate that I can. "Maybe we should suggest she rotate dresses like she does her matches."

I expect Samantha to react and tell Layla to knock it off, but she purses her lips and looks at me. "Jewel, may I suggest that you wear one dress to your coven union, one to the celebration, and finish with the gown you want Orlando to undress you out of and also bite you in for your transformation."

Evora claps her hands, drawing my attention to her. "That's a great idea, Sammy."

Layla glares at Samantha, who remains smiling at her Blood Match. I think it might be the only reason she doesn't call Samantha out for taking credit for her idea. Turning toward the rack, Layla plucks out a puffy as hell dress that sparkles with diamonds along the bodice. "This one would be perfect for your private celebration. Make him work for it."

I raise my eyebrows and swivel to glance toward the corner of the room where Kingston taps away on his tablet. It took him swearing not to murder the Vaduvas a dozen times before Orlando agreed to let him stay instead of Austin. And he's been surprisingly well behaved.

He doesn't look up, knowing that since I'm looking, the Vaduvas are looking as well. I'll have to give him some extra cuddles for managing to stay in control, uninvolved, and absolutely expressionless while listening to the Vaduvas discuss my Blood Vow, one we both want him to be a part of.

"Um, I don't think I'll be in any state for undressing after my Blood Vow," I say, running my fingers over the fabric of the pretty dress. "Orlando told me that vampire venom hurts a lot and that I could black out."

Merrick laughs. "It hurts like hell." I try not to react. Because I know. "Which is why the ceremony is an all-night affair for board members. It's customary to allow a few hours between the vow and the bite for those promising eternal love. Orlando will have plenty of time to fulfill your every desire. Or you know, change his mind and decide to perform your final donation."

I swallow and nod. "Oh."

"Aw, Mer. You made her nervous," Samantha says, reaching out to pat my knee. "Everything will be perfect. Orlando won't change his mind. Look at the trouble he went through to get you."

"I know he won't kill me, Samantha," I say, bouncing my feet on the floor.

Layla tilts her head and drinks me in. "Oh, wow. You're nervous about the other part. You haven't had sex with him yet, have you?"

My cheeks burn, my whole face threatening to catch fire.

"Layla," Samantha says.

Layla narrows her eyes. "What? It was just an observation."

"But I have a question," Merrick says. "Why not? He's sexy, powerful, way above your league, to be honest. I bet he's an even better time than Diego." She licks her lips and side-eyes Kingston in an attempt to get under his skin.

It works. Kingston materializes next to me and releases a scary ass growl. Merrick smiles wider, but Layla's smirk fades, and Samantha pouts her lip.

"Sammy, I think I'm ready to go," Evora says, speaking up. Her fear instincts are probably going off like crazy. It's enough to draw Kingston's heated gaze away from the Vaduvas. Just like me, it's obvious that Kingston forgot Samantha's Blood Match was quietly hanging out.

"Me too. We should pick out our own dresses for tomorrow. For once, you won't have to wear white since it's Jewel's special day," Samantha says, pulling herself up. She turns to her sisters. "You two should come. I think we've worn out our welcome. Heidi wanted Jewel's choices for the party fifteen minutes ago, anyway."

"Aw, but it's so much fun getting to know our soon-to-be ally," Merrick says, flashing her fangs at me. "It's our duty to give her all the advice she could ever need. It would be quite sad if she turns out to be such a disappointment to Or—"

"Out!" Kingston yells. "I will not allow you to attempt to make Jewel doubt herself or freak her out about tomorrow. She is the most incredible being in the universe that I wish I could stand with tomorrow. Orlando could never be disappointed with her. He'd be crazy if he were. If anything, Jewel's going to blow his fucking mind."

Kill me now.

Merrick raises her eyebrows and helps Layla to her feet. They turn and stroll to the door without responding until they're far enough to get a head start. Then Merrick leans into Layla and whispers, "Sounds like you were wrong about which one would be disappointed."

They disappear too quickly to see go, and Kingston lifts me onto his shoulder, rushes to the bedroom, slams the door, and tosses me onto the bed. He lands next to me, bouncing the mattress. Rolling on top of me, he pulls me in for a passionate kiss that leaves my whole body buzzing.

"I never thought they'd leave," he mumbles against my mouth.

"That was awkward."

"I know. They should know better than to question your sexual prowess. You know you're perfect. Everything I want and need."

I shift and pull back from his mouth to meet his gaze. "That wasn't the awkward part. Your unintentional pep talk in regards to me having sex with Orlando was. I didn't even know sex was expected. Do you think he will want to?"

He looks at me like I just asked the most ridiculous question. "Uh, fuck yeah. Don't you see how he looks at you? But he knows better than to expect it. If you don't want to bang him, you don't have to bang him."

I turn my gaze to the ceiling.

"If you want to bang him..."

I frown.

"Sorry, babe. That's none of my business. But so you know, the idea doesn't bother me as much as it did," he says. "You know why?"

"Because I love you and every single moment we have together?" I say, smiling.

He chuckles. "Not what I was gonna say, but yeah, that works."

Before I can ask him his reason, he devours my mouth in another deep kiss that awakens my whole body. I moan under his fervent touch as his hand glides down the front of my shirt to sneak up to caress the skin of my stomach. I stop him from tugging my shirt over my head and lock my fingers to his instead. I yank it off him, breaking from his mouth to kiss down his neck to lick and suck down to his shoulder.

I hear the familiar click of Kingston's fangs extending. "Mmm, that mouth of yours. I want it all over me."

I smile and push him over so I can climb on top of him. "You might have to wait a bit. I'm feeling a little bitey. I'm going to have to stop in a minute."

"How hungry are you?" he asks, exploring my body underneath my clothes, gently shifting my bra out of the way to play with my breasts.

I rotate my hips to feel his arousal through his pants. Leaning down, I suck his earlobe into my mouth for just a second. "Starved," I whisper, making him shiver. I gently graze my teeth down his neck and over the small hickey I left behind on his shoulder, my tongue practically tasting his blood already.

"Then bite me."

I suck in a deep breath and pull back, pressing my hands into his chest to keep a few inches of space between us. "Bite you?"

He nods and curls the corner of his lips in an irresistible smile. "Mmmhmm. I wasn't joking about wanting your mouth on me. Give me a better mark. Let me satiate you how you like."

I don't respond, searching his midnight eyes. He tilts his head to the side and silently invites me to him. Sliding his arm around my back, he pulls me closer. I close my eyes and breathe in a small breath of his sweet, warm scent. But I don't bite. Something inside me won't let me. Fear over my control, or lack thereof, or maybe something else. Maybe because he's teased me about it a dozen times that I'm too nervous to proceed, even if he begs.

"Jewel?" Kingston asks, relaxing under me, allowing my body to push him more into the pillow. "You okay?"

I try to open my mouth to tell him yeah, but only a small breathless noise comes out.

He grabs my hand, pulling it to his mouth to kiss. "You don't want to." It's not a question. He knows me well enough to read me without me having to say the words. "I made too big of a deal about it."

"Kingston," I say quietly. I shift off of him to lie on my back to stare at the ceiling.

He rolls onto his side and rests his head on my chest. "I'm sorry, babe. I hope you know that I really was only kidding...most of the time. The idea of your bite never scared me or anything."

I hug my arm around him and comb my fingers through his messy hair, playing with the black strands. "Don't apologize. I don't know what's up with me."

"Could it be that we're about to go through a life-changing event tomorrow in front of a bunch of people we barely tolerate?" he asks, running his fingers along the smooth skin of my stomach.

"Don't vampires ever party with people they like? I mean, is it possible to have a good time with people outside our coven?" I turn onto my side to face him. "Or possible to only invite like half a coven?"

He raises an eyebrow. "I know it seems like that, but that's only because...fuck. Vampires are assholes when it comes to humans, unless the humans belong to them or have previously served them. You should've seen those donors the Vaduvas—you know what? Never mind. I swear, next time we throw a party, you'll be in charge of the guest list."

"So, basically only Heidi and Viorica from the Vaduvas. Maybe Zara from the board." I mean, the board member of the Aku Region wasn't super weird or mean. She was nicer than Viorica when we met, even if it was because I agreed to let her taste my blood in a deal for access to her region.

"Heidi, huh?" Kingston says.

I smirk. "She doesn't talk much. Or try to flirt with you."

He laughs. "I'm not her type."

"Even better. I might also invite Ros."

"The prick who I had to let beat me up? Seriously, babe?" He releases a small growl. "I take it back. You are so not in charge of the guest list."

"Oh, come on," I tease. "You can't blame Ros. He was protecting..." My voice trails off as I think about Turner, who also makes me think about his grandmother. Liz died trying to protect me, and I have mixed emotions about her because of what she did.

Kingston releases the most dramatic groan in existence and sits up. "You better not."

"Huh?" I ask.

"Kill my boner."

I tip my head back and laugh, making Kingston smile. Reaching for his pants, I unbutton them and slide them down enough to lace my fingers around him and rub the length of his erection. "Pretty sure that's friggin' impossible."

"What's impossible?" Diego asks, tapping his finger to the door.

I laugh harder, and he takes the lightness of my voice as permission to come in. Kingston leans back on his elbows and grins like a cocky ass bastard, because Diego enters before my mind has the chance to catch up with my body to tell me to chill the hell out.

"Damn," Diego says, turning around to walk back out. "Sorry, Jewel. Kingston usually doesn't make you laugh while you're—"

"Diego, wait," I call. "We're not doing anything."

Kingston chuckles. "Uh, pretty fucking sure this counts as something, babe."

I release Kingston and scramble out of bed, cracking up as Kingston tries to snatch my leg but drops his pants to the floor in the process. He lets me cross the room, kicking out of his pants and making me laugh all over again as he rips my shirt right off me.

Diego spins at the sound of my footsteps and holds his arms open. I jump into them, wrapping my legs around his waist and let him spin me around. He buries his face in my cleavage, and I laugh harder, my eyes watering in the process. I must be loud as hell, because Austin peeks his head in to see what's going on.

"Austin, catch," Diego yells.

"Oh, no you don't." My words turn into a squeal as the world blurs around me.

Kingston beats Austin and tosses me back toward the bed. "Time to lose the pants. I'm at an unfair disadvantage."

I unbutton my jeans but don't pull them down. "I don't know. I kind of like that."

Kingston grabs my jeans by the ankles and hangs me upside down, making me crack up as I fall to the bed with my pants past my hips.

I flip over and glance down. "Did you really just fail to undress me?"

Austin dodges past Kingston. "I promise I won't."

Screeching, I roll off the bed and grin, curling and uncurling my fingers to invite Austin to me. "You can try."

Kingston knocks him out of the way, and the two of them laugh as I grab a pillow and chuck it. Diego catches it midair and swings it at both of his brothers.

I laugh again and throw another. "I guess I'll just have to take off my own pants."

Orlando appears in the doorway, drawing my attention from Kingston as he rushes toward me. He takes advantage of the distraction to toss me back to the bed. Hooking his fingers to my jeans from my ankles again, he tugs them hard enough to pull them off while dragging me to the edge of the bed. He holds me upside down and kisses my ass cheek, making me crack up and squirm as he tries to rip the fabric of my lacy underwear off with his teeth.

"Your laughter is going to bring every vampire in the vicinity onto our property," Orlando says, grinning at me as I hang upside down.

Kingston sets me down without completely undressing me with Orlando strolling into the room.

I sit on the edge of the bed and wave my hands in front of my face, trying to calm down. But damn it do I love when my guys act so playfully. "I'm sorry."

"Don't be. It's the best thing I've heard all night," Orlando says.

Kingston grins at me. "Oh, we were just getting started."

I scramble away from him again in an attempt to run to Diego. Orlando dodges around Kingston and grabs my extended hands only to spin me off my feet to toss me to Austin. I screech and laugh, landing in Austin's arms. I pat my hands to his bare chest and pause.

"Wait, what? Weren't you wearing a shirt?" I ask, grinning like crazy.

He chuckles. "I don't recall." Setting me down, Austin spins me around to face his brothers. "Do you guys?"

I gape at Diego and Orlando, who now stand shirtless as well while Kingston poses on the bed with his hands behind his head, his knee bent, while he flexes every, and I mean every, muscle on his body.

"You guys!" More laughter bursts from my mouth so hard that I friggin' snort. "This is dangerous."

The four of them look amused as eff, and I suck in deep breaths, trying to calm my suddenly racing heart. Because damn. They know exactly what to do to get my whole body tingling and begging for every bit of their affection.

"Ah hell," Kingston says. "I forgot our girl told me she was hungry."

My laughter fades under the weight of their stares. "Famished," I say. "It's been a long night."

"Let me take care of you then," Austin says, his voice lowering.

I freeze at the scent of his blood and swivel around to face him, taking in the sight of his bleeding bite mark. Goosebumps prickle over my skin, and I shift on my feet, trying my best to control my urge to throw myself at him.

"Maybe you should use a glass," I whisper.

Big hands slide around my stomach, and I automatically lean my back against Diego's firm chest. "Or I could hold you."

I hook my hands over his and turn my face to get a better look at him. "Are you sure you guys are willing to risk it? I mean, I'm pretty sure my body is set on devouring you, and I know we still have to go over things for tomorrow. It's our last night."

"It's also our time to celebrate," Austin says, offering his arm to me again. "Usually we'd celebrate after our union, but with the Blood Vow happening afterward, we won't have time for possibly days."

Kingston appears beside us. "He's right, babe. I don't want to wait. This is our time to celebrate our coven union with you."

I glance at Orlando, and he remains smiling as he drinks me in. "Well, what did you have in mind?"

Austin presses his arm to my lips and steps in close enough that I can feel his excitement through his pants. His sweet, tangy blood coats my mouth, and tingles tickle my throat with each of my swallows.

"We can start by feeding you," he says.

I hum under my breath, sucking his arm harder. Diego slides his hands up my stomach to slide into my bra.

"And then satisfying you," Diego whispers, kissing my neck.

"While reminding you how much you mean to us," Kingston says, linking his fingers through mine.

Orlando takes my other hand. "And assuring you that tomorrow will be everything we've promised."

Austin eases his arm away from me, testing to see if I'll let him go. He quickly replaces his arm with his lips and kisses me, sandwiching me between him and Diego. "We want to make sure you're perfect. You have no idea how excited I am."

"We're all fucking excited, babe," Kingston says, swinging my hand.

I slide out from their circle and give each of them a long once-over. "I can tell."

Austin smiles. "What about you, Jewel?"

Reaching my arm behind my back, I unclasp my bra and let it fall to the floor. Each of them sucks in a breath, their gazes smoldering over me and making me squirm.

"Are you excited, beautiful?" Diego asks, repeating Austin's question.

I don't know if it's because of the looks of anticipation on their faces or how their excitement is so palpable that I can feel it deep in my soul, but I want nothing more from this moment than to make them all happy. To show them that I love the direction our lives head together, and I too am excited about tomorrow.

Stepping closer, I stop in front of Diego. I take his hand in mine and guide it to the waistband of my thong. "You tell me."

Diego fingers the lacy fabric and slides his fingers down incredibly slow to touch me between my legs. He releases a deep moan with the action, and Austin releases a long breath next to him.

"Jewel," Austin whispers, drawing my attention to him.

I place my hand over Diego's, and he slowly pulls away. "It's Austin's turn to find out."

Diego licks his lips and nods, his breath panting. I take a step toward Austin and stand in front of him, still feeling the weight of everyone's gazes roving over my skin in anticipation. Stepping closer, Austin surprises me by kneeling in front of me.

My heart threatens to crash through my chest as he slides the fabric of my underwear out of the way so that he can bring his mouth to taste what Diego felt. I clutch onto his shoulders and moan, my legs threatening to give out on me. If Austin didn't pull away and look up at me, I'm pretty sure they would have.

Austin hums his enjoyment under his breath, his eyes flashing silver. "Just the way I like."

I smile and pat his cheek, and he gets back to his feet. I

turn to Orlando next, my heart pounding even harder, especially thinking about what I now know about the ceremony tomorrow.

"Jewel, it's okay," he says softly, mistaking my hesitation for something it's not. "I'm happy just to see the smile light your face and know that I finally get to fulfill the promise I made you about our lives together. That my brothers can too."

His words resonate with me so deeply that I close the space and press my lips to his, meeting him for a kiss. His hands slide around my waist and pull me close so that our bare chests touch together.

"Thank you for saying that," I whisper, breaking away first. "It means the world to me."

"To us," Austin adds.

Kingston holds out his hand to me, and I laugh as he tugs me close. "Okay, enough with that. I want to know how excited you are too."

I bite my lip between my teeth. "You do, do you?"

He nods his head and reaches out his hand to me, but I grab his fingers and bring them to my chest. Releasing a playful growl, he grazes his fingers over my boobs instead. I reach down and slide my fingers into his boxer briefs, pulling him out as I close the space. He moans and shuts his eyes as I stand on my tiptoes and guide the length of him between my legs, just rubbing the tip over my skin.

I grin and pull away, strolling by myself to the bed. "Is this okay?" I ask, undressing completely. Kicking my leg, I send my thong at Diego, and he lets it land on his head. "I mean, this is what you had in mind to celebrate the union of our coven, right?"

"Whatever you want, Jewel," Austin says.

I motion for him to come closer and ease my legs open for him to stand between them. I unfasten his pants and watch as he finishes taking them off. "I want to know what you guys want."

"I would love to feed you," Orlando says, speaking up.

Kingston glances at him. "Damn, she is hungry. Look at those eyes."

Orlando strolls closer and peers down at me, brushing my hair from my cheek. "Striking."

I pat the bed next to me. "I'd love that." Turning to Diego, I motion him closer. "What about you, Diego?"

He smirks and touches my mouth with his thumb. "I want to test our nutrients match."

I lick my lips and nod. "My mouth's already watering."

Kingston groans.

I look at him and smile. "Kingston?"

He flashes his fangs. "You're making me so fucking hungry."

Holding my hands out, I invite him to come closer. "Let me help you with that."

Kingston closes the space and motions for me to move over, so I climb into Austin's lap, making him release a breathless moan.

I align his body to mine and sink onto him, gasping at the good pressure between my legs. I slowly roll my hips up and down as I get the hang of the position.

Austin runs his hands over my hips and adds more pressure with his fingers, slowly drawing circles over me. Orlando silences my moan with a soft kiss before bringing his bleeding arm to my lips, grazing his hand over my breast. His blood fills my mouth, setting me off, and I pick up my rhythm with Austin, making him pant.

Kingston kisses my hand, bringing my attention to him. I turn my head slightly to look at him, my body buzzing as he strokes himself, watching the pleasure crossing my face. He draws my arm to his mouth and extends his fangs, and I squirm on Austin's lap, pushing my body harder into him in anticipation to be bitten.

Kingston's fangs pierce me so quickly that I don't even feel the pinch, and he captures me in his midnight eyes while he glides his tongue over the rivulets of blood seeping from my arm, not letting a single drop escape him.

"You're so sexy," Diego whispers, standing in front of me. He strokes himself a few times, and I reach out my free hand to graze it over the length of his shaft.

Austin guides my body up and down on his, sending amazing sensations exploding through me.

I suck in a breath, releasing my mouth from Orlando's arm only long enough to guide Diego closer to me. I bend forward slightly and lick my lips, bracing one hand to Diego's hip. I lick over the smooth skin of his tip, tasting the sugary taste of his building excitement. Taking a deep breath, I suck him into my mouth, making Diego moan.

Orlando's fingers trail from my breasts and down my stomach, gently touching me where Austin left off. I moan, my voice vibrating over Diego. He touches my cheek, and I gaze up at the lust darkening his features.

My whole body sings under the desperate attention my guys give to me, and I pull away from Diego to gasp and clutch both Kingston and Orlando's knees as I reach the point of release, my body clenching and relaxing as I orgasm, releasing a loud ass moan that has Austin clutching me tighter to stand me up. He thrusts into me faster and harder as I bend forward, gasping, my legs shaking so hard that I'm nearly certain only he's holding me up. He finishes, rocking into me a few more times until he slows and pulls me back with him on the bed.

"Damn," Diego says, touching my cheek as I gasp.

"So fucking hot," Kingston says, tugging my hand to touch the length of his excitement.

Austin kisses my shoulder. "Here, why don't you breathe for a minute?"

He eases me off of him and onto the bed. Diego stands in front of me, and I invite him to sit where Austin was while Austin scoots back to rest on his back. I spread his legs slightly to get between them, fully intent on giving Diego exactly what he wants.

I mold my lips over him and slowly suck him into my mouth. He plays with my hair, combing his fingers over my scalp as I work over him. Orlando slides off the bed and onto the floor next to me and kisses my exposed skin where Diego lifts my hair.

"Jewel, I want so badly to touch you," Orlando says, his voice a whispered plea into my ear. "To show you how much I'm in love with you."

I nod my consent, my heart picking up pace. Orlando trails his hands down the length of my back, and I stiffen with nerves for a moment as he slides his finger into me, getting me to part my legs.

"Fuck," Kingston whispers. "I should've thought of that."

I reach out and run my fingers over Kingston's thigh, blindly feeling my way over his leg until he guides my hand to where I want to it to be. I grip his erection under the sudden explosion of amazing sensations Orlando creates.

Austin rejoins us at Kingston's murmur, and he touches my shoulder, just wanting to be close to me.

Diego moans deep in his throat. "Jewel, I'm gonna cum."

A moment later, Diego finishes, clutching my head for a moment to slow me down. His sweetness fills my mouth, tasting as rich as his blood and unlike anything I can describe. He truly is my nutrients match. I moan and pull up, swallowing as he watches me lick my lips.

"The best," Diego says, his whole face lighting with a smile. "So hot, beautiful."

I grin at him, my face flushing, only to have my smile disappear with another moan. I rest my head on his knee, enjoying the electricity zinging through every cell on my body. Orlando continues to work his hand over me, and Kingston helps me rub him the way he likes.

"Let's move our girl onto the bed," Austin says.

Austin helps Orlando set me on the bed, and I arch my back and reach my hands out for something to hold onto. Kingston shifts next to me, and I start where I left off, running my hand up and down over and over again until he stops me to sit up.

"I'm going to finish in the bathroom," he murmurs, starting to get off the bed.

I grab his hand and pull him closer. "I want to see."

He chuckles and raises his eyebrows. "Fuck yeah."

I grin at him as he kneels next to me, stroking himself until he tips his head back and moans, finishing across my chest.

"You're driving me crazy, babe. Please fucking bite me. Right now," he says, shifting to lean his shoulder close to me.

Diego laughs. "I knew you wouldn't be able to resist, bro."

"She's so hot," he says. He takes my hand. "Babe, please devour me."

My body suddenly tenses as Orlando brings me to the point of release, and I pant so hard, squirming, just wanting so badly for my body to explode already.

I clutch onto Kingston, sitting up as good spasms roll

through me and give in to his pleas, sinking my teeth into the taut skin of his shoulder.

He grunts and tenses, his blood filling my mouth. "Fuck."

"Hell yeah. Look at that mark, Austin," Diego says.

I throw myself back, covering my face with the pillow, excitement and a tiny bit of embarrassment washing through me as I hear even Orlando intake a breath through his teeth.

Kingston's solid body slides next to me, and he gently rolls me onto my side to spoon me from behind. He kisses my shoulder and moves the pillow to lean up to press his cheek to mine.

"Babe, that was nearly as good as banging your brains out," he says, cuddling me close. "Best coven union celebration ever."

I don't say anything but giggle, still trying to catch my damn breath. This was definitely something.

"Get our girl some blood," Diego says.

Extending my arm, I wave it into the air. "More cuddles too."

Kingston chuckles. "But first, a shower."

I turn in his arms and let him carry me with him to the bathroom. My whole body still buzzes, and I know there's no friggin' way I'm going to manage to stand on my feet. Austin beats us there and turns on the hot water, holding his arms open to take me from Kingston.

"I love you, Jewel," he says. "I had a great time."

"The most amazing," Diego adds.

Orlando grins, draping his arms around his brothers. "To our future with Jewel. May it be like this always."

I laugh and cover my face with my hands. "Fuck. Me."

FACE THE WORLD

"HAVE I EVER TOLD YOU how stunning you are? More ravishing each time I see you," Orlando whispers, his soft voice sending a good shiver through me. *"Each day that passes where I can't hold you in my arms causes me unbearable pain."*

I slowly pull away from his embrace, my heart racing out of control at his words. Puffing out my bottom lip, I frown at him. He leans closer, his eyes leaving mine to trail down my face to stop at my mouth.

I hold a finger up to his lips and keep him back. "Good. Maybe you'll think twice today before you abandon me."

He chuckles at my response and takes my hand between his. "I think twice, three times, a dozen, every time the sun shifts across the sky. Do you know how easy it would be for me to pick you up and leave? It takes all my restraint to go without you."

"What if I told you that I wanted you to take me with you?" I ask. "That I don't want to stay here anymore."

He releases a deep, throaty noise, pushing me back on the sidewalk. His weight falls on top of me, and I gasp a breath as my body molds to his, allowing him to rest between my legs. His hands press the ground on the sides of my head, and he bends down to brush his lips to my jaw without kissing me.

"If I give you what you want, there is no coming back," he whispers into my ear.

I swallow, my nerves bunching at his words. "I just—I'm so tired of—I want to remember you. I want to be able to come outside and smile the second I find you waiting for me. I don't want to have to relive the fear of you over and over. I hate it. We don't deserve that."

He releases a small breath and closes his eyes. "I'm sorry, Jewel. The arrangement I have with your father—"

"Is bullshit and you know it. This is my life. Don't you feel bad every time you take the best part of me away?" Tears burn my eyes, and I blink to clear my vision. "I might not remember, but I can feel it."

"Jewel," he whispers.

I push my hands into his chest, and he sits upright to pull me with him. "The shadows are moving. I should go."

Enveloping me in his arms, he hugs me tight, resting his

forehead to mine. Our panting breaths mingle, our lips grazing but never fully meeting. I keep my eyes closed, hoping that if I do so long enough, Orlando will relent and leave me with my mind intact.

"Things won't always be this way," he says. "I know it doesn't feel as such, but your future is mine. You will never be a donor. This life here, it's fleeting."

Footsteps sound from around the corner, coming from the direction of The Boxes. Orlando sighs but doesn't move.

"Orlando, what are you doing here?" Mom's soft voice trickles through the air. "You shouldn't be here. Noah said Jewel could go for another week at least."

"In another week, Jewel would be too ill to even leave your home. Noah is growing careless in her maturity. Depriving her of what she needs will not make her stronger. It doesn't do Jewel or your family any favors." Orlando rests his head on my shoulder, still hugging me.

I don't turn to look at Mom. I can't. But I can feel her gaze on my back.

"You can't have Jewel pay her dues, Orlando," Mom says. "If Jewel needs more blood...I will pay. But please, you mustn't tell Noah."

"Helena, I wouldn't go against our agreement or put Jewel at risk by breaking Donor Life Corp law. These extra moments with Jewel are enough." Orlando shifts back to look into my eyes. "Offering your blood to me is unnecessary. The only reason I ask that of your husband is because he must not take things for granted. He must know that our arrangement comes at a great cost to me."

"But it doesn't have to," I say, finally swiveling to look at Mom. "Orlando is good to me."

Her eyes sheen over. "Jewel, honey. You don't know what you're saying."

I purse my lips. "I do. I can't live like this anymore. It's unfair. What Dad asks of Orlando—I hate it."

"It's for your safety," she says, her voice growing quiet.

"Are you sure? Wouldn't it be safer for me to know? What if something were to happen to you? I'd have no idea how even to survive. Orlando will guarantee I do." I get to my feet and close the space to my mom, leaving Orlando in the shade.

"Helena, I love your daughter. This last year—"

"Year?" Mom's voice squeaks. "You've been seeing him for a year, Jewel? Oh, honey, you should've..." Her voice trails off as she realizes that her words are pointless.

"Should've what? Told you?" I laugh, my voice sounding strangled. "I would have loved to!"

Mom brings her hand to my mouth, muffling my voice before I can yell louder. "I—I'm sorry, Jewel. I truly am, sweetie. I never wanted this for you. Your dad is so insistent, I just—" She snaps her mouth shut. "I'll talk to him."

Surprise furrows my brows. "You will?"

"He might need some extra convincing, but I'll see what I can do." Turning to Orlando, she straightens her shoulders and struts right into the shadow to face him. She wrings her hands in front of her and looks at him straight on. "I will not tell Noah about this, but you have to promise me that you will not take her from us unless it's absolutely necessary. I—I can't lose my daughter."

"Mom," I say.

She shakes her head. "No, Jewel. That's my stipulation. I will not lose you sooner than I have to. I love you."

"You have my word, Helena," Orlando says. "As long as Jewel is safe, we'll stay in the city."

She reaches out and touches his shoulder. "Thank you. Now, we must go. Noah will be home from work shortly." Turning to me, she motions me closer. "Please keep your word. I can't go against my husband, but I'll try to convince him. But not for you. For Jewel. Understand?"

I inch away, moving into the sunlight. "Please, Mom. No. Don't make him do this. I hate it."

She frowns. "I'm sorry, Jewel."

I spin to run, using the sunlight to my advantage, but Orlando pulls his jacket up and braves the light to push me into the nearest shaded area by a building. I squeeze my eyes shut, refusing to look at him. My chest heaves, my breath hard to come by.

"Sweetie, this is for the best. I know how brave you are, and we can't risk you doing something against your good senses. Orlando's not the only one who lurks in the shadows," Mom says.

"Helena, leave us. I'll send Jewel home shortly." Orlando rubs his fingers along my back, just hugging me as my mom's footsteps disappear.

I clutch him close, burying my face into the crook of his neck. "Orlando, please. No one has to know."

"But your mother's right about you. Such a fighter. Brave. I can't risk it. Not yet." He breaks away from me to cup my face. "I know this is difficult, precious Jewel."

"You have no idea."

His fingers brush over my cheeks, grazing my eyelashes. "I do."

I snap my eyes open. "Then you wouldn't—"

Orlando bites his arm and brings it up to my lips. His nose touches mine with his arm between our mouths. His sweet blood gushes down my throat, sending tingles into my stomach. His vibrant blue eyes stare into me like he can see beyond my flesh and blood to my very soul.

"Jewel, I promise you that I'll come again as soon as I can," Orlando whispers.

My eyes burn with tears as my body slackens in his embrace. "No," I mumble, but it's too late. He locks me in his gaze. I can't speak and beg him to stop. I can't get my mouth to pull away from him.

"Go straight home and hug your mother, and stay out of the shadows."

"No!"

"No," I repeat, the sudden shifting of the bed waking me

up.

Diego groans into my ear, pulling me close to him. "I don't want to wake up either, beautiful, but we have a big night."

"I think you can sleep a few minutes longer." Austin kisses my shoulder, snuggling into my back. "No one will mind."

Turning over, I arch my back and stretch my arms over my head. I push the dream of Orlando and my mom away and blink the sleep from my eyes. Diego props up on his elbow and traces his finger across my cheek, pulling the dark strands of my hair out of the way to reveal my neck and breasts to him.

"I definitely won't," Diego says, leaning down to kiss me.

Austin gently grabs my chin next and caresses his lips to mine. "Me either."

I smile and stretch my arms over their chests, attempting to touch Kingston and Orlando, but they're not in bed. Sitting up, I frown at their empty spaces.

"Babe, I fucking love that one of the first things you did was look for me," Kingston says, sitting on one of the beds in the study with Baby curled up on the pillow next to him.

"Why are you way over there?" I ask, scooting out from in between Diego and Austin.

He smirks, flicking his gaze to his brothers before scratching Baby behind her ears. "The kitty was lonely."

"Don't let him fool you, beautiful," Diego says, nudging my side with his foot. "Kingston and Orlando bolted the second you fell asleep. Baby didn't even hop up with Kingston there until a few minutes ago."

Kingston fake glares.

I laugh. "It's okay, Kingston. Your brothers should thank you for sparing them."

"Oh, we already did," Austin says, tossing a pillow at Kingston.

"Where is Orlando, anyway?" I ask, planting my feet to the floor.

"He went to finalize the contracts for our unions. Should be back any time," Diego says. "We'll go over everything, including your Blood Vow, together. As soon as we're done, then that's pretty much it. The board, excluding Mitchell because of his conflict of interest, and the rest of our guests are already arriving. Should be interesting since this is the first union not to happen at the Blood Match Center in Dark Terrace Ranch."

"Really? I guess it's better this way," I say.

"Hell yeah," Diego says.

I stand, my knees wobbly, my thighs aching in a good way, reminding me of our time together. Shivering, I stretch my back and force myself to move my legs. It takes everything in me to get walking without groaning, and I suck my bottom lip into my mouth.

"You all right, Jewel?" Austin asks.

My face burns so friggin' hard, but I only nod instead of looking at him. Kingston meets my gaze with a raised brow and motions for me to come to him. He looks amused as hell, his smirk turning into a chuckle as he watches me cross the room.

"I think our girl discovered some new muscles," Kingston says, pulling me onto the bed with him. Flipping me onto my back, he raises one of my legs and gently massages his fingers into the sensitive skin of my thighs.

I groan and release an embarrassed breath. "Shut it, dude...but don't stop. That feels amazing."

He chuckles. "Can't have you walking funny now, can we?"

I stick my tongue out at him. "It's a good thing I have you to carry me around."

"Damn straight."

Austin disappears into the bathroom and comes over to hand Kingston a small bottle of something I'm sure will ease all of my aches. I grab the hem of Austin's boxers, stopping him from pulling away, and pucker my lips, silently asking for a kiss he eagerly gives.

"I'll be back with breakfast," he says. "All your favorites."

"And I gotta go check on everyone in town," Diego says. He gets out of bed and stretches just for me so that I can drink in every one of his delicious muscles as he stands in his boxers.

"You can show Viorica the results. Everyone has a clean bill of health," Austin says, shrugging into a T-shirt.

I puff a breath through my lips. "Thank friggin' God. I'm so relieved."

Austin comes back and pats my cheek. "You're not the only one."

He and Diego disappear, leaving me with Kingston. I sink back onto the bed and cover my eyes with my folded arms, just enjoying the feeling of his fingers working pressure into my aching muscles as he rubs in the cream Austin gave him.

"Better?" he asks when he's through.

"Mmmhmm. Much."

"I hate that I'm going to say this, but we should probably get dressed." Kingston slides off the bed and holds his arms open for me.

I turn over. "That's the unsexiest thing I've ever heard."

He chuckles and scoops me up, kissing me all the way to the wardrobe. I stroll straight to my T-shirt drawer and tug out the one I saved for Kingston from the bottom and shrug the soft black fabric over my head.

Kingston slides up from behind me. "Not exactly what I thought you'd pick out to wear for me, but—"

I spin around and place my hands on my hips, twisting my lips to the side. "Okay, fine. Why don't you—"

Kingston's eyes drop to my chest as he stares at the logo of what Diego said belonged to his favorite back-world band. "You gotta be fucking kidding me. Where did you get that?"

I laugh. "You like it?"

"Like it? Come here. I'm going to bone the hell out of you right now."

I laugh and hold my hands up, shaking my head. "I'll wear it again on our night. Promise. But only if you serenade me."

He releases a playful growl. "Maybe."

"I guess I'll see."

I finish getting dressed and follow Kingston out of the wardrobe to find Orlando sitting at the table in the study. He glances up and gets to his feet, meeting me in the doorway to the bedroom.

"I hope you slept well, Jewel," he says, leaning in to kiss my cheek.

"Up until the dream I had about you and my mom was great," I say, keeping my voice even.

Orlando touches my shoulder, getting me to look at him. "Your mother was a marvelous woman, Jewel. She would be so happy for us today."

"You think so?" I ask.

"Unlike your father, she wanted what was best for you. I do regret how things ended, but I still wouldn't have changed everything that happened after. Because it brought us a better future than I could have planned alone." He looks at Kingston to include him, and Kingston hugs me from behind.

"As long as I can survive tonight," I say.

"We'll assure it." Orlando motions for me and Kingston to join him at the table.

Kingston starts reading over the stack of papers Orlando sets out before him. "You sure about this?" he asks, pointing to a paragraph. "This position should go to Jewel since Brayla isn't here."

Orlando glances to me and then trains his eyes on Kingston behind me. "I've thought long and hard about it, and I know Jewel was hesitant by the thought because of not being able to fully transition, so I decided you would be most fitted for the task. If you accept, that is."

I lean over and read the paragraph that sounds like Orlando is welcoming Kingston as his next in line, meaning if something happens to Orlando, Kingston would lead our coven. And I'm so happy Orlando asked him. With Brayla being formally filed as an outcast, someone must take her place, which thank the universe it isn't me.

"I do," Kingston says, hugging me tighter.

Austin and Diego soon join us, and the five of us—well, the four of them—look over all the contracts and sign everything to finalize what they need for their coven union. I sit and eat quietly until Orlando sets down a stack of papers in front of me.

"Is this the Blood Vow?" I ask.

He nods. "I hope you approve."

Seeing my name typed as Jewel Ortega sends butterflies through me. It's the first time I have seen it on paper, making this feel utterly real.

I point at a paragraph toward the bottom. "You want me to agree to renounce all of my human heirs? But—"

"Noah is a Blood Rebel. You cannot have ties to them.

This will prevent any future complications if he tries something that jeopardizes Donor Life Corp. Any association to him will weaken our alliances." Orlando leans over me, resting his hands on the table. "It has to be this way."

I look up at Kingston. "Is that true?"

He nods. "Yeah, babe. But it'll be fine."

"Okay," I say. I take a breath and sign the paper, sliding it to Orlando. "I guess this is it."

He smiles. "We're going to be great, Jewel. Promise. Now, if you'll excuse me, I must take this all to the board. I'm entrusting you to get Jewel safely to the ceremony, brothers. And remember, all eyes will be on us." In other words, we can't slip up and do something that could jeopardize my Blood Vow contract.

Orlando disappears, leaving me with my guys, and I stand up and motion them to surround me. The three of them engulf me in a hug, smothering me in their muscular goodness just the way I like.

"Why am I so nervous?" I ask, bouncing on my feet.

"Maybe because you just signed your life away," Kingston says.

Diego rubs his big hands up and down my back. "Don't listen to him. The only thing you're signing away is your donor title."

"It feels like more than that," I murmur. "I just hope this is really the right thing."

"You doubt Orlando?" Austin asks, keeping his voice low.

"I don't think it's that either. I just—I want this to be you guys too. So badly. I want to publicly vow to you. Each of you has a part of my heart, and I can't help feeling like it's wrong that I have to exclude you."

"You're not excluding us, beautiful," Diego says. "And we'll get our vows as soon as we get through this. We already have everything planned."

My eyes widen. "You do?"

Kingston whacks him. "Thanks for ruining the surprise."

My whole face lights up, and I smile. Diego bumps Kingston's shoulder to get him to look at me, and his face softens. Austin slides his hand through mine, and I try my best to wrap my arms around the three of them.

"I don't think anything was ruined for our girl," Diego says, smiling at me. "Look at her."

"So radiant," Austin says.

Kingston kisses me. "This is exactly how I want you to wake up every night, babe."

"With you guys, always," I say.

I take a few minutes to show each of them exactly how much they mean to me. I can't believe this is actually happening. I had no idea that my life would lead to this moment, where I'd stand in front of the board and pledge my life to my guys as part of the Ortega Coven. Jewel Jordan would ask if I was shitting her about this. Jewel Divine might tell me to run away as fast as I can.

But the me here now, the me who trusts my guys most in

the world. The me who can finally see this amazing future with everything I could ever dream of. This me is ready to straighten my shoulders and accept whatever the world has to throw at me. Because I get the forever I didn't think was possible.

And my guys get to share it with me.

Austin brings my hand to his mouth and kisses the back. "Ready to face the world, Jewel?"

I bob my head. "I think so."

"Good, 'cause we got ya, babe," Kingston says.

Diego smiles. "Forever."

COVEN UNION

I PULL AUSTIN TO ME by the lapels of his tuxedo and kiss him a dozen times all over his face. He laughs and secures me to him by my waist and captures my lips with his to kiss me tenderly, just allowing me to taste his sweetness.

"You look so handsome," I say against his mouth. "I can't wait for our next night alone so that I can give you all my attention."

"You think you can't wait," Diego says, coming up behind me.

I pull myself from Austin to face Diego. I bob my head, bouncing the tendrils of my shiny hair. "As much as I loved our group bonding adventure, I'm not sure I can handle so much bliss all the time."

Diego chuckles and kisses me. "You're our badass. We'd make sure of it."

Kingston cuts in and twirls me away, hooking his arm around my waist while linking his fingers through mine to dance slowly to the song humming through the surround sound. "But I'm so fucking happy that you still want alone time with me. Only twenty-four to thirty-six hours to go...depending on how you react to Orlando's venom."

I pout my lip at his words. That part of the Blood Vow, which is obviously the most important if I could actually transform, had been shoved to the back of my mind.

"We're not looking forward to it either," Diego says, spinning me from Kingston to dance with me next. "Hurts like hell."

"Wait, he's going to bite you too?"

Diego twirls me to Austin, who hugs me close, swaying with me without moving his feet. "It's tradition. Signifies a transformation since we've already been transformed."

"Oh." I rest my head on Austin's shoulder. "Anything else I need to be warned about?"

"The sacrificial virgin," Kingston says.

I gape.

He laughs. "Kidding."

I glare at him. "Maybe for our coven union."

Pressing his lips together, he goes expressionless.

"Seriously?" I ask, grimacing.

"Super not serious."

Kingston tips his head back and laughs at the same time Diego does. Austin shakes his head and pulls me close, spinning me away from his brothers, sending the hem of my dress sweeping around my legs.

"Everything is going to be perfect," Austin says. "The ceremony is rather short, and all you have to do is stand by and watch."

"Speaking of ceremonies, it looks like Orlando's ready for us," Kingston says.

I break away from Austin and touch his cheek. Sauntering to Kingston next, I hold his hands for a second and just drink in how hot he looks in his tuxedo. It's been a while since he's worn one, and I've missed it. Kingston nudges me to Diego, and I grab the front of his jacket and pull him close, returning a smile as bright as his own.

"I know I've been kind of a pain about this whole thing, but I want you all to know that your decision to do this has done nothing but make me the happiest I've been in my life," I say, opening my arms so we can hug.

"And you make us the happiest," Austin says.

Diego lifts me off my feet and follows behind Kingston, who leads the way. Austin protects our backs, though it would be insane for anyone to try anything right before the ceremony. Ombre Noire is the most guarded it has ever been. Every board member supposedly brought in their own security teams since this isn't neutral territory.

No one would tell me anything about the location of the

ceremony, keeping it a surprise. While the estate has hundreds of rooms, none of them are big enough to accommodate the board, their covens, and the rest of the guests who have come to bear witness to what's supposed to be the most significant coven union, considering there hasn't been a new board member...ever. Orlando is the first replacement since Mitchell killed Pierce of the Townsend Region.

"What happened with the tension in the Townsend Region?" I ask, unable to control my curiosity now that the thought is on my mind.

"Babe, really? Why do you always have random ass questions at times that we need to focus?" Kingston asks, slowing down to peer over his shoulder at me.

"Deflection," Diego says. "Jewel talks the most when she's nervous."

"And you all distract me when I'm alone with you," I add.

Kingston stops completely and turns to face me. He kisses me in Diego's arms and nuzzles his nose to my ear. "Everything will be fine, Jewel. We got you. Always."

"And if you really want to know, the Townsend Region has been divided among the board members, but all current covens remain in power, and all donors remained where they were. Pierce's next in line took over his city, but Orlando beat him for power, which is why he got the seat on the board," Austin whispers. "Our region comes from what Orlando acquired from Katherine and the Duchannes, part of the Townsend Region, and a few abandoned regions that board members gave up for one reason or another. It was what Orlando preferred. He wanted us to start mostly from scratch."

"So, you good, babe?" Kingston asks.

I nod and rub my lips together. "I think so."

"Good, because everyone's waiting."

Kingston opens the front door of the estate, and I try to remain expressionless at the sight before me. The last place I expected the coven union ceremony to take place was outside among the glittering night sky, so exposed to everything.

Diego sets me on my feet, and Orlando materializes at the bottom of the steps that lead to the pathway that enters the garden. Offering me his arm, Orlando smiles at me, sweeping his gaze slowly over my fitted white dress that shows off every single one of my curves. Crystal beads sparkle from the lace embroidery that follows the deep V-cut to enhance my cleavage how my guys like. Orlando's eyes flash silver, a mixture of hunger and desire, and he wraps me in an embrace to bring our bodies together.

"I have never felt so enchanted in my existence," he whispers, moving my hair from my shoulder.

"You look quite handsome, yourself," I say, playing with his black bowtie.

Orlando greets my guys next, hugging each of them while pressing his forehead to theirs. I've never seen such a weird ass sight, and I must be making a face, because Kingston snickers and sticks out his tongue at me, making me laugh.

"Our girl is jealous of our bromance," Kingston says, poking my nose.

I scrunch it and swat at him. "No, definitely not. It's just new to me. I assumed your affection came in the form of punches, shoves, growls, and occasionally a fist bump."

Diego howls a laugh. "Let's just say you brought us closer than we could have ever expected, beautiful. We're more than a coven sharing power. We're part of Team Jewel, and we know how much you like hugging over fighting."

"Plus, strong bonds are rarely tested," Austin adds.

Kingston squeezes my ass. "You can thank all that naked soul baring."

"And we can thank you, Jewel," Orlando says. "This wouldn't be possible without our girl."

My heart picks up pace at his use of how Austin, Diego, and Kingston refer to me. The four of them offer me the most amazing smiles, their sudden excitement so palpable it fills me up with everything amazing that I love. My nerves settle, and I straighten my shoulders, sliding my hand through Orlando's arm to allow him to guide me down the path and around the house to the garden.

Twinkling lights decorate every possible surface—from lining the pathway to twining around the trees and stringing across the air above us. The soft glow of the warm lighting sparkles off the glass greenhouse. Bouquets of a rainbow assortment of flowers decorate around the circular platform adorned with a clothed table with a satin pillow. It's then that

I realize the table isn't for the coven union. It's pre-positioned for my Blood Vow later in the night.

"We oversaw the decorations ourselves," Orlando says, nodding as dozens of vampires stand and offer deep bows in our directions.

I keep my eyes trained on the stone walkway. "It's perfect."

Viorica, Zara, Ademar Duchanne, and Mr. Bellamy, whose first name I've never learned, stand up from their seats in the front row. The four of them remain expressionless as we walk toward them, and it's the first time I gaze around to glance at the gathered crowd with many faces I've seen around the Blood Match Center but have thankfully never had the misery of meeting.

Samantha smiles at us, closing the space to kiss Austin on the cheek. She looks the happiest, unable to stay as stiff and expressionless as everyone else. They look bored as all get-out, and I wonder why they even bothered to show.

"This formality isn't what everyone has gathered to bear witness to," Orlando whispers into my ear. "They're truly here for you."

I squeeze his arm tighter, not really wanting that reminder. He gently pats my hand and strolls with me up to the platform and motions for me to stand in front of the table. Turning to the board, Orlando greets each of them with a short bow before they abandon us to return to their seats.

Kingston, Diego, and Austin join me, facing the crowd,

and I lean forward and look at all of them, though they don't turn to me. I can feel a dozen gazes burning over me, some of the vampires only seeing me for the first time. It takes everything in me to ignore them, but it's what I should do in this situation. I can't risk offering even an ounce of my attention.

"Thank you all for joining us to witness this union of power that will elevate the very core of Donor Life Corp and our regions," Orlando says, linking his hands in front of him. "My brothers stand before you today to swear their loyalty to the Ortega Coven and to blend our bloodlines to unite our strength, influence, and prestige as one." He turns to us and nods. "Please join me, Kingston."

I reach out and touch Kingston's hand, smiling at him as he steps forward. Nerves flutter through me, and I lean my back against the table, gripping onto it to keep my hands from shaking.

"Breathe, Jewel," Austin whispers, grazing his pinkie to mine.

"Kingston," Orlando begins. "Do you accept the Ortega name and the status as my next in line, vowing to serve our purpose in this existence, protecting and seeing our region grow and flourish?"

Kingston turns to his brothers. "I do."

"Then give me your hand."

"Shit balls," I whisper, never taking my eyes from Orlando as he rolls up Kingston's sleeve, extends his fangs longer than I've seen, and bites down hard enough to make Kingston grunt.

Shadows edge my vision, and I stumble on my feet, pushing too hard into the table that it shrieks back, shifting out of place. Heat blooms up my chest and into my neck, burning my face so brightly that I feel like I'm glowing.

Diego steadies me and smiles, trying his best to assure me that everything will be okay. But something sneaks inside me, tying around my heart to squeeze my chest. I struggle to breathe, expecting the worst at any second.

Orlando glances at me but continues and bites his own arm to drip blood over the mark he left on Kingston. They finish with a handshake that turns into a hug, and Orlando motions for me to step forward.

"Jewel, it is customary to welcome the new member of our coven with a kiss," he says.

I swallow and step forward, letting Kingston pull me in for a hug. I kiss him sweetly on the cheek and pull back and smile.

"Welcome to our coven, Mr. Ortega," I say, trying my best not to crinkle my nose.

"Thank you, Ms. Ortega," Kingston says. He leans in closer, bringing his lips to my ear. "I expect a proper, hot as fuck kiss the second we're alone."

He pulls back with a smile that relaxes my nerves and suppresses the strange, growing fear inside me.

I release a breath and allow him to guide me back to my spot. Kingston lifts me up to sit me on the table while taking his place next to me. Orlando motions to Diego next, and he joins him in front of us to greet the crowd.

He repeats the same thing to Diego, naming him the head of our defense, and Diego comes to me to accept a kiss and welcome into the Ortega Coven.

"Defense, huh?" I ask, grinning. "You'll be amazing. I always feel so safe with you."

Diego hugs me again and joins my side to watch Orlando call upon Austin. Austin turns and smiles at me, his green eyes flashing silver. Orlando names him head of the donors division of our region, which Austin graciously accepts. It couldn't be a more perfect position for him in our coven, and it crushes any doubt I had carried about this being what's right for our future together.

Austin stands silent and stoic as Orlando bites him and blends his blood, pouring it over the bite mark. The two of them share a hug, and I hop from the table and greet Austin, clutching his head in my hand to kiss each of his cheeks.

The four of them sandwich me in the best hug ever, each stealing a kiss to my lips that no one in the awkwardly silent crowd that watches us can see. After a minute, my guys pull apart and Orlando takes my hand, pulling me to him.

One look into his startling eyes sends fear blasting through me. He locks his fingers to me, lifting me off my feet. Kingston, Diego, and Austin all growl, and I struggle to break free, my whole body tensing and igniting in fear only triggered by the threat of danger.

"Kill him," Kingston commands, his deep, threatening voice scaring me so badly that I shove Orlando hard enough to get him to let me go.

I eat shit, falling on my ass, only to be knocked flat on my back by blurring figures above me.

I don't have time to react as Kingston, Austin, Diego, and Orlando all freeze, and for the first time I catch sight of an unfamiliar vampire restrained between them. Blood spills across my body, splashing my face, and Diego kicks the vampire's head a second before it lands on top of me.

And then the four of them laugh.

So does the crowd.

All I can do is swipe the blood from my face and push up to look around.

What the fuck did I just get myself into?

NO TURNING BACK

AUSTIN HELPS RINSE THE LAST of the blood from my hair. As my human health keeper, he was the only one able to leave the party to celebrate the union of the Ortega Coven, and there was no friggin' way I was going to parade around with some jerk's blood all over me. It's one thing to do so with my guys', but being drenched in the blood of someone who wanted to test the strength of our new coven before we even left the stage was friggin' intolerable.

"I should've told you about the possibility," Austin says, wrapping me in a fluffy towel. "We thought it was highly unlikely, but whoever the guy was must have been offered something he couldn't refuse to even try such a thing."

"Do you think it was Mitchell?" I ask, wringing my sopping hair out.

He shrugs. "Don't know."

"I guess it's a good thing I decided to follow through with Layla's suggestion to wear multiple gowns tonight," I say, looking over the rack. "But I guess this one isn't necessary since I'm missing the party." I move the short, strapless dress that sparkles with sequins away from the other two. If I'm not going to be dancing, I'm not showing off any more skin."

"*That* was your party dress?" Austin asks, smirking. "Kingston was sure you picked that for Orlando."

I inhale a soft breath through my nose and point at the puffy, full-length white gown Layla had suggested. "I picked that one for my Blood Vow."

"He'll love it," Austin says, kissing me sweetly.

"I just—Orlando and I never got the chance to talk about expectations or anything. I don't want him to assume," I say, my voice shaking. "Though last night..."

Austin pulls me in for a hug. "I can't speak for him, but I don't think he would risk jeopardizing everything he's worked toward with you because of a back-world tradition this particular type of Blood Vow carries."

I brush my lips to his. "Thanks for saying that. I know it can't be easy for you."

"We'll have our moment, Jewel, and it'll be way better than this spectacle to appease the board. It'll be something amazing, intimate, and everything the both of us imagined when you accepted my proposal." He smiles at me. "I promise."

I grin and kiss him again. "Then let's get this shit over with. All I want is to send everyone away and start my life with you, Mr. Ortega."

He chuckles. "The name sounds perfect coming from your lips."

Austin helps me dress in the poufy gown, the soft, diamond speckled fabric catching the light to sparkle with tiny bursts of rainbow color. I sway in front of the mirror, sweeping the gown back and forth, watching it move with my body. Lifting my hair, Austin helps me fasten the vow necklace Orlando gave me, his drop of blood reflecting red on my skin.

I sigh, feeling the weight of it on my chest. "Is it weird that I miss the roses? I know they were your crests as Divines, but they still were your promises of forever to me."

"Don't worry, Jewel. Orlando's vow won't be lonely for long," he whispers, kissing the crook of my shoulder.

A soft knock on the door draws our attention away from my reflection in the mirror, and Diego peeks his head in. Kingston stops short in the doorway and takes a moment to drink me in. I grab the skirt of my gown and sway it.

"What do you think?" I ask him.

Diego closes the space to me first. "Stunning, beautiful. I'll struggle to keep my hands off you."

I look at Kingston. "What? You don't like it?"

"I—" Rushing to me, he scoops me up and kisses me, spinning me around with him. "I'm so fucking jealous that I can't rip it off you, though I'm also so damn relieved it's not that tiny number over there, because then I know I couldn't keep myself away."

"I did pick that one out with you in mind," I say, smirking. "Because you make me so hot...dancing."

He releases a low cross between a growl and a moan, expertly managing to sneak his hand up my dress to spread my legs so that I can feel his body through my soft satin short-cut styled underwear. "This might be our last chance to be alone for days. I think I can slip it in for a quickie before people wonder where you are."

I shiver under his desire. "Kingston."

"Fuck, babe. This is so hard for me."

I reach between us and touch him. "I think it's hard for me too."

He groans softly, squeezing me tighter. "I love you. So. Damn. Much. You're so beautiful and funny and sexy, and I kind of want to murder Orlando so that I can step in his place and vow myself to you in front of everyone."

I kiss his pouty mouth. "If you're not completely on board—"

Kingston holds me away from him, untangling my body from his so quickly that I can't finish my sentence. "Babe, I'm on board. I just—someone take her. I don't trust that I'll make it to the ceremony with her without ruining her dress or not showing up at all."

Austin takes me into his arms, and Diego slides his arm

over Kingston's shoulders. My eyes water, my chest tightening with nerves. I can't believe this is actually happening. I think my guys can't believe it either. But it is, and there's no going back.

"Jewel," Austin whispers. "No tears. This is a happy occasion."

I sniffle. "I know."

"We'll officially be a coven in the eyes of Donor Life Corp," Diego adds.

"No one will ever threaten you again. They will never look down on you or question you," Kingston says. "Everything we're doing—it's really fucking legit. You're our girl."

Austin kisses my cheek. "Our forever."

Diego touches my shoulder. "Now, let's get you out there. Orlando's waiting."

"You guys will stay with me, right?" I ask, resting my cheek to Austin's chest to listen to his heart beating seemingly only for me.

Kingston nods. "The whole time."

Diego takes the lead and rushes through the estate at a vampire's pace. My hair swirls in the wind created by Austin, and when we stop on the front porch, Kingston smooths my hair and kisses my cheek. He and Austin each take one of my arms, and Diego strolls along the same path to the garden. All signs of the dead vampire have been removed. I release a long breath, drawing everyone's gazes to me, and everyone blurs to find their seats.

Kingston squeezes my hand and whispers how much he loves me again before letting me go. He blurs up the aisle and to Orlando's side where Orlando waits with his hands together in front of him. He captures my gaze from across the room, sending my heart thrashing around my chest. A dozen memories of me and Orlando together flit through my mind—from our times sneaking around the shadows, to the moments he stole after my Blood Matching and to everything that has happened over the last few months and every moment I share of him with Kingston, Austin, and Diego. Every little piece scatters into a path that leads me right to him like he promised.

Whispers trickle to me, dozens of vampires talking about me, unaware that I can hear everything. Like how the man in the last row thinks Orlando's making a mistake with the type of vow, and how another man gives me a few months before I'm cast to the shadows for betraying him.

Austin and Diego both squeeze my hand, lending me their strength to walk through the cacophonous hum of everyone who doesn't think I'm worthy of joining what they suspect might be the most powerful coven since the Divine reign.

A soft melody fills the air, drawing my gaze from the path and back up to the platform where Kingston plucks a slow tune on a guitar he took from the music store in town. I recognize the song from his collection he put together for me that he always plays when we're alone together.

"Dude," I say, a smile breaking through my tight jaw.

He grins right back at me, and I'm nearly certain I'm going to melt into a puddle before I even make it to the stage. If Austin and Diego weren't guiding me along, I'd probably stop in place and just listen.

The music fades with the appearance of the other board members, and I nearly trip over my heels as they stand in front of the stage to block our way. Diego steadies me on my feet, touching his big hand to my lower back.

Viorica steps forward and extends her hand to me. "Ms. Ortega, you have been found worthy of a life beyond your mortal bonds. Congratulations."

I nod without saying anything.

Zara steps before me next and kisses my cheek. "Please do not take such for granted. The position you will hold is coveted by many."

Mr. Duchanne gathers my hand in his and brushes his lips to my knuckles. "Be aware that our expectations for such a Blood Vow are high. Do not disappoint us or your new coven, Ms. Ortega."

"Seems such a waste to give up another blood source. The Ortega Coven would thrive regardless." Mr. Bellamy crosses his arms. "With saying that, this is your last chance to speak your mind to the board, Ms. Ortega. If you believe you are unfit of such a position or have decided to embrace the life you were born to lead, speak now."

It takes everything in me not to glower.

Viorica turns to Orlando. "Very well. Mr. Ortega, you

may proceed."

The board members return to their seats, and Diego and Austin lead me to the stage where they take their places behind Orlando and next to Kingston. Orlando takes my hand and twirls me around to get a view of all of me in the dress. Pulling me in close, he cups my cheeks and stares deeply into my eyes.

"This is everything I could ever hope for, Jewel. You have given me so much in such a short time that I can only hope to return in our eternity." Orlando leans in and brushes his lips to mine in a kiss that leaves my body tingling.

"Damn," Diego whispers under his breath only low enough that we could here.

I wiggle my fingers at him on Orlando's shoulder, and he chuckles.

Orlando steps away from me, still holding my hand, and he turns me toward the crowd. I peer over the dozens of vampires watching us intently with various expressions lining their faces. I meet Samantha's gaze in the crowd, and she leans in and whispers something to her Blood Match that I can't hear, but it makes Evora smile wider.

"On this marvelous night, I, Orlando Ortega, present to you the woman I have chosen to vow my love to and to give her the gift of eternity. I thank you for joining us on this unforgettable occasion and ask that you fondly carry this moment within you as I will." Orlando faces me again and takes both my hands in his. "Jewel Jordan of Dark Terrace Ranch, will you accept the Ortega name and join my coven in a binding vow of our love forever?"

I swallow, afraid that my voice will refuse to come. "I do," I say, the words sounding loud and clear and more confident than I expected.

Orlando's smile widens. "With this vow, I promise to protect, to love, to teach, and to respect you in your transition into a better version of yourself. I vow the strength of our coven to hold you up and to give you everything that your heart could ever desire. This moment may be fleeting, but I swear to you that the memory will always live through every word I speak, every touch I give, and every passing second we share. As a reminder, I give to you my ring with my very life force to hold close always."

Orlando lifts my hand and slides a platinum ring with glittering rubies and diamonds with a square vile of deep crimson blood. Bringing my hand to his mouth, he kisses the ring softly and pulls me to him.

"And now, you may share a few words of your own," he says, keeping my body close to his.

"As we stand in front of those who think so little of me and find me undeserving of the life you offer, I vow never to disappoint you, Orlando. Nor will I take for granted, throw away, or betray you like those who bear witness tonight surely expect." For the first time, the crowd draws completely quiet. "From this moment and for the rest of eternity, I offer my love freely, unashamedly, and unconditionally in return for a place by your side and in your coven. I vow to protect you, to share the best pieces of my life with you, always." I shift my gaze and smile at Kingston, Diego, and Austin and they return he gesture, knowing I'm referring to them.

"It's all that I ask," Orlando whispers.

"So, Mr. Ortega, will you accept my ring and always carry a part of me close to you forever?" I take the ring Kingston holds out for me and slide it on Orlando's finger.

"I do."

Orlando meets me for a kiss so passionate that he steals my breath only to return it with his. His hands roam down my back to my waist, and I moan softly as every part of me lights ablaze with a dozen emotions that rip at my very soul to break pieces of myself I thought were gone forever. Pieces of the girl from Dark Terrace Ranch who fell for a vampire in the shadows. The same girl who had no idea her heart was big enough to withstand loving four.

Orlando slowly eases away, a handsome smile softening the hard features of his face, and he spins me around to let Diego, Austin, and Kingston engulf me in the best hug ever. They each kiss my cheek and surround me with so much love that this whole moment feels utterly surreal.

"That was the best and sneakiest vow I've ever heard, babe," Kingston whispers.

I laugh. "I try. I could never exclude you guys. You're my everything."

"And you're ours," Austin says.

Diego squeezes my hand. "I especially love how you called all those assholes out."

"What can I say? I'm your badass girl."

"Please rise and enjoy the celebration of the union of the Ortega Coven and my Blood Vow to dear Jewel," Orlando says. "The rest of the ceremony will continue an hour before sunrise."

Orlando holds out his hand for me and slides our fingers together. A blip of fear sneaks into my heart, and I tense, half expecting for a thousand angry vampires to storm the estate in an attempt to destroy everything we worked hard to build here.

But nothing happens.

"Have fun, babe," Kingston says, pursing his lips.

I stick my tongue out at him. "You too, dude. All of you."

Orlando motions for Kingston, Austin, and Diego to come closer, and the four of them sandwich me in one more hug.

And then Orlando lifts me off my feet, and I inhale a long breath and hug him as he carries me away. I suppress my nerves the best I can as he slows down outside his study and sets me on my feet.

"Jewel, I hope you know that you've made me the happiest man tonight," he says softly. "I know that it hasn't been easy for you, and I know you've had your doubts, but I promise you that I'll be and do the best I can for you. I love you."

I stare into his eyes, letting his words sink in, feeling the weight of them on my soul. I open my mouth to respond, but footsteps sound out and Baby hisses from inside the room. Orlando releases a soft growl and disappears from in front of me to fling the door open.

He roars.

COMMITTED

"HOW DARE YOU INTRUDE ON the most significant moment of my life," Orlando says, lowering his voice to a pitch as to not draw attention from the vampires on the estate.

Diego materializes in front of me, blocking my view of the room. "Come on, wait with me over here."

I don't move, resting my hands on Diego's chest. He searches my face as intensely as I search his. But he doesn't say anything, just tips his chin toward the table with a blooming bouquet of roses that wasn't there when I left.

"If you don't leave right now, I will rip your throat out. You have forgotten your place," Orlando says, his threat keeping me frozen, resisting against Diego's gentle push to get me to move.

"You wouldn't. Not with Jewel standing right there," Hayden's voice sends a dozen nerves clenching my insides. "You wouldn't risk her seeing you as the monster you are. She'd never forgive you."

Orlando releases a growl. "You don't know her like I do, Mr. Andrei. She will accept what is right for this coven. I have her vow."

I hold my breath at his words, my mind and body warring with each other in an attempt to interpret what he means.

"She might hold compassion, but she also carries a fierce protectiveness that you must tread lightly around with your next words. I will not stand by and allow you to cause her any more distress," Orlando continues.

"I'm sorry, Orlando. I understand. I just—it couldn't wait," Hayden says.

I push past Diego and stand in the doorway, catching sight of Hayden and Orlando facing each other in the middle of the room. Hayden's eyes dart to mine, worry lining his face. It's enough to draw me a step forward.

"What's going on? Is everything okay? Did something happen?" I ask, keeping my voice soft as to not let it break.

The expression Hayden gives me ignites a thousand horrible thoughts in my mind. I can't help but think the worst, especially with so many vampire guests in our region. Viorica knows about the humans he brought in, but no one else does.

"Jewel, it's about Ramona," Hayden says.

I bring my hand to my chest. "Is she okay?"

He nods. "Yes, but—"

"Stop." I raise my palm to him. I can't help it. "If she's okay, then whatever you need to tell me can wait. I just vowed my forever to Orlando and our coven, and I will not let you or anyone else ruin a moment that will stay pure and perfect in my mind."

Orlando's face softens at my words, and I bring my gaze to his and smile. I don't know where my thought came from, but it's the most certain thing in my life right now. From now on, I no longer have to worry about my mind getting manipulated. I don't have to despair losing moments precious to me because of some power play my dad insisted on to control me.

Accepting Orlando's Blood Vow was more than cementing our futures together, but it also assures that my life from now on will remain clear. Every decision—every decision I make with Orlando, Kingston, Diego, and Austin will be for us, for me, no matter how selfish that might be. But I don't care. Everyone fights for their own interests. Now, I'll fight for ours.

"Jewel, please," Hayden says.

I shake my head and turn to Diego. "Will you please escort Mr. Andrei from the estate, Diego?"

Hayden waves his hand. "You're making a mistake, Jewel."

Diego materializes behind Hayden and covers his mouth with his hand, disappearing before he has a chance to argue any more. I stroll to the door and peer into the study, the noise of their departure fading to only leave the sound of my and Orlando's hearts beating.

I close the door, activating the lock, and turn my back to rest on the cool wood for a moment. Orlando remains in his spot, watching me without a word, his chest still heaving, his eyes flashing. I comb my hair from my face and swallow the rest of the unwanted feelings Hayden unleashed inside me.

"Jewel, I'm sorry that Hayden ruined tonight," Orlando says softly. "I did not expect his intrusion."

I rub my lips together, wishing with everything inside me that Orlando would smile. Combing my hair over my shoulder, I expose my neck to him and stand straighter to show him nothing was ruined. I'm used to interruptions. "The only thing you need to apologize for is all of this space between us."

He releases a small breath, his face relaxing as he smiles at my words. "Jewel."

It's me who moves first, but Orlando's quick to close the space and wraps me in his arms, just hugging me for a long moment while his heart slows.

Orlando eases away and touches my cheek. "What you said to Hayden—"

"Was true. I want this night to be amazing...for the both of us," I say, my sudden excitement sending my heart thrumming against Orlando's. "I mean, I know there's a certain expectation, and I—"

He kisses me softly, cutting off my words in the best way possible. "The only expectation I have tonight is to give you whatever you desire. I want you to be happy."

"So, if I want to hang out and watch a movie?" I ask, smiling.

He chuckles. "I have all of your favorites ready."

"What if I want to...?" I let my words trail off, my attraction to Orlando burning through me so hotly that I lean my head on his shoulder to hide my face. "Orlando." His name whispers on my lips so that I'm not sure he heard them.

"Jewel, please look at me." He touches my chin, guiding my face up to meet his gaze. "I love you, and I know you still have reservations about us. I cannot blame you for that. Sometimes, the love I hold for you infuriates me. You poke at my very nature with your wild, untamed, and free heart, because you are my weakness. It has made me do things I know were unfair to you. Things I want to regret, but I can't. Your passion and bravery, your fierceness, it drives me crazy."

I slide my arms over his chest to hook around his neck. "I don't know if I can ever forget the things that happened between us, and honestly, I don't want to, but I do forgive you. I understand how hard it is to fight against who you are. I mean, look at me. Half the time my body wants nothing more than to devour you. How you, or your brothers for that matter, can get past that awful part of me, I don't even know."

He tilts his head. "But you do know, Jewel. You've done it with us, to which I'm grateful."

I smile. "You have no friggin' idea how thankful I am to have you."

"I might."

Standing on my tiptoes, I meet him for another kiss. "Can I show you?"

Orlando eases away and smiles, desire darkening his startling blue eyes. He stands utterly still, his breathing quickening as my fingers slowly trail up his stomach along the buttons of his dress shirt, feeling the ridges and grooves of his taut body through his clothes.

I step around him, drawing my finger across his muscular shoulder and graze my lips to the back of his neck along his collar. Tugging off his jacket, I let it drop to the floor. He spins so quickly, capturing me with his mouth to steal my breath with a kiss that sends tingles through me.

I work my hands over the buttons of his shirt, my fingers desperate to pull them free. Breaking away from his heated kiss, I trace my tongue along his jaw and down his neck, tasting the sweetness of his skin as I open his shirt completely to touch his rippling muscles.

Orlando picks me up, bringing my lips back to his, sliding his tongue into my mouth. I kiss him deeper, exploring the softness of his tongue until it turns fervent with my hands reaching between us to unfasten the button on his pants.

My back hits the bed, and Orlando kisses my neck, sucking my sensitive skin hard enough to ignite a lust and need so intense inside me that I push him up only to get him to roll over. I straddle him, my gown spilling over the bed, and Orlando slides his hands under my skirt to push it out of the way to rub his fingers over my thighs. I arch my back at the sudden sensation of his fingers shifting my underwear away to rub how I like.

I clutch his legs, rocking my body with the good pressure he creates all while feeling the hardness of his excitement as I grind against him. Slowly easing away, Orlando glides his hands around my waist. They travel up my sides and to my back where he pulls the zipper down to expose my bra to him.

Leaning up, Orlando gathers the fabric of my gown and pulls it off me, tossing it to the floor. He drinks me in, his fangs peeking out from beneath his lips. I reach behind me and unclasp my bra, baring my breasts to him. He intakes a breath at the sight of me, how I expose myself for him and only him in this moment.

I roll my hips against his, teasing him without breaking my gaze. He trails his hands over my legs and to my thighs, playing with the hem of my underwear before quickly ripping it free. I gasp as he pulls me higher up his body until my thighs rest at the sides of his head. He slides two fingers between my legs so that he can draw his tongue over me in such a way that leaves me squirming and panting and pleading his name.

He holds my body still, moaning every time I squeeze his head with my thighs. Good pressure builds and builds, my heart crashing into my ribcage, every nerve ending screaming inside me in the best possible way as I release a loud ass moan that turns my whole body weak so that Orlando's the only reason I'm still upright.

He slides me back and sits up, hugging his arms around me to roll me off of him only to shift with me to rest between my legs. Smiling down at me, Orlando brushes the hair from my cheek before kissing my heated skin, still tingling under his touch.

"To hear my name on your lips fills me with everything I could ever want in life," he murmurs, kissing me softly. "I want nothing more than to continue, Jewel. May I?"

I bite my lip and reach down to graze my fingers over his pants. "I'd like that."

He smiles and undresses for me, kneeling between my legs so I can appreciate how sexy he looks with his anticipation to take our relationship to a level we've both thought about dozens of times. But none of those times were right. None of those times were undiluted by the circumstances my life threw at me. But now, as I lie before Orlando, everything is perfectly clear. I'll carry this moment, feel his love, his protection, his everything for the rest of eternity.

I reach out for him, linking my fingers through his. "Orlando, I love you. I love you despite your faults. Despite everything. I hope you know that and will be careful with me."

"I will do better," he says, lying on top of me, taking my hand with his to hold over my head.

"You already do."

I shift beneath him and open my body completely. With his free hand, he adjusts himself to me, never taking his eyes off mine as he teases me for a second, testing me, and then sinks so deeply that I gasp and close my eyes, arching my hips to feel the blissful extent of him.

He moans deep in his throat, just enjoying my body entwined with his. Our lips meet and he kisses me softly, caressing his mouth to mine until I suck in his bottom lip and graze my teeth over it. His fangs extend, and he bites his lip, sending drops of blood over my tongue. I awaken under the taste of him and suck harder, breaking my hand from his to map down the length of his body to pull him closer by his ass.

My body stays in rhythm with his, and he braces on the wall, thrusting harder and faster, gasping through a dozen kisses, only stopping to whisper my name. I draw my hands to my knees to pull them higher until he stretches one of my legs up over my head, sending electricity through me so intense that I scream out, scratching my nails over his back. I lean up to press my loud mouth to his shoulder to muffle the sound the best I can.

I sink back into the pillow, my breath heaving, my heart pounding. Tingles course through my veins, and Orlando smiles at me. He holds my gaze, thrusting into me, capturing my mouth to his until he finishes.

Rolling over, he takes me with him and hugs me to his chest, combing his fingers through my hair. His heart thrums in beat with mine, and he embraces me in silence, just soaking in the love I've given him in the life I've committed to him.

"You've made me the happiest man, Jewel. To see you

smile, to feel your body, your love, your soul completes me. I never knew you'd give me so much," Orlando says, stroking his fingers over my arm. "I can only hope to return just as much or more."

I shift and kiss him, pressing my boobs into his chest. "You will—you do. I never imagined more to life than what my father gave me, what Donor Life Corp tried to ensure, but with you and your brothers, I know there will always be more. I just hope I can keep up," I tease. "But I also hope that I never let you down or prove the board right. I still worry what my existence means for yours."

"Please don't worry. You have to trust us and yourself, Jewel."

Orlando rolls me off of him but doesn't untangle our legs. He pulls the blankets up so that I can cuddle him, warming his side. I draw circles over the taut planes of his chest, thinking about his words. I shouldn't worry. Because I trust them, and I trust myself with them, now more than ever. I might've been a little freaked out the other night about my self-control, but they're strong enough to handle me— especially together.

"You're right," I finally say. "It's just hard to accept that my life could be more than what I was as a donor."

"What have I told you since the first moment I met you alone and away from your father in the shadows?" he asks.

"That I deserve more. I was always meant for more," I say, thinking about that moment where he sat with me on the curb in the shadows around the corner from the market. We talked for hours as he asked me questions about my life and family, how he said he wanted to know every little thing about me, things I had yet to even know.

"And I stand by it, Jewel."

I hug him close. "So what happens now? Do we go back to the party? Stay here? Can we just send everyone home and have our own private celebration just the five of us?"

He props himself up, taking me with him so that I sit on his lap with my legs around his waist. "I was hoping we could feed each other. Possibly let me enjoy you for a bit longer. We don't have to return for another few hours."

I smile and kiss him. "That sounds perfect."

"Yeah?"

I shift my hair off my neck and expose it to him. "I want nothing more than for you to bite me."

Hugging me close, he brings his lips to my ear, breathing softly. "You first."

THE BITE

I SIT IN BED, MY shower-damp hair hanging down my back. Orlando combs his fingers through it, stopping to kiss my shoulder, then my neck, gently trailing his tongue over my healing bite mark. His fingers slide around me to brush over another one at the top of my breast, and then he kisses a third on the back of my shoulder. But they're nothing compared to the marks I left on him.

Sliding my hands up, I hug his arms to me. "And you said I'd be the one to beg you to drain me dry."

Deep laughter erupts near my ear, his body shaking against me with the movement. "My brothers weren't joking about the wonders of your mouth, Jewel. While I'd gladly die in utter ecstasy under you, I'd fight to live to experience such a thing over and over. Your need—I have a strong desire to satiate you above myself."

I get off the bed to stand between his legs only to turn around to face him. "You have always loved feeding me. I wouldn't deny fulfilling your desires again, if you'd like."

He grins in my arms and pulls me to him, kissing me until I push him back and climb on top of him. I lean down to caress my lips to his neck, but he flips me off and kisses mine instead, pinning me down with his weight in a way that ignites my lust to set my body ablaze.

Slowly easing up, he meets my gaze, his eyes flashing silver. "Jewel, I want nothing more than to give into you again."

"Then do it." My voice comes out softly, pleading for him to close the space between us.

His jaw tightens and he suppresses a frown. "We only have a few more minutes. We've missed our Blood Vow celebration completely."

I inhale a sharp breath and push him back so that I can sit up. "Shit. The whole thing?"

"No one cares, Jewel."

"But Diego, Austin, and Kingston—"

"Are slightly bored, jealous, hungry, and in serious need of cuddles, but fine." Kingston's voice trickles through the door, drawing my attention away from Orlando.

"Dude," I say. "I thought you all would be enjoying the party."

"We did," Austin says. "Don't let Kingston mess with

you. We've only been out here for a bit."

Kingston chuckles. "That shower sounded amazing, though. I've never heard you make that noise before. Hot."

Orlando grins and I smack him on the chest, my whole body bursting into tingles and heat, a mixture of embarrassment and pleasure all at once.

"I'd punch Kingston for pointing that out, but he's right, beautiful," Diego says.

Both he and Kingston groan a second before two thuds sound through the air. I rub my face with my hands and leave Orlando on the bed to cross the room to the double doors. I swing them open to find Diego and Kingston sitting on the edge of one bed, looking suspicious as all get-out as they pretend to have been sitting there all this time. Austin sits across from them, holding Baby on his lap, not even caring that white and orange fur gets on his black tuxedo.

The three of them smile at me, and I scrunch my nose and narrow my eyes before I can't resist smiling back. Opening my arms, I invite them to me, and Diego carries me into the bedroom only to spin me around and toss me back to Orlando. He catches me and kisses me, sitting me down on the edge of the bed.

"I swear if you guys start high-fiving or fist bumping or whatever, I'm leaving," I tease, noticing the four of them sharing sneaky ass looks at one another. "And Kingston, I swear if you ask Orlando to tell you what we did in the shower, I'll—"

"Be the most satisfied and satiated babe all the fucking

time," Kingston says, putting his words in my mouth.

I laugh. I can't help it. "What am I going to do with you?"

He wags his eyebrows at me. "I have a list of suggestions if you need help."

Shaking my head with another wide ass grin, I let my hair spill over my shoulders. "Okay, OG body match, I'm going to come up with my own list too. One of things to do outside the bedroom."

Diego laughs before Kingston can even respond and says, "Careful, beautiful. You're going to give him the wrong idea."

Kingston shrugs. "What wrong idea? If our girl wants some adventure in other places, I'll be happy to provide it."

"Okay, okay. I'm going to have to set some new rules if my body's ever going to survive." I reach over and grab a pillow from the bed and chuck it at Kingston. He lets it hit him in the face and fall to the floor. "Starting with our next nights alone. I'm insisting you take me at least into town. Bonus points for somewhere new."

"What can we get with bonus points?" Kingston asks.

I laugh. "I guess you'll just have to wait and see."

Kingston fake pouts. "Ugh, that's way too many hours away."

"I guess that means you should get dressed, beautiful," Diego says. "The sooner you complete your ceremony, the sooner we'll get our lives back."

I fall silent at Diego's words, the excitement and playfulness my guys rouse in me drains away with the warmth in my body. Scooting back on the bed, I curl my knees to my chest and rest my chin on them.

Austin sits beside me and slides his arm behind my back. "What's wrong, Jewel?"

"I—I don't know if I can do this," I murmur.

"Of course you can, babe," Kingston says, stepping closer to stand in front of me. "Um, have you looked at yourself? It looks like you let Orlando practice."

Diego punches him and shakes his head. "She's not worried about the bite, bro. Our girl is a badass. She knows she can handle the venom, probably better than you. You've complained at least twice tonight."

I lift my chin and look at Kingston. "Come here, dude. Let me see it."

Kingston crosses his arms. "Not gonna happen."

"What if I offer to kiss it?" I tease, smirking.

Diego steps in front of Kingston, blocking him from me. Kneeling in front of the bed, Diego motions for me to scoot closer. Austin slides with me, and Orlando eases my hands from my death grip on my legs to lace his fingers through mine.

"We are here, Jewel. We're not leaving you, ever. Period. You don't have to be afraid, okay?" Diego says, sliding his hand behind my legs to pull me a bit closer. "We won't allow anyone to get within a foot of you in your vulnerable state."

I lick my lips and nod. "Can't you just pretend to inject

me with your venom, Orlando? What if it makes me worse? You know, all of these side effects weren't so bad until my matches bit me with their venom before Haven Springs."

Orlando brings my hand to his lips to kiss. "If we weren't under such scrutiny, I wouldn't. But Jewel, the board might be able to tell."

"He's right," Austin says. "The only reason the board didn't know for you was for the fact that there was a lot of commotion, and they were more concerned about watching their backs because of Mitchell."

I groan. "Don't remind me. I'm surprised that monster hasn't tried to crash our night already." The four of them look at each other, and I bring my hand to my mouth. "What? You're shitting me. He didn't."

Orlando stands and pulls me to my feet. "It's nothing we want you to worry about. Mitchell will not get within a mile of you, promise. We planned the night properly. If it goes in our favor, we won't have to worry about him anymore. If it doesn't, we'll still never be in harm's way."

I blink a few times at his words, trying to process them the best I can. "Are you saying you knew he'd come?"

Again, the four of them look at each other.

Shifting, I look at Austin. "Tell me everything."

"Don't do it, Austin," Kingston says. "We talked about this."

"No, we discussed how and when we'd tell Jewel, not how we'd keep it from her if she asked," Austin says.

"Yeah, after everything is done," Kingston says.

My chest clenches with fear, and I stand up and stroll a few feet away from them, turning my back. It takes everything in me to control the sudden hurt and anger washing through me. I know that there was a lot going on, and I'm not exactly innocent when it comes to doing things without discussing it with all of them either but shit.

I clench my hands at my sides. "Someone better tell me right now."

Silence falls between them, but still, I keep my back turned. The fact that I was nervous to begin with makes this worse.

"Jewel," Orlando says softly, his light footsteps coming up behind me. "Don't blame them for my decision."

I stroll toward the wardrobe, keeping space between us. "I don't blame them. I blame all of you. I thought we were past this. I thought that the union and the Blood Vow would finally put a stop to you trying to protect me by keeping me ignorant over everything."

"Beautiful, that wasn't our intent," Diego says.

I enter the wardrobe and pull the simple white dress I chose for the venom bite and slip it over my head. I quickly run my fingers through my hair, braiding the pieces along my hairline in a crown and letting the rest of my tresses hang over my shoulders. I look at my silver flashing eyes in the wall mirror for a moment, trying to get them to stop. Nothing works.

Emerging from the wardrobe, I stand in the doorway,

clutching the frame. "I know upsetting me wasn't your intent. And I know you all had my best interest in mind, but you *have* to tell me these kinds of things from now on. I mean it. You *have* to. I'm not the only one who needs protecting. Have you forgotten what I am? What I'm capable of?"

The four of them close the space to me, surrounding me so that if I tried to storm away, I couldn't. Not that I would. Never again.

"The reason I—*we*—chose not to tell you was because this is an important night for you. I know you want to know these things. You want to worry about them. But just because you want to, doesn't mean you should have to," Orlando says. "Every day of your life since your father left you in Dark Terrace Ranch has been you stressing and worrying about your future. I did not want this night to be that."

Diego reaches out and takes my hand, getting me to loosen the tightness in my muscles. "Tonight is supposed to be celebrating the fact that we got you. You're our girl. You should be able to relax and enjoy the life you deserve. You shouldn't have to worry about the plans Donor Life Corp set into motion with Mitchell."

I pout my lip and look at the ground. "Of course they would use this as an opportunity to advance their power."

"Mitchell is a threat not only to us but to them. As former Divines, we knew he wouldn't be able to resist coming here," Kingston says. "And here, we have the advantage."

"We also know where he is, so you don't have to worry.

He can try all he wants, but he won't stop us," Orlando says.

I take a few breaths, trying to calm my nerves. It was one thing to worry about the bite in front of everyone or the fact that I'll have to play the part of a vampire, but it's another to freak the hell out about the monster who wants nothing more than to bathe in all our blood and ruin humanity crashing my Blood Vow—or at least trying.

"Give me a weapon or something," I say, rubbing my hands up and down my arms.

Kingston smirks. "What happened to the babe who trusted us to take care of her?"

I stick my tongue out at him. "She realized that she was a better fighter than you and can watch your ass that way I can smack it later."

Kingston releases a chuckle. "Are we still in trouble?"

I fake glare and nod. "So much. You just wait."

"I don't know if I can."

Austin kneels at my feet and lifts up my dress, making me shiver as his hands trail over my thigh to buckle a knife holster in place. "Before you two get carried away, we really have to get going."

Diego holds up a pair of stilettos to me. "These can be used as a weapon as well."

I crinkle my nose. "Someone's going to have to carry me."

Orlando scoops me off my feet while Diego fastens on the too high heels. My heart thrashes around my chest while my guys' heartbeats remain perfectly even and in sync, seemingly beating as one around me.

Diego leads us to the door and stops before exiting. He turns to face me and comes in close to press a sweet kiss to my lips. "You're going to be amazing, okay? We got you. You're our girl."

"And you're my guys," I say, patting his cheek. "My brave, sexy as hell, powerful protectors. I love you all so much."

Diego kisses me again. "Love you, beautiful."

Austin comes up next and touches my cheek, smiling at me as he leans in to caress his soft lips to mine. "Don't worry about the venom. Your body can handle it. I'll make sure you're not in any pain, okay?"

I hug him. "Thank you, Austin."

Kingston steals me from Orlando and curls my body up to his face to bury it in my cleavage. "You're so fucking hot. All these dresses—they don't stand a chance on my night."

I bring my mouth to his. "Watch your brothers' backs, okay?"

"You bet."

Orlando takes me from Kingston, and the three of them step into the study, giving me a moment alone with Orlando. He kisses me tenderly, sucking my lip into his mouth, tightening his arms around me to hold me close.

"I love you, Jewel," he says. "I hope you can forgive me for tonight and for putting you in this position."

I rest my head on the crook of his neck. "I already do, but please, let's just get through this."

"Together," he says.

I force myself to smile. "Always."

The loud music fades in the night with our arrival. Soft voices murmur through the air as Orlando carries me in his arms back to the stage.

Everyone watches from their places, and I catch sight of a few vampires feeding on donors lying on tables brought out for the party. I'm kind of glad I missed that part of the party, though I wish I had gotten to taste the amazing looking chocolate cake.

Austin materializes in front of me and Orlando. Like he read my mind, or maybe he just saw me looking longingly and drooling at the cut cake, he holds up a forkful to my mouth. "A bite to enjoy one last time."

It takes everything in me not to frown. Because even though I know it's not the last time I can eat cake or any solid food for that matter, I have to pretend it is. And I also have to pretend that the idea doesn't bother me.

I let Austin feed me and savor the rich, chocolaty flavor that reminds me of him. My stupid body chooses to react at the memory, and I release a soft moan at the blossoming tingles between my legs.

"The cake must be exquisite," Orlando murmurs into my hair.

"That was not a food moan," Kingston whispers too lowly for anyone but the five of us to hear.

If everyone wasn't so invested in watching this moment, I'd kick him in the shoulder.

"It was too," I say, smiling at Austin. "It just also happened to remind me of something."

Kingston tilts his head. "What?"

I shake my head. "Not telling."

Before Kingston can beg me, Orlando motions for them to continue to walk us to the stage. The table with the pillow remains as we left it, and Orlando sits me on it. I stare at the audience, the vampires and humans taking their seats, looking happier from their night of partying. Even the board members smile, not looking bored as hell for once.

Orlando, Kingston, Diego, and Austin all stand together in front of me, staring at the audience. "We wanted to thank you for attending the festivities tonight. We hope you've enjoyed the first of many events we plan to host," Orlando says, speaking up.

"To the Ortegas!" someone shouts from the back row.

People applaud, and Orlando turns slightly to smile at me. "And to my precious Jewel, who sits before you on the night of her transition. May she gain our strength, resilience, and power."

The four of them return to me, Kingston standing in front of the table by my feet to watch the crowd. Austin stands at my head, combing my hair out of the way. Diego adjusts the hem of my dress and positions himself by my feet. He smiles and winks at me. Finally, Orlando strolls around the table so that he faces the crowd. He perches on the edge, gathering me in his arms to hug me against him.

Silence draws over the crowd, everyone seemingly holding their breaths.

Orlando takes a moment to kiss and hug me close. I hear the familiar click of his fangs near my ear, his strong arms tightening around me, a hand sliding to my back as the other gently guides my head to bend my neck.

My heartbeat pounds in my head, my body choosing now to tremble with both fear and anticipation. I dig my fingers into Orlando's back. My stomach suddenly twists, and I jerk forward, letting him go to clutch myself. Coolness slides over my body, and an alarm rings through the air startling me.

"Something's wrong," I say, pulling back to stare at Orlando.

The shock alarm shuts off, and people stand, orienting themselves from the blast of the noise. My ears ring, and I try to look around, but Orlando doesn't let me.

"It's all good," Kingston says, tapping the screen of his tablet. "Security intercepted Mitchell exactly where we expected."

Orlando motions to the board, and they nod their heads, getting everyone to take their seats. All focus returns to us on stage.

"Relax, Jewel. All is fine," Orlando says.

But my insides scream. My heart refuses to believe his words. It doesn't feel fine. Something is wrong.

I lick my lips and swallow. "It's not," I whisper, keeping my voice low so that no one apart from Orlando hears me. "I know it."

He leans away and cups my face, staring into my eyes. "Let's just get through this so that we can take you away. We can't postpone."

I slowly nod my head, going against everything inside me to pull my hair from my neck. Orlando leans in and kisses me softly, and Kingston, Austin, and Diego inch closer to us, surrounding me in a way that helps suppress the panic storming through my heart.

"Take a breath, Jewel," Orlando says. "This will hurt."

I close my eyes and take a breath, feeling Orlando's fangs sink deeply into my neck. I startle at the pain, my body tensing. And then fire burns my skin, blazing from his bite to creep away to devour the rest of me.

Eyes watering, I try my best to suppress a whimper, and Orlando holds me close, kissing my cheeks, then my forehead, to finally meet his lips to mine.

He eases me to lie down on the pillow with my shadowing vision. My fingers curl into my hands, my nails digging into my palms, but it does nothing for Orlando's bite resonating pain through me deep in my bones.

It's worse than all of the venom bites I received before, and I feel my body giving in to my mind's desire to save me from myself.

Orlando steps away from me to greet the crowd once more. "Thank you again for bearing witness to the expansion of my coven. Please welcome Jewel as an Ortega and may our future be everything she desires."

The board members stand and stroll over to greet me. I blink through my tears, my body convulsing with pain.

Viorica hovers over me and touches my cheek with a smile. She whispers something to me, but I can't hear it as the world shifts from shadows to light, my consciousness threatening to abandon me.

Zara touches my hand, pulling my focus from the pain. She only smiles down at me before disappearing. Mr. Bellamy bows to me without touching me and turns to shake Orlando's hand. He steps off to the side to allow Mr. Duchanne to greet me, and fear explodes through me the second our eyes meet.

I thrust my body away, jerking so hard that the world spins as I fall off the narrow table. Diego's quick to catch me, pulling me to him, and I catch sight of Mr. Duchanne drawing a blade from beneath his jacket.

I try to open my mouth to call for Kingston, but he's too focused on me. Everyone is. Pushing against Diego, I throw myself forward, catching him off guard.

I can barely see through the pain, but my action was enough to draw Mr. Duchanne's attention away for a split second.

I can't do anything as he rushes me, blade drawn.

He swings his arm back, his fangs flashing, but I can't move. I can't do anything.

All I can do is wait to die.

ENEMIES

BLOOD POURS OVER ME, SOAKING my white dress to stain it red. Mr. Duchanne's head lands right on my lap, his eyes still open and his sharp fangs extended. I freeze, sucking in a breath, my body wanting nothing more than to lick the blood coating my hands in an attempt to satiate the pain and need burning through me from Orlando's bite.

"Get Jewel out of here," Orlando commands. "Austin, Kingston. Get the rest of the Duchannes. Only kill them if they fight."

"Heidi, you're with us. The rest of you, assist them," Viorica commands her daughters. "Evora, go with Mr. Ortega."

"I'm not leaving her," Samantha yells.

"You don't have a choice. Now go."

I remain staring at the glittering night sky, silently praying that my body blacks out, but the fear rolling through me fights for my consciousness. Everything happens so fast, I barely have time to process. Diego lifts me into his arms, cradling me against him. He bends down and motions for Evora to climb on his back.

Evora reaches over Diego's shoulder and takes my hand, frowning as she looks into my eyes. "Don't worry, Jewel. We're going to be okay," she says to me. "Our covens are the fiercest I have ever seen."

I lick my trembling lips, my throat burning at my attempt to push air through to respond. Nothing comes out, and I give up and rest my head on Diego's shoulder. The world blurs around us, and he relocates us inside and to Orlando's room.

Loud pops ring through the air, startling me a second before I hit the ground, my chest heaving as the air escapes my lungs.

Diego releases the scariest roar I've ever heard, jumping back to his feet. Evora rolls toward me, shielding me with her body. I can't do anything, paralyzed by fear and pain. All I can do is watch in shock and horror as Hayden fires his weapon over and over at Diego, staining the front of his shirt.

Another man steps out from the wardrobe, taking Diego from behind. I groan, my body bucking beneath Evora. She doesn't even try to fight, fully determined to just keep me down and the both of us out of the way of the flying bullets.

"Da-da-dagger," I force myself to say, clutching the sides of my dress.

Evora shifts to help me pull up my dress to grab the dagger hidden on my thigh holster. She clutches it in her hand and looks to me before looking at the back of the guy still firing at Diego, who can't move under the force of the attack.

"I'll help him," she says, getting to her feet.

I try to stop her, pushing myself to my knees, but I can barely get up by the time she rushes the man. Hayden stops his fire to shout, but Evora stabs the guy right in the back. He spins around to attack, and Evora drops to the ground and kicks him in the balls with the point of her stiletto. It's enough time for Diego to move. He spins and grabs the guy, lifting him off his feet. Diego extends his fangs and bites him, making the guy scream.

Hayden takes the opportunity to rush me, but Evora jumps between us to attempt to get him to stay back. The asshole swings out and punches her away, sending her falling to her knees. Hayden closes the space and grabs me under the arms to drag me up onto his shoulder.

My scream draws Diego's attention. He drops the guy on the ground and spins, rushing to me. Hayden fires his gun at him again, slowing him down. My ears ring, my head spinning, and I struggle even to lift my arms to fight Hayden off. I pound my fists into his back as he shuffles toward the double doors, continuing to shoot at Diego.

"I got her!" Hayden shouts to someone I can't see. "Let's go."

A strange vampire materializes from behind us and takes me from Hayden. Diego roars, pushing to close the distance, his brutalized body threatening to give out on him. And then it does. Diego drops to his knees, unable to withstand the extensiveness of the surprise attack.

"Jewel!" he yells, still trying to get to me. "Fight!"

But I can't.

The strange vampire restrains me against him, and Hayden jumps on his back, slapping something over my mouth to stop me from trying to bite. Evora rushes to Diego, holding out her arm to him instead of trying to come after me. The last thing I see is Diego sink his fangs into Evora before the world blurs around me.

Cool air whips through my hair, and I can't concentrate on the commotion breaking through the estate. I thrash, doing everything I can to get the vampire to let me go, but he only holds me tighter.

"Jewel, I warned you. It didn't have to be this way," Hayden says, talking over the pounding in my head. "I wanted us to work together, but you just let them control you. You know that, right? They pretend that you have a choice, that you get to help make the decisions, but when it comes down to it, if your decision goes against what they want, they will deny you. They don't care about you or your family. All they want is for you to feed them, pleasure them, obey them."

Anger rushes through me at his words, pissing me the hell off. I buck my body harder, my emotions tapping into my deep-seated nature, and I manage to throw the vampire off course enough to get him to loosen his hold. Jerking my arm, I ram my elbow into his nose, and he drops me. I crash into the ground, rolling over and over, the hard terrain scraping and cutting my skin, ripping my dress, and tangling weeds and leaves in my hair. My back hits a tree, and I curl in on myself, unable to scream as the air escapes my lungs.

I blink, trying to clear my vision. The vampire materializes in front of me, and I punch out in fear, sending him sprawling back and off his feet.

He lands with a thud on the ground before me, and I push up to my feet, using the tree to help steady myself. My heels sink into the ground, tripping me, and I land right on top of the vampire. But he doesn't move and blood coats my fingers.

"Holy shit balls," I mumble against the tape over my mouth.

My hand sinks into the vampire's chest cavity, crunching against shattered bones, soft tissue, and a whole lot of blood. I yank my hand back, sending guts splattering across the ground. Gross, sour liquid coats my tongue too late for me to realize I popped my bloody finger in my mouth, and I gag and spit, for once tasting a blood of a vampire I find disgusting.

"Jewel, don't move," Hayden says, his footsteps crushing the terrain beneath his boots. "Don't scream, either. I will shoot you."

Ignoring him, I open my mouth and shout, "Orlando!"

A loud pop echoes through the air at the same time pain explodes in my leg. I clutch my shin in anguish, the pain too unbearable to deal with along with the vampire venom burning through my veins.

"You just can't listen, can you?" Hayden asks, stepping forward.

I curl in on myself, the world closing in around me.

Hayden bends down and lifts me up. "This is your own fault, you know."

I can only glower at him through my hazy vision.

"But don't worry. You'll be just fine where I'm taking you. For once, you'll actually be free."

"Honey, you can't stay mad at me forever," Dad says, resting his hands on my shoulders. "You know you can't keep living your life like this. What you're experiencing isn't love. You're just trying to fill the void he created in the first place."

I squeeze my eyes shut. "That void was caused by you, Dad. You couldn't just leave everything alone. You couldn't just see what I need. What I want for myself."

"Don't be stupid, Jewel. I raised you to be strong. Clear-minded. Able to see the world through the eyes of our ancestors. Your grandpa didn't sacrifice his life to see you lie down at the feet of a vampire who wants to own you as a possession."

"He sacrificed nothing," I say. "Neither have you. Only I've been sacrificing anything. What you've done to me—what you had Orlando do—"

Dad slaps me across the face, startling me. "You will not speak to me like this."

The world spins, and my back hits the wall of a building. "Jewel, I'm taking you away."

I gasp my breath and fling myself at Orlando. He gathers me in his arms and lifts me off my feet. Rubbing his hand up my back, he smooths away the trembles shaking my body.

"Don't you even think about it, Orlando," Dad says, his deep, threatening voice stabbing fear right into my heart.

Orlando growls and sets me on my feet, spinning around to face my dad. Dad unsheathes a gun I've never seen before, and I step forward and touch Orlando's shoulders, getting him to halt in his tracks.

"You will have to kill me to take her," Dad says, glowering. "I will turn you in to Donor Life Corp for kidnapping a minor, entering a territory without authorization, and for treason against your kind."

Orlando grabs Dad and shoves his back to the wall, forcing him to drop his gun. "How dare you think you can threaten me."

"What's it going to be?" Dad asks.

Orlando turns his attention to me. "Jewel, cover your ears and close your eyes. I want you to count to sixty."

I frown, meeting my dad's gaze. "What?"

"He's going to kill me, honey. Look at this monster you think you're in love with. He'll kill me and leave our family defenseless. Your mother will barely be able to make the proper donations to care for you and your sister."

"Your mother and Ramona will live life just fine," Orlando says. "Don't let him trick you otherwise. If I don't do this, it jeopardizes our future. He doesn't care about you, Jewel. He wants to use you against me."

"Orlando," I say softly. "Just be quick."

Dad's eyes widen, and he yells.

I jerk my hands up to cover my ears, squeezing my eyes shut. A million emotions coil around my heart, stealing my breath. Grief washes over me, but Orlando is right. Dad will never agree with our life. He hates vampires too much. He will force me to fight them until I die. I know it.

Dad's yells cut off, and I release a small whimper, my chest heaving.

A gentle hand touches my shoulder, and I snap my eyes open to look at Orlando, but Mom stands before me. She holds out her hand to me, pulling me from the ground to hug me.

"Sweetie, it's going to be okay," she says, rubbing her hand on my back.

"I—I'm so sorry. I'm sorry. I don't know what else to do," I say, tears burning my eyes. "I love him, Mom. I'll die without him."

"You will not, Jewel," Dad says, his voice making me

gasp. "You will soon be able to take care of yourself."

"D-Dad?" I ask.

"You broke my heart, honey. You chose a vampire over me. How could you?" he asks, flaring his nostrils.

"Noah, stop," Mom says. "Don't be so hard on her. She's young. Naïve. She'll learn."

I shake my head. "You need to learn. I'm not like you."

Mom meets my eyes with a frown. "I'm sorry, honey. I have a deal with Orlando. I won't lose you. Not yet." She motions to Orlando. "I trust that you'll follow through with our agreement. Please respect my family's wishes."

Orlando closes the space to me, wrapping me in his arms. He rests his head against my shoulder, breathing in the scent of my hair as he regains composure. "I'm sorry, Jewel. Your mother is right. My behavior today was unacceptable. Please forgive me."

I hug him tighter. "Just run. Take me. I can't stay. I can't do this anymore."

Orlando eases away to meet my gaze. "I'm sorry. It won't be like this forever. Now forget me."

I scream out and thrash in his arms, trying to fight him. "I hate you, Dad!" I yell. "I'll never forgive you."

Dad comes up to Orlando's side. "Fix her feelings about me too."

"Noah."

"Do it now."

I scream.

A hand slaps over my mouth, muffling my voice. "Screaming won't do anything to save you, Ms. Jordan," a familiar, masculine voice says. "We are too far away for your masters to retrieve you now."

"Miles, be nice to Jewel. She's hurt and afraid." Mrs. Diggs' soft voice sounds over the beating of my heart. "I don't see why it was necessary for you to shoot her, Hayden. Hasn't she been through enough?"

"It was either shoot her or let her kill me. She punched Claremont's heart so hard that it pulverized under her touch," Hayden says. "A bullet hole is nothing. She's already healing. Orlando's venom is quickening her regeneration. Who knew?"

"But still. You made this harder on her than you had to," Mrs. Diggs says.

"She deserves it. She's so selfish that she doesn't care about anyone but herself," Hayden snaps.

Mrs. Diggs sighs, crawling closer in the back of the van with Dougie sleeping in her arms. She waves Mr. Barton away, and I glare at the back of the old man's head.

I should've known that my instincts about him were right from the moment I met him. He was a Blood Rebel, pretending to be an innocent council leader to Haven Springs.

Picking up my hand, Mrs. Diggs squeezes it. "Jewel, I'm sorry for all of this. I know you thought you loved those vampires, and how can anyone blame you? You're still young, impressionable. You got two eyes and hormones. The Ortegas were quite charming."

"Please," I whisper. "Don't let them do this."

Mrs. Diggs frowns. "Do what? Take you home? Come on now, Jewel-babewel. You know your mother would want your family to stick together. Fight the good fight like your father's trying to do. If she were alive, she'd be sick with worry until she knew you were safe."

Her words summon rage inside me. How I ever felt pity for Mrs. Diggs is beyond me. She probably knew what to expect all along. She played me as good as Hayden did.

They both know friggin' well that I'm not the traitor to humanity they claim me to be. They used my need to help the kids and their mothers of Haven Springs to their advantage. But why take me? Hayden claimed my dad was crazy, how he didn't care about his people.

"But don't worry, Jewel. We're going to take you right to Noah, where you belong," Mrs. Diggs says, smiling at me. "Ramona will be so relieved to unite with her child's father. I can't imagine what she's going through without Hayden there to support her. Why you just couldn't help him is beyond me."

I scoff, yanking my hand away from Mrs. Diggs. "This is about Ramona?" My voice screeches through the air with my annoyance. "Hayden, I told you that if Ramona asked for help, I'd help. What are we even doing?"

"Trading you," Hayden says, twisting in his seat to look at me. "I can't be away from Ramona anymore. She needs me. Our daughter needs me. They'll ruin her if I can't get her away."

I scrunch my nose. "Daughter? How do you know?"

He looks at me like I'm stupid as hell, his short, strangled laugh getting on my nerves. "Because some human doctors care enough to share that information unlike those who work for Donor Life Corp who treat us like breeding animals."

I wring my hands together. "I don't understand. Why trade me? Why not just go to The Orchards and be together."

"Because they want her!" Hayden shouts. "They will take her away from us, and we'll never see her again. Don't be stupid. Why do you think Noah remained in Dark Terrace Ranch? Why do you think your grandparents gave their lives to get your family there? They were safe after The Divide and purposely turned themselves in to the city they escaped. Your parents were pardoned, but they were not. They did it so your mom could raise you and Ramona. Your dad loved her enough to make it happen. And that's what I'm doing."

"You don't have to trade me for her," I say. "I can help you. My guys—"

"Would never allow it," he snaps. "I'm sorry, Jewel. They're too far deep into Donor Life Corp now. It was different when it was just Orlando, but your matches changed him. It has to be this way. Your dad won't make the same mistake twice. If he doesn't have you to give to the elders in The Orchards, he'll give my daughter."

"But you don't even know if she'll be symptomatic," I say.

"Doesn't matter."

I clench my fingers into fists. "You can't do this."

He huffs a breath, clutching the steering wheel. "Jewel, it's already done."

NEW PLAN

I TUG AT THE TIGHT restraints, anchoring me to the wall of an old, rundown house in the middle of friggin' nowhere. I couldn't stop myself from dozing on and off as Hayden drove us along a straight, wide road for hours in the direct sunlight. We changed cars twice, and it wasn't until dusk that Hayden blindly navigated us to this shitty house in an area I've never been to. Because the van he drove is so old, I couldn't even see where we ended on a map.

"Get some sleep, Jewel," Mrs. Diggs says, rocking Dougie in her arms. He cries and cries, unable to settle down.

"I can't sleep," I say. "My neck hurts too badly." The venom bite on my throat still burns, but somehow I manage to stay aware. Maybe because my body friggin' knows it better keep its shit prepared to fight.

Mrs. Diggs adjusts Dougie on her hip and walks him to me. "Here, take Dougie. I'll see what I can find to help you. I thought I saw a first aid kit in the kitchen."

Setting Dougie on my lap, Mrs. Diggs strolls from the small bedroom and shuts the door behind her. I struggle to keep my hold on Dougie with the damn restraints, and he stops crying with the bouncing of my legs. Wiggling his body, he squirms away from me too fast for me to grab and toddles toward the window.

I pull against my restraints, trying to summon the strength to break myself free. "Dougie, come here. Don't go over there. You could hurt yourself."

"Tin-Tin!" he says, his sweet voice squealing as he shifts the curtain to press his hands to the window.

"Tin-Tin?" I ask, tilting my head. My heart flutters at Dougie calling Austin's name. "Is Austin out there, Dougie?"

"Tin-Tin!" he repeats, yanking the curtain with his chubby fingers.

It swirls out of the way, and I gasp, catching sight of the unfamiliar vampire flashing his fangs at Dougie through the window.

"Fuck, Dougie, get away from there," I say, pulling on my restraints.

The vampire taps his finger to the window, pointing at the button to unlatch it. I realize he doesn't want to smash it and cause noise that even humans can hear and attempts to get Dougie to unlock the window.

"Tin-Tin. Tin-Tin. Tin-Tin," Dougie chants, slapping his little hands to the glass.

"Dougie, stop. Please, come back here. Get away. That's not Austin," I say.

The vampire turns his attention to me, his eyes flashing silver. His lips curl into a wider smile, and he gives up on coaxing Dougie to punch the window. Glass shatters, cascading on the floor around Dougie. He startles and starts crying, and all I can do is fight against my restraints.

"Don't touch him!" I scream. "Stay back!"

My eyes dart to Dougie, clutching his hands to his face, so startled and scared, he remains frozen in his spot crying.

"Tin-Tin," he says, wailing with another sob. "Ouchie. Tin-Tin."

The vampire flares his nostrils, sucking in a breath through his teeth. My heart rams in my chest the second I realize what happened. Dougie cut himself on a piece of glass from the window, and the vampire smells it.

Panic races through me, and I thrash my hands, yanking so hard against the restraints that I'll either break my wrists or break chains. At this point, I don't friggin' care. I have to get free. The vampire lifts up Dougie, and he suddenly stops crying.

"Don't hurt him, please," I beg, jerking my hand so hard that one of my restraints snaps, the sound of the metal hitting the wall drawing the vampire's gaze to me. I hold out my arm.

"You can bite me. I don't care. Just don't hurt him."

"Tin-Tin," Dougie says again, waving his chubby arms around while the vampire strolls closer.

"Have you been bitten before?" the vampire asks, speaking for the first time.

I purse my lips. "Does it matter?"

He shrugs. "I've never given someone their first bite."

Swallowing, I shift my hair away from my neck on the opposite side that Orlando sunk his fangs into my neck to inject me with venom. "You can be mine. Please, just let him go."

"Tin-Tin!" Dougie calls as the vampire sets him down in a portable crib. "Tin-Tin."

The vampire closes the space to me and brushes his finger across my cheek. "No scars. Can I see your arms?"

I press my lips together and hold out my free arm. "I can't bring down my other one."

"Why are you chained?" he asks, locking his fingers to the restraints. "What do the rebels plan to do with you? Sell you for safe passage? I might accept their offer. You are...hypnotic. I can't seem to take my eyes away from you. Will you look at me?"

I inwardly groan, disguising the sound as I clear my throat. "Help me break free first."

Without questioning, the vampire rips my other restraint from the wall. "Better?"

I rub my hands together. "Much."

"Tin-Tin," Dougie says, clapping his hands. "Up! Up!"

The vampire tips his head to look at Dougie, his eyes flashing silver. He tenses and locks his fingers through my hair, yanking my head to the side.

"You bitch, you lied to me. You've been marked. You're claimed." He releases a growl and jerks his head back, fully set on biting me now.

Swinging my arm, I punch him so hard in the nose that it sinks under my hand.

He roars, his voice startling Dougie, making him cry again. I draw my arm back to push him off, but the vampire disappears from in front of me.

"Tin-Tin!" Dougie cries.

I rush to grab him, but a figure blurs in front of me, snatching Dougie up. I scream out and jump forward, only to have two hands grab me by the waist to yank me back. The world blurs for a second as I fight, thrashing with everything inside me to break free.

"Beautiful, I got you," Diego says, spinning me around to face him. "Take a breath. Bite me if you need to. Just don't rip my heart out."

I break at the sound of Diego's voice, my body relaxing to sink against him as he pulls me up to cradle me in his arms. Clutching his cheeks, I shower him with a dozen kisses, determined to brush my lips over every inch of his face.

"You found me," I say, swallowing the burning in my throat.

"Fuck yeah, we did," Kingston says, slamming the bedroom door wide open. On his shoulder, he carries an unconscious Mrs. Diggs. "Sorry it took so damn long. Traffic." He laughs at my look of confusion. "Just kidding. Only a bunch of annoying vampires getting in our way."

"Mama." Dougie's sweet voice draws my attention back to him. "Say hi, Tin-Tin."

Austin sits on the floor with Dougie on his lap, tending to the small cut on his foot from stepping in the glass from the shattered window.

"All done, Dougie," Austin says, standing from the floor and carrying him on his hip.

Dougie stretches his leg out in front of him. "Kiss boo-boo."

Austin chuckles and kisses the bottom of Dougie's little foot, making him clap his hands. "All better."

"Here, Kingston. Take Dougie. I need to examine Jewel," Austin says, handing Dougie to Kingston.

I laugh. I can't help it. Kingston obeys his brother but holds Dougie out and away from him as far as possible, dangling him in the air like Austin asked him to take care of a bomb. "Dude, get over here. Diego, take Dougie. I don't want Kingston to drop him accidentally."

"I'd never," Kingston says, practically tossing the little guy into Diego's arms the second Austin takes me from Diego.

Austin hugs me close for a moment, just savoring the affection I offer him. I kiss him slowly, letting him suck my bottom lip into his mouth like he can't get enough of me. He strolls to the cot and sets me down, his eyes roving over my body to stop at the broken chains still attached to the metal cuffs on my wrists.

"Kingston, go get the key from Hayden. I don't want to break these off and hurt Jewel anymore. Her wrists are bruised and swollen from her struggle." Austin reaches down and picks up his medical bag, setting it beside us. "Did the vampire hurt you at all?"

I shake my head. "No, he wasn't out of his mind starving. Just drawn by the noise, I guess. He thought Hayden wanted to trade me for safe passage. I might have told him he could bite me if he broke my chains."

"I bet he wasn't expecting you to break his nose," Diego says. He holds his hand open for me, and I give him a high-five. "I'm proud as hell of you, beautiful. You strategized perfectly."

"He's lucky I didn't pulverize his heart like I did to the dickhead who helped Hayden kidnap me," I murmur. "And that guy was lucky he tasted nasty as eff."

"I love our blood snob," Kingston says, returning into the room. He hands Austin the key to my restraints. "You hungry, Jewel?"

I bob my head. "Starved. Where's Orlando anyway?"

A soft chuckle sounds from somewhere in another part of the house. "Jewel, you're going to make your nutrients match jealous." Orlando peeks his head in, holding Hayden in front of him. "Just give me a few minutes to take care of Mr. Andrei."

I clear my throat. "Orlando, don't kill him."

His eyes flash silver. "Jewel, he took advantage of our situation with Mitchell. He never informed us that his sources gave him fair warning. I think you've given Mr. Andrei far too many chances."

"He's right, babe. Did you know he jeopardized our alliance with the Vaduvas? Samantha lost her shit over Evora giving Diego her blood to help him. That's a breach in contract. If Evora wanted to gain exemption status, she now could."

I frown and rub my hands over my face, my wrists aching with the movement. "Does she want it?"

"Lucky for Diego, no," Kingston says.

Diego groans. "Jewel, I'm sorry. I—"

"No apologizing. Your brothers would have done the same thing. You tried your best," I say. I turn my gaze to Orlando. "But my answer stands. Don't kill him. Ramona and my niece are going to need him."

Austin intakes a sharp breath. "Niece?"

"Yeah, did you know you could learn the sex before birth?" I ask him. "Because I didn't. Hayden told me."

"Babe, there are movies that show the back-world way," Kingston says.

"Movies that cover anything in regards to human conception, or in our girl's words, expanding the donor population, are on the do not watch list," Diego says.

I twist my lips to the side. "So you all knew. You could've told me."

It's Austin's turn to frown. "I just assumed the humans in Red Canyon Crest Grove didn't have that kind of technology. The human health practitioners do check here, but that information is kept confidential with either Donor Life Corp or the household the human is contracted to. They don't pay much attention because the chances of being born male are high, and no one would risk sharing the sex if the fetus were female. They're more desirable."

I groan. "That's not what I wanted to hear." I forgot that vampires call The Orchards something different. Diego once told me that it took power, wealth, and status even to get there. My guys swore that if Brayla went there with my family, she was never coming back, but no one told me exactly why.

Austin takes my hand. "I'm sorry, Jewel. I did offer to teach you and go over human conception, remember?"

I laugh and cover my mouth. I can't help it. "After we had finished having sex."

"Fuck, Austin," Kingston says.

Austin blushes and leans his elbows on his knees. "You don't have to tell me, bro. We were having a heart-to-heart and I wasn't thinking clearly."

I sigh and get to my feet, catching Orlando trying to sneak out of the room with Hayden. "Nu-uh, Orlando. I told you. You're not going to act now and beg me for forgiveness later. I know you all hate the guy. I friggin' hate him too. But the reason he kidnapped me was to get Ramona away from The Orchards."

Orlando releases a soft growl and pushes Hayden forward. He falls flat on his face and doesn't move, trapped under Orlando's mind manipulation. I bet he had planned to use the vampire I killed in Ombre Noire to protect his mind, and I ruined that plan for him.

I startle at Orlando closing the space and sitting me back on the bed before I can realize I no longer stand on my feet. He kneels between my legs, taking my hands into his and holds them against his heart.

"Jewel, I can't see how you alone could've helped him retrieve Ramona from Red Canyon Crest Grove. Whatever he told you, he lied about it," he says.

I close my eyes to shield myself from the intensity of all my guys staring at me. "No, actually. He was quite honest." I pick up and drop the chain. "Hence the restraints. Apparently the Blood Rebels gave up on me and decided to change focus to my future niece. My dad is going to force Ramona to give her up to them to be trained so that she doesn't turn out like me."

Kingston growls and punches the wall, startling Dougie and making him cry. "He's a fucking dead man."

"Kingston, language in front of Dougie," Austin says.

Kingston scrunches his face. "What? I heard Jewel say fuck to him from a mile away."

Austin sighs and takes Dougie from Diego and leaves the room to calm him down. Kingston holds my glare for calling me out on swearing in a moment I thought some asshole vampire was going to hurt us. Diego shoves Kingston toward the door, and Kingston snarls and snaps his teeth at Hayden on the floor.

"Jewel, what you desire to do is dangerous," Orlando says, drawing my attention back to him. "I'd like you to think about what it means. The place your sister resides in is not under the Donor Life Corp territory. It's a place frozen in time between the fall of civilization and the rise of vampires. There is no structure there. No civility. Donor Life Corp doesn't even bother with that unclaimed region because it's not worth the effort. The board thinks that it'll eventually take care of itself."

"Oh," I say. It's the only thing I can think of.

"I don't want to take you there," he says. "Please don't argue. We need to go home, and you need to let us take care of Mr. Andrei. We have other things that take precedence."

Hayden's words from earlier sneak back in my mind, and I can't help wondering if a part of what he said was true. When it comes down to it, do I get a choice? Am I really in a position to ask for one?

I squeeze Orlando's hand. I am. I know I am. "Orlando, no. I don't want to help Hayden, but I want to help my sister. If he thinks trading me could get Ramona out, can't we use that to our advantage? We can set a trap. Get my family and

Brayla back."

Orlando's jaw twitches, and he clenches his teeth. My heart picks up speed as I look at him, waiting for the answer I'm afraid to hear, the answer I'm nearly certain will come to prove Hayden right.

Orlando shakes his head, releasing a groan. My heart falters at his response, but then he says, "You know I have the most difficult time telling you no, Jewel. If this is what you feel we should do, then let's have a coven meeting."

My mouth falls agape. "Really?"

He releases a breathless laugh. "Why do you sound so surprised?"

I throw my arms around him, knocking him back on the bed. Cupping his cheeks in my hands, I lean down and kiss him until he laughs and asks me to show him some mercy because I'm testing his restraint.

I get to my feet and stroll over to Hayden. I nudge him from his stomach and onto his back to peer into his open eyes. "You were wrong about them, you asshole. You hear that? I told you so. They aren't just using me to feed and pleasure them."

Kingston materializes next to me, "He fucking said that?"

I nod.

Kingston kicks Hayden back over to face the floor. "You definitely got that wrong, douchebag. We exist to feed and pleasure our girl, not the other way around."

I raise my hands at him. "Dude."

Kingston chuckles. "What, babe? I'm damn proud of it. Now, come on. We've missed you. Let us take care of you."

My grimace turns into a smile. "Now how could I ever resist that?"

STRONGER

"SHIT! DON'T TOUCH THERE," I say, snatching Diego's hand as he brushes it through my hair to pull it back.

Diego freezes, his eyes widening. "Let me take a look at it, beautiful."

I bring his hand to my mouth and kiss his knuckles. "I'm fine. The bite mark is just really friggin' sensitive."

Kingston tries to shift my hair next. "Babe, if you're in pain—"

I cover Kingston's mouth with my other hand. "I just need more to eat. It's been rough. My nerves are shot. I can't stop thinking about everything that happened. I mean, you guys didn't suspect Asshole Duchanne at all? The Beast was part of his coven. So was Creepo Caruthers."

Diego tugs his shirt off, distracting me. I inhale a small breath and pout, taking in his seriously bruised stomach and chest, still not completely healed from Hayden's attack. "Come here. I think there's a place you can bite on my shoulder. Or I could take my pants off, and you can try something new and bite my thigh."

Kingston shudders. "Fuck, Diego. That's freaky ass shit. You're not nervous she might get carried away?"

Ignoring Kingston, I move onto Diego and hold his face in my hands, straddling his lap. "You are way too injured still."

"Here, let me take care of our girl," Kingston says, scooting closer to Diego to pull me into his lap. "Maybe you can let Diego have at you for a minute."

I extend my arm to Diego. "He's right. Let me feed you. You're probably in so much pain."

"I'm good, beautiful. Austin said not to just yet. He's not certain if you're hiding your pain or actually okay. The fact that you nearly broke my hand when I barely touched your shoulder..."

I gawk at him. "I did not."

Diego lifts his hand and shows off the red handprint over his fingers. "You can't tell me you did this because your skin's only a bit sensitive. Looks like you're getting even stronger."

Tipping my head back, I stare at the ceiling. "Fine, it hurts like hell. Worse than any of the ones I got before. And I have a massive headache. My wrists hurt too. I just—ugh—

Kingston, please give me more blood already. I'm feeling super friggin' bitey. Zombie, not love bites."

Kingston's lips stretch downward as he frowns for a split second at my words. He might actually look a bit nervous. He hesitates, searching my face, and then pulls me back with him to spoon me from behind. The click of his fangs sets me off, and I squirm, now a little bit nervous as well.

"Ah hell, I think Orlando's venom bite broke our girl," Kingston says. "She just got scared."

I shift onto my back. "I'm not scared."

Kingston puffs out his bottom lip in response, grazing it over mine. "It's okay. I can live eternity without ever biting you again, babe. But look, I'm just biting myself. For you." Extending his fangs again, Kingston bites his arm. I must make a face or some shit, because he calls out for Austin and Orlando.

"Here, we can sit up," Kingston says.

I shake my head and pull his arm around me so I can drink from him in his favorite blood exchanging position. My wild heart picks a rhythm to finally stick to, slowing down the longer I drink from Kingston, letting his sweet and spicy blood send tingles down my throat and to my stomach.

I moan softly, sucking harder, feeling tons better the more I drink. Kingston's body awakens against mine, and he somehow manages to hike my dress up enough to rest his flexing bulge between my legs, even with his pants on.

"Austin? Orlando? Come the hell on. One of you better

get your ass in here before Jewel takes my final donation. She's starving." He slides his free hand over my hip, digging in his fingers to rock against me. "And I'm so fucking horny, babe," he whispers into my ear, making me shiver.

I hum my agreement under my breath, reaching behind me to try to touch him.

"Let me stick it in. If I'm sacrificing myself to you, I want to die with a bang."

I squeeze his boner between my thighs, fully considering his request. But then the rest of his words sink in, and I ease myself away from his arm and take a breath. "No going out with a bang. I can't spend eternity without you."

Kingston chuckles. "Thank fucking God."

Orlando appears in the door, followed by Austin, and the two of them stop short to assess what they probably thought would be me latched onto Kingston.

"About time," Kingston says. "I could've been dead already."

I roll my eyes and whack his arm, making him swear. He inwardly growls, the noise nearly inaudible in his throat, just his body reacting to what I'm pretty sure is pain that I caused him. I must have hit his own venom bite. He's quick to compose himself and sits up, motioning to Orlando.

"If you're going to feed our girl, I suggest you face her. You kind of broke her," Kingston says.

I raise my hand to smack his arm again and stop short at the way he tenses. "He didn't break me, and you're totally in pain too. Let me see, dude."

"You're in pain, Jewel?" Austin asks, crossing the room to beat Orlando. Kingston gets up so that Austin can take his place on the bed, and he slowly reaches up to touch my hair to shift it out of the way.

I swat his arm, my body reacting without my permission. Gasping, I cover my mouth with my hand. "Shit, I'm sorry, Austin."

He smirks and shakes out his hand. "I'll be careful. Just let me take a quick look. I won't even touch it."

Cautiously reaching out for my hair, Austin stops short and quickly retracts his hand at my reaction of his fingers getting too close. He looks at his brothers with wide eyes. Diego howls a laugh from my other side, and Kingston gawks at me with furrowed brows. Orlando moves closer, coming up beside Austin.

"She totally growled at you, bro," Kingston says. He turns and punches Orlando in the shoulder. "What the fuck did your do to our girl? That sounded more possessive than painful. I should know."

"There is one way to find out." Austin remains expressionless with the words but looks at Orlando. "You try."

I hold my hands up, palms out. "You guys. Seriously, stop talking about me like a wild animal. I'm fine. I swear. I just need more blood."

"Someone listen to her before she turns into a savage," Kingston says.

Diego gets to his feet and drapes his arm over Kingston's shoulder, forcing him to turn away from me. The two of them whisper too low for me to hear. They break away and look at me, and I narrow my eyes at them, making Kingston release a play growl.

Orlando closes the space to me completely while my attention is on them and reaches for my hair to move it. Again, my body reacts and I swing out, knocking his hand away. Kingston tips his head back and laughs and returns to my side to hook his arm around me.

"It's not possessiveness," Kingston says. "She's just being stubborn. Right, Brat Babe? Now, maybe if one of you would listen to me and satiate that hunger burning in her eyes, she might chill the fuck out."

"Kingston," I say.

Austin extends his fangs, startling me, and I throw myself back on the bed in embarrassment. The four of them suddenly surround me as I lie on the bed, my heart racing, my body tensing even though I don't want anything to do with the crazy ass reaction.

"Told you. Orlando broke her with the venom bite," Kingston says. "Her fear instincts go crazy every time she hears our fangs extend."

No one responds to him, but I can smell Austin's sweet, tangy blood from my spot without even having to look at him. I lick my lips and wiggle my fingers, wanting nothing more than to get the four of them to stop staring at me with pouty as hell faces.

"If you spill any of that blood, Austin..." I warn, the tightness in my chest easing as I meet his gaze.

He smiles at my teasing words and comes closer to lie behind me to cuddle me to him like Kingston had. I moan softly against his arm, reaching behind me to dig my fingers into his hip. Just like with Kingston, I feel his excitement building to press between my legs.

"Jewel," Orlando says softly. "Is there anything else we can do for you? The last thing I ever wanted was for you to fear our bites."

I pull back a bit from Austin's arm to mumble, "I'm not scared." I don't have to look at any of them to know they don't exactly believe me. "I don't know why my body's being dumb."

"I think we just need to remind that sexy ass body of yours that it'll only experience pleasure from our mouths from now on," Kingston says, getting in front of me. He takes my hand and kisses my palm.

"Now's probably not a good time, Kingston," Diego says.

Kingston smiles at me without his fangs. "It's always a good time."

Pulling back from Austin again, I say, "I want you to catch me up on what happened with Mitchell first. That's what you can do for me to help me feel better."

Kingston groans. "That's not what we had in mind on the list of things we could do."

"Please, Kingston. If you tell me, I'll let you try to remind my body," I say, licking my lips. "I'll accept all the distractions." I bring my mouth back to Austin's arm and suck harder, making him moan into my hair.

"Fuck, you heard our girl," Kingston says, rolling away from me to give Orlando space. "Let's get on with it."

Orlando eases on the bed and lies in front of me. His eyes flash silver as he watches me drink from Austin, a longing in his face that sends butterflies fluttering through my stomach. I love the way each of my guys looks at me like they want and need me, like I'm the best thing in the world despite the shit show that seems to follow my existence around.

Orlando gathers my hand between his, leaning in to watch me suck on Austin's arm. "First, before anything else, I need to apologize. I underestimated Mitchell's influence. The danger of an attack should have never gotten so close to you, nor should it have given Mr. Andrei an opportunity to take advantage. I'm sorry our Blood Vow didn't go as expected. This was not how I wanted you to remember it."

My eyes glass over at his words but not because I'm sad for me. I know everyone underplays the meaning behind vampire traditions, and I know Orlando didn't want to make a huge deal over the Blood Vow because he knew I was unhappy that I couldn't publicly accept one from Austin, Kingston, and Diego too. But seeing his frown, gazing into his eyes, I know that it was important for him that everything was perfect to me, and he now thinks he failed.

I ease my mouth from Austin and press my fingers to his puncture wounds to better look at Orlando. "Orlando, all the bullshit that happened is a total blur. You know what I remember the most about the night?"

"Hmm?" he asks, the corner of his lips pulling up slightly.

"How happy you all looked. How relieved I was that we're finally all officially together as a coven," I say. Arching forward, I graze my lips to his and then bring my mouth to his ear. "But I'll remember our moment alone the most. Just thinking about it..." I shiver and sink into him, relaxing as he brings his arms around me.

"That was the best moment of my life too," he murmurs.

I release a small shudder and pull myself away from him. "Now that you said that, I want to know the rest. You nearly succeeded in distracting me."

He chuckles and motions for me to roll over to face Austin. "You can't fault me for trying."

Austin grins at me, grabbing my hands to hold them in his. His green eyes capture mine, and he remains expressionless as I stiffen just a little at the sound of Orlando's fangs clicking. Orlando shifts me up enough to rest his arm under me, and I ignore the ache of my neck as pressure from the position prods at the venom bite.

Frowning, Austin notices my reaction, but he doesn't say anything because I distract myself by sucking on Orlando's arm. Kingston and Diego join the three of us, sitting close to touch me while showing that they're here.

"So, about Mitchell and Mr. Duchanne," Orlando finally says, knowing that I won't let it go. "It seems that Mitchell managed to arrange an alliance with him without us knowing."

"Obviously," I mumble against his arm.

"You know, we had discussed the possibility of repercussions with Ademas, but his region was weak already. Mitchell took advantage and beat us to him, winning him over by revealing that your matches were the ones responsible for the deaths of Roger and Katherine, acting on your behalf. Because he told him, it revealed that I had lied about ending Katherine's life over a possession feud."

I pull away and turn to face him. "You told Mr. Duchanne that you killed Katherine?"

He nods. "It was in my right to do so since she had tried to take you, even if the board didn't recognize you as next in line to fulfill the Jordan blood debt. Kingston, Diego, and Austin did not have the right to end her. The proper thing to do would've been to file a grievance with the board to let them determine whether or not they had the right to end her life." Orlando presses his lips together, hiding them in a thin line. "It's one of the more complex laws of Donor Life Corp to prevent blood feuds and wars between regions and covens."

I shift and sit up to look at my matches. "You guys. Always breaking the rules for me."

Diego grins. "And we wouldn't change a thing."

"Obviously," Kingston murmurs, sliding closer, begging

me with his eyes to show him some attention. "I mean, we're in this piece of shit house with a few Blood Rebels about to do something crazy as hell all for the bitch who I can't even say her name."

I stretch out my arms, wiggling my fingers to him. "We're not doing this for Ramona or Hayden, dude. We're doing this for my niece and cousins. For Brayla. Our family."

"Not to mention our future," Austin says. "Imagine if the rebels actually raised a dhampir? I'd hate to think what would happen."

"Nothing to you. You're my guys. I'd protect you," I say, looking at them.

"We know, beautiful," Diego says.

"I mean, who the fuck else would be brave enough to risk that mouth of yours?" Kingston asks, scooting to lie on top of me between his brothers. "Plus, you're especially badass when you're hungry. I'd feel sorry for anyone who tried to mess with your blood source."

I snap my teeth at him, making him chuckle. "I can't help it. You're mine."

Orlando touches my cheek, drawing my attention to him. "Exactly how we want."

Kingston clears his throat. "So, about the distractions..."

Laughing, I capture Kingston's lips with mine, devouring his affection as his hands map my body to hike up my dress. He shimmies lower, dragging his fingers down my body in a way that leaves me arching up into him.

I shift and reach for Austin, who leans in and kisses me sweetly. "I hope you don't mind, but I need to check on Dougie."

My mouth forms an O. "Uh, yeah. That's fine."

Orlando strokes his fingers across my cheek. "I need to take care of a few things with Mr. Andrei as well, Jewel."

I frown.

Diego bends down and kisses me next. "And I need to sweep the area and prepare the house for sunrise."

Kingston rests his elbows on the outside of my legs. "Will you be okay with just me?"

Smiling, I nod my head. "I love our time together."

"Fuck yeah, me too."

Without even waiting for his brothers to leave, Kingston rips the side of my dress without bothering with the zipper and yanks it off so fast that my body doesn't even move. I tip my head back and laugh.

"Damn," Diego murmurs, glancing at me from over his shoulder. "Have fun, beautiful."

"But take it easy," Austin says, looking more at Kingston.

"Yell out if you need anything," Orlando adds.

Kingston rests his weight on me. "Uh, maybe don't come if it's Jewel who yells out."

Giggling, my face flushing, I grab at the back of Kingston's shirt and pull him higher up to kiss my lips. The door clicks closed, and Kingston brings his mouth to mine to kiss me deep enough to send my heart racing.

"You have no idea how good it sounds to hear you laugh, babe," Kingston says. "I've missed you. We were all going crazy on the way to find you."

"How did you, anyway? I'm not wearing my bracelet," I say, hooking my hands around his neck.

"Your ring," Kingston murmurs. "Your vow necklace too. Ours will have trackers as well. Orlando's already does."

I inhale a small breath. "Should I be worried that you guys feel you need trackers for yourselves?"

He shakes his head and runs his fingers down my stomach and between my legs to touch me through the satin and lace lingerie I had worn under my dress. "No, babe. Just precautions in these uncertain times."

"Okay," I say, sucking his lip into my mouth.

He tugs the fabric of my panties aside and slips his finger gently inside me, just feeling the warmth of my excitement. "Now, no more talking."

"No more talking," I repeat, moaning softly.

"All the touching."

I reach down and hook my fingers to his belt. "All the touching."

Kingston shifts up so I can unfasten his belt and open his pants. He flexes his erection under my fingers as I pull it out without undressing him. I stroke the length of his shaft, playing with him while he plays with me, rubbing his finger in small circles, creating the pressure I love.

Adjusting his body, Kingston spreads my legs wider and

grazes his body to mine, just teasing me without undressing me. I moan, my chest rising and falling with my building desire.

"How badly do you want me?" he asks, shifting my panties to slowly enter me just enough to make me gasp.

"So bad," I whisper, rolling my hips in an attempt to make him sink deeper inside me. "I crave you. I need you."

Kingston slowly shifts his weight, continuing to push inside me. "I need you too, babe. I need to enjoy you, to savor you."

"Kingston." My voice comes out whispery, pleading his name. "Whatever you want."

Meeting me with his midnight eyes, Kingston drinks in my face, his lower lip puffing with his quickening breath. I cup his face and kiss him, sliding my tongue into his mouth to graze over the sharpness of his fangs. He gently nips my tongue, moaning at the taste of my blood igniting desire through him.

I draw my hands down his body, working over the buttons of his dress shirt, and he shrugs out of it to toss to the floor. My fingers explore the muscles of his chest, and I break away to kiss down along his shoulder, flicking my tongue across his skin, shimmying myself lower down his body as he holds himself up over me.

Kingston lets me roll him over, and I yank his pants off so fast that he can't stop the wide ass smile from crossing his face. I drag my fingers down his abs, grazing my nails over every one of his bone-hard muscles until I reach his boxer briefs and hook my fingers along the hem to pull them off.

He tries to grab my hands to pull me on top of him, but I wag my finger and shift his legs so that I can rest between them. Moaning from deep in his throat, Kingston sinks back on the bed, gripping the blankets in his fingers as I glide my tongue over his thigh, tracing my way to his raging boner.

"Jewel," he whispers, my name sounding so incredibly sexy on his lips.

I lace my fingers around him and work my mouth back up and suck, tasting the sweetness of his building excitement. Taking a breath, I open my mouth and inch my way down as far as I can go. Kingston combs his fingers through my hair, massaging my head, moaning more than I've heard him before.

"That feels incredible," he murmurs, his breath gasping. "Let me take care of you too. I need to taste you so bad, Jewel. Please, let me."

I ease my mouth away from him and smile, licking my lips. His mouth hangs slightly open with his heavy breathing, and he reaches for me to kiss my lips. Lying back, Kingston repositions on his side and I lie opposite of him, allowing him to rest his head on my thigh. I gasp as he kisses me between the legs, sucking just hard enough to make me release a loud moan before his tongue caresses over me in circles.

We continue to taste and explore each other with our mouths, Kingston's moans humming between my legs in the most amazing away. I shudder as he builds tingles inside me so crazy good that I ease my mouth away from him to close my eyes and just relish in the sensations. Hooking his hands to my hips, Kingston rolls with me so that I'm on top of him and straddling his head. I lean forward and rest on his hip, unable to stay upright because of the pleasure rolling through me in wave after wave until my muscles tense so hard that Kingston inhales a surprised breath and then chuckles.

"Whoa, fuck. That was awesome," he says under his breath to himself.

"Hmm?" I ask, words unable to come to my lips.

He shifts me off him to smile. "Just you. Delicious. Incredible. That orgasm. Amazing." He wipes his face on the sheet and chuckles again at the confusion puckering my brows. "Come here. I'm desperate to experience that all over again."

This time I laugh as he flips me onto my back and nestles between my legs to sink inside me. He moans as I wrap my body around his, resting my ankles on his sides. I don't know if it was because he was scared of losing me or because he's still amped up from the ceremony and the start of our lives as a new coven, but Kingston's happiness and desire wash over me in waves I want to drown myself in.

Our bodies move in perfect sync, Kingston's motions fast and deep, desperate almost. He grazes his mouth to my throat and whispers how he can't ever get enough of me in my ear. The old bed creaks with our movements, hitting the wall in loud thumps. I moan in bursts with his thrusts until he gasps and stays in me as he finishes.

We lie together for a long while, our bodies entwined, our hearts crashing together. It's not until soft voices grow in volume through the wall that I shift myself away to stare at the door.

"Fucking Hayden," Kingston mutters under his breath. "Come here, babe. You should ignore them and try to get some sleep."

But I can't ignore the commotion.

Neither can Kingston.

The door flies open, crashing off its hinges, and I screech out as a body hits the floor.

DONOR TRADING

KINGSTON TUGS THE BLANKETS OVER us, pressing me into the bed so I can't move or see anything that goes on. A strange growl sounds through the room, igniting my fear instincts, and I cling onto Kingston and bury my face into the crook of his neck.

"Get up and face me," Orlando says, his deep, threatening voice booming through the small room. "You will be held accountable for illegally trading protection for donors."

"I'm unregistered. You can't do shit," a guy says. "I don't need Donor Life Corp's handouts."

"So you have more donors," Austin says, his voice remaining even. "Acquiring donors and imprisoning them without work contracts, personal donation contracts, or blood debts is prohibited regardless of whether or not you're regis-tered and receive blood benefits from Donor Life Corp."

"Fuck you. My donors fall into fair trade. They're not unwilling. The rebels find it honorable to volunteer. They choose to come with me so that their people can have safe pas-sage through the groves."

"And what about the donor you came for tonight. The female?" Orlando asks.

The unfamiliar vampire releases a strange ass noise that makes me shudder under Kingston. "Hayden said she was willing. That she liked vampires. Loved being bitten. And if he lied, I'm sure I could've convinced her otherwise."

"Ugh," I say, digging my fingers into Kingston's shoul-ders. "Is he talking about me?"

"She's here," the vampire says. "Hayden made a deal with me. The female is mine. If you don't give her over, my coven will—"

Another crash sounds out, followed by a yell, and then utter silence.

I inhale a deep breath near Kingston's ear, my body war-ring with itself between wanting to suck in another deep breath of the weirdly inviting scent trickling through the sheets, even stronger than Kingston's sweet skin, and the part of me that wants to curl in on myself and hide.

"Kingston, you and Jewel should get cleaned up and dressed. If this guy has a coven nearby and they're involved in donor trading, then they'll come looking for this asshole," Diego says.

Kingston gets off me and stands up, not even caring that he's naked. I hold the sheet to me and gaze around the room, but Austin steps in the way and closes the space to block my view of what I'm certain is a bloody body.

"I brought you something for the pain of the bite," he says, pulling a tube of cream from his pocket. "May I carry you to the bathroom and clean it?"

I barely get a chance to nod before Austin scoops me up in the sheet and kisses me the whole way across the room and into the hallway where the small, dingy bathroom is located in the middle of the rundown house.

"There's hot water," Austin says, turning on the shower. "We assume this house is used as a meeting point for rebels traveling between cities."

"I can't believe rebels just trade themselves," I say, peering at the closed door. "They hate vampires."

Austin purses his lips. "People do what they feel is necessary, especially regarding their families. Look at you."

He's right. If my cousins were in danger, I'd trade myself for them. I practically did with the Blood Match Program. But that was different. These vampires, helping the humans, they seem to be lawless and disregarding of Donor Life Corp. I guess they'd be considered rebel vampires. Orlando was one before he established his position.

I take a small breath, trying not to let the complexity of the world get to me. Because no matter how hard I try, I'll never learn about all of it. I'll always have questions about life outside of Dark Terrace Ranch.

"I guess so," I say way too late.

Austin leans in and kisses me, touching my hair to brush it away from my tender neck. I tense, my body reacting, and he pulls his hand away without touching me.

"Why don't you move your hair so that I can take a look at the bite?" Austin says, smirking at me.

I puff out my bottom lip, dimpling my chin. "I don't want to. It's gross."

"Will you show me yours if I show you mine?" he asks, rolling up his sleeve.

Kingston groans as he opens the bathroom door, squeezing inside with us. "Don't you dare ruin that game for me and Jewel."

I tip my head back and laugh. "He's right. I'd much prefer to see something...sexier."

Kingston raises an eyebrow. "Babe, I have nothing left to take off. I'm showing you everything."

I stick out my tongue. "Not you. Him."

Groaning, Kingston turns and laces his fingers behind his head. "I fucking love when you get all playful, Jewel. Austin, just do what our girl wants."

Austin chuckles and unbuttons his shirt, slowly teasing me by showing a little bit of his chest and abs first. I try to grab him to help him along, but he steps back. I giggle, full-on giggle, when he tosses his shirt on my head.

I clap, bouncing on the sink. "You guys crack me up."

I absently comb my fingers through my hair, playing with it, and Austin rushes closer. He links my hands with his, catching me off guard. I realize I moved my hair for him to see the bite mark, and he totally took advantage of the situation.

"Not fair," I say, drooping my shoulders.

"All's fair in taking care of our girl," Kingston says, stepping closer to clasp my arms. "Especially because you're stubborn as hell."

Austin gently runs his cool finger over the skin around the venom bite, and I do my best to remain still. "I'm going to apply the cream now. It will numb it, but I think we need to keep an eye on it. It looks worse than the last time you were bitten with venom."

"She said it hurts way worse too. Diego thinks she's stronger."

"I wish I could ask Brayla how hers was," I murmur. Orlando did transform her. I might not transform into a vampire, but I'd think the effects would be similar.

Austin turns his arm over, palm up. "Here, you can look at mine for comparison."

I suck in air through my teeth, twisting to look at my reflection in the mirror. Austin hangs his arm over my shoulder so that I can get a look at his and mine together. Mine is worse. Much worse.

"I'm actually kind of surprised you're conscious," Kingston says. "Last time, you were out for days."

Austin slides his other arm over my chest, snuggling his cool chest to my back. "Because we all bit her. There might be new side effects too. Orlando's venom is strong."

"I did black out, and I'm really friggin' exhausted now, but I just—I don't know. It's like my senses won't stop going crazy. My body says nope to the whole succumbing to weakness thing." I turn back around to face Kingston and Austin directly. "Doesn't help that this house sucks."

"Well, why don't you and I go lie down for a bit?" Austin says. "Kingston's shift is over."

"Shift?" I ask. "You make me sound like a job."

Kingston pokes my nose. "One I want to work over and over again. And technically, it's Austin's shift that's over. We're rotating guarding the premises. I should've slept while I was with you, but...who are we kidding? Being with you is a constant adrenaline rush, though Austin could use the rest."

Austin smirks, shaking his head. "I switched with Diego. He needs the rest."

"Can I feed him yet?" I ask, pursing my lips.

"You sure you're up to it?" Austin's eyes search mine, and he holds my hand up, drawing soft circles over my skin.

I nod. "I need to take care of him. He's so injured."

"In pain too," Kingston adds. "But don't tell him we told you."

"He knows he can't hide it from me," I say.

Austin touches my cheek before leaning in to brush his lips to mine. "Have we told you we loved you in the last ten minutes?”

“It’s been eleven.”

He chuckles. “Let me grab my kit. I’ll meet you in the room.”

I press my hands to his chest and push him back. “I’m good, Austin. I got this.”

“Jewel,” Kingston says, his eyebrows lowering. “You reacted to—”

I pat his cheek and slide around him. “I said I got this.”

The two of them look at each other, remaining expressionless. “All right, babe,” Kingston says. “Make sure you try to get some sleep too. It might be a crazy ass journey.”

Twisting my lips, I sigh. “That always seems to be the case.”

“See, I told you I had it,” I say, lifting my hair to show off Diego’s bite mark on his favorite spot on my shoulder.

Diego grins, proud as all get-out that I practically attacked him with my mouth the second I saw him lying on the bed waiting for me. It was almost like the first time we bit each other all over again, my body reminding me that my guys may bite but the most amazing sensations come with it.

“Looks like Diego had you too,” Kingston quips. “Pretty sure that mark is worse than the venom bite, Savage Babe.”

Warmth blossoms in my face, and Diego closes the space to Kingston and hooks him in a headlock while punching his stomach. The two of them blur in a play fight, and I screech and rush out of the way before one of them accidentally knocks me on my ass. Orlando spins me off my feet, and I wrap my arms around him, burying my face in the crook of his neck.

"I think we're ready to relocate," Orlando says, adjusting my body so that I wrap my legs around his waist.

Kingston and Diego stop fighting and close the space to us. Austin appears in the doorway with Dougie propped on his hip. I frown at the sight of Mrs. Diggs, Hayden, and Mr. Barton sitting on the floor against the wall, just staring at nothing. It's eerie to see them still under mind manipulation.

"Do you have to keep them like that?" I ask, strolling forward.

"It's easier," Orlando says, leaning back to lock his gaze to mine. "I know it upsets you, but Hayden will fight, Mr. Barton wants nothing more than to yell, and Brayla's Mom is quite the gossip. They're not in any pain."

I open my mouth to argue and then think best of it. "Okay."

Kingston releases a dramatic gasp. "What? No Brat Babe?"

I roll my eyes. "I made you a promise that we come first. I know you guys already have hesitations about going through with this, and I have no friggin' clue about what we're getting into, so...you guys are in charge. I trust you."

"Thank you, Jewel," Orlando says, interrupting whatever Kingston was going to say. "We won't let you down."

"I kn—"

The sound of tires crunching on asphalt draws my attention from Orlando. Spinning, he tosses me to Diego, who silences any sort of noise I make by pressing my head into his shoulder. I get my shit together to stop from yelling out, and Austin materializes in front of me and hands Dougie over for me to tuck between mine and Diego's bodies.

"Must be the coven of the douche who thought he could have our girl," Kingston says, sliding a knife from beneath his jacket. "What do you want to do, brothers? Sounds like five of them. No, four. One human."

"Don't attack first," Diego says, adjusting his arms around me. "If they're way out here, there might be something they want. If they accept donors in exchange for safe passage through the grove, they know the area. We could use them."

"Mr. Andrei," a masculine voice calls. "It would be in your best interest to show yourself."

My guys glance to one another and to Hayden in the hallway. Orlando clears his throat and disappears with Kingston behind him. Austin remains with the rebels, guarding the door. Diego situates me near the wall, using his body as a block so if someone enters they won't have a clear view.

"I'm afraid Mr. Andrei can't respond to you." Orlando's voice trickles to me, remaining even. "And if you're looking for your coven brother, I'm sorry to say he's been found guilty of trading donors and was decapitated under Donor Life Corp law. File his death within the Bellamy Region and his estate will be properly divided and transferred."

"Huntington is dead?" the same masculine voice who called for Hayden asks.

I stiffen, expecting to hear a helluva fight but laughter bursts out.

"What did I tell you, Paris? Huntington was a fucking idiot. I told you he'd get in over his head with the rebels. And what did he get for it? A few donors he couldn't even keep alive," another vampire says.

"Brother, show some respect," the vampire, who I think must be Paris, says.

"Fuck no. Look at the mess he left us with. He refused to even register so all of his shit will go to waste. We can't even keep this donor because he's a kid."

Another vampire sighs. "We were never going to."

"But—"

"He's fifteen," Paris snaps.

"I'll be sixteen next month," a familiar voice says.

I suck in a small breath and jerk my head to face Diego. I can't believe I recognize the voice. I for sure thought Raul was taken by outcast vampires or dead. We found his brother's body among the destruction left behind by Mitchell when he attacked the Blood Rebels and started a war.

"Damn it," Kingston says, speaking up for the first time, stopping whatever the other strange vampires were about to say to Raul. "Jewel heard him."

"Jewel?" Paris asks. "Isn't that the female donor Huntington went on and on about?"

"I think so," the other guy says.

All four of my guys growl in unison at the sound of my name on someone else's mouth. I wiggle in Diego's arms until he puts me down and hand Dougie to him so that I can leave the room.

I clear my throat and channel my best Vaduva impression. "Lover, no need to take offense. I'm sure this coven had no idea Mr. Andrei took advantage of the Divine attack to kidnap me from our Blood Vow ceremony."

Austin tries to block my way to stop me from heading to the living room where I can hear the strange vampires listening to my approach.

Orlando sighs. "Brother, it's okay. Let Jewel meet the..."

"Mercy Coven of Shadow Hill Pointe. I'm Paris Mercy," he, who I assume is the coven leader, says. "These are my brothers Angel, Dallas, and Rio."

I hover in the archway to the living room and freeze as way too many gazes lock onto me. And while I'm glad I'm not wearing the bloody dress Kingston ripped off me, I wish I was wearing more than Diego's long shirt tied with a knot on the small of my back to cinch the waist.

A ruggedly attractive vampire with dark skin, cropped hair, and a neatly trimmed beard materializes in front of me. I half expect all my guys to throw themselves in my direction to tear him apart for invading my space, but Austin only presses his chest to my back.

"You must be the enchanting Jewel." The vampire smiles, showing off his straight white teeth before flashing his fangs. "It's a pleasure to meet the infamous donor responsible for breaking the Divine power."

I remain expressionless though keep my gaze trained on him. "Former donor."

He extends his hand out, and I cautiously allow him to take mine to kiss the back. "My apologies, Ms. Ortega. A newly transformed vampire still carries a semblance of humanity that misleads one's judgment."

Trailing his gaze away from my eyes and the rest of me, Paris studies me way too friggin' hard for comfort. I brace myself to have him ask me to bare my fangs or some shit. The only thing that stops me from fidgeting with nerves is the fact that even if I mess up, it won't be a huge deal. My guys will assure no one leaves here to tell the world I'm a fake.

"It's *Mrs.* Ortega as my precious Jewel accepted my Blood Vow with a promise of love," Orlando says, breaking from his position standing between the rest of the Mercy brothers and me and Austin. "And if you'll excuse us, we will be taking the rebels and going. My Jewel is still recovering from her transition."

"And starving," the buff as all get-out vampire next to Kingston says. He smirks at me, his hazel eyes crinkling in the corners. "You know, we won't tell if you suddenly want a snack. The kid would deserve it for—"

"Shut it, Angel," Paris snaps.

"You guys are dumb motherfuckers." Raul's sharp tone jerks my attention to him. He balls his fingers into fists, scowling like he'll attempt to fight the room full of vampires even though he knows he'll lose.

Paris disappears from in front of me and smashes Raul's back into the wall. "Give me one good reason I shouldn't rip your throat out."

"Because I know something that might interest you," Raul says.

Kingston moves to try to rip Raul from Paris, but the rest of the Mercy Coven cuts him off. Orlando holds up his hand to stop Austin from joining Kingston. Diego looks about ready to toss Dougie to me as well.

"We're listening," Paris says.

Raul curls his lips. "Jewel doesn't drink donor blood."

Shit. Shit. Shit. A friggin' lunatic teenage boy who only has had asshole Hayden as a role model is about to blow my act.

"You're right, little man," Kingston says. "She's a worse blood snob than I am."

"Fuck off. That's not what I meant." Raul thrashes in Paris's hold. "She craves you."

Kingston remains expressionless. "Can you blame her? Look at me. OG Body Match."

My cheeks burn, and I say, "Dude, knock it off."

That makes the Mercy brothers laugh.

Paris gets into Raul's face and locks him in his gaze. Raul slackens in his arms, trapped under the influence of Paris's mind manipulation. "Don't speak. Don't scream. Just sleep."

Raul closes his eyes, his mind unable to resist Paris's control, and the vampire drops him to the floor and turns to look at me. "This is why I don't like dealing with Blood Rebels. My brother Huntington had this wild idea that running with rebels was some kind of game. He was addicted to havoc. Sometimes untamed."

"And a fucking piece of work," the dark blond vampire says, pushing his long tresses back.

"So right, Dallas," the last brother with black hair and deep tan skin says. "I knew we should've cast him to the shadows after the accident."

"Accident?" I ask, finding myself engrossed in their conversation.

Orlando slides his hand around my waist and spins me. "Excuse us for a moment, please."

Diego hands me Dougie as Orlando guides me by him and leads me down the hallway and back to the room. I adjust the sleeping little guy on my shoulder. I'm kind of surprised that none of the Mercy brothers questioned why we're babysitting a toddler, and I wonder if it has something to do with the fact that vampires know better than to pay attention to kids. Raul is almost an adult and annoying as hell so that he would fall in the who-knew-he-was-underage category.

"Jewel, your curiosity is getting the best of you," Orlando

whispers. "I must ask you not to engage or open up any more lines of conversation. We don't have an alliance to this coven."

"Oh," I say. "Sorry if I was trying to gather as much intel as possible to use to our advantage."

He chuckles and shakes his head. "If that's what you say. But please, keep in mind that we have to be careful."

I purse my lips. "Fine. I still don't think it would hurt to find out about what kind of accident dead douchebag was involved in."

Orlando surprises me with a hug, lifting me off my feet to spin me around once. I laugh at the speed and hold him tighter, knowing it's what he wants. "If finding out will satiate that dangerous curiosity of yours, then I suppose you can ask."

I comb my fingers through his hair and smile. "I thought you'd tell me no a lot more than you have, you know."

"Those blue eyes and pouty mouth make it impossible now that I know you're mine."

I frown. "Yours? Orlando, you know you can't claim me like that."

His eyes flash silver, and he takes a small breath. "Forgive me, Jewel. You make it easy to forget how you share your love so freely when we're alone."

I nod and slide out of his arms, just holding my hands to his neck. "I hope you always feel that way. I don't ever want you guys to feel like you only get a part of me."

A strange noise sounds through the air, drawing our attention to the bedroom door. Orlando spins me around, placing me against the wall with Dougie to block us. The ground shakes under my feet, startling me, and Dougie starts crying in my arms.

"What was that?" I ask, cradling Dougie, trying to get him to be quiet.

Orlando doesn't have a chance to respond. The door flies open, and Paris charges in the room, carrying Raul on his shoulder. He drops him to the floor and rushes to meet his brother Angel to grab Mrs. Diggs from him. Diego slides past them with Hayden in his arms, and Kingston lugs in Mr. Barton by the back of his shirt.

My heart rams against my ribcage, fear stealing my breath, my fear instincts going crazy. I grip the back of Orlando's shirt as the house shakes again.

"He found us," I say, my voice barely coming out a whisper.

"Who is she talking about?" the blond vampire, Dallas, asks.

I lick my lips, the panic growing more intense. I'd recognize the cause anywhere. "How did he find us?" I ignore Dallas's question.

Orlando grabs me and spins me away from the wall, setting me in the middle of the room. He tugs out a dagger from beneath his jacket and glances over his shoulder at Diego, Kingston, and Austin.

"It seems the board failed," Orlando says, tightening his jaw.

I clutch Dougie against me. "What do you mean?"

"If Mitchell's here, then the board lost." He keeps his voice even.

"I thought you were handling it." My voice quivers, and I brace myself through another round of ground-shaking trembles.

"We left to come after you, babe," Kingston says.

I groan and snuggle my face into Dougie. He's as scared as I am, and he doesn't even know why. "What do we do?"

"Our priority is to take care of you," Orlando says.

"Fucking Huntington," Angel mutters from behind me. "Of course he managed to drag us into a blood feud even after death."

"You guys are free to go. If you feel you must surrender to the last Divine, we will give you a head start," Orlando says to the Mercy brothers.

The four of them look at each other, their eyes flashing silver, weapons already drawn.

But none of them get to respond.

I don't even get a chance to react.

The house shakes hard enough to knock me back into Austin's arms, and the ceiling collapses.

MERCY BROTHERS

"JEWEL!" KINGSTON CALLS, HIS VOICE breaking through the ringing in my ears.

"I got her," Austin says, releasing a growl. "But I need help."

I blink the stars from my vision and peer through the dust clouding the air. Austin stands hunched above me, bearing the weight of a huge beam on his shoulders. Dougie's strangled cough, followed by a wail, startles me, and I roll on my side and see him sitting up next to me. Dirt clings to the both of us, the air hard to breathe.

"Sh-shit balls." With my words, I cough so hard that I gag, tasting the dust coating my tongue. I stretch my arms out and pull Dougie closer, curling my body around his to protect him from the debris raining down as Austin struggles to keep the section of the roof off of us.

"Jewel, don't panic," Austin says. "Pull the shirt over your face. Breathe slow and easy."

I adjust Dougie to tuck him under my shirt and pull the neckline over my face. Being close and cocooned against me settles the little guy down enough that I finally manage to hear the murmur of voices as his wails dissipate.

"That's good. Just like that, Jewel," Austin says, grunting while tightening his jaw. He sweeps his gaze over the rest of me, trying to assess if I was hurt or not.

"Ki-Kingston," I say, swallowing the burning in my throat.

"Almost there, babe," he says. Something crashes, startling me, and more dust and drywall rains across me.

"Diego? Orlando?" I call. "You guys okay?"

Silence greets me, sending panic through my chest. I dart my gaze to Austin, and he closes his eyes, listening to something I can't hear over the pounding of our hearts. A few growls sound through the air. I tighten my jaw and hold Dougie close.

"Shit," Kingston mutters. Something crashes again.

"Need a hand?" Angel asks from somewhere to my right.

"Yeah, Jewel and Austin didn't make it out," Kingston says. "Can you help me clear this? I think they're here."

I listen to the thuds of Kingston and Angel shifting debris out of the way. A hand touches my back, surprising me, and I swing my arm only to have someone yank me and Dougie away from Austin. Crisp air engulfs me, and I tug the shirt from my face and gasp a fresh breath.

A loud boom echoes out, and I jerk my attention to the house, watching it cave in. Fear clenches my chest, but before I can scream out for Austin, he bends over me and touches my cheek, combing my dirty hair from my face.

Austin kisses my trembling mouth, pulling me into his lap. He quickly pulls Dougie from my shirt and sets him on my lap, examining him the best he can in the dark. "I need you to try to keep him as quiet as possible."

I nod my head. "What happened? Where are Diego and Orlando?"

Austin points his finger, and I turn in the direction to see blurring figures rushing around in a fight. "Mitchell's brought the fight to us."

I groan. "Damn it."

"Come on, Austin. We gotta move," Kingston says. "We lost sight of Mitchell. He wasn't expecting us to be with another coven."

"You're welcome," Angel says, dusting off his pants.

"Yeah, yeah," Kingston says. "You'll be rewarded and all that bullshit."

A soft plea for help trickles through the air, and the three of us turn our attention back to the house. I gasp in a breath at the realization that I don't see any of the rebels. They are all still in the rubble.

"Oh, no. Mrs. Diggs," I say, pushing to my feet. Kingston wraps his arm around my waist, supporting me as I find my footing. "Kingston, we need to help them."

"No, Mrs. Ortega. We need to go before Divine returns with a better thought out plan of attack," Angel says, stepping to block my way back to the house.

I glower at him. "You want me to leave them?"

Angel flashes his fangs. "They're fucking rebels. Useless."

Kingston groans and holds me tighter. "Back the fuck up, man. Jewel's a wild one when someone pisses her off. Unless you hate living, I suggest you move."

Angel hesitates, trying to decide if he's going to stand his ground against me, but something in my expression gets him to step out of my way. Probably the look of murder in my eyes. If Kingston wasn't clutching me, I'm pretty friggin' sure my body would've reacted before my mind had a chance to catch up.

"Control yourself, babe," Kingston whispers. "If you rip that guy's heart out, they could decide to trade sides and aid Mitchell. We already killed one of their brothers."

I dig my nails into the palms of my hands.

"Luckily my least favorite," Angel calls, still too close that he can hear.

I whip my head and glance at him. "You're welcome."

That makes him chuckle, and Kingston relaxes his hold on me a bit. We stand just outside the house and peer at the mess of wood, concrete, and drywall. The putrid smell of burning tickles my nose, but the house doesn't smolder. Someone must've put out the flames caused by the small explosion.

"Careful, Jewel," Kingston says, stepping into the debris. "Austin will kill me if you so much as break a nail. He's barely keeping himself together."

I swivel and look at Austin, who watches us intently from his spot on the ground, rocking Dougie in his arms. He tightens his lips, his eyes flashing crazy silver. Kingston's right. He looks fully prepared to rush to my side to snatch me away at any second.

"Fucking damn it." Hayden's low words sound through the rubble, drawing my attention.

"The blast must've shocked him enough to break the mind manipulation," Kingston says.

"Someone get me the hell out of here," Hayden calls. "I know you hear me."

Kingston stops in his place and turns to me. "Babe, please don't make me help him."

I sigh and comb my fingers through my hair. "What if we work on finding the others first?"

Narrowing his eyes at me, Kingston locks me in his gaze, considering my suggestion. "Fucking fine."

"Hayden," I call. "Do you see the others? Are they with you?"

"Raul and Miles. But they're both dead," Hayden responds.

I crinkle my nose and pout at Kingston. And now I'm friggin' pissed. "This is your damn fault, Hayden."

"You don't think I know that?" he asks, coughing. "I should've never recruited him and his brother. They'd still be alive if I hadn't. But I won't take blame for Miles. He's the fucking one who brought Mitchell here. I see the damn tracker on his wrist. He—"

"Shit, don't look, babe," Kingston says, cutting Hayden's rant off.

Kingston's not fast enough to cover my eyes before I see a head of blond hair face down under a heavy ceiling beam. My chest tightens, and I cover my mouth with my hand. My body acts, my mind unable to catch up, and I rush forward and drop to my knees next to Mrs. Diggs. My fear pushes my body to gather all my strength, and I lift the beam and drop it next to Mrs. Diggs, creating a cloud of dust.

"Mrs. Diggs," I say, my breath gasping. "Mrs. Diggs, can you hear me?"

I roll her over and release a strangled cry. Kingston scoops me off my feet and relocates me so fast that my head spins. Clutching my knees, I heave, my stomach clenching. Kingston rubs his hand on my back, leaning closer.

"Deep breaths. Don't throw up. Vampires don't get sick," he whispers.

Dropping to my knees, I curl in on myself. "I don't friggin' care. Mrs. Diggs is dead. She's dead!"

Kingston gets on the ground behind me and molds his

body to mine, just holding me as I try to grasp what the hell is happening to my life. The last few months have been out of control and uncertain. Mrs. Diggs has been questionable. But it doesn't change the fact that I grew up knowing her. That she took care of my cousins in Haven Springs. How she and my mom were friends. God, she's Brayla's mom. How the hell will I tell her that we let this happen? What about Dougie? Shit.

"Babe, I'm so sorry," Kingston whispers. He clutches my hands, hugging me tight against him even though he shouldn't.

"Jewel," Austin whispers, sitting down in front of me. "We're going to make him pay. We will avenge everyone he hurt in your life."

I sniffle, trying to suppress my sobs. "I just want the fighting to stop. I don't want anyone else to get hurt."

Austin shifts Dougie so that he can reach out and graze his fingers to my cheek. "I know, and we're going to do our best."

Growls and yells drag my attention away from my grief, and Kingston lifts me to my feet to hug me in his arms. He spins to assess the situation, and I catch sight of Diego cutting off a vampire that flies in our direction. Yanking the back of his shirt, Diego throws the guy into the air. A figure blurs under the snarling vampire, and a moment later, his head splits from his body to roll across the dirt.

"Hell yeah!" Diego says, high-fiving Orlando.

The two of them stop short, their smiles fading the second they look at me in Kingston's arms. Diego closes the space first and gathers me to him, taking me from Kingston. He searches my face, trying to decipher what happened without me having to say the words.

"Finally." Hayden's voice ignites rage inside me, and I thrust away from Diego and charge him as he stands next to Angel, who took over in pulling him from the debris.

Hayden doesn't get a chance to react, and I collide into him, knocking him back into the rubble. He gasps, his eyes widening, and he attempts to shove me off him, but I pin him down. Swinging my arm, I punch him in the face, jerking his head to the side. Blood peppers the ground next to him from a cut on his lip. Just the sight of it sets me off even more, because there isn't enough of it. I can't stop the desire to spill more as it rages through me.

A strong hand locks onto my wrist, stopping me from socking Hayden again with my crazy strength. Orlando drags me back, and I kick and flail, screaming so loud that he slaps a hand over my mouth. I bite him in response, making him release me.

For the first time in a long time, I crash hard to the floor, no one breaking my fall.

"Someone, restrain her," Orlando snaps, shaking out his bleeding hand.

I push to my feet, fisting my fingers. The edges of my vision shadow, and I spin around, attempting to go after Hayden again despite Orlando standing in front of him.

"Kill him!" I yell. "I want you to kill him!"

Kingston slides his arms around me and drags me away from Orlando and Hayden. Instead of covering my mouth with his hand to shut me up, he spins me and presses his lips to mine in an attempt to steal my voice away.

I gasp in surprise, the shock of his gesture bunching my nerves because I feel the weight of too many intense gazes locked on us. "Kingston, my vow."

"I don't fucking care. I'm not going to pretend we aren't madly in love while you lose your shit," he says, clutching me, forcing me to focus on him. "You're my babe." His claim on me settles my nerves, turning me ultra-aware of our surroundings.

"Dude."

"What? Orlando tested it on you earlier. Plus, you are *my* babe. I'm *your* dude." He kisses me again, sliding his hands to my ass to get me to wrap my body around his.

Austin appears behind Kingston and closes the space. "Good work, bro. She's calming down."

The second Dougie wiggles in Austin's arms to look at me, my eyes water all over again. Kingston swears and kisses me a dozen more times. It takes Diego touching my back to get us to pull apart. He offers me a smile, though his eyes don't light up with the gesture.

"We gotta move. It's not safe," he says to me and Kingston. "More outcasts are gathering, waiting for Mitchell." He motions toward the endless stretch of dirt where I spot a dozen vampires closing in on each other to form a group.

I groan. "Fuck. Can't you guys just kill them all?"

"We could, but we need to contact the board and find out what we're dealing with," Orlando says, drawing my attention to him. "We need to strategize accordingly."

"What you need is our help," Hayden says. His voice drags all sorts of fury from me all over again.

"Babe, chill," Kingston says, pinching my ass.

I startle in his arms. "I thought you wanted him dead. I'm giving you permission to kill him now."

Kingston purrs deep in his throat, his hard features softening with a smile. "That's the sexiest thing you've ever said to me."

"Don't make me beg," I say, locking my gaze to his.

"Fucking fine." He tosses me to Diego, making me screech. "You're a dead man, Hayden."

Orlando cuts him off, stopping him from getting within a foot of Hayden. The two of them bare their fangs at each other, but Kingston backs off.

He returns to my side. "Sorry, babe. Be mad at Orlando for denying you what you want."

I huff a breath and turn to Orlando. "Seriously? You're going to let him live? After everything?"

Orlando tightens his jaw and struts closer. I cross my arms over my chest, not giving him the chance to hold my hands, though he looks ready to try anyway. But Kingston stands close, glaring at Orlando as hard as I am.

"Jewel, I want to. I do. But I don't think you mean what you say," he says, rubbing his hand over the sides of his face.

"Yes, I do," I snap.

"Seriously, Jewel?" Hayden asks.

Austin materializes in front of Hayden, startling him with a deep ass growl. Diego intervenes and pulls Austin back before he loses control and murders Hayden on my behalf with Dougie in his arms.

"Maybe give me Dougie," Diego says quietly to Austin.

Austin shakes his head. "No. Holding him is the only way I can assure he's safe."

Diego glances at me, and I nod that it's okay. Dougie is probably the safest one in this moment in Austin's arms. I know he'd never allow anything to happen to the little guy. Austin comes to my side and stands close enough to touch, so I rest my chin on his shoulder, using him to anchor me in place as Hayden steps closer, keeping his hand near the weapon on his belt.

"Everyone good?" Orlando says, keeping his eyes trained on me.

"Yeah," I say. "For now. But what's the plan?"

Orlando turns his attention to the silent Mercy brothers, who stand tense and ready to fight any nearby threats. "Mr. Mercy has kindly offered his knowledge of the area to help us get where we need to go."

"And where's that?" I ask, bouncing on my feet.

"To Red Canyon Crest Grove," Orlando says. "Just like we planned."

My brows pucker with my frown, and I dig my chin deeper into Austin's shoulder. "What about Mitchell?"

"I've decided to take Mr. Andrei up on his offer. If he stays good on his word and aids us with the help of his people, we'll assure your future niece's safety," Orlando says, looking at Hayden.

Hayden nods. "I swear."

Stepping around Austin, I close the space to Hayden. "If you betray us, I will kill you myself."

"I won't," Hayden says.

Kingston takes my hand and pulls me close. He bares his fangs at Hayden. "For Jewel's sake, I hope you're fucking right."

REBEL VAMPIRE

"THIS IS AS FAR AS we go," Paris says, coming to a stop about a hundred feet away from a giant ass wall that cuts right through the middle of a grove of various fruits. Haven Springs's orchards can't even compare to this area. It was the strangest thing to go from a desolate wasteland to this place, thriving with enough fruit to feed everyone in Dark Terrace Ranch and then some.

Dallas rocks on his heels, staring at the wall. "If you travel a few miles south along the wall, you'll come to one of the entrances. Be careful, though. There are no Donor Life Corp allies around here. Trust no one. Everyone fights to kill regardless of being human or vampire unless you know someone. Huntington happened to...have history with a rebel nest.

If you can find a guy named Newport, tell him you know Huntington but don't tell him he's dead."

"The accident," I say, drawing the Mercy brothers' attention to me. "Was Huntington a Blood Rebel?"

None of them has to say anything for me to know that he was. Unlike my guys, this coven doesn't mask their feelings as much.

"He was a shithead with a death wish," Rio, the quietest of the brothers, says. "But yes, he was a rebel. Transformed only a few years ago by the outcast who exchanged blood for blood to some donors. The rebels had the guy convinced that transforming Huntington would elevate his power, but the rebels tricked the both of them, intending to grow their own vampire blood supply. Paris found Huntington chained up during a sweep—we work for the Bellamy Coven—and felt bad."

"He insisted we take the asshole in," Angel says. "Proved to be a huge fucking mistake."

Paris sighs and runs his fingers over his cropped hair. "Yeah, yeah. You didn't complain when he had rebels lining up to be personal donors."

Angel shrugs. "Can't complain about giving up gen. pop."

Footsteps sound from deep within the grove behind us. Fear claws through me, my instincts going off like crazy. I automatically reach for Austin and Dougie, my hands trembling as I step closer to slide under Austin's arm.

"Our girl senses trouble," Austin says, drawing everyone's attention away from the trees and back to me.

Rio makes a weird noise in his throat. "You guys keep saying that. Claiming her. I thought she accepted a vow from him." He motions to Orlando.

"I made a vow to all of them." I can't stop the words from tumbling from my mouth.

Angel raises his brow. "Interesting."

"Perhaps the infrastructure of our coven is none of your business," Orlando says.

None of the Mercy brothers have a chance to respond, the shuffling of feet growing louder as the people head in our direction.

"Sounds like three people. Too quiet to be human. Probably outcasts looking for donors trying to pass through the grove unprotected. They hang out around here because they know Donor Life Corp doesn't give a shit about this region," Dallas says.

"We'll head them off," Paris says, turning to Orlando. "They're wild as hell out here."

Orlando shakes Paris's hand. "Thank you."

Paris nods. "I'll reach out to Brock Bellamy again."

Because no one responded from the board. A part of me knows that Orlando might've been right and that their plan really did fail. What that means for Donor Life Corp and the rest of humanity? I have no idea.

"Your help will not be forgotten nor will it go unrewarded," Orlando says.

The four Mercy brothers disappear without so much as a goodbye, vanishing seemingly into thin air. Diego motions for me to get onto his back, and Kingston helps me up, sandwiching me to his brother for a moment like he can push his strength into my body if he tries hard enough.

"You take the asshole," Kingston says to Orlando, motioning to Hayden. "I'll bite him if you don't, and you know how jealous our girl gets."

I don't react to his words, snuggling my face into the crook of Diego's shoulder, shifting his jacket to kiss his bare skin.

Kingston sighs. "Not even a pity laugh, babe?"

I blink my eyes and shift. "Sorry, dude. Ha-ha."

Kingston, Austin, and Orlando all frown at me, standing in front of Diego. Friggin' pouty as hell vampires.

"You've hung around Kingston too much, Orlando," I say. "I like you better when you're all serious."

He tightens his mouth, hardening his features. "Better?"

I shrug. "I don't think anything will get better until we're out of here. This place creeps me out."

Orlando nods. "Then I suppose it's time to go."

Picking up Hayden, Orlando leads the way at vampire speed. Wind burns my eyes with tears, and I hide my face against Diego's shoulder to block it the best I can. He rubs his big hands up and down the length of my arms, doing the best he can to calm my racing heart as it bangs into his back.

He finally gives up and flips me forward to press his mouth to mine, still managing to keep his attention on his brothers though most of it grabs hold of me. I sigh against his lips, just letting the softness and sweetness of his mouth explore mine until I can't even think of anything else beside the tingles washing through me at Diego's affection.

I don't even realize we've stopped moving until Diego eases back and smiles at me, his smile genuine as it wrinkles the corners of his eyes.

"I can't wait for this to be over so that I can give you everything you want," he murmurs, kissing me softly once more.

He shifts me to his back to free his hands, and I feel Kingston slide his fingers down the length of my body to squeeze my ass. He stands right behind me, protecting my back but also taking advantage of our closeness just the way I like.

"He's right, babe," he whispers into my ear. "If you think you've experienced ecstasy with me before, you just wait."

I shiver and lean my head so that he can kiss my forehead. "No, *you* just wait. I'm so tired of all this bullshit that I've decided that I'm never leaving our house again. You get your wish about spending the rest of eternity in bed."

He chuckles. "Damn straight."

A gunshot sounds through the air, startling me, and I nearly fly from Diego's back to attack Hayden as he shoots Orlando in the stomach. Orlando grunts, clutching his bleeding stomach, but no one moves. No one tries to help him.

"Don't let her go," Orlando commands, his fangs peeking out from beneath his lips as he looks at me.

I realize that Kingston still locks me in place, not letting me move even though I begin to thrash.

Hayden raises his gun again and pulls the trigger, shooting Orlando a second time. Kingston covers my mouth with his hand, risking getting bit as panic ignites inside me to set my whole body ablaze with despair.

"Jewel," Austin says, covering Dougie's ears, somehow managing to keep him from crying. "He's going to be okay. Just stay calm."

"He just shot him," I mumble, trying to break free of Kingston's grip.

"That was the plan," Austin says. "Didn't you hear us...damn it, Kingston. You distracted Jewel."

Kingston releases a soft growl near my ear. "With good reason. She'd have argued about this, and we don't have time."

"Wait, this was planned?" I ask, managing to get control over myself.

"Yeah, and now you have to bite Diego. Give him what he loves," he whispers.

Kingston releases me, and he and Austin disappear, taking Dougie with them to hide in the trees. I clutch onto Diego in confusion, watching Orlando drop to his knees on purpose. Hayden friggin' shoots Orlando again, and he falls forward and hits the ground face first with a thud.

Diego squeezes my hand. "Come on, beautiful. You heard Kingston. Give me what I want. Nice and hard."

I hesitate for a moment, but the sound of someone yelling out kicks my ass into motion, and I sink my teeth into Diego, biting him hard enough that he grunts.

His syrupy blood fills my mouth, and I automatically swallow, humming in my throat. He tastes so good. I didn't realize how hungry I was through all the adrenaline pouring through me.

"Shit," Diego whispers. "This is driving me crazy."

The world spins, and Diego surprises me by flipping me onto my back. He flashes his fangs like he's going to bite me, and I totally bend my neck to expose it to him. Leaning down, he brushes his lips to my throat, before thrusting himself off me, turning me with him. He raises his arms over his head, taking my hands with his, and I pant and straddle him, my chest heaving.

"Again, beautiful. Bite hard and brace yourself. They're coming," Diego says, shifting his body beneath mine like he's trying to escape my weak hold.

A growl sounds through the air, setting me off, and I bend forward and sink my teeth into his chest, biting hard enough to fill my mouth with blood. I can't stop myself from pulling his jacket open to lick my tongue across his skin. His body reacts beneath mine, and I wiggle lower to feel the sudden excitement bulging from his pants as he feeds off my own desire.

And then someone rips me away by my waist.

I roar—and I mean full-on roar and snarl, my body wanting no part of being taken away from Diego.

"Calm down and don't attack me," a deep voice says in my ear. "You don't have to be afraid. I'm on your side, dhampir."

I gasp a few breaths, trying my best not to lose my shit and fight the vampire who holds me in place.

"I can't let you kill him. It would be such a waste of a blood source," he adds, breathing in my ear. "Hasn't anyone taught you that? You'll end up dead otherwise, and this guy looks like he can be tamed. I mean, he didn't even put up a fight. I think he likes you."

The vampire releases me and strolls toward Hayden. "Nice shot with this one, but you didn't kill him. He's only playing."

Orlando releases a deep growl but doesn't move.

"I'm going to assume you're her guardian? You're either really lucky or you like to wait for her to finish them off. Where'd you pick her up anyway? How much do you want?"

"She's not for sale," Hayden snaps.

The vampire smiles, flashing his fangs. "What if I show you the most effective way to kill this guy without needing your charge's help?"

Grabbing Orlando by the front of his shirt, he hoists him off the ground just enough so that he sits upright. The man pulls a friggin' silver stake from his jacket and waves it in the air. Orlando growls but doesn't fight much. The creepy ass vampire must not know who he is or else he'd know a few bullets are only inconveniences to him. He probably thinks he's an outcast since the Mercy Coven said there are a lot out here.

"So, what you want to do is aim up from the side or through the back. Breaking through the sternum would be a real bitch for you. Not to mention, you have to force the heart cleanly out or we just start to regenerate. Once you get yourself past the hard bone here—" The vampire jabs Orlando with the stake, piercing it an inch into his chest, and I try not to react because Orlando doesn't. "You'll have yourself a nice vulnerable area to thrust the rest through. Push the thing out the back, and boom. You're a real badass. Let me demonstrate."

I rush forward toward Orlando, my scream ripping through the air. It's enough to distract the vampire for Orlando to shove him off and overpower him. Kingston materializes from the trees and joins Orlando, and the two of them restrain the guy as he snaps his teeth.

"Are you a fucking dumbass?" Kingston asks. "Hayden can't even protect himself, let alone our girl."

"You're her guardians?" The vampire flares his nostrils. "But there are four of you."

"Uh, she's a member of our coven, so we protect her, yeah. I don't know what you mean about this guardian bullshit or why you're so surprised that there are four of us. You act like you know dhampirs. If you did, you'd know how insatiable they are. It takes all of us to keep her satisfied, satiated, and safe, or what I like to call the three S's."

"Dude, shut up. You think I talk a lot, but you're spilling all of our damn business," I say, placing my hands on my hips.

He play growls at me. "What? We're just going to rip off his head anyway."

Austin emerges from the tree with Dougie, seeing now that we have the situation under control. Diego scoops me off my feet and hugs me against him, and I tease him a little by licking my bite mark on his shoulder.

"Careful, bro. Jewel looked ready to tear your clothes off and devour you just the way I love a second ago," Kingston warns.

"Jewel? Her name is Jewel?" the vampire asks. "Descendant of the dhampir Jordan line."

Orlando leans into him, baring his teeth. "You must know her father. Word has it he arrived here a few months ago."

"So, you're looking for a reunion? From what I've been told, Jewel was lost to Donor Life Corp," he says, glancing at me. "Jewel, would you like me to take you to Noah? I'm sure your...coven mates have enough to pay for your safe passage."

"I'm willing to cover the cost of all of us," Orlando says.

The guy flashes his fangs. "Not happening. Jewel and the donor may come. You guys cannot."

I press against Diego's chest until he sets me down. "Are you friggin' kidding me?"

"Oh, the child. He may come too."

I strut forward and stand next to Orlando to face the vampire. Jerking my finger, I stab him in the chest hard enough to make him wince at the pressure. "If you think for one second that I'm just going to abandon my guys out here to go with someone who thought Hayden was willing to *sell* me, then you are sorely mistaken."

His jaw twitches.

"Beautiful, careful. You know you tend to punch hearts out when you're upset," Diego says.

It takes everything in me not to react.

I can't tell if Diego said it to really remind me or to freak the vampire out. Either way, his words resonate with both of us because the vampire heaves a breath and looks away from me.

I square my shoulders. "What you're going to do is take us all within the walls. We were told to find a vampire named Newport and that he would get us to my dad."

"Newport, huh? Who told you about him?" the guy asks.

"Huntington," I say.

He blinks, keeping his face expressionless. "Fine. I'll allow two of your blood sources to come, but they will cost double."

I glance at Kingston, Austin, Diego, and Orlando. None of them look happy about the deal, but none of them immediately reject it either.

"We accept your deal," Orlando says. "But you must provide shelter for Kingston and Diego from the sun."

"Which one of them is Diego?" he asks.

Diego steps forward. "Me."

The guy looks at Austin and Kingston. "Which one of you is Kingston?"

Kingston only nods his head.

"Who are you?" the vampire asks, motioning to Austin.

"Austin," Orlando says for him. "And I'm Orlando. We're part of the Ortega Coven of Ombre Noire."

Orlando sets the guy on his feet, and he straightens his jacket. I half expect him to bolt for it, but he remains composed and unfazed by my guys' intimidation that makes even me a bit nervous.

"So where is this damn shelter?" Kingston asks, crossing his arms.

"You won't need to know. I said two of Jewel's blood sources could come, and one of them will be you." The guy looks to Austin. "And you will be the other one."

"That was not the deal," Orlando says.

"Do you really think I'm going to take your coven's strongest with me? No. Either accept my choice or don't. You have five seconds to decide before I change my mind."

Orlando growls, but I step in front of him and place my hand on his chest. "You'll provide safe passage back too, right?"

The guy nods. "As long as you don't cause any trouble."

I purse my lips and glance to Kingston. He gives me a why-are-you-looking-at-me shrug. "Okay, it's a deal. But I swear if anyone tries anything stupid, I'll punch their hearts out."

The vampire smirks. "It's a good thing you say that, because to go where we're going, I'm going to need you to do just that."

BLOOD SOURCES

FOR THE FIRST TIME IN a long time, I really friggin' hate my guys' sensitivity to the sun. Sure, I wish they didn't have it in the first place, but it never bothered me. Scared the shit out of me when they had to brave the day, but other than that, it's been fine. But now? Holy mother-effin' shitballs. This place is dark. I can't see anything. If Kingston wasn't carrying me, I don't think I could get my body to overcome the panic threatening to freeze my insides.

I concentrate on our surroundings, listening to four distinct footsteps—three feather light and one loud as hell. The thuds of Hayden's boots nearly make me ask Kingston to pick him up instead. My fear is crazy intense, and I'm afraid some monster will hunt us down and attack us because of the noise.

"We're almost through the tunnel," Kingston whispers into my ear, keeping his voice too low for anyone except me to hear. "Don't worry. There's no one living here."

My rebel mouth releases a small whimper. I know he doesn't mean living as inhabiting this place, which means he must see some dead bodies that I can't.

Kingston strokes his hand up and down my back, playing with my hair, and I distract my mouth by kissing his sweet skin, sucking it hard enough to leave a hickey. Kingston's breath quickens, his body reacting to mine.

"Jewel, you're torturing me," he whispers, sneaking his hand lower until he grazes his fingers across my ass. "I want so badly to distract you. I mean, I'm pretty fucking sure we can manage. It's dark as shit."

I release a breathless laugh. "Not happening."

He brushes his lips to my temple. "Your loss."

"Dude."

He chuckles. "That's better. I knew it would get you to stop shaking."

Tilting my head up, I blindly attempt to kiss him, brushing my lips to his chin. He flicks out his tongue and licks the tip of my nose on purpose, and I stretch up and lick the side of his face.

"You're sneaky," I whisper.

"And I'm about to flip you upside down so that you can lick me again...lower."

"Don't you even think about—"

A gust of wind cuts off my words, and I twist in Kingston's arms to peer in front of us. Trickling water drips from somewhere nearby. I squint my eyes in the dark, glimpsing strange, eerie shadows.

"You guys wait here," the vampire says, his voice echoing around us. "I'll be back in a few minutes."

"Wait, you're leaving us?" I ask.

Austin's familiar touch brushes across my back. "I'm sure it'll be fine, Jewel. There is a ladder leading up. He's probably just checking the area or paying the guard."

"Listen to your blood source, dhampir. And so you know, it's not you who should be afraid." The soft tapping of boots on metal sounds out as the vampire leaves without waiting for my response.

Kingston releases a low growl. "This guy is cockier than fucking Hayden."

"I was thinking the same thing," Hayden responds. "But about you."

I rest my head on Kingston's shoulder. "Ah hell, Austin. I think the world might be ending at any minute. Kingston kind of just agreed with the asshole."

Austin chuckles.

Kingston surprises me with a light smack to my ass. "Not funny, babe."

Something crashes nearby, startling me, and I don't get the chance to respond. Austin feels for me and places sleeping Dougie in my arms so that I sandwich him between me and

Kingston. Kingston's muscles tense, and I can feel him reach for his hidden knife under his jacket. He only holds onto me with one hand, and I do my best to tighten my grip on his shoulder without squishing Dougie too much.

A bright light flashes on, blinding me, and both Kingston and Austin growl. I tense, my whole body screaming with fear until my eyes adjust and the light turns from us to aim at the ground.

And I wish it friggin' hadn't.

The annoying vampire waves the flashlight over the dead body seeping fresh blood over the dirty concrete ground. "Anyone else hungry?"

"What the hell?" I ask.

He shrugs. "A vampire's got to eat, and this guy was new. I guess my contact forgot to tell him the rules about this territory."

"What rules?" My big mouth. I swear. I should know better than to let my curiosity get the best of me. Kingston pinches my ass, trying to remind me too, but all I do is squeeze his shoulders.

The vampire flashes the light into my eyes again. "Nothing to concern your pretty little head over. The rules don't apply to you."

Hayden crosses his arms. "And the rest of us?" I'm glad he asks, because I knew my guys wouldn't have.

"That's yet to be determined." The vampire spins. "Now, come along. Dhampirs first."

Kingston sets me on my feet at the bottom of the ladder. "I'll go first, babe."

The vampire materializes next to us and hits his flashlight on the metal rung, the banging noise piercing my ear through the eerie quiet of the tunnel. It's loud enough to wake Dougie, and Austin quickly takes him from me, bouncing on his feet to settle him down before he starts crying.

"I *said* dhampirs first," the vampire says, flashing his fangs.

Kingston's eyes flash silver, and I touch his cheek, getting him to look at me instead of the jerk. I know if he doesn't focus his attention elsewhere, Kingston will react and start a fight that will end with us without a guide.

"It's fine, Kingston. I can handle it," I say, lacing my fingers around the cool metal rungs. "You taught me to be brave, remember?"

The vampire releases a weird ass sound, almost like a snort and a snicker. "It's not always about being brave. Brave people die because they think they have to be fearless when they should actually be smart."

"Which our girl is too, dickhead," Kingston snaps.

Taking a breath, I test my weight on the rung, bouncing on my feet for a second. Kingston stands close behind me, practically keeping his arms around me and only staying a rung below me. He could fully take advantage of my position if he wanted by allowing me a bit of space, but for the first time in a long time, he's not in a playful mood. It probably kills him that I lead the way in a place none of us knows where we're going, and without half my backup to protect me.

Cool air blows my hair, sending strands in my face. I climb the last few rungs to a hatch that remains open with a view of the glittering sky overhead. Slowly, I ease my head out to peer around. The quiet night remains empty, and I close my eyes and inhale a breath of fresh air.

Fear prickles over my neck, and I snap my eyes open and screech. Kingston locks his hands around my waist the same time another vampire digs his fingers into my wrist to yank me up and out of the tunnel. Our guide grabs Kingston, and he loses his grip on me, the two of them crashing into the others on the ladder.

The vampire that pulled me up rushes and slams the hatch to the tunnel closed and spins to flash his fangs at me. I scramble back, my good senses telling me to run away as fast as I can, but another far more spontaneous, reckless, dangerous part of me explodes to steal my good senses away, sending me running to the guy.

"Well, don't you look delectable," the vampire says, giving me a once-over while spinning out of my reach. "Mind if I get a little taste?"

He disappears, and I automatically kick my leg back, expecting him to sneak up behind me. My foot hits solid muscle, but the vampire takes advantage of me and grabs my leg, pulling my feet out from under me. I hit my back to the ground, my lungs burning with my watering eyes.

He tips his head back and laughs. "I do love a fight. If only you didn't make things so easy."

Bending forward, he tries to grab hold of me. I roll over out of his reach and onto my knees to push back to my feet. But I'm not fast enough. The vampire latches his fingers to my ankles and drags me back, sending my long shirt rolling up my legs to reveal my thighs.

My body tenses, fear crashing through me, and I flip back over and glower at the vampire's smug-ass smile as he drinks me in, trailing his gaze slowly up my bare legs like he can undress the rest of me with his eyes.

And it pisses me the hell off.

But I don't react and attack.

Instead, I clutch the ground and release a small whimper, scooting back to put space between us that he quickly closes.

"Come on now," he says, biting his lip. "I'm not going to hurt you."

"Then just let me go," I say, my voice cracking with my words.

"I can't do that either," he says. Extending his arm, he holds out his hand for me. "So don't make this hard on yourself. If you get up nicely, I won't bite you unless you ask."

I don't move. "And if I don't?"

"All those people that came with you will be dead come sunrise."

The vampire smiles at my frown, and I gingerly hold out my hand, my fingers shaking like crazy. Wrapping his cool hand around mine, he starts to pull me to my feet, thinking that I'm actually going to comply, and I surprise him by jerking my foot up between his legs. I wrench him back, flipping him over my head to land on the ground.

He roars and tightens his grip on my hand, yanking me toward him. I resist for a second and then relax, throwing him off balance. I land on my knees next to him and swing my arm, punching him in the throat. His growl cuts off with his airway, and my body kicks into action. I jump on top of him, pinning his arms with my knees, and I pull the strands of his dark hair to expose his neck.

I bite down so friggin' hard that he bucks under me, managing to get me off but not without ripping his flesh. I hock it right into his face, surprising the hell out of him. His hesitation leaves him open, and I swing my arm back and punch toward his chest, aiming for his heart.

A hand catches mine, locking around my wrist, stopping my swing. "Jewel, I'm going to need you not to kill this guy. He's my brother."

Fury at the sound of our vampire guide's voice ignites in me, and I slam my fist into his stomach, sending him sprawling back to skid across the ground.

"Fuck yeah, babe!" Kingston shouts, his proud as hell voice the only thing stopping me from launching myself at the jerk as he scrambles to get to his feet. "You show these assholes what they get for messing with you."

The vampire who yanked me from the tunnel rubs his

hand over his groin. "She impressed me, Colton. I think that was the first time I thought I might actually die." Colton, huh? I didn't think I'd ever learn the guy's name.

"You would've if your brother hadn't intervened. I hope you enjoy your bruised fucking cock, though," I say, making Kingston laugh harder.

Austin materializes in front of me and runs his fingers through my hair, inspecting every inch that he can of me while still holding Dougie in his arms. I catch sight of Hayden standing a few feet away from Kingston with his arms crossed over his chest. Colton closes the space to us and drinks me in for a minute, making me super uncomfortable.

"Do you mind?" I ask, glowering at him.

He smirks and looks to his brother. "What do you think, Oakley? Did she pass?"

I twist my lips. "Pass what exactly?"

"Your worthiness. Those who lie placated beneath vampires don't gain passage here. You passed with fucking flying colors. Look at this bite, brother." Oakley pulls his collar down to show off the nasty ass zombie bite I gave him. "If she wants to meet with Noah, I think she deserves it."

"Man, Diego would be so proud and jealous as hell, babe," Kingston whispers. "That's the worst one I've seen you do."

Heat floods my face, and I suck in another shaky breath as my nerves finally settle. Whatever twisted test this was has me more annoyed than anything, and it takes Austin squeezing my hand to get me to not give into my murdery need to go after Colton to punch the smug smile off his face.

Colton risks my guys' growls to step closer to hold his hand out to me. "Come on, dhampir. Let's get you where you need to go. The sun will rise soon, and I'm sure you wouldn't want us to get trapped in the trees for the day."

I ignore his hand and motion for Kingston to pick me up. "There better not be any more tests," I say. "If you pull this shit again, I will rip your heart out. And eat it."

He raises his eyebrows. "It's a shame you've found yourself vowed to a coven."

I glare at him. "It's the best thing that's happened to me."

Oakley glances at his brother before turning to me. "Don't tell anyone else that while you're here."

"Why?"

He flashes his fangs. "They'll never let you leave."

My guys weren't kidding about The Orchards being dangerous. I've never seen so much disorder and fighting in my life. Why my dad would ever want to bring us here is beyond me. Outside the wall isn't the only place filled with hungry outcast vampires. Colton and Oakley fought ten feral and famished as hell vampire guys already. Except these aren't like the vampires I've seen outside the cities. These ones don't have any tattoo marks. Nor do they have covens. I'm pretty friggin' sure they don't even know the civilized world.

"Oh, look. That guy looks pretty clean. Are you hungry,

Jewel? We don't mind holding him down for you," Oakley says, smirking at me. "No fighting necessary."

I scrunch my nose. "Yeah, no. Not happening."

"You know, it's rude to deny such an offer," Colton says.

I roll my eyes. "It's even ruder to offer me something equivalent to gen. pop. blood by your standards when you know I have these delicious, perfect matches of mine standing right here who do a better job at feeding me than you ever could."

Austin touches my cheek, grinning at me.

Kingston snuggles his face into my shoulder. "Damn straight."

Colton hums under his breath like he doesn't believe it's possible. He keeps his thoughts to himself, taking the position on the other side of Hayden. It kind of annoys me that they're discretely protecting him in the form of walking on both his sides. They should be backing my guys up, but then again, I'd never hear the end of it if I told Kingston and Austin as much.

"The compound is coming up," Colton says after a few more minutes of silence. "There are a few rules you must follow upon entrance." He glances over his shoulder at us to make sure we're listening to him.

I raise my eyebrow, silently telling him that I am.

"One, vampires must not show attention to any humans. Two, the word donor is extremely rude here. Any vampire who uses it will rightfully take a knife to the gut."

I side-eye Kingston to make sure he's paying attention.

Narrowing his eyes, he glares at me for even looking at him with the thought that he'd call someone a donor. But we both know if he's angry enough, he lets it slip.

"Any blood exchange must be made in private. Vampires caught biting will lose their fangs. Most won't risk it. I suggest you refrain as well. We do not treat humans as food here." Again, Colton looks at my guys.

I place my hands on my hips. "They don't treat me like food." I don't know why I feel the need to defend my guys, but I don't like the way Colton or Oakley looks at them.

Colton remains unfazed to my annoyance. "Fair enough. I just thought I'd make it clear in case."

"What about rules for humans?" Austin asks.

Colton shrugs. "Be nice? Don't admit your love of vampires? I don't know or care. This is where we part ways."

"Wait, you're leaving?" I ask. "Where do we go once we enter?"

"You'll find Newport waiting. He's expecting you," Oakley says. "He'll take you to Noah."

"We'll return for you tomorrow an hour past nightfall. Just tell the guardian at the gate you're with the Daring Guides."

"Daring?"

Oakley nods. "That's right. We're two of five and the only coven permitted in all of Red Crest Canyon Grove. All the others are kept wild. We wouldn't want Donor Life Corp to think they can suddenly divide this place."

"Oh." It's all I can think to say.

"Good luck, dhampir," Colton says. "Send Noah my regards."

Colton and Oakley vanish, leaving us outside a tall concrete wall with buzzing electric wires running along the top. Austin and Kingston peer around, assessing our situation. Hayden takes initiative and struts to the wall and walks along it a few dozen feet.

He disappears from view for a minute before popping his head out. "Hurry the hell up. I'm not risking getting attacked out here."

Kingston and Austin guide me forward, each holding one of my hands. Dougie sleeps on Austin's shoulder, quietly snoring, and I can't stop the smirk that crosses my face. Austin returns my smile and squeezes my hand. Kingston remains serious, jaw tense, body rigid. I have to shake our hands to get him to loosen the death grip on my fingers.

"This better be worth it," Kingston whispers under his breath.

I rub my lips together. "I'll make sure it is."

He heaves a sigh and tugs me faster, and I pull Austin with us. Hayden waits in an alcove with a gate that leads inside the compound. The thick metal door doesn't have a handle or anything, so Kingston bangs his fist on it.

A slot opens, and I spot the light brown eyes of the guardian on the other side of the door. He just looks at us without a word.

"We're here to see Newport. Huntington sent us," Kingston says.

The guy doesn't respond. He doesn't even look at Kingston. Instead, his eyes remain trained on me.

I shift awkwardly on my feet and glance at my guys. "Did Colton mention some sort of passcode?"

Austin shakes his head. "No, but he did make it sound like our roles were reversed here."

"Fucking A," Kingston mutters. "I only like this shit with our girl."

I step on his foot, getting him to shut up before he says something he most definitely shouldn't. Clearing my throat, I meet the guy's gaze again and say, "Will you please let us in? We're here to see Newport."

"Name?" the guy asks, finally responding. It looks like Colton wasn't kidding.

"Jewel Ortega," I say.

The guy's eye twitches without a word. He doesn't open the door, either.

"Uh, did you hear me?" I ask.

Hayden steps closer. "Tell Newport that Hayden Andrei is here. I'm looking for Noah."

The guy flicks his attention to Hayden. "Sorry, Hayden. You have not been granted access."

Anger ignites inside me, and I fist my hand and punch the guy right in the face through the slot. Kingston jerks me back into his chest, wrapping his arms around me, covering my mouth to stop me from yelling.

"Fuck, Jewel. Use your damn family name, and I will let you in," the guy says, cupping his nose.

My mouth drops open. "Seriously? You ignored me because I called myself Jewel Ortega? What the actual hell?"

He glares at me through the slot. "Name, please?" Seriously. This. Guy. He composes himself and acts like I didn't just hit him. His nose twitches and a drop of blood trickles down, and grossly, he doesn't even wipe it, just lets it splash on his lip.

I tighten my jaw. "Jewel Jordan." It takes everything in me to say the name. Kingston squeezes my hand, doing his best to keep me calm.

"How many are in your group?" the guy asks.

"Five. Three do—humans and two vampires." Shit. Kingston raises his eyebrow at me, silently gloating that it was me who nearly broke the rule by referring to myself as a donor.

The guy shuts the slot, and I listen to a few beeps followed by a strange hissing sound before the door retracts into the wall. I step forward first even though I know Kingston wants to, but he relents to letting me be in charge like this jerk clearly wants.

"Welcome to The Orchards, Jewel. Hayden. While your arrival was unexpected, it is quite welcome. I had expected my brother to be coming alone with Jewel. What changed?"

I frown. "Your brother?"

"Huntington," the guy says.

Giving him a once-over, I take in his features. I nearly missed the fact that this guy looks identical to the jerk who thought he was getting me from Hayden. Only slightly older.

"You're Newport? But you're—"

"Human? Yeah, I know. My brother caught the plague a few years ago. I hope you know that whatever Donor Life Corp tried to feed you out there in the wild was utter shit. There is no vaccine."

"There's no plague, either," Austin says, drawing the guy's attention to him.

The guy suddenly jerks his hand forward, punching Austin in the stomach. Austin releases a growl, and it takes Kingston extending his arm across the both of us to stop us from attacking. Austin grunts and touches his stomach. The sweet scent of blood permeates the air at the same time a ruby stain blossoms like a flower across the front of his dress shirt.

"What the actual fuck!" My voice screeches through the air, and I swing out my arm in an attempt the smack the guy, but Kingston continues to block me, and the guy steps back out of my reach.

"It's a crime for vampires to speak freely, especially in regards to the bullshit lies Donor Life Corp used to placate the human population before we knew any better." Newport swipes his finger across the side of his blade, wiping off the blood before popping his finger into his mouth. "I must ask you to control your blood sources, Jewel. Until you check them in and get them situated for the day, they must remain silent. I will not warn you again."

"Shit," I whisper. I glance to Austin. "What the fuck. This isn't worth it."

Austin and Kingston don't reply to me, keeping their intense gazes trained on the ground. I bet it takes everything in them not to react. And I can't blame them. They've never had to experience being considered less than like I have. Like all donors in the vampire world outside of this place.

"We've come all this way," Hayden says, glancing to me. "Your matches are tough. Maybe they'll actually learn something while we're here."

Turning to face Kingston and Austin, I push them a few feet away and whisper, "What do you guys want to do?"

"As much as the thought kills me, Hayden is right. We came here on a mission, and if we turn around now, we won't get what we want. Mitchell is currently out of control, and none of us even know who to trust...except for the people who hate us most," Kingston says, pursing his lips.

"And what if they don't help us?" I ask.

Austin squeezes my hand. "Then they don't help us. Our trip won't have been wasted. We'll get Brayla and your cousins."

"And Ramona," I add.

Kingston huffs. "That's still up in the air."

"Kingston, my niece."

"You're right. I'm sorry, babe."

I nod and straighten my shoulders, turning to face Newport. He crosses his arms and waits for my response. "Lead the way." Asshole.

Newport turns and struts down the path in front of us, not even checking to see if we keep up. He clomps as loudly as Hayden and not the soft footsteps of the human staff I'm used to. Loud and proud. I'm sure I could find that slogan around here somewhere.

After a short walk, we arrive in front of what looks like the entrance to an underground bunker. A man stands guard over a metal hatch with the word *Beware* slapped across the top in a faded sticker warning.

"Hey, Dixon. Checkin' in two blood sources. Property of Jewel Jordan." Newport looks cocky as hell as he says the words.

But his attempt to get to my guys doesn't work. They know they're mine. I'm nearly certain Kingston might make a joke about this later. I wouldn't put it past him.

The guy, Dixon, nods and bends down to open the hatch. Stale air wafts from the underground room, and I peer down the set of wooden stairs. Soft light glows from within, but I don't hear much inside.

I step forward first, but Dixon cuts me off. "The accommodations are adequate. You don't need to check."

"Accommodations for what exactly?" I ask, swiveling on my feet to eye my guys.

"Your blood sources. You're checking them in for the day."

My mouth falls agape as I realize what it means to check my guys in. They're not asking me to sign their names on some log to track them. They literally want me to leave them here in this dank ass looking bunker.

"Ugh, no. They stay with me," I say.

"Not happening," Dixon says. "They either stay here, or I'll put them in the cages."

I grimace. "The cages?"

He points to a fenced in area in the middle of a lawn. "Over there."

Gasping, I cover my mouth with my hand. I can't even believe what I see. The cages he refers to look to trap vampires. And not just to lock them up. Whoever is inside would be exposed to direct sunlight if stuck in there during the day.

"Are you friggin' kidding me?" I ask. "What is wrong with you people?"

"Babe, they're super serious," Kingston whispers too quietly for the rebels to hear.

"What is wrong with *us?*" Newport asks.

It takes everything in me not to react.

The thought of even forcing my guys to take to the shade all day freaks me out.

Because while they don't explode or burn, it's uncomfortable. It's hot. I can't imagine what a day in direct sunlight would do. Even a minute leaves them blistering. A whole day? I shudder even to think about it.

"If you think for one second that putting a vampire in the

cage is wrong, then you are seriously delusional. They put us in cages. They kill us. Torture us. Treat us like food. Like we're beneath them," Newport says. "Vampires divide families. Force humans to live meaningless lives. They are not good. Here, we treat them as they deserve." Newport scowls at me, his chest heaving at the words.

If Austin didn't squeeze my hand, I would snap and scream and tell him that he knows nothing. Because all vampires aren't like that. They're not all monsters.

"Hayden, please take the child," Newport continues saying while turning to Dougie, unaffected by my reaction.

Hayden takes Dougie without question.

Newport motions to the guard. "You will follow Dixon. He will take you where you want to go."

Dixon doesn't give Hayden a chance to say anything before he shoves him forward, assuring he strolls from us. I shift uncomfortably on my feet, watching them walk away with Dougie. Hayden glances back with a frown but doesn't do or say anything.

Fear rises in my chest, and I reach out and clutch both Kingston and Austin's hands.

"What about us?" I ask, my voice coming out low with my nerves.

A few clicks sound behind us before something pokes me hard in the back—a gun. I'll never forget the feeling of one pressed against me.

"You will be joining this blood source here in the bunker," he says, pointing at Austin. "As for your other one, he'll spend the day in the cage."

I stand in shock. "What?"

Newport straightens his shoulders. "Guardians, seize them."

THE CAGES

AUSTIN COVERS MY MOUTH, SILENCING my screams as the guardians bind Kingston. He doesn't even put up a fight, unwilling to risk the fact that one of them continues to train a gun on me. I don't get the chance to watch them take Kingston. Two hands shove me in the back, sending me falling down the flight of stairs.

Wrapping his arms around me, Austin breaks my fall, heaving a breath as he collides into the concrete floor. The hatch closes above us, cutting off the view of the sky, and we remain motionless on the floor.

"Shit, Austin," I say, rolling off of him. "What are we going to do?"

He takes a few slow breaths. "We're going to stay calm.

We still have an hour until sunrise."

"But Kingston—"

Austin kisses me softly to stop me from screaming out in despair again, hugging me to him. "Kingston will be okay."

"He'll burn."

"He's strong."

I blink tears from my eyes. "I don't care how strong he is, what they're doing is wrong. Barbaric."

"They're getting revenge for the injustices they've faced since the uprising, Jewel." Austin sits up and peers around the dimly lit room. Pushing to his feet, he helps me off the floor with him and closes his eyes for a second, just listening to the world around us. "We're in Blood Rebel territory. Some of these people might have descended from those who managed to escape The Divide."

"Still," I say.

Austin pulls me in for a hug, just smothering the trembles from me. "I know, Jewel. It sucks that we're here in this position."

I rest my head on his shoulder. "Especially considering we're not the bad guys."

"To them, we are."

He's right. I can't even imagine what life is like for a Blood Rebel, or for anyone else for that matter. There was a reason my parents fought to get us away from here. There was a reason my dad gave in to the donor life. But losing my mom made him lose sight of that. He came here out of desperation—at least, that's what I hope.

Austin lets silence fill the air, and I continue to hug him like his arms are the sole reason that I haven't fallen apart. Because this is all my fault. I was warned by Colton not to admit that I liked vampires, and I guess standing up for them and protesting was enough to set these guys off.

Easing away, I meet Austin's gaze. "I'm sorry."

He frowns. "For what?"

I shrug. "Uh, this complete shit show." I reach down and caress my fingers over the blood stain of his wound. "Does it hurt?"

Austin tugs his shirt up knowing well enough that I want to check the damage for myself. If it were Kingston or Diego standing in front of me, neither of them would show me, brushing off that they're fine, but Austin doesn't see this kind of a thing as a weakness. His injuries prove how strong he is.

"It's not so bad," he murmurs, touching his fingers to his bloody skin. "It's already coagulating."

I gape at his fingers and cringe at the fact that I totally find them appealing. Austin notices too but doesn't tease me or comment that I should control myself. Instead, he brings his fingers to my mouth.

"Better to not let it go to waste and wipe it on my pants, right?" he asks, smirking at me, still managing to remain calm and in control even under these circumstances.

"Austin..." My voice fades away as he grazes his fingers across my lips, my tongue automatically darting out to lick the blood off.

"Come on, why don't you let me satiate you while I get a better look around," he murmurs, lifting me into his arms without waiting for my response.

I swallow and hug him. "I shouldn't."

"Of course you should. Plus, I could really use the distraction. You're the only thing stopping me from trying to break open the hatch," he says, rubbing his hands on my back.

"Why don't we?" I ask.

"I won't risk them separating us," he says.

Bobbing my head, I take Austin up on his offer to drink from him. He pulls his collar down a bit, dead-set on me biting him instead of biting himself to make it easier. I don't know if it's because he doesn't want to set me down or if he's nervous even to flash his fangs, but I give in and sink my teeth into his skin until blood fills my mouth.

Austin moans softly, rubbing his hand up and down my back. I keep my eyes closed and let him carry me around as he inspects the room. It's no bigger than Orlando's study with no other exit apart from the stairs. I'm surprised even to see a cot.

Moving toward the too small bed, Austin sits on it, allowing me to straddle him while I continue to suck on his skin. My desire ignites at the most inopportune time, and I can't stop my body from rubbing against his, creating friction between us with my movements.

"Jewel," he whispers.

I break away to meet his lips. "I'm sorry. I can't hold still.

I just—"

Austin surprises me by flipping me onto my back and lying on top of me. I gasp, only to have him steal the breath from me with so much passion that I don't even care that we've found ourselves locked in this gross room. All I want is to let him help me forget that I've made a huge friggin' mistake by coming here. He obviously wants to forget too.

Sliding his hand between my legs, he traces his finger softly over my warm skin. I reach down and return the favor, feeling the extent of his desire pressing against his pants. I quickly unfasten and unzip them, grazing my fingers along the front of his boxers until I find what I want.

Austin moans softly, his fangs clicking in my ear. I open up completely for him, not even bothering to take off my underwear, and he shifts them out of the way with his finger to push inside me with a hot desperation I don't think I've ever seen on him. Austin assures my rebel mouth remains quiet by kissing me fervently, sucking my lip into his mouth just far enough to nip me to make me bleed.

Our bodies move together, Austin thrusts quick and deep while his mouth remains soft and gentle as he continues to kiss and suck my lips, grazing his tongue against mine. My fingers travel up his chest and to his neck until I link them through his blond hair to play with the soft tendrils. He slides his hands under my ass, pulling me even closer somehow managing to keep the cot from squeaking under us. I pull back from his mouth and tip my head up, just savoring the crazy good sensations Austin creates, building more pressure until I gasp and dig my nails into his back.

I cover my mouth with my hand, managing to muffle the sound of my body wanting Austin to know that I'm on the verge of imploding with my release, my muscles tightening, clenching him as he picks up his speed even more.

The sexiest friggin' noise in existence escapes his mouth in a soft tone that makes me shiver as I relish in the feeling of our bodies together. He slows, kissing me just as passionately as when we started and sinks his weight on top of me while he catches his breath.

I breathe against his neck, holding him close until he eases off me and fixes his pants, desire still flashing silver in his eyes. He pulls me to him to cuddle me in his arms, hugging me quietly as time passes.

"I for sure thought that would get the universe to interrupt us to get someone to open the door," I murmur, pressing my ear to Austin's chest to listen to his heartbeat.

He laughs loudly, the noise filling the room and my heart at the same time. "You always know exactly what to say to make me feel like the world's not going to burn as long as we're together."

I frown. I can't help it. A burning world isn't something I need to be reminded about. Austin realizes that his words bother me, and he stands up, taking me with him to climb back up the stairs to the bunker door.

We both listen for sounds of people outside. I don't hear

anything apart from Austin's breathing in my ear, making me shiver.

He clears his throat. "Kingston? Can you hear me?"

I close my eyes, waiting for a response.

"Kingston," Austin calls louder.

"Yeah, I'm here." Kingston's voice trickles through the air, bringing me relief just knowing that he's still okay. "Trying not to be jealous that I'm preparing for my imminent demise without the bang."

"Kingston, I—"

Kingston chuckles, the lightness to his voice easing the guilt inside me over allowing my body control over my brain. "Hey, I'd be fucking you too if I were Austin. I'd also never let Austin hear the end of it if he didn't seduce you. I know you're freaking out."

I squeeze Austin tighter. "What about you? Are you hurt or anything?"

"Hardly. But it's coming. The fuckers took my clothes but left me a knife," he says.

I stare at Austin's green eyes with Kingston's words. "A knife?"

"To show me that they're better than me, because they're showing me mercy," Kingston says, growling with his words.

I cover my mouth with my hand. "Shit. Shit. Shit. What the eff?"

"Take a breath, Jewel. What did I tell you about Kingston?" Austin asks, hugging his arms around me.

"That he was strong," I murmur.

"Not that strong," Kingston says. "You do realize I'm about to burn my fucking cock off and not even to risk a sun adventure banging our girl."

I cringe at his words.

So does Austin.

"Kingston, I'm not going to let that happen," I say despite having no friggin' idea what the hell I'm going to do. "Is there anything you can do to cover yourself?"

"I wish. I'm standing on concrete. I tried to break the cage open, but the fencing is electric. If I touch it too long, I'll knock myself out, so I'm saving that as a last resort. But the sun's coming soon," he says. "There are assholes gathering to watch the show."

I frown at Austin. "I want you to break the door. I don't care if they try to separate us. I'll distract them and you get Kingston."

"Fuck no, babe," Kingston says. "You're going to stay put and keep that sexy ass of yours safe. I'm going to need you to take care of me come nightfall."

I groan. "Absolutely not."

"What? The staying safe or taking care of me?"

I glare though he can't see me. "You know I'll always take care of you."

"All right then. Austin, Jewel's going to flip out in twelve minutes. I'm going to need you to cover her ears, smother her with love, bone the hell out of her some more, whatever you need to do to distract her."

"Kingston."

"Eleven minutes, brother," Kingston says instead of responding to me.

Clutching onto Austin's face, I force him to look at me. He remains expressionless as Kingston's words sink in. Austin can't stand the idea of Kingston burning in the sun either, his anger clear to me in his silver flashing eyes.

"We can't just ignore this," I argue.

Austin releases a breath. "I know. So we'll do things your way." He says the words so quietly that Kingston won't be able to hear them to complain.

Through the hatch, human noises sound through the air, growing louder with the oncoming dawn. Kingston wasn't lying about people gathering to watch. Some swear at him. Some laugh. But then I hear a distinct cry.

"Fuck, close your eyes and go inside, Fallon," Kingston says. "Only your cousin can see me in all my sexy naked glory."

"What is going on here? What are you doing? He's going to burn!" Fallon screams the words. "Uncle Noah!"

"Stay away from the cage, girl," a masculine voice says.

Fallon screeches, and something thuds before a deep groan sounds out. Whatever she does makes Kingston laugh. "You guys can't do this. Uncle Noah! You have to stop them. That's Kingston."

"Ramona, grab her and take her inside." Dad's familiar

voice hums to me. "Lock her in her room."

"Aw, come on, Jordan," another man calls. "Let the girls see."

"Shut up! Who accepted his entrance? Where is my other daughter? Her blood sources wouldn't leave her unattended," Dad says.

His questions are greeted with silence by the people around him.

"Dad, Hayden said he was coming here. He said that things with Donor Life Corp were getting crazy, and he couldn't stay." Ramona's soft voice trickles to me. I have to focus past my racing heart to even hear her. "What if he told them where we were?"

"You got that right, Ramona," Kingston says. "He didn't just tell us. He came with us. The asshole last night said he was taking him to you."

"What?" Ramona asks.

"Someone shut the blood source up." It's Newport. His voice sends fury racing through me. "Noah, take your girls back inside and wait for my call. Things have been a bit crazy around here, so I just haven't had the time to inform you of Jewel's arrival."

"You didn't have time?" Dad's voice bellows through the air.

"Austin, hurry. You have to hurry and break the hatch," I say. "Kingston, get ready. We're coming."

"Jewel, no," Kingston says. "The sun's too close."

A gunshot rings through the air, startling me, and Austin shoves his shoulder into the hatch, trying to force the door open. Fallon and Ramona both scream, and fear clenches my heart. I want so badly to see that I help Austin, putting all my strength into the door.

"I said get away from the cage, you little brat!" a man says.

"Kingston, grab this. Ramona, shove through your jacket to him too. The sun!" Fallon yells. Her voice rips through the air, and it sounds like people start to fight.

The metal door quivers under Austin's force, but it just won't give. Kingston swears, and my insides twist and turn as he growls and then groans. I don't have to look at the sky to know the sun rises.

"Dad!" Ramona screams.

"Fuck!" Kingston shouts.

Austin shoves against the door one more time, and it suddenly flies open. He growls at the burst of sunlight, sending him falling back into the dark bunker. I rush out, leaving him behind, pushing my legs to move as fast as I can.

Smoke wafts from the cage in the middle of an open field with a slab of concrete. Kingston lies on the ground curled in on himself with two small pieces of clothing covering what he considers his most important parts.

"Jewel!" Fallon yells, drawing my attention to her.

My heart rams into my ribcage, threatening to spill out. Several people fight each other, all guys from what I can tell. I spot my dad ramming his fist into an old man's stomach before pushing him to the ground.

"Kingston," I yell, gasping a breath. Without thinking, I tug my shirt over my head and shove it through the metal bars of the cage. A jolt of electricity shocks me, knocking me on my ass. I hit the ground hard and don't get the chance to move before someone locks their hands around my wrists and drags me back.

"I got you, beautiful," Diego says, his soft voice wrapping around me, snuffing out the fight inside me.

"Diego," I say, my chest aching so hard. "Get Kingston, but be careful. It's electric."

"On it."

Diego sets me on my feet, slapping a dagger to the palm of my hand, and then disappears. My body refuses to stand here and do nothing, so as soon as Diego rips a large wooden beam right from the front of one of the ancient looking houses, I dash behind him.

I don't get more than ten feet from the spot he left me before someone collides into me, knocking me off my feet. Strong arms wrap around me, and I roll a few times and gasp when the world stops spinning. I land on top of Austin in the shade under an awning.

He presses his lips to mine, silencing any noise I could make.

Diego roars, drawing our attention to him as he braves the sun with only his jacket pulled over his head. Shots ring through the air, but he doesn't stop, swinging the beam at a couple of guys to knock them off their feet and out of his way. Another figure darts through the sun, throwing guys off their feet.

I can't take my gaze off Kingston and Diego, though. Diego rams the wooden beam into the cage hard enough to bend the bars on the side wall. Sparks fly, the wood smoldering. He pulls it back again so hard that the cage goes flying over his head, detached from the ground. A man screams as it lands on top of him before falling silent.

"We have to go to them," I tell Austin, trying to push myself up.

He lifts me with him and darts toward his brothers. People yell out, confused by the chaos that no one even tries to stop us. Diego picks Kingston off the ground, and I cry out at the sight of his blackening flesh along the side of his stomach.

"This way!" Ramona calls out, and my guys don't even hesitate to follow her between two buildings and into a shaded spot.

I jump from Austin's arms and rush to put my arm to Kingston's mouth. "Fuck, dude. Drink. Come on. You have to drink."

"No biting, babe," he murmurs, his chest heaving. "I like my fangs."

Without thinking, I lift the dagger I still clutch to my arm. Austin intervenes and grabs it from me before I slash it across my skin. Instead, he cuts a small incision that immediately seeps blood.

Kingston snatches my arm so fast that I have to steady myself against Diego before I fall into them both. "This fucking hurts," Kingston murmurs through mouthfuls of my blood. "How's my cock, babe? All I can feel is the pain in my leg."

I release a breathless laugh, humoring him to pull the shirt up enough to glance at his naked body. "I can't be certain until we're alone."

He groans. "Then someone get us the hell out of here."

My guys look to Ramona, and she hugs herself and looks around. It's the first time I really get a good look at her, and I can't stop my eyes from darting to her bulging belly. I don't know why surprise washes over me. I knew she was pregnant, but part of me might not have believed it.

"We just need somewhere to wait out the day," Austin says, speaking when Ramona doesn't react.

She sucks in her bottom lip. "Hayden..."

"We'll find him, but we need to get out of the sun," I say, speaking up. I turn to Diego. "Where's Orlando?"

He shrugs. "All he said was to get to you and that he'll find us."

A figure blurs, rushing toward us, making my guys react. It's too short to be Orlando, but it's definitely a vampire.

"Don't attack," Brayla says, holding Fallon in her arms. "It's just us. Now, come on. Hurry. This way. Someone grab Ramona."

Austin motions for Ramona to close the space, and I hop up on his back while he lifts her in his arms. Brayla disappears, and the world blurs around me. The noise of the chaos fades, and Brayla forces my guys to brave the sunlight once again.

REUNITED

I LIE ON THE FLOOR behind Kingston, spooning him for once, hugging him and allowing him to drink from my arm for the third time. His skin already looks tons better as it regenerates and heals. But still, my heart hurts so much that we weren't fast enough to get to him and that he had to experience such torture at all.

For the first time, I have no pity for these humans. These so-called rebels who look to protect and save humanity. They're far more concerned with revenge than figuring out a way to create a better future. Their better future consists of wiping out vampires. But they're delusional to think that's even possible. Vampires aren't going anywhere. There is no returning to the back-world. Apart from my love for my guys, this is one of the only other things in which I'm certain.

"Jewel, I know you want to take care of Kingston, but you need to rest," Austin says, squatting down to brush his fingers through my hair.

"Just a little more," I murmur, rubbing my free hand over Kingston's chest across the smooth spot of new skin.

Kingston releases my arm and kisses my sensitive skin, aching from the incision he keeps breaking open instead of using his fangs. I rest my chin on his shoulder, embracing him with both my arms until he relaxes.

"I'm good now, babe. Thanks," Kingston says without turning to face me. "Why don't you go with Austin and let him take care of you now? I think I'm going to sleep for a bit."

"I can cuddle you until you do," I offer, brushing my lips across his healing shoulder.

He groans softly. "Save that thought for later when I can properly snuggle you back."

"Okay. Just call for me if you need more to eat."

Austin helps me to my knees, and I lean over and meet Kingston for a soft kiss that makes him smile. His midnight eyes flash silver, and it takes everything in me not to press my arm back to his lips to get him to drink more. Even the spots of his skin that he managed to cover with the help of the clothing Fallon and Ramona gave him still glow pink with a tender sunburn.

Sliding his arm around my back, Austin guides me from the closet-sized room without windows, and we leave Kingston in the dark. Soft voices hum from the living room but fade with my arrival. Brayla gets to her feet from a lumpy, stained couch and meets me for a hug.

I release a breath, the force of her death grip squeezing the air out of me. I embrace her tighter, making her laugh, and we silently rock back and forth on our feet for a few minutes without anyone daring to break us apart.

"I'm so mad at you," I say, pulling back to meet her brown eyes. "How dare you break off our Blood Vow."

She crinkles her nose, pursing her lips. "I'm sorry, Jewel. I'm the worst best friend ever."

I shake my head. "I was only teasing. You're the best. You stayed with my family when they needed someone to look out for them. You didn't have to do that."

"Yes, I did. They're my family too." Brayla hugs me again. "Your crazy ass dad would have gotten them slaughtered otherwise."

I glance at Ramona, sitting on the loveseat between both my cousins. She hugs them to her, resting her head on Dana's shoulder. Dougie claps his hands on Fallon's lap as she bounces her knees, and I break away from Brayla to meet them.

Ramona shocks me by scooting closer to Dana to offer me a spot between her and Fallon. My eyes burn with tears at the gesture, and it takes everything inside me not to start bawling my eyes out when all three of them sandwich me in a hug that leaves me laughing.

"I can't believe you came here," Ramona says.

I slowly ease myself from her hug and rest my elbows on my knees. "I'll be honest. I wasn't going to. Not until I knew for sure about..." I wave my hand at her stomach, not wanting to say the words out loud.

Ramona puckers her bottom lip. "I guess I should've listened to Dad's speeches on procreation, huh? I just—I love Hayden."

I release a small breath and pat her knee. "I know. And he obviously loves you. He's infuriatingly brave and reckless, still a total asshole, but he wants to do right for you so I can't be too mad."

"You better not be," Hayden says, emerging from the kitchen. "Or else you won't be getting any of this."

Austin materializes in front of Hayden and snatches the plate before he has a chance to react. Closing the space, Austin sits down on the floor in front of me and sets the plate beside him to wiggle his fingers to get me to pull away from my family to join him on his lap.

Fallon laughs. "Don't you know never to threaten to withhold food from Jewel? Austin takes feeding her seriously."

I smirk and smack my cousin on the knee. "God, I missed you girls."

"We missed you too," Dana and Fallon say in unison. "This place is nuts. We thought Haven Springs was bad, but these people...they're crazy."

"They're soldiers and fighters," Hayden says. "They train people to help those in the world who need it."

"Then why the dramatics of getting Jewel here?" Diego materializes in front of me, holding two glasses of blood in his hands. He offers one to Austin, who takes it with a tight mouth. I gaze at the glasses and try not to react, but I'm curious as hell to know where they got blood from. It wasn't from me.

A strange man steps from the kitchen, pressing a towel to his arm, and I tense. Brayla moves across the room to him, biting her arm. She offers it out to the man with a smile, and he silently drinks from her, closing his eyes, looking like he enjoys the blood consumption more than even me.

I gawk at the two of them, unable to help myself. Brayla flicks her gaze to mine, her cheeks erupting in rosy color. She guides the guy to the front door and cracks it open just enough for him to squeeze through without drenching the room in sunlight.

"Did you know I'm the first female vampire to have come to The Orchards?" she asks, totally pretending all of this is normal.

"So they haven't locked you in a bunker only to let you out for time in the cages?" I ask.

"They wouldn't dare. I'm the future blood source of that little beast," Brayla responds, pointing at Ramona's belly. "...maybe."

"Oh." Her words leave me with mixed emotions. Relief that she never experienced the torture this group of Blood Rebels seems insistent to cause but also fear at the prospect of my future niece experiencing life from within these walls.

"She's the only vampire I trust," Ramona says quietly. "I can't...do what dad did to you to my daughter. I had no idea that he set you up for this. I also can't allow whatever the hell these people want to do with her."

"I don't want that either," I say, reaching out to touch her leg. "Which is why I agreed to come. Orlando—"

"He's here?" Ramona makes a face, twisting her lips down. "Where?"

I glance at Diego, who shrugs. "Don't know. He had plans to talk to Dad about working together to—"

"Wait, you left him alone to go after Dad?" she asks.

"Uh, yeah. Why?"

Ramona's fear widens her eyes. "Jewel. He's going to kill him."

"I know it's hard to believe, but Orlando isn't some terrible guy—"

"To *you.*"

Anger rushes over me, and I can't stop myself from getting to my feet. Austin follows my lead, abandoning my untouched food on the floor. Diego joins us in the corner of the room where I watch my sister watch me. Hayden closes the space to her, taking the spot I had filled and gathers her into his lap to kiss her.

"We need to find Orlando," I whisper too low for anyone to hear.

Diego rubs his hand over my arm. "He said he'd find us

and will most likely wait until dusk."

"I can't wait that long. I *need* to find him. I need to. I can't explain it other than I have a bad feeling. Ramona didn't help it, either." I bounce on my tiptoes, taking a moment to look at Austin and Diego individually, letting them see for themselves how serious I am.

"Beautiful, I'll go. You and Austin stay here and look after Kingston. He's too injured to come with us," Diego says.

Austin takes my hand before I can argue. "Jewel, he's right. It's too dangerous out there."

"For you," I say to Diego. "So let me back you up. I'm capable."

Diego and Austin stare at each other, having a silent conversation about me with only their eyes. Neither of them looks like they want to leave the safety of Brayla's house on the outskirts of the Blood Rebel compound, and I can't really blame them.

"You two are wasting time. You know I'm going. You're not going to tell me no," I say, placing my hands on my hips.

Diego raises an eyebrow. "Damn it. You're right."

"Which is why I'm going to tell Kingston so that he can do it for us," Austin teases, managing to pull his frown into a soft smile.

I clutch his hand. "Don't you dare. He needs rest."

Austin pulls me a bit closer. "So do you."

"I'll rest when I find Orlando. I have to make sure...he's okay." Wow. That wasn't what I was going to say, but the words come out anyway. And I'm pissed at myself because it should've been what I had planned to say, what I should be worried about, but Orlando's safety wasn't what was on my mind. It was my dad's safety.

And both Austin and Diego realize it.

"Jewel..." Austin lets my name hang in the air.

I purse my lips. "I'm sorry. I know it's crazy. I shouldn't care about my dad."

"You wouldn't be you if you didn't," Diego says.

I sigh. "Will you still take me? I just—I have a bad feeling."

"We'll go, but you have to know that we can't intervene. We need to stay hidden. It's not safe," Diego says.

Nodding, I glance to Austin. "Stay here and look after our family?"

He frowns, looking pouty as hell and unhappy by my request, but he doesn't argue. Instead, he leans in and brushes his lips to mine. "Be safe, Jewel. Take care of my brother."

I smile. "Always."

Diego doesn't waste any time. Without even a word to my family, he lifts me up and whisks me away.

"What the fuck?" I whisper from Diego's arms. "Are they actually just talking?"

Diego sets me on my feet in the shade created by a building. "Looks like it."

"Take me closer."

Diego peers around in search of another shadow closer to where Orlando and my dad stand on the porch of the first ancient house overlooking the now destroyed cages.

I shudder just looking at the twisted metal, the awful memory of Kingston curled on his side flitting through my mind.

"Brother, Jewel. Join us." Orlando looks up in our direction like he can feel the weight of our stares. "It is safe now. The Blood Rebels no longer pose a threat."

Diego bolts from shadow to shadow until we close the distance.

Orlando opens his arms for me, begging for me to hug him, but my steps falter because of the look Dad gives me. His expressionless face morphs into a scowl, not unlike the many I've seen on his face from before—from when he started taking me to Orlando in the shadows when just bringing me his blood no longer sufficed.

I square my shoulders and turn my attention away from Dad. I slide into Orlando's arms and rest my head to his chest, just breathing in his scent.

Diego stands next to us, and I reach out and squeeze his hand, needing the extra strength to pull myself back to face my dad once more.

"Stop looking at me like that," I say, meeting my dad's eyes, the same color as mine, straight on.

Dad's jaw twitches, but he doesn't comment.

"Jewel, don't let it get to you. He can't help it that he's

incapable of wanting to see you happy," Orlando says.

"Shut up or the deal is off," Dad snaps. "You want our help? You better remember that you're no longer in Donor Life Corp territory."

Orlando refrains from reacting and says, "Fair enough. My apologies, Noah. Just know that it is in everyone's best interest that you lay aside your hard feelings and step up to do what you were born to do for all of humanity's sake."

Dad surprises me by nodding. "You're right."

"He is?" I ask. I can't help the question from escaping.

Turning his gaze back to me, Dad nods. "Yes, honey. The fact that Orlando was willing to come here, and bring you with him, proves the seriousness of the situation with Donor Life Corp. Our sources from the cities confirmed it. Mitchell sent word out that Donor Life Corp was undergoing a shift in power and that..." He swallows without continuing.

"Please don't tell me—"

"Yes, honey. The regions will undergo another round of divisions," Dad says, inhaling a sharp breath.

Icy dread cools my veins, stealing all the warmth from me. I tilt my head up to look at Orlando for confirmation, but he doesn't say anything except, "None of the regions are responding to my calls."

"None of them?" I ask, needing him to confirm what I already know is the worst, that the Vaduvas, our strongest allies, fell by Mitchell's hands.

"I'll keep trying," is all he says.

I turn and hug Diego. I didn't necessarily like the Vaduvas, but Viorica kind of grew on me over the last few months. She stood up for me. She agreed to take Brayla into her coven because we had to outcast her from ours to complete the union without her. Now? I don't even know what's going to happen.

"But try not to worry. Our first concern is taking care of the threat Mitchell poses," Orlando says.

"And how do we do that?" I ask.

"We bait him."

I frown. "Bait him with what?"

He smirks at me.

Diego growls. "No, brother. I don't think so."

"The only thing stronger than his need to kill us is to kill Jewel," he says.

I hate to admit he's right. Mitchell blames me for losing his heirs. He blames me for the shift in power. He blames me for everything despite it being him who caused his own life's destruction.

"We'll assure she's safe," Orlando adds.

"Okay," I say.

Diego squeezes my hand. "Jewel, no. There has to be another way."

"There might be, but we don't have time. We need to put a stop to this before he makes new alliances. Before anything else bad happens." I suck in a breath through my nose. "I couldn't live with myself if things shift for the worst. We were so close to creating an amazing future. I—I can't risk it failing. I have to do this—for our sake. For humanity's sake."

"So it's settled," Orlando says. "Gather your people, Noah. We'll meet at dusk."

TEAM JEWEL

I LICK MY LIPS. "MORE."

"Whatever you want," Diego whispers, tilting his head the other way. "Whatever you need."

I grind against him for a moment, brushing my lips to his skin, just savoring the pressure his fingers create as they dig into my hips. He releases a breathless moan, dead-set on letting me suck on his neck to my heart's content.

"Jewel, you might want to take it easy," Austin says, touching my back. "This is more than you usually drink."

"You're going to get blood bloat," Kingston adds.

I groan and rest my head on Diego's shoulder without biting him. "Thanks for the reminder."

Diego cups my cheeks, drawing my attention to him. "I'll

stop you before that happens. Drink some more." Turning to his brothers, he says, "And you guys go check on the plans. They looked fine to me, but I want you to triple check Orlando's strategy."

"And I want a moment alone with Diego," I say, hugging him. "Don't worry. I'll make time for you."

Kingston hums deep in his throat, coming up behind me to rest his hands on my shoulders to press his body into my back. "I need another hour and another drink before I can properly take care of you."

"Go talk to Brayla," Diego says, tracing his fingers under my shirt to play with the skin of my lower back. "She'll hook you up."

"Try to keep everyone else away too. Tell them I'm sleeping," I murmur.

"Damn," Kingston whispers to Austin. "Maybe we should stay."

"She does look ready to drain him," Austin teases, leaning in to kiss my cheek.

I wave my hand behind me and graze it against his leg. "I might, so you two better find safety or I'll come for you next."

"That's the plan," Kingston says, kissing my other cheek. His innuendo makes me blush crazy hard with more desire.

Diego chuckles. "You better listen to our girl."

The door clicks closed, and I bite down on Diego's shoulder. Moaning, he squeezes my hips, rolling my body against his to let me feel how hot and excited I make him even through our clothes.

"I love you, Jewel," he whispers, sliding his hands up my shirt to tug it over my head, not wasting a moment of our stolen alone time where we should be resting. But I can't. Neither can he. We both lasted all of five minutes trying to sleep. Our nerves are way out of control, so Diego offered to feed me, and now I'm offering him this. My whole tense body begs for me to let Diego help us both relax.

I break away from his shoulder and arch my back to bring my breasts to his mouth. He kisses along the fabric of my bra, quick to unclasp it to suck my sensitive skin into his mouth. I moan, clutching my hands around his head, running my fingers through his hair.

"I love you, Diego," I whisper, bringing my lips to his. "There's nothing more I want right now than you."

He hums his agreement against my mouth as I press my body harder into his. "Is that so?"

"It's all I can think about. It's all I *want* to think about. It's been days since I got to be alone with you. If things go bad—"

"They won't," he says, cutting me off. "Don't think about that."

I nod. "Okay."

"Just think about me."

Diego shifts me off of him so that I stand between his legs. He drinks me in, his chest heaving, and slowly reaches forward to slip the pair of jeans I borrowed from Brayla off until they fall to the ground. I step out of them and bend forward to undress the rest of him. He arches up so that I can tug his pants and boxers off to drop them on the floor with mine.

I bite my lip and smile, just standing naked before him. He leans forward, sliding his hands around my waist to tug me closer. Brushing his lips to my stomach, he kisses my navel and scoops me off my feet to set me next to him. We both lie on our sides, facing each other, and he takes his time to explore my body with his fingers, teasing my skin inch by inch until I open up for him. He nestles between my legs, bending my knee to hold on to.

His lips meet mine, and he positions himself to align our bodies. I gasp under the incredible sensation of our bodies connecting completely. Diego kisses me harder, using my body to brace himself as he rocks against me, knocking his hips to mine with his fervent movements.

Diego's breathing matches mine in hard pants, my whole body begging me to wrap myself around him. I clutch his neck, resting my forehead to his chin. He brushes his lips to my hair and slides his hand under me to squeeze my ass.

I could survive on his attention and love, the desire he drags from me in wave after hot wave as he steals my breath with every kiss. He moans, his voice low and whispery, and he tilts his head to watch our bodies meet as one.

It's so friggin' hot, the passion he shares with me in a moment we should care about the world, but all I care about is how he feels, the softness of his lips, the warmth building to explode through me.

He captures my mouth to silence it, chuckling when I bite down on his lip, my mouth refusing to let go. Piercing his fangs into his lip, he teases me with his blood, knowing how much I crave him in this moment on every level the way he craves me—our bodies and souls clinging to each other to assure we're always together.

Diego rolls with me to thrust a few more times while I'm on my back so that I can hold onto him as he finishes. He kisses me once more before sinking his weight on me, so there is not a single inch of space between us.

"Jewel," he whispers. "I don't want you to be the bait." He says the words so softly like he's afraid how I'll react.

They're not the words I had expected to hear, and it catches me off guard, making me frown. He rests on his elbows and meets my gaze with his stormy gray-eyed intensity, pleading with me without saying the words.

"Orlando is being reckless with you," he adds. "I just—I can't agree with the plan."

"But you said it looked fine," I say, resting my hands on his neck. "The four of you will be there to assure nothing goes wrong. This place is full of fighters. Isn't it better to lure Mitchell to us rather than just wait around for the next attack? Or to let him have his way to re-divide the regions? Who would even take over on the board?"

"I don't have those answers," he says, his brows puckering. "The only thing I know is that I can't agree with this.

Please, change your mind."

"Diego." I huff a breath with his name. "I wish I could but—"

Diego rests his head next to mine, pressing our cheeks together. "But nothing, Jewel. You shouldn't feel like you have to do this. We can do it for you. He wants us dead just as much as you."

"It won't work like that. He'll know you're baiting him. It has to be me," I say.

"There has to be another way."

I lie with Diego in silence, just letting him hold me close. A dozen thoughts cross my mind as I try to think of another way to get Mitchell where we want him to fight back and stop this madness. But everything I think of ends up with my guys hurt or dead or worse, captured and chained for the rest of eternity, however long that may be.

"So you really don't want me to do it?" I ask quietly, getting Diego to lean back to look at me. "Even though you have more confidence in my ability out of everyone?"

"We all know you're a badass, beautiful," he says, offering me a small smile. "But just because you are, doesn't mean you have to be. I'm not willing to put my faith or your life in the hands of people who only want to use you. I know these are uncertain times and we're desperate, but I'd rather lose everything and go to the shadows than risk ever losing you."

I lean up and brush my lips to his, kissing him like he's my sole purpose for being. And in this moment, I'll gladly exist just for him. His words are exactly what I need to hear to know that the world could crash down around us, but everything would still be okay because we're together. We're stronger together. If Diego feels this way, I'm sure Austin and Kingston do. As for Orlando? I guess we'll find out. He's still learning that things go beyond my desire. What we all desire is the most important to me.

"Okay, I won't do it. We'll think of another way," I say, kissing him again. "But if I'm not going to be the bait, neither are you guys."

His eyes flash silver. "It'll complicate things. Could put a strain on any sort of alliance Orlando's trying to build with the rebels."

"I'll handle that," I say. "I can talk to my dad."

He frowns. "I don't know, Jewel."

I cup his face in my hands. "Will you trust me?"

"I always do. It's the rest of the world I don't trust."

"Your plan sucks. It requires us to be too far away. Do you know what could happen in a matter of seconds?" Kingston's voice booms through the small room. "I don't know what the hell kind of plan you went over with Diego, but it wasn't fucking this. He'd never say it was fine."

Oh, boy. It sounds like Kingston took Diego up on his suggestion of asking Brayla to hook him up with some extra blood, because he sounds like his crazy, sexy, passionate self again. And I love how he isn't afraid to call something out.

"Then we can move here and here," Orlando says. He taps his finger on the first paper map I've ever seen in real life. "It'll be risky to be this close, but if you're that against securing the fate of our coven—"

"Oh, don't fucking give me that bullshit. I'm a fucking master of playing games, and I'm not going to allow you to try to manipulate Jewel into thinking that I don't care." Something crashes, and I tense, squeezing Diego's hand. "Hey, babe. Come on in and stop eavesdropping. I want to show you this half-assed plan."

I bare my teeth at Diego, making him chuckle, and pull him from the small hallway with me to where Orlando and Kingston hover around a table. Austin bounces Dougie in his arms in the corner, and Hayden sits on the couch with Ramona asleep with her head in his lap. I don't see my cousins or Brayla anywhere. I'm surprised no one came rushing in at the sound of Kingston throwing a chair at the wall.

I straighten my back. "It's okay, Kingston. I don't need to see the plan. I'm not doing it. We're going to come up with something else."

"Whoa, what? Are you serious?" Kingston asks. "I was pretty sure I was going to have to lock you in a closet to stop you from going all save-the-day on us."

"Super serious, dude. Diego told me he didn't want me to, and if you're not all on board..." I shrug. "We're a team. A coven."

Kingston narrows his eyes. "Do you know how many

times I didn't agree—"

I close the space to him and place my hands on his shoulders. He snaps his mouth shut without finishing his complaint, and I hug him until he lifts me off my feet and practically crashes his mouth to mine.

"I'm sorry you don't always get what you want, but after seeing you in the sun today, how willing you were to suffer to assure that I stayed safe, I can't go through that again. I *won't* go through that again."

Kingston rocks me back and forth. "I love you. So. Damn. Much. Can I ask for my moment alone with you now? I'm in serious need of feeling your body against mine."

I release a gasp of a laugh as he drops me a few inches lower and humps me through our clothes, not even caring that everyone, including Hayden, watches us. Patting Kingston's chest, I get him to calm down for a second before he takes my lack of response and smile as silent permission and locks us in the room.

"Actually—"

Kingston groans. "I hate when you deny me. It kills me. Torture."

I laugh. "I'm not denying you. I just have to do something first."

Pouting his kissable mouth, he heaves the most dramatic sigh in all of existence and sets me on my feet but doesn't let go of my hand like he can't stand the thought of ever letting me go. And I let him, enjoying his need to be close. I'll never tire of my lack of personal space nor will I ever take Kingston's wild heart for granted.

I turn to Orlando, who quietly watches the two of us without so much as a flash of silver in his eyes. "I know you think this is a good idea, and it might possibly be if it works, but I think we can come up with something better."

"What exactly?" Hayden asks, speaking up for the first time. "The rebels aren't going to work beside anyone but you. They would never trust a vampire to lead them anywhere. This whole deal depends on you doing what they believe you were born to do, Jewel."

So much for Kingston sticking by my side. He releases me to stand in front of Hayden, yanking him from his seat and startling Ramona awake in the process. I rush to them in time to get Ramona to put down a silver stake she tugs from her jacket. Jeez. I wonder if Blood Rebels ever go unarmed.

"Dude, put him down," I say. "Now."

Kingston softly growls at me. "Only because you're fucking irresistible when you talk to me like this."

"Don't even start," I say.

"Yeah, please don't," Ramona says.

He growls at her next, making her shudder with her uncontrollable fear instincts. I hold my hands up, motioning for everyone to chill the hell out. Kingston heads to Austin's side, standing to face the corner. Diego closes the space to me, taking my hand in his to assure Ramona doesn't spontaneously attack. We never know with her.

Orlando scoops the map from the table and crumples it up in his hands, throwing the ball of paper at Hayden. I expected a lot more argument with him, even half expected him to tell us that he will make me do it anyway, but all he does is step forward and open his arms for me.

I sink into his embrace, smelling the sweet scent of his skin through his dress shirt, the same he wore for our vow ceremony. Trailing his hand over the back of my head, he plays with my hair for a minute, remaining silent as he gathers his thoughts.

"If this is what you want, then I respect your decision," Orlando says, tilting his head down to gaze at me. "But we need to leave immediately."

I nod and stretch up to kiss him. "Thank you."

"You know I'll do anything for you, Jewel."

Pulling myself away, I turn to face everyone. Austin, Kingston, and Diego close the space to join us, enclosing me in the best muscular circle. I spin slightly to run my hands across each of their chests, feeling their beating hearts under my fingers.

"There's one more thing we need to discuss," I say, standing on my tiptoes to glance at Ramona and Hayden.

"Babe, it'd be a terrible idea to take them. The Blood Rebels would possibly come after us," Kingston says.

"We can handle them," Austin says. "You know how Jewel feels. That's our niece."

I throw my arms around Austin, my heart refusing to stay

away from him after his declaration about Ramona carrying *our* niece and not just mine. Kingston groans at my reaction, and Diego drapes his arm over his shoulder, half hugging him and half shaking him.

"We have to take the Diggs' heir as well," Orlando says. "Brayla expressed her desire not to leave him behind since her father..." He doesn't finish his sentence.

My heart clenches at his words, and I feel like a total failure as a friend. I've been so concerned about everything else that I haven't even talked to Brayla about her mom and what happened. And now her dad? Shit.

Orlando squeezes my shoulder. "There will be time for grieving and comfort later. Brayla is strong. Our focus is now getting out safely. The Daring brothers should be near to assist."

I had almost forgotten that they said they'd meet us where they dropped us off. I can imagine they'll ask for something more when they see Orlando and Diego followed us instead of staying behind and that we have a few extra people. But Orlando doesn't seem fazed. His composure is the only thing stopping me from freaking the eff out.

A low groan from somewhere in the hall draws my attention away from my guys. They step back to give me space so that I can see Brayla half carrying a man from where her bedroom must be. My cousins trail behind her, carrying two duffle bags, and I turn my attention to Orlando.

"Brayla was preparing for our trip by stocking up on extra

blood," he responds, answering my silent question.

I bob my head. "Oh, okay. I wouldn't mind providing to her if need be." My mouth says the words, but my body shivers at the thought.

"Thanks, Jewel-babewel, but I'm good. I even have enough for your boy toys if things turn to shit. Even you have your limitations," she says.

I smile. I can't help it. "That's sweet."

"Hey, we're a coven...in a year." Orlando must've told her the new arrangement.

"Unless the board is dead," Kingston says. "No board, no one to see that we follow through."

As much as I like the idea of not having to follow through, a part of me hurts at the thought of having to deal with the aftermath. We still have to take care of Mitchell.

"I guess we'll see," Brayla says.

"And soon. Is everyone ready?" Orlando asks.

Kingston slides his fingers through mine while Orlando offers his hand to me to hold my other one. Brayla takes Dougie from Austin, and Austin and Diego pick up my cousins. Diego carries Dana on his back while Austin carries Fallon.

"Diego, will you please also take Mr. Andrei?" Orlando asks him. "Kingston, you can take Ramona."

I cringe and step on Kingston's foot before he can react. "Actually, Orlando. I'd feel better if you took Ramona."

Kingston smirks and lifts me up into his arms, beating

everyone to the door, as ready to go as I am. Reaching out, I open the door for him and tense in his arms.

"Jewel, honey," Dad says, standing with a group of men outside of Brayla's door. "You have no idea how happy I am that you've come to your senses. I just wanted to introduce you to a few of the elders and view the plans one more time."

"Oh, uh, sure." I wiggle from Kingston's arms and glance behind me.

Orlando nods.

I straighten my shoulders and add, "Why don't you all come on in?"

THE ELDERS

"IT'S NICE TO SEE EVERYONE here," Dad says, shifting on his feet in the middle of the room.

Five men stand behind him, nothing elder-looking about any of them. One of the guys barely looks older than Orlando, who is physically forever in his mid-twenties though it's sometimes hard to tell. He's handsome yet ageless. Like with Kingston, Austin, and Diego, his eyes tell another story, though they've all adapted to life with me.

"Jewel, come here and give your dad a hug," Dad says.

I don't move from Kingston's side. "I'm sorry, no."

He frowns, stepping closer to try anyway.

All my suppressed memories from my real life growing up with him and not the one Orlando created come exploding back to me, making my head spin. I jerk my hand out and shove my dad hard, feeling muscles I had no idea he had, muscles he put on after leaving Dark Terrace Ranch.

"Get back. You lost your right to act like I mean something to you the second you abandoned and betrayed me. You severed our bond completely when you attacked Orlando and dragged my family to this awful place." My sharp voice cuts through the air. I hope he can feel the pain he caused me whip across his heart with my words.

"Calm down or the vampires go to the cage, Jewel, and the deal is off. I'm not playing these games with you. If you cannot act like the daughter I raised, then you will be treated like the traitor to humanity our people accuse you of being." Dad's words sting, but I remain expressionless despite the fury boiling through me.

"Mr. Jordan, I'd advise that it's in your best interest not to threaten us," Orlando says.

Austin and Diego join him to stand with me and Kingston. It takes everything in me not to grin like crazy, loving every second of discomfort our presences bring to this group of assholes as they reach for their weapons.

"And I'm not a traitor, Dad," I say, clenching my teeth. "I was never a traitor. I care about humanity, but I also care about those who have agreed to fight for me and with me to assure an eternity I want to live."

"As a blood slave," one of the men says, a guy with a shaved head and thick brunette beard cut close to his boxy jaw.

I step closer, my guys flanking me as we move together as one, and glare. The man's heart picks up pace, pounding crazy out of control, and I can't help but smile. I know it's not me poking at his human rationale that forces him to be afraid, but it still feels damn good that he realizes his words were a big friggin' mistake.

"Jewel, I'm sorry," Dad says, holding his arms out to keep the elders in check. "I didn't come here to upset you or to start problems. And even if you don't believe me, I love you. I do want to work together. I never intended for you to be put in this position. We want what's best for you even if it means working with your blood sources. My future granddaughter counts on us to come to a mutual agreement. She will have the life she truly deserves with you here to help. The life you will assure she gets by providing your future niece the perfect guardian and blood source."

I slowly turn to meet my guys' gazes. They all remain expressionless to my dad's words. They'll humor him and the rest of these Blood Rebels for as long as they need to. But, I mean, what the actual eff? It sounds like my dad thought I planned to stay here permanently after taking care of Mitchell.

"Excuse me?" I finally manage to say. "What do you mean that I'll provide her a blood source?"

"Honey, a dhampir doesn't need an entire coven to satiate her needs. One is just fine, and you have four. I know how...obsessed...these blood sources are with you, so you convincing one of them will assure they do not build an attach-ment nor start an unhealthy relationship with another gift to humanity the universe bestowed us with."

Holy shit balls. I knew my dad was a little weird, but he's out of his damn mind if he thinks that I'm just going to offer up one of my guys as a blood source to be treated as food. I can't even stand the thought. They're mine.

"Don't react, Jewel," Kingston whispers under his breath.

"They don't know that you're different than any other dhampir the Blood Rebels have supposedly encountered. You've been bitten with venom...a lot, remember?" Austin adds quietly.

Without having to ask, I know they're right. We're still trying to figure out the extent of my ability and what I can do. The Blood Rebels don't know. And they never will. I won't tell them. I'm not staying. Neither is Ramona.

I open my mouth to tell them as much, but Orlando takes a step in front of me. Diego joins him while Austin and Kingston each come to my side. The room falls completely silent as the elders and my dad decide to start a glower-match with my vampires.

"What is this?" Dad asks. "I'm in the middle of talking to my daughter."

"I'm sorry, Mr. Jordan. Jewel's finished talking to you. Everything you say from now on will be directed to me."

"The hell it will," the same man who called me a blood slave says. "Whatever truce you think we have will be over.

We don't deal with vampires here."

"Jewel," Dad says. "Don't be stupid. Control them. You have it in you."

I tighten my jaw and slide my hands between Diego and Orlando, getting them to allow me to stand between them. I keep my chin raised, meeting everyone's glares as they wait for me to do or say something.

I flick my gaze to Brayla in the corner of the room, tilting my head just enough so that she knows I want her to get to my cousins. Hayden grabs Ramona's hand as well, preparing to make a run for it if need be.

The elders sense what's coming and yank their weapons to point at us.

I clear my throat and hold my arms out. "Everyone calm down. We don't want to fight."

"Then come to me, honey," Dad says. "We don't need your blood sources to help us. You will be good enough. Our people already stand ready. We're not afraid, and we damn well don't need vampires thinking that they can control us."

I shake my head. "No. I'm sorry. We're leaving."

Dad scoffs, his eyes widening. "The only way you're leaving is with me."

"Dad, please," I say. "We don't want to hurt you."

Dad reaches into his pocket and pulls out a small black device. Diego stiffens next to me, and Kingston tugs me back. Orlando stops Austin from bolting forward. It's the first time I've seen them really hesitate.

"Noah," Hayden says from his place with Ramona. "Don't be stupid. You'll kill us all."

"Only if I have to," Dad says. "But I know my daughter. She's smart. She'll listen."

My hands tremble with sudden fear. "Dad, what is that?"

He tightens his jaw. "Come on, Jewel. Come to me. We're leaving."

"What? No," I say.

"Jewel, it's going to be okay," Orlando says. "Go ahead and go with your dad."

"Orlando," Kingston snaps.

"It's not worth the risk to see if he's bluffing, bro," Diego says to Kingston.

Austin keeps his eyes trained on the device in Dad's hand. "You know how Blood Rebels are. They'll sacrifice themselves and try to take us all with them. We might survive the explosion but Jewel might not. Her family won't."

I suck in a shuddering breath. "What? That's a bomb?"

"A detonator," Diego says. "It's probably been here this whole time because of Brayla."

"Jewel, you have five seconds to decide," Dad says.

It only takes me one to step forward and away from my guys. Dad and the elders walk slowly toward the door, their weapons raised. Dad motions for Hayden and Ramona to get my cousins and Dougie. Strong hands lock onto my shoulders, keeping me from turning to see which elder holds onto me.

"If you try anything stupid, they will kill her," Dad says, strolling in front of me to get the door.

"Dad," I whisper. "Don't do this."

"I'm sorry, honey. It's the only way. We all have to do things in life that we don't want to," he says. "But think about what your sacrifice will mean. This is the future of humanity."

"And what about *my* future?" I ask.

"You will not die in vain."

Dad pushes me out, and I struggle to look behind me, watching as Orlando stops Kingston, Austin, and Diego from moving. Brayla comes up next to them and touches Kingston's shoulder.

"Don't do anything to piss them off," Kingston says. "We won't let them get far."

Austin's eyes flash silver. "Stay on guard, Jewel."

"Remember everything I taught you," Diego adds.

Orlando rests his arm on Austin. "Show them the fighter you truly are."

"I love you all. I won't let you down," I say.

Someone shoves me hard in the back, sending me forward. I nearly eat shit on the walkway but manage to get control of my legs. I spin around to hit the asshole who pushed me, and the oldest elder, a man with streaks of gray through his dirty blond hair catches my arm and twists me around, locking me against his chest. And eff is he strong.

He grips me against him and turns toward the cabin, ignoring the deep growls coming from my guys within. "Noah, do it now."

I don't have time to react as the old house explodes before me, shaking the ground. The sound of the blast rings in my ears, stealing my hearing. Someone lifts me into their arms and binds my wrists. Then someone pulls a bag over my head, stealing my vision too.

"Relax, Jewel-babewel. You're with family now," Dad says.

"You're not my family," I mutter.

"You are to me." Dad hugs me to him, far gentler than the other man. "And now honey, I need you to be brave. So very brave."

"Attack all covenless vampires on sight." The familiar voice pulls me from counting my breaths. One-thousand seven-hundred and two have passed in my attempt to keep my cool. "It's time we sever all cordial ties with vampires. Blood sources will be imprisoned."

"What about your brother, Newport?" a guy asks.

"If you can avoid conflict, do, but he's a Mercy Brother now," Newport says. "They're standing by for instructions." What? I can't friggin' believe it. The Mercy Coven wanted nothing to do with Blood Rebels. They thought Huntington was crazy for even humoring such a life...but then again, they hate Mitchell. I wonder if Orlando has something to do with their involvement. If he did, no one mentioned it to me.

"What about the girls, Noah?" Hayden asks, drawing my

attention to him next.

"I can escort them to the safe house with Donnie's girls. It'll keep them out of the way," a man says.

"Yeah, the baby too," Dad says. "We're all he has left."

I frown. I want to ask what happened to Brayla's dad, but I don't. All I do is try to remain calm through the commotion of everyone preparing for a war there is no friggin' way they're going to win.

"I'm staying with Hayden," Ramona says, her voice sharp. Defiant.

"The hell you—"

Someone heaves a breath a second before a thud, sounding like a body hitting the ground. I should know. I hear those types of thumps all the time when my guys mess around and play fight.

"Mona stays with us," Hayden says, his voice turning low and scary. He's definitely hung around vampires enough to have learned exactly how to be threatening.

"Fine, but she has to fight," Newport says.

I shift in my dad's arms, trying to shake the bag off my head so I can see what the eff is going on. There are too many voices humming through the air to distinguish but not as many as the times people gathered in Haven Springs.

"Stop wiggling, Jewel," Dad says.

"Just put me down," I say. "I won't run or fight."

Dad sighs and sets me on my feet. He doesn't stop me as I tug the bag off my head and toss it on the ground. My wrists ache from the metal binds, but I don't ask him to take them off. I'm just glad I can still use my hands with them on.

Swiveling on my feet, I look around. And holy shit balls. I'm standing in the middle of an army. Hayden used to tell my guys that they had no idea how far of a reach Blood Rebels had, and I'm pretty friggin' sure he was right. And they're quiet as all get-out. I would've sworn that there were fewer people here. All men. I don't see a single female apart from Ramona and my cousins.

"Jewel," Dana says, her soft voice drawing my gaze from the closest guys around me. "You okay?"

I nod my head, afraid to say anything out loud.

"Come on, girls. Wish your uncle a good fight," Newport says, motioning for the two of them to head with the jerk elder who called me a blood slave.

The second I meet Newport's eyes, I can't stop the fury from rushing through me. I break into a sprint, closing the distance inhumanly fast, and collide into his chest. We fall to the ground, and I land on top of him. My anger enhances my strength, and I snap the flimsy chain bindings and punch him in the face.

"You're just like your brother," I say, gripping the front of his shirt. "And like him, I'm going to see that you meet your final donation."

Newport freezes beneath me, confusion wrinkling his forehead before realization sets in, tightening his brows. "Huntington is dead."

"Damn straight. He deserved it." I never thought telling someone that their family member is dead could feel so good. I should feel bad, but I don't. And now I'm determined to hurt him to give him something more to cry about, if he's even capable of the act.

Newport manages to break his arm free and swings to punch me off him. I snatch his wrist and slam his hand into the concrete. Someone drags me off him, yanking me to my feet, and I still in Hayden's arms for the first time not wanting to punch him. He might be the one person still on my side.

"Calm down, Jewel," he whispers. "Your coven will kill me if you get hurt under my watch."

"Your watch?" I ask, relaxing in his arms.

Hayden's mouth remains pressed against my ear. "Yes, my watch. You know as well as I do that your coven is powerful enough to survive an explosion. They're only keeping back because they don't trust your dad not to do something stupid."

Hayden's right about that. I never once thought something happened to my guys. He holds his arm out to anyone attempting to step closer, making it seem like he's restraining me and trying to get me to calm down. So I purposely struggle.

"He already is," I mutter. "What do they expect to do? Stick to the original plan? Without my guys standing to back them up, they don't stand a chance."

"Don't underestimate them, Jewel," Hayden says. "They

haven't spent their lives placated at the servitude of vampires. They've been preparing to fight."

I shake my head, peering around at the crowd. "You mean to die."

"It's worth it to them."

"It's also stupid. What do they even plan to do? If they manage to rise against Mitchell, there is still the rest of the cities. They'll just be wiped out eventually." Because it's true. Each region has a hierarchy. Each coven has a place.

"I know," he murmurs. "Why do you think I chose to work with Orlando instead of Noah? I'm how he kept tabs on your father, even after he faked his death. I don't want to see people die unnecessarily. I don't want humans to end up in literal cages. The cities are bad enough. This—these rebels choosing to fight until they die, they're only setting up the world for complete devastation."

I close my eyes, taking a breath. "God, what do we do?"

"We comply and we wait," he says. "We stick to the original plan."

"Well, that doesn't work for me."

Reaching down, I snatch Hayden's knife from his belt and rip it free. Hayden holds his hands up in surrender, choosing not to fight me, and I slice the blade through the air at anyone who dares come near. A gunshot rings out, startling me, and I freeze.

"Put that thing down," Dad says, standing between me and Newport, who holds the gun awkwardly, clenching his teeth, because I'm pretty friggin' sure I broke some of his fingers. "You can't hurt Jewel. We need her for this to work. Our source says Divine is outside the Bellamy Region. They're willing to meet us there for the trade."

"How do you know we can even trust Paris now? He didn't say anything about Huntington," Newport snaps.

"Because he doesn't know," Hayden says. "The Ortegas took care of his body."

"I think Hayden's right," Dad says. "And we can use that knowledge. They'll want revenge. They'll assure this plan works. All we need is for Mitchell to know we have Jewel. He'll come for her, and we'll be ready."

I heave a few deep breaths. "I hope you're right, Dad. If you're not, everyone will die."

"If that happens, the work we've put forth will help future generations. Our legacies will still live on."

"Keep telling yourself that," I mutter. "You will be responsible for the loss of all of humanity."

CHANGE THE WORLD

"JEWEL, IF YOU FIGHT AGAIN, you'll be given to the Mercy Coven gagged, chained, and blind," Dad says, his voice sharper than I've ever heard it.

It reminds me of the time he caught Orlando and me in the shadows about to kiss after Mom's death. The coldness of his voice sinks deep inside me, pulling the grief I haven't felt in a long time right from me.

"Now, I don't want to have to do that, honey. I want you to be able to fight. I want you to survive. I love you," Dad adds.

"I wish it were you who caught the flu." My voice shakes as I say the words, struggling to breathe under the bag Dad put back on my head. "Mom would've shoved you in the shadows herself for what you're doing."

"Don't speak of your mother like you know what you're talking about," Dad snaps.

The world falls out from under me, and I screech and huff as I hit my back on the solid ground. I roll to my side, curling my knees to my chest. I've been waiting and waiting for my guys to arrive or to whisper that I shouldn't worry because they're nearby. But they haven't. And I'm more than worried. I'm freaking the hell out.

"Someone else take her." Dad's boots crunch next to me. He stops somewhere above my head. "Not you, Hayden. I trust you to care for Ramona."

"I will gladly watch her," Newport says.

"Not you, either. I don't trust you. Hey kid, come here. You're from the South Compound, right?" Someone shuffles forward, stopping near my dad. "How do you feel about accepting a handler position? If you get Jewel safely in and out of the fight that will ensue at the fake exchange, I'll see to it myself that you're heavily rewarded and given the opportunity to transfer to the East Compound."

"Don't say no, kid," another man says. "I'd give anything for that opportunity. You can't pass up the chance to help ensure the next generation. Most men who end up there find their wives there."

What the eff.

"That's if he can manage to impress someone," another guy says with a laugh. "I hear the women only go for the best of the best considering all the options."

OhmyfrigginGod. Now it makes perfect sense as to why I haven't seen a single female apart from my family. They weren't where we were, and it sounds like the Blood Rebels probably keep them somewhere far away from any possible vampires. I guess the whole coveted because they're female crosses into this place too.

"So what do you say, kid?" Dad asks. "Do you want the chance? It'll be dangerous but worth it if you succeed."

"Yes, sir."

My whole body screams with fear at the familiar sound of Cyprus's voice. I'd remember it no matter what. And I can't believe he's here.

The bag lifts from my face, and I scramble back to put space between me and Cyprus. There is no friggin' way I'm letting him get within an inch of me. If he's here, that means—

I open my mouth to scream, to tell everyone to run, but someone lifts me from behind and slaps a hand across my mouth. I bite down hard, and a man hollers and drops me. A heavy foot rams into my back, sending me sprawling forward. I can't catch my breath, the words unable to come out.

Dad lifts me to my feet and shoves a ball of fabric into my mouth before slapping silver tape across my lips. He unlocks my restraints only to flip me over to secure my hands behind my back and then ties up my feet. I thrash, rolling away, trying my best to get to my knees, but every time I try, someone else kicks me down.

"Dad, stop!" Ramona yells. "Stop!"

"Hayden, shut her up or I'll gag her too," Dad says.

"But, Noah—"

Dad shoots his gun into the air, cutting off Hayden's words. "Say another word, and it'll be your last. You're lucky to even be here after the godforsaken arrangement you made with that devil of a vampire."

Says the man who made one too.

But I can't scream it. I can't say anything.

All I can do is continue to thrash as Dad motions at Cyprus to pick me off the ground. Cyprus holds me out for a second, tilting his head to the side as he drinks me in. He looks thinner, his dark skin ashen, his eyes hollow, the flecks of gold no longer sparkling from their brown depths. I'd recognize the reason anywhere. He's given blood, possibly too much, yet here he is among these Blood Rebels. But how? I have no idea.

"I'm going to take good care of you, Ms. Jordan," he says, using my human-born name. He situates me on his shoulder, digging his hard bone into my stomach. "I bet you regret ever giving a damn about these donors. But don't worry, Jewel. I have you. This will all be over soon. Promise." The words come out in a whisper so that no one can hear them.

I try to scream, but the action makes me gag on the cloth, and the last thing I want to do is throw up.

"Just relax. Remember, us traitors stick together," Cyprus

says, reaching up to pat my back.

I hang placidly, deciding against wasting my energy fighting now when I'm not sure what lies ahead of me. Right now, I'll lose any fight. I'm bound and gagged, but at least no one thinks to put the bag over my head. At least if I can see, I can expect what's coming. If I expect what's coming, I can strategize the best plan to survive. My guys would give me hell otherwise. They taught me better than to give up so easily.

Staring at the back of Cyprus's dirty shirt, I focus my attention on my surroundings, listening to the quiet conversations between the rebels. They're crazy for even talking at all. Their footsteps are loud enough. It's like they either don't know or don't care that vampires can hear them.

"Newport, Hayden, new kid—"

"The name's Cyprus."

Dad hums gruffly. "Cyprus. You three stay by my side at all times. Jay, Tito, and Alonzo, grab two of your best men to back us up. The rest of you, head to your posts. No more talking. Be ready to fight on my command. Do not show yourselves until we have a clear view of our target."

"Yes, sir," a couple of guys say in unison.

A hand touches my head, and I'm forced to look at my dad squatting behind Cyprus. "Honey, you're so strong and brave. I know you'll do what's right and fight with us. Just remember that this blood source wants nothing more than to end your life because he's afraid of you. Time to prove to him that his fear is warranted."

I glare at my dad, my eyes burning, but I refuse to cry. Instead, I channel my heartache and anger to my very core, feeling it burn away whatever feelings I might've had left for my dad. For these people.

The murmur of voices falls silent as the army of rebels splits up. I train my gaze to the ground, watching the terrain change from dirt to asphalt. The night grows lighter the longer we march toward our destination, and I hear the familiar hum of electricity radiating from a nearby city. But that's not the only thing I hear.

"Vampires," I mumble, trying to speak, but the words come out as just a whiny noise.

No one responds to me.

"Vampires." I try again. "Vampires. Vampires. Vampires."

The growls grow in the distance and not because we near a city on the edge of the Bellamy Region. My heart pounds in my head, my fear instincts driving me crazy. I can't hang onto Cyprus's shoulder for a moment longer.

"Jewel, shut up, or you're going to get us all killed," Dad says, whacking me on the back hard enough to make my muscles stiffen.

I don't shut up, though. I try to scream the best I can.

The hairs on my neck rise, and I arch my back, attempting to search the night around us. My long hair veils my view, but I spot the flash of silver eyes in the distance. Another pair appears and then another. I stop trying to yell as a fourth vampire materializes from the darkness, hope lifting me up that my guys have arrived.

"The Mercy Coven will meet us by the third spotlight along the wall," Newport whispers, standing close enough to dad that I can clearly hear his words. "There are five—four of them. They owe me a huge favor, so they'll—"

A small huff sounds through the air, and I tense at the sound of a muffled yell that fades too fast for anyone to notice. The group focuses all their attention at the supposed threat before us rather than what lurks in every direction.

"Easy now, Jewel," Cyprus says. "Don't try anything stupid. My eternity counts on getting you there safely."

Eff this.

Rocking as hard as I can, I flip my body from Cyprus's shoulder and land on the ground. My shoulders and arms scream at my weight slamming on top of them, but it pushes me to sit up, using every ounce of strength in my core instead of rolling over to my knees. Cyprus grabs me by the hair and drags me a few feet. Ramona screams out my name, her voice cutting through the air.

Hayden swings and punches Newport in the face before he can react to Ramona. Dad raises his gun at Hayden. Ramona pulls him back, getting between the two of them. No one sees another guy in the group disappear, snatched away by an outcast vampire.

I try to scream again.

Hayden aims his gun at me. "Let Jewel go."

Cyprus pulls me up higher, using me as a shield. "You're going to have to shoot me."

"Hayden, put the gun down," Dad says. "You're going to get us all killed."

Hayden steps forward, sliding in front of Ramona, ignoring Dad. People shuffle around in our group, moving closer like they'll tackle Hayden. I spot silver flashing eyes behind Ramona and thrash hard enough in Cyprus's arms to get him to release me. Hayden aims his gun at Cyprus but spins and shoots, hitting a vampire in the chest.

"We were set up," Hayden says, firing his weapon again.

Cyprus takes the chance to try to grab me, digging his hands under my arms. "Jewel, stop your fucking fighting. I'm not going to hurt you. Mitchell needs you alive."

Ah, hell.

"Kid," Dad says. "Behind you!"

Cyprus releases a strangled laugh but doesn't turn. Dad raises his gun at us, and my eyes widen. A vampire flies right past us at my dad. He fires his gun, slowing the guy down, but the vampire shoves into my dad hard, knocking him off his feet. I clench my jaw as the vampire bends down, trying to bite my dad.

I scream, nearly choking on the gag, but it's enough to draw Ramona's attention away from Hayden in his own fight. She rushes to our dad and shoves a silver stake through the vampire's back. The guy snarls and releases dad, reaching for Ramona.

Fear cascades through me, and I ram my head back into Cyprus's nose. His blood spills all over me. The outcast vampire freezes, jerking his attention to us, and Dad swipes a knife through the vampire's throat.

"Jewel, fight," Dad says. "Fight!"

I jerk my arms as hard as I can, breaking the restraints with my sudden strength. Cyprus reacts with a shout, trying to grab onto me, but I spin on the balls of my feet and punch him in the face. The sudden movement sends my tied feet right out from under me, and I claw back as Cyprus runs toward me again.

A shot rings through the air, piercing my ears. I hit my back against someone before two arms wrap around me. But I don't react. I don't move. All I can do is stare at Cyprus clutching his stomach, his blood seeping through his hands. He stumbles forward at me, and I jerk my hands up, feeling his bones crack under my fisted fingers.

"Jewel, here," Dad says, waving a knife at me. "Take this. We have to go."

I drag the knife through the ropes on my ankles and then rip the tape off my mouth and spit out the rag, coughing and gasping, my whole body shaking with fear and anger. I thrash away from Dad and crawl the few feet to the vampire lying on the ground but still managing to move because Ramona injured him but didn't kill him.

I grip his shirt and roll him over. He flashes his fangs at me and suddenly stops. Without him having to utter a word, I know he sees the silver flashing in my blue eyes. He sees my nature peeking through the vulnerability of my human half struggling to make sense of what happened.

"Where's Mitchell?" I ask, holding the knife to his chest.

"Waiting," he says. "Whoever brings you unharmed will get a spot on the Divine Coven. If we don't, we'll be killed."

A wave of ice trickles through me, and I heave a breath. "How many of you are there?"

The guy doesn't respond.

I sink the knife down an inch. "Tell me!"

"Enough. More waiting. You're the priority. You must be brought unharmed or the deal falls apart."

The vampire tries to lock his hands around me, but I shove the knife down until it hits the solid ground. Grabbing the front of his shirt, I hoist him up so hard that my hand follows, punching through his chest. The vampire slumps under me, and I slide my hand out and stare at the dark blood coating my fingers.

I try to resist my urge to lick them, but my body begs me to give in. It's been a while since I've eaten, and my nerves are out of control. I'm freaking the hell out.

I bring my hand to my mouth and lick my fingers, tasting the somewhat weird blandness of the vampire. He's neither sweet nor sour, but it's better than nothing.

"Come on, honey. We have to go," Dad says, touching my back, unfazed by the fact that I'm still straddling a dead vampire pretty set on devouring him.

"Go? Go where? We've been set up. Cyprus somehow managed to get into The Orchards. I tried to warn you that he was with Mitchell." My voice comes out low, and I keep my eyes trained on the blood on my hands. "You should've never done this, Dad."

Dad squats next to me. "Jewel, I had to. Donor Life Corp is weak. We've been waiting for the opportunity for the regions to go to war with each other so that they couldn't prepare for our coming."

"You didn't have to do it this way. You should've trusted me. I would've come up with a better plan. Now, I don't even know where my guys are or if they're okay. And Brayla. Dad, you ruined everything." I swipe my hand over my face, pushing my hair away.

"I'm trying to change the world."

"So am I!" My words screech through the air, and Dad tries to cover my mouth. Swinging my elbow back, I knock him away and get to my feet to face him. "I don't even know why I bother with you. Mom should've never left me with such an impossible task."

Dad frowns. "What are you talking about?"

"The fight. She wanted me to remind you that there was more to life than the fight," I say, shifting on my feet to peer around the night. "But that's it for you, isn't it?"

"Honey, please. I'm doing this for our family. For humankind. I didn't sacrifice everything just to—"

I hold my hand up. "If you sacrifice everything, you have

nothing else to lose. You have nothing left to fight for!"

Charging forward, I knock my dad away from me. Newport tries to grab me next, but I punch him, and he trips over Cyprus's unmoving body. My chest heaves as I listen to the silence. His heart no longer beating. I killed him. The first human I've ever killed.

Searching around the ground, I find a discarded knife and pick it up. I turn to Hayden and point it. "Get everyone out of here. Take shelter until the sun rises and leave."

"What about you, Jewel?" Ramona asks, her blue eyes crinkling in the corners.

"I'm going to find Mitchell," I say.

"And then what?"

I shrug. "I don't know, but I hope it gives you time. I love you Ramona-babona. Tell the girls I love them too."

I turn to leave, and Ramona surprises me with the first real hug she's given me since the day we both left Dark Terrace Ranch. Sinking into her, I hug her close and kiss her forehead before bringing my hand to her belly for just a moment.

Without a word, I break away from her and turn around. I can't find my voice to speak again, to tell her to take care of herself and my niece.

I don't feel the need to warn her about what happens if she's born a dhampir. I can only hope that her life is far better than mine. That so many people won't fight against her. That she'll find the home and love I got from my guys.

I peer behind me once, watching Hayden and the others head in the other direction. All I can hope for now is that I'm strong enough to get through whatever happens next.

Strolling toward the wall of the unfamiliar city, I head toward where Newport had supposedly arranged a meeting with the Mercy Coven. If Cyprus was with the rebels, I doubt the coven is even there, but I don't know what else to do. The few vampires that had attacked us have disappeared, though they must lurk somewhere nearby because I can't shake the feeling of doom rising inside me.

And then I spot a few figures up ahead, illuminated by the third light pole right where the Mercy Coven was supposed to be.

"Paris?" I call, my voice echoing through the quiet air.

"Jewel, you're safe." The sound of Orlando's voice cuts through the air, igniting so much relief inside me that I can't stop my legs from charging forward.

He meets me halfway, opening his arms wide to engulf me in a hug. I jump up, wrapping my arms around him, burying my face into the crook of his neck. I can't believe he's here.

"You have no friggin' idea how happy I am to see you. Where are my matches?" I try to keep my voice even as I ask. Because they wouldn't deny smothering me.

"Are you hurt?" Orlando asks instead of answering me.

I shake my head. "I'm fine. Mitchell somehow found out about the plan and sent vampires after us, but we managed to escape. I—I killed Cyprus." My voice shakes as I say the words.

"That's quite the shame, Mrs. Ortega. He'd have made an obedient heir." Mitchell's voice pierces me through the heart, stealing my breath away.

Orlando tightens his hold on me. "It's okay, Jewel. He's not going to hurt you."

"What's going on?" I ask, dread seeping through me. "Where are Austin, Kingston, and Diego?"

Orlando doesn't respond right away, his blue eyes flashing silver.

Panic engulfs me, and I try to push away from him, but he only holds me tighter. "Jewel, I know you're upset, but you have to understand. This was the only way to protect you."

Jerking again, I manage to loosen Orlando's hold on my arms. I swing out and punch him, getting him to let me go. Someone catches me, pressing their chest to my back, and I stiffen at Mitchell's unsettling familiarity as he spins me to get a better look at the figures I thought might've been the Mercy Coven.

Kingston, Austin, and Diego kneel on the ground. Chains wrap around their arms and torsos, keeping them restrained.

Black bags cover their heads, and blood stains their clothes. None of them say a word to me, but their hearts pick up pace, listening to my intake of breath.

"Don't worry, Mrs. Ortega. I still manage to hold my

former heirs dear to me," Mitchell says. "And that's why I'll allow you to pick one to grace with my mercy. A few decades in my care will remind them that we were once family."

Fury explodes through me, and I jerk my head back, head-butting Mitchell in the chin.

My strength knocks him off balance, and I rush forward to my guys. I get my fingers around the bag covering Diego's head, but Orlando hooks his hands around my waist and yanks me back. But it doesn't stop me from tugging it off to see Diego.

He flashes his fangs, snarling, before his eyes meet mine. "Beautiful, I'm so sorry."

Mitchell stands before Diego and punches him in the face, cutting off his words. "No talking!"

"Don't touch him!" I scream, flailing in Orlando's arms. "Don't fucking touch him!"

Mitchell materializes in front of me, tipping his head slightly to study my face. "Do you choose Diego to spare?"

"I—"

Mitchell returns to Diego and pulls a blade from his jacket. He strolls behind him and locks his fingers through his hair, exposing his neck.

Diego snarls, but Mitchell holds him in place. The knife sparkles in the soft light from above, and I gasp, my whole body screaming as a drop of blood seeps from Diego's neck.

"Your answer, Jewel. Do you choose to spare Diego?" he asks.

Diego meets my gaze. "I will not make you choose. I love you, beautiful. I love—"

Mitchell swipes the blade across Diego's neck.

I scream.

BETRAYED

THRASHING AGAINST ORLANDO'S HOLD, I break free and rush toward Mitchell. Something dark inside me snaps, and I lose myself to my nature, letting the fighter in me break free. Mitchell's eyes widen as I fly at him at an inhumanly fast speed, now more powerful than ever. He thrusts Diego forward into the dirt and disappears from my view.

"Remember the deal, Orlando," Mitchell calls from a few dozen feet in the distance. "If you want the re-division to happen in your favor, it must be this way. It's going to happen regardless."

I crouch next to Diego and pull him onto my lap, sticking my arm to his mouth. "Diego, drink. Please."

He opens and closes his mouth, the gaping slit on his

throat stopping him from responding to me. I pierce myself on his fangs and let my blood seep into his mouth, but it spills down his chin.

"Jewel, stop," Orlando says. "You have to stop."

"Fuck you!" I yell, moving my arm to Diego's throat instead, gently pressing it to his wound, praying it helps him heal faster. "How could you do this to us? I—I gave you everything."

"And I'm trying to do the same!" Orlando growls, his fangs extending. "I promised you eternity. I promised you I'd protect you. But with the way our lives are heading, I can't. I can't keep putting you in danger. You're mine, Jewel. You've always been mine. This is the only way. You can live as you are. You don't have to pretend to be a vampire. You don't have to give so much. We will get an entire territory, build new regions."

His words stab me deeply. Pain tightens my chest, stealing my breath away. I don't understand. How could he do this?

"I never wanted that!" I pull my arm away from Diego's mouth and reach over to pull Austin's bag from his head next. "And I'm not yours. I will *never* be yours! Never again."

"Jewel," Orlando says, attempting to come closer, but something stops him.

I scramble to tug Kingston's bag off next. "Don't! I choose them. All of them." I glower at Mitchell. "If you want to hurt them, you'll have to get through me."

Scooping up the dagger, I point it at Mitchell while I tug at the chains on Austin first, trying to loosen them.

"Last chance, Orlando. Control her or the deal is off," Mitchell says.

Orlando disappears from in front of me, and I swing my arm out behind me, expecting him to try to tackle me. I hit empty air but spin fast on my feet, hitting something solid over Austin's head. Orlando catches my wrist as I drag the knife across his chest and squeezes so hard that I have no choice but to drop the blade.

Orlando kicks my legs out from under me, sending me crashing forward to knock Austin down. Yanking me to him, Orlando pins me, capturing me in an embrace I flail against. I sink my teeth into his chest, biting him hard over and over again, trying to get him to let me go.

"Don't, Jewel. He'll kill you," Orlando says. "Please."

"Babe, I fucking love you. Don't let him get you. You're our girl," Kingston says.

Mitchell roars, but I can't look behind me. Orlando holds me too tightly. Fear radiates through me at the strangled noise Kingston releases, and Austin yells his name. Loud pops ring through the air, startling me, and I catch the sound of clomping boots thudding across the asphalt.

Orlando growls and releases me, dropping me to my knees.

"Let her go!" Ramona yells from behind him, clutching her bloody silver stake.

Hayden and Dad aim their weapons at Mitchell, shooting him over and over again, forcing him to step away from my guys. I take advantage of the sudden distraction and launch myself at Orlando, knocking him into the ground. He flares his nostrils, flashing his fangs, and I slap him across the face.

"I trusted you," I say.

"I'm sorry," Orlando says. "Everything I do is for you."

"I never asked for any of this." Tears burn my eyes. "You betrayed me. I gave you my love, my body, my promise and you—I hate you. I fucking hate you. I'd rather live in the shadows than ever spend another second with you."

"Jewel!" My dad's voice rips through the air, calling my name.

I shift and look behind me, catching sight of Mitchell holding my dad from behind, bending his neck to expose his throat. Mitchell extends his fangs and bites down sending blood gushing from my dad.

Orlando shoves me off him, and I screech as I land hard on my back, expecting him to tackle me. He disappears and surprises me by rushing toward Mitchell. Mitchell pulls away from my dad and pushes him forward. Dad's body thuds into the ground, and he struggles to get to his feet. Mitchell dodges Orlando and grabs my dad, lifting him up by his head.

My eyes shadow, and I cover my ears and spin away. I can't watch. I can't listen. Ramona screams out, her voice piercing my ears even through my hands. More gunshots ring through the air, and I force myself to spin around to see Ramona going after Mitchell and Orlando as they blur in a fight.

Arms wrap around me. "It's me," Austin says, before I have a chance to react. "Come on. We have to go."

"Mona!" Hayden yells, and I automatically push from Austin.

Ramona stands frozen in Mitchell's arms, blood seeping from her neck. Austin abandons me and charges in their direction. He rips Ramona away from Mitchell, and Hayden fires another round of bullets at him.

Mitchell materializes behind Hayden, and I don't get the chance to scream out before Mitchell stabs a long dagger right through Hayden's chest and pushes him to the ground. His eyes dart to where Austin kneels over Ramona, and I push my legs to race me forward. Mitchell turns his attention to me, a bloody smile crossing his face, his eyes glowing solid silver. I don't have the chance to react and brace myself.

A figure darts in front of me, and I scream, feeling pressure push against my chest. I clutch Orlando's shoulders as Mitchell jams his hand into his chest so hard that I can feel the bulge of his hand through Orlando's back as he falls into me.

"No!" My voice rips through the air.

Diego materializes behind Mitchell and locks him in place. Kingston jerks a dagger so hard through Mitchell's arm that he cuts it off. Austin grabs Mitchell's other arm, and the three of them restrain him. Orlando falls into me, and I catch him, stopping him from hitting the ground. Mitchell roars again, thrashing, managing to break his arm free of Austin.

I've never seen the full extent of Mitchell's power, and I heave a breath, fear rushing through me as my guys struggle to restrain him long enough to kill him. Mitchell throws himself back into Diego, knocking them all over, and my legs kick into action. I charge forward and land on top of Mitchell. He thrashes and snarls, his severed arm bleeding everywhere, making his body slick and hard to hold onto.

"You want the new territory?" Mitchell says, gritting his teeth. "I'll give it to you and your matches."

I pin my hands against Mitchell's chest.

Mitchell growls. "You can have control of Donor Life Corp."

Adjusting my hands, I push them harder into Mitchell, feeling his heartbeat thrum against my fingers. His eyes widen, his fear palpable, setting off something dark and deadly inside me. My stomach twists and burns, and I can't stop staring at the blood seeping around my fingers.

"Sons, don't let her do this!" Mitchell yells. "I gave you everything!"

"No, *we* gave you everything," Austin says, grinding his teeth.

"We wasted our lives serving you," Diego adds.

Kingston punches Mitchell in the face. "No more."

"You ungrate—"

I ram my fist into Mitchell's chest, crushing his bones with the power of my strength. He hollers and bucks under me, but my guys restrain him. My hand slides into his body, my fingers sinking into the soft tissue of his heart, feeling it pulse. I squeeze it harder and twist my wrist, slowly tugging it free, hoping it hurts him as much as he hurt me. His silver eyes lock on mine, and he opens and closes his mouth, but Austin silences him with is hand.

My whole body trembles as I clutch onto Mitchell's heart and stare at his blood coating my hand. I chuck it as far away as possible and slide off Mitchell, stumbling to my feet. Austin, Diego, and Kingston take no chances and sever his head before ripping the rest of him apart. I turn away and hug myself, afraid to look around me.

"Precious Jewel." Orlando's soft whisper trickles through the air, drawing my attention to him as he lies on the ground, his cheek pressed into the asphalt.

Kingston materializes in front of me, blocking my way. "Babe, we got him."

I release a small shudder of a breath. "Let me talk to him."

"Jewel."

I rest my head against his shoulder. "Please."

Kingston growls softly and turns to Diego and Austin. They materialize in front of me, and I release a small sob at Ramona's body in Austin's arms.

"We have to go," Austin says. "She's dying."

"I'll grab Orlando," Diego says.

"Diego, please—"

He turns his gaze to me. "I won't hurt him unless you want me to. Please, just let Kingston hold you."

I nod my head and sink against Kingston, burying my face into the crook of his shoulder. He squeezes me against him, kissing the side of my head a dozen times. The world blurs around us, and I keep my eyes closed so I don't try to glimpse my dad or Hayden's bodies. They were supposed to leave. They shouldn't have come after me. But because they did, I'm alive and so are my guys. I'll never forget that my dad, even after losing himself in the fight, finally decided what was most important to him. His family. Me.

The world comes to a standstill, and I pull away from Kingston's neck to peer around the same abandoned house Hayden had brought me to what feels like forever ago. Kingston sets me on my feet but doesn't let me go, and I turn and face Diego still holding Orlando.

"Austin?" I call, peering around.

Kingston squeezes my hand. "He took Ramona into Shadow Hill Pointe to a medical facility."

"We have to go there," I say, trying to pull him to the door.

"Not yet, beautiful. We have one more thing to take care of." Diego's soft voice draws my attention to him, and he strolls to the couch to lay Orlando down, who is too injured to put up a fight.

Orlando flutters his eyes open and meets my gaze. "Jewel."

I can tell it takes everything in Kingston to let me go, but he relents and releases my hand but stays right behind me, pressing his chest into my back. I stop for a moment next to Diego and hug him, needing all the strength I can get from my guys.

"Jewel," Orlando whispers again. "Please let me explain."

I tense, my muscles reacting to his words, and I reach out and shake him by the shoulders, making him groan. "I've heard enough, Orlando. You betrayed me. You betrayed our coven. I can't stand to even look at you."

His fangs click under my anger, peeking out from beneath his twisted lips. "I know it feels like that, and I know I don't deserve your forgiveness, but it had to be this way to get to Mitchell. None of you would've gone for this, so I took your safety into my own hands. Mitchell wasn't ever going to stop. He'd have kept going after us until you died. Until the world found out about you. I couldn't allow that to happen. Any other plan, using you as bait or your matches—it wouldn't have ended well. So, I contacted Mitchell directly and told him he could have my brothers if he let me keep you."

I slap him, sending his head jerking sideways. "People died, Orlando! My dad—"

"Never deserved you. The rebels would've continued to fight. I gave Mitchell their location so that they could fight each other," Orlando says. "So that everyone would stop coming after you. But then your dad managed to get you away from me. I underestimated both him and Mitchell. I thought Mitchell would send his army of outcasts into Red Canyon Crest Grove, but he sent Cyprus alone. I couldn't risk Mitchell realizing it was more than about you. Cyprus knew too much."

I clutch the front of his shirt, twisting the fabric between my fingers. "You just stood there when he almost killed Diego."

"I know, and I'm sorry." Orlando turns to Diego. "I truly am, brother. I had faith in our girl to stop it."

"I'm not *your* girl! I can't be. Not when you do things that jeopardize us all. Not when you keep secrets or don't consult us. We're supposed to be a team."

Orlando closes his eyes, expecting me to smack him again, but I cover my face instead, my heart breaking. He gently touches my shoulder. "Forgive me. I'll always think of you as my girl, Jewel. And I knew I risked losing the part you so selflessly gave to me, but I don't regret what I did. You're safe and Mitchell is dead. You'll now have the time to focus on who you were born to be."

A tear slips from my eye, and I swipe it away before it can fall. "Orlando, I—I can't do this."

"I know, I'm not asking you to do anything," he says, grazing his hand up to my cheek. "That's why I'm not going to put you in the position to decide or to move past this. I can't be who you all need me to be for you. I can't hold a position of power and keep you safe. So, I'm leaving, Jewel. My legacy as the leader of the Ortega Coven will end here. Everything with my name will pass along to you and your matches to do as you please."

I frown. "I don't understand."

He props himself up to meet my gaze. "The regions still have their leaders apart from Bellamy and Duchanne. The Vaduva and Aku Regions remain strong in wait. My brothers will declare me dead by Mitchell's hands, and I'll live my life as I deserve."

"As you deserve?" I ask, my lip quivering, my head and heart battling it out over how I should feel. But right now, I'm just really friggin' confused.

"I'll return to being a ghost to the system. You're safer with me in the shadows. You can have the life you want. You'll no longer be vowed to me. You can love my brothers freely." Orlando closes the space between us and grazes his lips to mine. "I love you, Jewel. Take care of my brothers. Take care of Brayla. Please don't hold this against her. She went along with this for you. She's family."

Orlando eases himself off the couch and sways on his feet. Turning to Kingston and Diego, he pats them both on the shoulder. "Please give Austin my apologies, and take care of our girl. I'm counting on you, brothers. Give her the eternity she wants and everything she desires."

Kingston and Diego flank my sides, and we silently watch Orlando disappear, leaving the door open behind him. I stand in shock, staring after him. My chest tightens as his words finally sink in with his departure.

I cover my mouth with my hand and release a small sob. I should be furious that he did this. I shouldn't feel like he took a piece of my heart with him. But I do. I can't help it. No matter what crazy ass shit he's done, Orlando was always there. He was my constant shadow. And now, I can truly feel his absence. He'll no longer haunt me. He'll remain with Jewel Jordan in my mind—the girl I'll never be again.

"Babe," Kingston says, drawing my attention to him. "Let us smother the hell out of you."

I release a breathless laugh with a sob and turn toward Diego and Kingston, letting them sandwich me between their muscular bodies until I no longer feel like I'll fall apart. They take turns kissing me a dozen times, and I finally manage to breathe without the pain in my chest squeezing my heart.

"Will you take me to Austin?" I ask, letting Diego pick me up. "I need us to all be together. I can't stand another minute apart from him."

Kingston squeezes my hand. "Don't tell Austin I said this, but same, babe. I feel the fucking same."

TOGETHER FOREVER

"JEWEL!" DANA AND FALLON YELL in unison. "Thank God! We were so scared."

Diego sets me on my feet as my cousins tackle me in the middle of the empty lobby of the Human Health Center of Shadow Hill Pointe. The small building is barely the size of one floor of the one in Dark Terrace Ranch, this city way smaller than the big ones I'm used to run by board members.

"How did you get here? How is Ramona?" I ask, peering over my shoulder to Diego and Kingston, but they shake their heads unable to answer. They don't know either.

Someone clears their throat, and I pull away from my cousins and spot Austin standing next to Brayla in the wide hallway before a set of double doors. Brayla clutches Dougie in her arms, her brown eyes lined with the sadness I know reflect in my own.

"I brought them, Jewel," Brayla says. "Orlando sent me after them for you and had me stay with the Mercy Coven."

Austin leaves her side and scoops me up, lifting me in his arms to give me a dozen kisses while I sneak in a dozen more, cutting him off every time he tries to talk. Tears burn down my cheeks but not from grief and confusion. I'm just so happy to be in Austin's arms as Diego and Kingston engulf the two of us in theirs.

"He's gone," I say, taking in a breath, knowing Brayla still listens. "He couldn't handle that he felt he had to betray us to assure my life. He decided the way he could take care of us was to return to the shadows and give up his power. We're to file his death."

Brayla releases a small cry, drawing my attention to her. My heart clenches, and I hold out my arm to her, motioning for her to come to me. For the first time, none of my guys growl at her, and they allow her to join our hug. Dougie giggles, his sweet voice pushing away all the despair trying to release itself as I pull myself back together.

"Jewel, I'm so sorry," Brayla says. "I'm so, so sorry. I never wanted it to be like this. When he told me—that's why he sent me away. He knew I'd tell your guys because I know you wouldn't have wanted it to be like this."

I swallow the burning in my throat. "I know, Brayla. And I'm so, so sorry too. You should've never been dragged into this mess. My dad—"

I can't even finish my sentence.

Austin takes Dougie from her arms so that we can hug each other tighter, and I rock her back and forth with me until we both stop crying. Diego stands with my cousins, hugging an arm around each of them, and Kingston yanks his shirt over his head and rips it in two, making both me and Brayla laugh as he wipes our faces with the fabric.

The whooshing of an automatic double door opening draws my attention from Brayla, and I stiffen at the sight of Rio Mercy wearing a mask and gown over his clothes. Austin hands Dougie to Fallon and crosses the room to Rio's side, frowning at the quiet words the Mercy brother says to him.

Austin glances at me, his eyes sheening over, and he scrubs his face with his hands. My heart slides into my stomach, my knees shaking as the realization sets in. Austin doesn't have to tell me for me to know that Ramona didn't make it.

Two strong arms wrap around me, catching me from falling, and I suck in a breath of Austin's citrusy scent. He holds me against him, letting me squeeze the hell out of him as I clutch my arms around his neck.

"I'm sorry, Jewel. Ramona's heart was damaged in the fight, and she lost a lot of blood. The trauma of the emergency delivery was too much for her body to handle. We tried everything we could to save her," Austin says, rubbing smooth circles on my back.

Kingston and Diego enclose us again, and Diego asks,

"Our niece?"

My heart clenches at his question, and I look up at Austin.

He offers me a ghost of a smile. "She's beautiful. Stable."

I gasp in a breath, covering my mouth with my hand, and start bawling my eyes out all over again. "Can I see her?" I finally manage to ask.

Austin nods his head, smiling at the relief and joy spilling through me to cool the burning heartache. I've never been so grateful in my life. Setting me on my feet, Austin leaves me with Diego and Kingston for a minute to return to Rio, who remains quiet in the doorway.

He glances at me and nods, motioning me to come over to him. I look to my cousins, who Brayla hugs to her, guiding them back to the sitting area. Diego and Kingston each hold my hand as we meet Austin and Rio.

"I want you to know that Jade is in the best hands," Rio says, pressing his lips together. "Our city is known for our birthing facility and advanced neonatal technology. We have the highest successful donor births in the whole Bellamy Region."

I nod my head, not really sure what to expect. The last baby I was around was Dougie, and I didn't get to even see him for a few months after he was born. The Human Health Clinic requires all newborns to remain under observation to assure good health. And for once in my life, I'm so friggin' relieved by Donor Life Corp's diligence and necessity to ensure population growth.

Rio leads the way into a sterile hallway. The floor is vacant this part of night, though I hear a few people somewhere in the back of the building. We turn into the second room where Rio waits outside for us to all take quick showers and change into medical attire with gloves and masks and everything, reminding me of the time the people from the lab came to take final donations during the flu outbreak. But this time it's our niece who needs protection from us.

"I must prepare you, Mrs. Ortega—"

"Jewel's fine," I say, cutting him off.

He bobs his head. "Jade was born prematurely and is quite small. She'll need around the clock care as she finishes developing. In cases like these, the Human Health Center keeps the infant into their first year of life and monitors them closely for another six months before releasing complete care to the mother."

"A year and a half?" I ask, gaping at him.

Austin squeezes my hand. "We'll arrange transport as soon as we have everything arranged to care for her."

"So who named her Jade?" I ask him, sinking closer to let Austin hug me again.

Rio clears his throat. "The mother."

"Ramona?" I ask, tears burning my eyes. "She knew of Jade?"

"I told her the story on the way here, trying to keep her conscious." Austin presses his lips into a line, his eyes glassing again. "I'm so sorry, Jewel. I tried everything I could. She just—"

I hug him tighter, knowing he blames himself for my sister's death. He'll go through everything over and over again in his mind, trying to think of something he could've done to change this horrible outcome.

"Austin, it's not your fault. It's Mitchell's, and he's dead. You did your best, okay? You don't have to ever apologize to me. I'm so happy that you saved our niece."

Austin hugs me tighter, and we stay together until he's ready to let me go. Rio guides the four of us into another room painted in soft green with chiming music to drown out the chirping of machines.

I hold my hand over my chest, staring at the small, clear bassinet with two human staff members gazing down at the tiniest little human I've ever seen lying within what looks like her own personal bubble.

"Whoa," I say, trying to calm my heart.

"She's fucking little as shit," Kingston says from beside me.

Diego elbows him. "Watch your mouth."

"She's little but strong," Austin says, smiling at me. "Perfect. Fierce like you, Jewel."

I close the distance, and Rio shows me how the bubble will move with my hand, creating a barrier but allowing me to touch her. Rubbing my finger across Jade's tiny fingers, I blink through my tears, taking in her wispy dark hair and her closed eyes.

"Hey, Jade. Auntie Jewel's here, okay?" Turning to my guys, I say, "You met your Uncle Austin, but I want you to meet your Uncle Diego and Uncle Kingston. We're going to take the best care of you. We promise."

"Forever," my guys say in unison.

I smile. "Always."

"Well, if this isn't a shit show, then I don't know what is," Kingston says, pacing in a fast circle around me. He blurs, unable to stay calm as we wait in the lobby of the Blood Match Center in Dark Terrace Ranch.

I narrow my eyes on him in an attempt to grab him by the shirt. He spins and lifts me off my feet, holding me while he speeds fast enough that he'll surely leave track marks on the tile floor. Tilting my head up, I kiss his pout and suck his bottom lip into my mouth. He slows under my touch, now distracted by my desire to caress my tongue to his, deepening our kiss until he stops completely to shift my body so that my legs wrap around him.

"More tongue," he murmurs, nipping me hard enough with his fangs to let my blood tease him. "More touching."

I pull away and pat his chest. "After we meet with Viorica and Zara."

"Can't wait," Kingston responds. "It could be hours."

"He's right, Jewel," Austin says, coming from down a hallway. "I snuck some food from the kitchen. Diego's checked our floor, and everything is how we left it. You look like you could sleep."

I twist my lips. "I don't want to sleep. I should really call Brayla and check on my cousins and Jade."

"Jewel, we're fine." Brayla's voice rings through the air. Diego steps off the elevator and waves a tablet at me before lighting the wall with Brayla's projection. "Fallon and Dana are passed out with Dougie." The video feed shifts, and I catch sight of the three of them fast asleep in the same room at the Human Health Center where we left them.

Big green eyes appear in front of the camera. "The baby is doing great too," Samantha says. "My sisters are with her. No one except the best doctors will get within a hundred feet of that pretty baby girl."

"They better not," Diego says.

Austin looks at the projection. "We trust you, Sammy."

"And we'll murder you all if they do. Got it?" Kingston says, releasing a soft growl.

Samantha nods. "Promise."

For the first time, I actually believe Kingston's threat. Samantha does too.

I can't stop the smile crossing my face at my guys' protectiveness, and I bring my mouth back to Kingston and kiss him. "You guys are extra sexy right now."

Kingston hums deep in his throat. "Is that so?"

Pulling back slightly, I comb my fingers through his hair. "So, it could be a few hours, huh?"

"Maybe longer," Diego says, shrugging. Samantha waves and disconnects the line without us telling her goodbye.

I turn my gaze to Austin. "You promise food?"

Kingston squeezes my ass. "And whatever else you want."

I bite my lip. "All of you. I want all of you."

The world blurs, and I screech out only to be cut off with a kiss from Austin from over Kingston's shoulder. I squirm against Kingston and reach for Diego, who kisses my neck up to my earlobe to suck it into his mouth.

I don't even realize we've left the elevator until my back hits the soft mattress of a familiar bed, and I sit up and stare around Kingston's old room under the Divine name on the top floor. Through the tinted glass, I spot a view of the ocean in the distance lit in afternoon sunlight, but my attention shifts to Diego, Kingston, and Austin standing at the end of the bed, waiting for me to encourage the next move.

I scoot forward to the edge of the bed. "What's with all the clothes?"

Kingston rips my dress off me so fast that it takes me a second to realize I'm suddenly in my undergarments. I crack up and throw the torn dress fabric at him, and he swats it to make it land on Austin's head.

"Dude," I say, wagging my finger at him before he tries for my bra next.

He meets me with a wide ass grin. "Wait, I thought you were asking me about *your* clothes."

I laugh again and stand up, closing the space. "Because of

that, I'm going to take my time. Don't you dare move."

Kingston licks his lips and glances to his brothers. "I think she's serious."

"I hope so," Austin says, smiling at me.

Diego reaches out to move my hair from my shoulder. "I love our girl like this."

"And I love you like this." I hook my fingers to Diego's shirt first and stretch on my tiptoes to pull it over his head.

I step closer, holding his hands between mine so that he can't touch me. He releases the sexiest noise from deep in his throat, his stomach muscles tightening as I graze my lips over his taut chest and kiss my way down.

Releasing his hands, I touch the button on his jeans. "Is this okay, Diego?"

"Hell yeah," he responds, smiling at me. "Whatever you want."

Desire rushes over me with his words, and I unfasten the button on his jeans and tug them down far enough for him to step out of. I draw my finger along his boxers, grazing lightly over the prominent bulge yearning for my attention. I lace my fingers around Diego's erection, working my hand over him as I undress him completely.

"Come sit with me, beautiful," he says, spinning me around so that I'm standing in the spot he left.

I smile and close the space, turning around to face Austin and Kingston as they watch Diego pull me onto his lap with only soft lace as a barrier between our bodies. Kingston hums in his throat, unable to wait a second longer, and undresses completely before I even make my move. He sits next to me and Diego and kisses my shoulder, grazing his fangs over my skin while dragging my bra strap down with his teeth.

I wiggle my fingers at Austin, and he bends down to kiss me softly as I tug his shirt off for him. Diego hooks his fingers to my hips, rocking my body against him, letting me feel his hardness between my legs. Kingston unclasps my bra to rub his fingers over my nipples, making me moan softly. I reach for Austin and can barely manage to unfasten his jeans, not even letting him kick them off before I grab him by the waist to bring him close enough to tease with my mouth until he nudges me back so that I scoot with Diego more onto the bed.

I lift my hips to let Austin finish undressing me, and Diego kisses my shoulder and eases me down on top of him. I moan so friggin' loud at the pressure he builds between my legs as he guides my body to roll against his in a motion that feels so good that I close my eyes and grip onto Austin's fingers as he stands in front of me.

Austin guides my hands over his body, letting me explore the planes of his stomach and the stiffness of his arousal, showing me what he wants from me. Kingston's hand slides from my breast and down my stomach, and I pant harder, unable to control my moans as Kingston draws his hand between my legs, vibrating his fingers against my sensitive skin until I bend forward, bracing myself on Austin.

Kingston lifts my head and kisses the moan from my

mouth, working his way over my shoulder. Diego moves my hips faster over and over again, unleashing so much pleasure inside me that I can barely take it. Austin studies my face, his eyes locking with mine, enjoying just watching my reaction. Diego releases a moan as he finishes, slowing my body down, letting me sit on him to catch my breath while he catches his. He eases me off him, and Kingston gathers me into his arms, pulling me higher onto the bed. I straddle his waist and kiss him, feeling him gently press his raging boner between my legs to test me for a reaction and to see if I'll let him continue.

I'm so ready to give into his need for me next that I kiss him harder and deeper, digging my fingers into his shoulders. I lift and drop slowly without letting him go farther than his tip, just enjoying his desperation for me build in his midnight eyes as they lock to mine.

"Jewel." My name sounds like a velvety plea on his lips, and I rotate my hips until our bodies join as one. He slides his hands under my ass with my knees bent around his body, using his strength to hold me to him. I trace my fingers over his flexing muscles as he swings my body into his to rock me against him. Austin shifts on the bed to kneel behind me, lifting my hair to kiss my neck. I reach up and touch his cheek, guiding him next to me so that our lips can meet.

I gasp the faster Kingston rocks me, slapping our bodies together in a rhythmic motion that I moan with every time we meet completely. I blindly reach out to run my fingers down Austin's abs until I find what I'm looking for. His breathing quickens under my touch, and the bed shifts behind me as Diego grazes his lips to my other shoulder and slides his hands around my chest to play with my breasts.

I tilt my head, knowing exactly what he wants, and give Diego silent permission to bite me. His fangs click, and he waits for Kingston to rock me away from him before biting me so quickly that I don't feel the pressure of his fangs and only his lips when he sucks on my shoulder, keeping in rhythm with my body moving with Kingston's.

"I love you, Jewel," Kingston whispers with his moan, slowing down. Diego releases my shoulder so that Kingston can kiss me, the three of them working together to see to it that I get everything I want from them. I've always felt so loved by them, but something about this moment, about being together in a way that has them close with all of me at once, drags out the best emotions inside me.

Kingston's feather-light kiss is so tender and full of love that I release Austin to hug Kingston for a moment, just breathing in the familiar scent of his skin. Lifting me off of him, Kingston touches my cheek and smiles, shifting me next to Austin.

I don't wait a moment with Austin and act first, stretching my arms out to him so that he closes the space to rest between my legs. Austin's mouth brushes to mine, and I glide my tongue across the seam of his lips, kissing him deeper, soaking in his desire for me that flashes silver in his eyes. I catch my own eyes flashing in his green gaze, and Kingston bites his arm to offer me his blood.

"Is this okay, Jewel?" Austin asks, holding his weight up on his arms.

I open myself completely for him, pulling away from Kingston's arm to hook my hands around Austin's neck. His eyes darken with passion, and he rubs himself between my legs, closing his eyes as our bodies join together.

Reaching out, I get Diego and Kingston to lie on both our sides so that I can explore their chests and stomachs with my fingers. I want so badly to be close to them all, especially after everything, that I can't keep my hands away.

Austin thrusts into me, moving his body just right that tingles explode through me, starting from between my legs to travel through the rest of me. I dig my fingers into Kingston and Diego as good pressure builds and builds with Austin's movement, the way his body creates friction in just the right place until I can't stop my rebel mouth from shouting my pleasure.

Kingston leans over and kisses me, smiling into my mouth. "That was hot, babe."

I release a breathless laugh. Blush warms my chest to flourish in my cheeks, and I arch forward to catch Austin's lips as his face scrunches so that he moans into my mouth. He kisses me passionately, pushing me back until he can lie on top of me, letting me feel his weight against me.

"You're everything to me, Jewel," Austin whispers into my ear, making me shiver. "I love you."

I hug him as he catches his breath, gliding my hands in smooth circles over his muscular shoulders. "I love you. You're so important to me." Reaching out, I lace my fingers with Kingston's. "And I love you. I hope you can feel it every day, in every way, always." Diego leans in and brushes his lips to my forehead. "I love you, too, Diego. You give me so much strength and bravery. I know we can face anything."

"Hell yeah, we can," Diego says, beaming his brilliant smile.

Kingston shifts so Austin can roll between us, only to pull me with him to lie on his chest. "Damn straight."

"No matter what," Austin says.

"No matter what," I agree.

POWER SHIFT

IT ONLY TOOK VIORICA AND Zara most of the day and half the night to finally call us to the grand boardroom of the Blood Match Center. I can't stop myself from gazing into the open office door that used to belong to Mitchell. A part of me fears he'll materialize out of nowhere, but he doesn't. His body remains where we left it outside the Bellamy Region, forgotten and left for the sun to disintegrate until his ashes disappear with every thought I hope to never have of him again once everything is settled and in order.

Kingston and Austin squeeze my hands, positioning me between them with Diego hugging my shoulders. Even though Viorica and Zara think I have transformed into a vampire and no one would dare touch me, my guys can't help their protectiveness. Not that I'll complain any time soon. Not with the room full of unfamiliar vampires—some from both Viorica and Zara's regions, some from the Duchanne and the Bellamy Regions, and even a few from the Divine Region, vampires I might have seen before but can't place names to faces.

"Thank you for all joining us tonight. As you've all become aware of, we've unfortunately lost four outstanding members of our board. We gathered you here to reassess and open Donor Life Corp to our region's best covens to apply for positions among our ranks," Viorica says.

So that's why everyone is here. I knew that Donor Life Corp didn't always take next in line for power, but it's strange to know that things are really changing. Whether they're good or bad, I have no idea.

"First and foremost, we'd like to offer Mrs. Jewel Ortega our deepest condolences for the loss of her mate during this unnecessary Divine War," Zara says. "Even as a newly transformed vampire, she managed to show undeniable strength and power, working with the rest of her coven to annihilate not only the threat of Mitchell but that of Blood Rebels."

I remain expressionless, allowing them to give me credit for the craziness that ensued with Mitchell sending outcasts after those humans from The Orchards. My guys don't have to tell me, but I know many died. But, I also know that Blood Rebels are resilient. It probably won't be the last time we ever hear from them—just hopefully not for a long, long time.

"Now usually in these circumstances, we'd offer the position of the board to next in line, but if Kingston agrees, we'd like to offer a spot on the board to Jewel as the new head of the Ortega Region. We'd also like to allocate a part of the Divine power and region to her coven to do as they see fit."

Kingston straightens his shoulders, remaining expressionless. "I see no problem if it's what Jewel wants."

I grimace, twisting my mouth. "Fuck no, dude."

He chuckles. "You heard our girl."

Viorica disappears from her spot to materialize in front of me. "I must ask you to think about it."

"I have, Viorica. My answer is still no. After everything I've been through and everything the board stands for, no. But, I do ask that you offer the position to Kingston. And—" I glance at each of my guys. "We'd like the Divinity Estate along with the Divine name."

"Really, babe?" Kingston asks.

"We're fine with remaining under the Ortega title," Austin adds.

Diego smiles at me. "I'll take whatever name you want, beautiful."

I rub my lips together, wishing we weren't under the scrutiny of a room full of vampires. Motioning my guys away from the table, I lead them to the sitting area and lean in close.

"I'm sorry I just threw the name thing out there. I know you have hard feelings about Mitchell, as do I, but...I don't think of Mitchell when I hear Divine. I think of us. I think of you. Of everything we've done together," I say, keeping my gaze trained toward the floor, afraid of their reactions.

Kingston scoops me up and kisses me right in front of everyone. "Thank fucking God. I was never going to get used to Ortega."

I laugh. "Me either."

"Same," Austin and Diego say in unison and then laugh.

We turn our attention back to the silent group of vampires. "So, is that okay?"

Viorica and Zara glance to each other and nod. "We suppose so."

"I'd also like you to recognize a formal Blood Vow between the four of us," I add.

"Jewel, that's not necessary. With the death of your mate, you are free to build whatever infrastructure you want within your coven," Zara says. "Blood Vows apply to blending power or transitioning donors into vampires. A union now serves no purpose seeing as you're already a coven."

I straighten my shoulders. "It does to me. Please. I promised my guys a Blood Vow, and I intend to keep it to all of them."

Viorica sighs. "Fine, Ms. Divine. We'll humor your still present donor rationale but just this once. The laws will remain unchanged for everyone else."

My guys all beam me huge ass smiles, and I bounce on my feet, barely able to contain myself. I can't believe it's happening—really happening. Officially. We'll finally get what we've always wanted.

Zara leans her elbows on the sleek wood table. "Now, on-to the board position. Kingston, will you accept a spot on be-half of your coven?"

Kingston smirks at me. "No fucking way. I'm going to be way too busy for all this bullshit ensuring our girl gets every-thing she ever could desire. Though, if you need a second opinion or guidance on how to run this place, you can call us."

I raise my eyebrows. "Really, dude?"

"Yeah, babe. I'm not missing another second of our eter-nity with you," he says.

Diego hugs his arms around me. "Don't bother asking me or Austin either, Vi."

Austin brings my hand to his mouth to kiss the back. "We have two teenaged girls, a toddler, and a baby girl to look after, right?"

I grin. "Right."

Kingston groans. "Well, when you put it like that—"

I whack him. "Dude."

Leaning in, he kisses me. "I wouldn't have it any other way."

Viorica and Zara look annoyed as all get-out, but neither of them argues with our decision. I expect them to excuse us, but Viorica starts where she left off and turns to another small group of guys, sitting expressionless across the table.

"It seems that the Divine seat is open," Viorica says.

"We'd like to offer it to your coven, Mr. Royale."

I turn my attention to the guy who eerily reminds me of Mitchell with the way he sits with his fingers linked together on the table. He doesn't react to Viorica's offer but instead turns to the four guys looming behind him.

They share a silent conversation with their eyes, and then the guy nods. "I accept."

Zara slides over a stack of papers across the table. "Welcome to Donor Life Corp. We look forward to the rise of the Royale Region."

The guy signs the paperwork and slips it to Viorica. "As do we." He stands from his seat and motions for the guys behind him to head to the door. "You know how to reach me."

I blink and the group disappears, leaving me in confusion. I look to Austin, who mouths *later* to me. Resting my head to his shoulder, I try to pay attention as Viorica offers positions to two other guys who accept, leaving one position open.

Viorica and Zara don't move from their spots as the room clears, and I shift under the sudden scrutiny.

"Last chance to accept our offer," Viorica says. "You can take over the Bellamy Region."

"We're good," I say. "We'll keep Ombre Noire and the Divinity Estate."

"You will no longer be allowed to expand," Zara says. "Your wealth will be limited to what's left from Orlando."

I bob my head. "That's fine. It's more than we could ever

need."

"Okay," Viorica says. She taps her finger to her tablet. "Looks like we have one last thing to discuss with the Divine Coven."

"You do?" I ask.

Viorica hums. "What do you want to do about Brayla? It seems we lost the outcast paperwork Orlando intended to file. Would you like to proceed? The offer of a spot for her among my coven still stands."

I shift and look to my guys.

"Brayla is head of the Shadow Crest Villa, and we ask that she be allowed to maintain permanent residency in Ombre Noire as the head of their donor division," Kingston says. "We also want approval for the residents of Haven Springs currently housed there if they want to stay with exempt status."

I smile at Kingston, knowing that he's requesting it because those were the people Hayden thought needed the most protection. Even though Hayden wasn't always on our good side, he did share our idea of creating a world where we could coincide. I hope to honor his legacy. Ramona's too.

Viorica nods. "Approved. I assume the four of you will maintain a close eye on Brayla while residing at the Divinity Estate?"

Diego nods. "Yes. We will assure everything remains up to Donor Life Corp standards."

Zara sighs, looking bored. "Very well. Then this meeting is over. Submit your Blood Vow paperwork within the next week for approval, but please don't expect the presence of the board considering you've denied the prestigious position of power among us."

"Fine by me," the four of us say together and then laugh.

Viorica and Zara stand, and Kingston takes my hand to pull me to my feet. Both women shake our hands, and Viorica surprises me by squeezing my shoulder. She offers me a closed lip smile and waits for Zara to leave before saying, "I do hope we can continue our alliance."

"Even though we didn't accept to run an entire region?" I ask.

"Especially because you didn't accept to run a region," she says. "I look forward to seeing everything you accomplish."

Viorica disappears, leaving us alone in the boardroom, and I open my arms for my guys to engulf me within their deliciously muscular embraces.

"That was better than I could've hoped for," I say, kissing each of them, taking a minute to celebrate with kisses that leave me breathless.

"Fucking same, babe," Kingston says.

"I'm slightly surprised you denied the board position, bro," Diego says, squeezing Kingston's shoulder.

Austin shakes his head. "Not me. He's always been clear about his plans for his ideal future with Jewel."

I laugh. "I still expect to leave the room, Kingston."

Kingston play-growls at me. "Maybe in a few weeks."

"I'll think about it," I say with a grin.

He sighs dramatically. "You'll *think* about it?"

"Mmmhmm," I say, humming under my breath. "I mean, a few weeks might not be quite long enough for me to properly celebrate with the three of you."

Austin grins. "I guess we should get going."

"Hell yeah. I never want to come back here again," Diego says.

Kingston picks me up. "Time to get our girl home."

"Home," I say. "Friggin' finally."

The three of them crowd around me, enveloping me in all their love and hope and faith for our future—a future I know will come. A future that'll be exactly as we want it to be. A future together where we can love freely, unconditionally, together. Always together.

And I know that's how it'll always be.

BLOOD VOWS

A SOFT KNOCK TAPS ON the balcony door, drawing my attention away from my vanity mirror. Brayla leaves my side and shifts the curtain out of the way. Her heart picks up speed at the silhouette through the dark tinted glass, and I push to my feet.

"Jewel, Brayla," Orlando says, his soft voice trickling to me.

Brayla swivels to meet my gaze. "Should I get your boy toys?"

I lick my lips, swallowing my nerves, and then shake my head. "No, it's okay. Let him in."

Brayla eases the door open and returns to my side. Orlando saunters in holding a bouquet of deep ruby roses. His blue gaze roves over me, starting from my face to trail down the rest of me. He sucks in a small breath, his heart picking up pace.

I hug myself under his scrutiny. "Orlando, you shouldn't be here."

His soft features harden. "My apologies, precious Jewel. I couldn't keep away on this special day. But I assure you, I've already visited with my bro—your matches—and they said it would be okay to visit with you if you chose to allow me in."

"They know you're here?" I ask, shifting.

He nods. "They do."

I side-glance Brayla. "Will you give us a minute?"

Brayla nods and closes the distance to Orlando. He sets the bouquet of roses on the nearby table and holds open his arms to her. She hugs him for a second and smiles. I don't say anything as they share a few quiet words I can't hear. I give them some privacy, knowing that Brayla and Orlando will always have a relationship with each other. He did create her after all.

The door to the room clicks closed, and a gentle hand touches my shoulder. Orlando spins me around and touches my cheek with a smile that reminds me of the hundreds he gave from our times meeting in the shadows, from the moments after when I allowed him to be a part of my life until the moment he broke my heart, no matter his reasoning.

"You look ravishing," he whispers.

I suck in my bottom lip between my teeth. "Thank you.

I'm assuming you know about tonight."

"Word travels in the shadows, and I couldn't resist stopping by." He glides his fingers down my shoulder and arm to test if I'll let him hold my hand.

I do. I can't help it. I wouldn't be here, getting ready for my Blood Vows to Kingston, Diego, and Austin if it weren't for Orlando. In his weird, twisted way, he managed to fulfill his promise that I'd get them.

"How are you holding up?" I ask, bringing his hand to my heart.

He shrugs. "That doesn't matter. I'd much prefer you tell me how you're doing? Are you happy, Jewel?"

I puff air through my lips. "Incredibly happy. We haven't had a single incident since moving back here. Ombre Noire is flourishing. Humans and vampires alike constantly apply to transfer. A curfew isn't even necessary. There aren't any vampire-only areas. Not a single human has even considered applying to Blood Match. Brayla has done an amazing job in human placement so that the vampire of the house treats the humans as equals. They take care of each other instead of being served. It's incredible."

"It is," he murmurs.

"You've been?"

He nods. "It's a shame you didn't accept the position on the board Viorica offered you."

"You know why," I whisper. "I can't pretend to be something I'm not all the time."

"I hope that one day that isn't always the case, precious Jewel. You deserve a world as compassionate, brave, beautiful, and as loving as you." Orlando leans in and presses a kiss to my forehead. "I'll continue to do what I can to see to it. For you."

I bob my head and slide my arms around him. "Do it for everyone, Orlando. For Jade. She's like me. Started showing symptoms last week." I can't help the frown crossing my face. I had hoped she wouldn't be a dhampir, but it seems the universe had another idea.

His eyes soften. "Don't look sad. Being a dhampir is a gift, Jewel. She's as precious and rare as you and will have an amazing life. I know you and your matches will assure it."

"I hope so."

He engulfs me in his arms again. "I know it."

Laughter trickles in from the hallway, and I shift my attention to the door. I turn away from Orlando at the sound of a knock before my cousins swing the door open. Dana claps her hands and Fallon grins. I expect them to freeze in their places at the sight of Orlando, but they race toward me.

I reach out to grab his arm, but I touch empty air. He's gone. Only the roses remain as a reminder that he's still around, hiding in the shadows, being his stalker self. Except now, knowing that makes me smile.

"You look so pretty!" Fallon says, hugging me with her sister. "Just like a real bride from the movies."

I grin. "That's what the Blood Vow tradition originated

from."

"Well, we love it," Dana says. "And Kingston, Diego, and Austin will too. Everyone's here, so whenever you're ready."

Pulling away from them, I smile one more time. "Come on. I'm so friggin' ready now. I can't wait a moment longer."

Brayla materializes in the doorway and motions to the three of us. "Then hurry your ass up, Jewel-babewel. Your forever awaits."

"Keep your eyes closed," Brayla says, linking her fingers through mine. "I mean it. Don't peek."

I laugh and wave my hand in front of me. "What happens if I do?"

"Kingston threatened to destroy the world."

I shake my head. "Seriously, dude?"

His soft chuckle sounds through the air, drawing my attention from Brayla. Three intakes of breath send my heart racing, and it takes everything in me to keep my eyes squeezed shut so that I don't look at the area around us.

Brayla stops me in place, my dark eyelids shifting red as light shines around us. Big hands lock to my hips, and I stretch up, puckering my lips to meet Diego for a sweet kiss. He hugs me for a moment, grazing his lips to mine.

"You look stunning, beautiful. I can't take my eyes off you," he whispers, tilting my head to kiss my throat.

A hard chest presses into my back, and Austin caresses his mouth to my shoulder. "Incredible. You're everything I've imagined. Diego's right about being unable to take our eyes off you. I can barely control my hands."

Kingston's alluring scent tickles my nose, and he kisses my cheek, swiveling me enough from Diego to glide his tongue across my bottom lip before sucking it into his mouth. "I don't plan to. My lips want to taste every bit of you. I can't wait to ravish the hell out of you."

Heat blossoms in my stomach to travel up my neck. "I can't wait, dude. I've missed you."

"Two days is forever," he murmurs. "But it just makes me want to love you more passionately than before. You just wait until we get this dress off you."

I shiver as his breath tickles my skin. "Fuck. Me." My body already reacts with anticipation. I love my alone time with each of them—our dates and days in each other's arms, the fun we have—but I really friggin' enjoy our time together too. And tonight is a night I've been dreaming about. It's the only dream I've had since... I push my thoughts away and turn to kiss Austin on the lips.

"We plan on it," Kingston says, chuckling. "But maybe not in front of our family."

"Or the Vaduvas," Diego adds.

"So open your eyes, Jewel." Austin leans away from me and smiles first as I gaze into his green eyes. His fangs peek out from beneath his lips, and he turns me to face the stone terrace with a view of the blooming garden and pond, one of my favorite spots on the Divinity Estate.

Kingston grins and spins me, dancing to his own beat to twirl me under the twinkling lights strung above us like glittering stars come to earth. I laugh and pat his chest, meeting him for another kiss as he twists me around so fast that Diego sweeps me off my feet to catch me before I fall. I grin at his affection, wrapping my hands around his neck to accept another kiss.

Diego sets me on my feet, and Austin kisses me once more, and the three of them hug me between their bodies. I couldn't have asked for a more perfect night to accept their Blood Vows for our future together. It's everything and more than what I could've hoped for.

"It's perfect," I say, smiling at Dana and Fallon.

Dana beams at Jade in her bassinet while Fallon bounces Dougie on her knee. My guys lead me to them so that I can hug them and gently run my fingers over Jade's tiny hand. It's only been a few weeks, but she's already grown so much as she gets the best care from her Uncle Austin.

A soft meow draws my attention to the ground, and Baby walks figure eights between Dana's legs, getting her to scratch behind her ears. I reach down to pet the cat, so glad that she's adapted well to life as a Divine, enjoying being here as much as I do.

Kingston clears his throat, drawing the small crowd's attention to us. "We'd like to thank you all—those we consider our family and closest allies—for joining us here tonight to celebrate the official promise of forever to the woman who changed our lives."

I grin. "You guys changed my life too."

"Please stand to bear witness to the blending of our power and to unite us in love for the rest of eternity," Diego says, taking my hand.

Austin holds my other hand. "Jewel, as the love of our existence, we promise you to fulfill your every need and desire."

"We promise to protect you by not only kicking everyone's asses who dare try to steal your smile but also by teaching you everything we know to assure you can do it yourself," Kingston says, sliding his hands around my waist.

"We also vow that our love and devotion, our loyalty and power, is forever yours," Diego says. "That you're forever ours."

"And you're forever mine," I say, kissing each of them. "In front of our family and allies as witnesses, I accept your vows and promise my own. I vow to love you all equally, in the forms you most enjoy, together and apart, forever. I promise to offer you my strength and protection and to stand by your sides no matter what. Because we're better together. Stronger together."

"Damn straight," Kingston says. "I do, babe."

"I accept everything you are, Jewel," Austin says.

"Hell yeah," Diego says. "We love our girl."

"I love you all too."

My guys each slide a ring onto my finger, each one connecting together in the prettiest setting with rubies and diamonds and a drop of each of their blood blended as one. I slide the rings I picked out for each of them on their fingers, my cheeks aching from smiling so much.

The small crowd cheers when I kiss each of them, and we turn together to glance around the Divinity Estate, our forever home.

"You ready to accept our bites, Jewel?" Austin asks, licking his lips.

Diego kisses my cheek. "After our private celebration."

"If we manage to survive that sexy pouty mouth of hers," Kingston adds.

I open my arms to hug them. "It's a good thing there are three of you," I tease, kissing Kingston's cheek. Hugging them to me once more, I breathe in the sweet scent of their skin, feel their love and desire pouring over me, and bask in their promise of forever. "And so you know, with you guys, I'm ready for anything."

The End

Thank you so much for reading *Blood Vows!* This series was so much fun to write. If you loved the *Vampire Heir* world, stay tuned for *Rebel Vampires,* book one in *The Royale Vampire Heirs* series.

Other Series by Ginna Moran

REVERSE HAREM

The Divine Vampire Heirs Series
The Royale Vampire Heirs Series
Academy of Vampire Heirs Series
The Pack Mates of Lunar Crest Series

PARANORMAL

Call of the Ocean Series
Demon Watcher Series
Demon Within Series
Destined for Dreams Series
Finding Nate Series
Going Ghostly Series
Spark of Life Series
The Merman's Spark Series
When Souls Collide Series

CONTEMPORARY

Falling into Fame Series
Life After Lila

ABOUT GINNA MORAN

GINNA MORAN IS a writer from sunny Southern California. She started writing poetry as a teenager in a spiral notebook that she still has tucked away on her desk today. Her love of writing grew after she graduated high school, and she completed her first unpublished manuscript at age eighteen.

When she realized her love of writing was her life's passion, she studied literature at Mira Costa College in Northern San Diego. Besides writing novels, she was senior editor, content manager, and image coordinator for Crescent House Publishing Inc. for four years.

Aside from Ginna's professional life, she enjoys binge watching television shows, playing pretend with her daughter, and cuddling with her dogs. Some of her favorite things include chocolate, anything that glitters, cheesy jokes, and organizing her bookshelf.

Ginna Moran loves to hear from her readers so visit her online at www.GinnaMoran.com. You can also find her on Facebook, Twitter, and Instagram. To stay up-to-date on new releases, sign up to her newsletter. You'll not only get exclusive access to extra stories, but you'll be able to participate in monthly giveaways!